The Spoils of Eden

*Saccharum
officinarum*

(sugar cane)

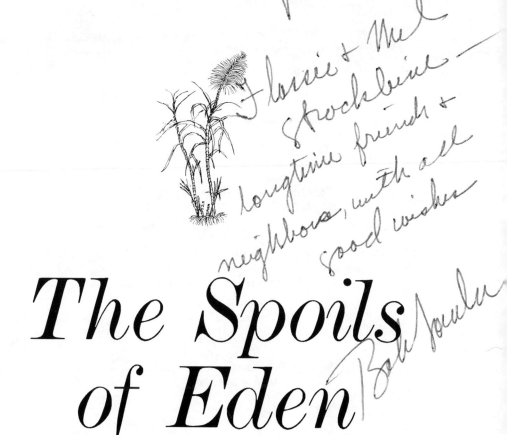

The Spoils of Eden

Robert H. Fowler

Dodd, Mead & Company
New York

Frontispiece map is from *The Economic Geography of Barbados* by Otis P. Starkey, Columbia University Press, 1939, and used by permission of the publishers.

Published by Dodd, Mead & Company, Inc.
79 Madison Avenue, New York, N.Y. 10016
Distributed in Canada by
McClelland and Stewart Limited, Toronto
Manufactured in the United States of America
Designed by Kay Lee
First Edition

Library of Congress Cataloging in Publication Data

Fowler, Robert H.
The spoils of Eden.

Bibliography: p.
1. Barbados—History—Fiction. I. Title.
PS3556.O847S67   1985   813'.54   84-21189
ISBN 0-396-08490-7

To Peter Campbell

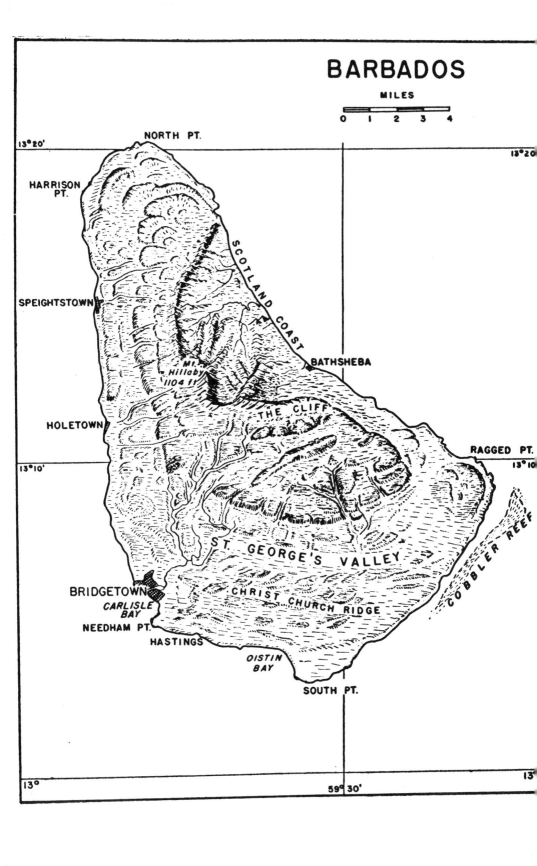

Acknowledgments

The history of Barbados as a resolutely British colony is far more complex than the average winter visitor to the now independent nation may realize. Despite its small size, the island was the wealthiest and most populous English-speaking settlement in the New World throughout most of the seventeenth century. It may well have been the most influential, too. Certainly the colony left its mark both on the West Indies and North America.

Not only was Barbados the linchpin of the English mercantile system in the New World; the island's House of Assembly, established in 1639, is one of the world's oldest legislative bodies, and its Articles of Agreement, signed in 1652, was England's first grant of partial self-rule to a colonial people. Furthermore, Barbadian emigrants, taking up land in the Carolinas and bringing along their African slaves, established the plantation system that dominated the American South until the Civil War. Trade between Barbados and North America flourished right up until the American War for Independence.

Fires and hurricanes have destroyed the island's earliest records, but, fortunately, copies of many were preserved in London and elsewhere, along with official reports, correspondence, and abstracts of local laws. So there is no shortage of documents to tell the story of Barbados, nor of books. Information from more than a hundred volumes went into the writing of this novel. Only the most readily available and useful are listed in the appendix at the back.

My wife, Beverly Utley Fowler, has worked with me as research assistant and editor. She joins me in thanking the many institutions and people who have helped us "get it right." We wish to thank the staffs of these libraries and museums for their hospitality and assistance:

In Barbados, the Department of Archives, the Bridgetown Public Library, and the Barbados Museum; in England, the Society of Friends Library in London, the Bristol Central Library, Saint Stephens Church Museum in Bristol, and the University of Bristol; in the Netherlands, the Rijkmuseum of Amsterdam; and in the United States, the New Cumberland (Pennsylvania) Library, the Pennsylvania State Library, and the New York Public Library. Numerous other institutions have lent us books under interlibrary loan.

Despite so much documentary information, we would not have got our story "right" without the guidance of many persons already steeped in various aspects of seventeenth-century English, Barbadian, and American history. We are grateful for the generous help of:

In the United States: Miss Anne Beale, managing editor, and Roy Baker, former editor, of *British Heritage* magazine; Pieter C. Kooistra; and Thomas R. Forbes, Ph.D., senior research scholar, History of Medicine, School of Medicine, Yale University. In England: Ralph Hyde, keeper of maps and prints, Guildhall Library; Don Rumbelow, official historian of the City of London Police; Dr. Patrick McGrath, professor of history, the University of Bristol; and Michael Crowder, consulting editor for *History Today* magazine. In Barbados: Catherine and Miles Rothwell; Gloria and Harold Manning, owners of Westmoreland Plantation; Bruce Bates, librarian at the Department of Archives, and David Williams, assistant archivist; Edwin Ifill, research librarian, the Bridgetown Public Library; Mrs. Ann Musgrave, proprietress of the Cloister Bookstore; Lieutenant Colonel Stephen Cave, owner of Saint Nicholas Abbey Plantation, and his mother, Mrs. Laurence Cave; and many courteous, patient citizens who gave us directions along the island's back roads.

For all our pains, students of Barbadian history will find some errors. A few of these have been made consciously, to serve narrative ends. For instance, no Quakers were "Barbadosed" or transported from Bristol quite as early as I have made it seem. It is doubtful that Charles II really did attend divine service at Saint

Paul's Cathedral on Sunday, October 30, 1664, and I have the Barbados militia wearing red jackets a few years too early.

I have taken some liberties in describing certain historical figures and even more in writing the dialogue of my characters, real and imaginary. While my wife and I tried to eliminate the most obvious anachronisms, we know that many must have slipped past us. Indeed, some are deliberate for the sake of clarity. To have given our characters the vocabularies or speaking styles employed in the seventeenth century would have made their speech nearly incomprehensible for today's readers.

Despite the care taken by myself and those already listed, this narrative would present a hopelessly inaccurate picture of seventeenth-century Barbados had it not been for the meticulous work of three residents of Barbados who graciously agreed to serve as an informal committee to answer my questions and catch me up on mistakes in the manuscript. They are Warren Alleyne, longtime student of Barbadian history and author of *Historical Bridgetown*; Ronald Hughes, research assistant in the Department of History, University of the West Indies; and Peter F. Campbell, editor of *The Journal of the Barbados Museum and Historical Society* and author of *An Outline of Barbados History*.

Mr. Campbell, who served as the chairman of my "truth squad," is an Englishman. After reading history at Oxford, he entered the British Colonial Service and first came to Barbados in 1943 and while there married a "Bajan." After a long period in Africa, he retired with his wife to a business career in Barbados and to the study of local history.

His letters and notes, incorporating comments from his colleagues, not only have been invaluable to our research, they could be made into a volume of their own. We are indebted to him for his contributions. The best way to thank Peter Campbell is to dedicate this book to him.

ROBERT H. FOWLER
New Cumberland, Pennsylvania

*Saccharum
officinarum*

(sugar cane)

Book One

. . . For two days have I sat holding this enormous ship's log, pondering how best to use its wealth of empty, ruled pages.

Newly brought here from London, 'tis a handsome volume, covered in coarse, brown canvas, with spine and corners nicely bound in red leather. The heavy thing rests upon my lap like a millstone. Thick with lined paper, it lies ready to receive some captain's daily notations as to conditions of the seas, direction of the wind, changes of watch, sails sighted, noontime azimuths, and approximate latitudes and longitudes. And landfalls and cargoes discharged or taken on.

" 'Twill help you pass the days whilst you are confined," my dear husband said upon presenting me with this great logbook.

"In what way help?" I asked. "My days are a burden to me, as I am to you. They hardly merit recording."

"Write down a history of your family in Bedford and an account of your girlhood days there. I should like to read your recollection. And the child surely would treasure your story someday."

"It seems wrong to sit about scribbling in the midst of all this destruction," I protested. "There is so much to be done."

"Nay, I forbid any work. After all you have been through, dear Charlotte, 'twould risk miscarriage for you to exert yourself. Truly, there are hands enough to repair our major damage in time and servants aplenty for the lesser chores meanwhile. With your library destroyed, you lack an occupation, I know. So, having lost your volumes, why not write your own? Think on it."

Well, I have thought on it hour upon waking hour, running my fingertips over the rough cover of this logbook, trying to push away my confusion and sense of loss, striving to focus my wandering thoughts and summon my reluctant will.

I used to find consolation in my book of Montaigne's essays. 'Twas a fine copy of Florio's third edition, given me by my father on my 16th birthday. It was destroyed with the rest of my books and papers, but I recall that Montaigne wrote with probing insight of Sadness and Idleness, saying of the former how it can "stun the whole soul and hinder its freedom of action," and warning that the latter leads to a mind that, with "no fixed aims," "loses itself." As he put it, for one's thoughts to be everywhere is for them to be nowhere.

I do need to fix my sad and restless mind on some purpose. I have toyed with the notion of composing a short history of our recent great calamity, but I shrink from reliving the awful events that have brought us all to ruin. In time, perhaps, but not now.

As for composing a little history of my entire life, I did begin keeping diaries when I was 6 and discontinued the habit only earlier this year, when I became 30. Except for the odd sodden page, they are lost along with my works of Shakespeare, Bacon, Donne, Montaigne . . . all my beloved books, and good riddance—to the diaries, that is. Little worth recording occurred during the first 19, nearly 20 years of my existence anyway.

On the occasions I read my old entries, I was ashamed of the self-centered, arrogant girl they reflected. Even now the memories of my former self embarrass me. The babe that I feel stirring in my womb, when grown, might be amused by such an account, true. But I shall not hash over early recollections, beyond saying that, matured by my recent years as wife to a man of prominence and tempered by my responsibilities as the mistress of a considerable estate, I see now that what others thought was true: The young Charlotte Foxley, she who grew up during England's drab, waning years of Cromwellian tyranny and the bright, waxing period of the restored Monarchy, was a spoiled bratling.

The youngest child and only daughter of a doting father, educated at his knee and deceived into regarding herself as cleverer than the general run of humankind, despising and despised by (with good reason) her three older brothers, at constant odds with her mother, scorning a succession of well-meaning suitors until almost beyond marriageable age, yet was this vain, misguided creature loved and admired far beyond her deserving, by a few persons.

How anyone abided me during my growing up, I do not know. I was an outspoken, ungracious, contrary-minded harridan with an overblown estimate of herself. I was vain of my book learning and horsemanship and disdainful of all that my mother wished for me, such as a smooth tongue, ladylike deportment, and early marriage.

Poor Mama. Unlike dear Father's, her reading was limited to the

Old Testament. She oft warned me that pride goeth before a fall. What would she say if she could see me in my present state, my hair fresh streaked with gray, grown large with child, living in a ruin? "How the mighty and the proud are brought low," she would say. But, mayhap, if she could look within my heart and see the compassion and humility finally rooted there ... well, that's no matter for the present.

So, I cannot bring myself to write of our great recent catastrophe, and I will not further remind myself of my girlhood. This is a ship's log. It was made to receive chronicles of sea voyages. Now, one does not begin such a journal whilst the keel of a vessel is being laid, nor whilst the ribs and thwarts are being fashioned. Nay, the log is opened only after the craft has left the ways, the masts, spars and rigging are in place, the crew recruited, and the anchor weighed, in other words when the voyage has begun.

Today is the 30th of October. All morning I have reflected on the significance of this date. This brooding hath not been for naught. It has helped me "fix my mind."

Yes, it was eleven years ago to this very day that the great voyage of my life really began, whether by accident or according to some predestination, I cannot say. But it hath been an often stormy and adventuresome passage, for me and my shipmates. And, with the clear vision of hindsight, I see that all that happened before this very day, eleven years ago, was merely prologue for us all. It hath been an incredible voyage.

Today is a Saturday. October 30 fell on a Sunday in 1664. I remember that morning as vividly as though 'twere yesterday. I had come down to London with my father to attend the annual Lord Mayor's Show ...

1

Hands on hips, with growing annoyance, Charlotte Foxley looked down at her father lying on his back in the bed of the darkened tavern room.

"The fresh air will do you good," she said.

"No such thing as fresh air in this damnable city. Nothing but smoke and the stench of too many people."

Charlotte opened one of the shutters and said with forced sweetness: "Never has there been a more brilliant Sunday morning in London. See how the skies have cleared. The streets are washed clean. They fairly sparkle."

Sir Robert pulled the covers over his face. "Close that damned thing. The light hurts my eyes."

Charlotte opened the other shutter and said in a harsher tone, "Then think of me. You left me here alone in these stuffy rooms in this miserable tavern last night while you enjoyed the lord mayor's banquet. And the king was at the Guildhall with Queen Catherine, not to mention the French ambassador. And I still say you could have taken me had you wished. Are you and Sir John Lawrence not old friends? And did he not send you a special invitation to see him made lord mayor? You simply did not wish me to accompany you. Well, sir, this morning is my turn to enjoy myself, and I intend to attend divine services at Saint Paul's."

"You had a book last night. You're never happier than with a good book."

"I read books enough at home. Really, Father, had I known you would neglect me so, I never would have agreed to accompany you to London. I am bored."

"I have promised to take you to that damned Killigrew

play tomorrow. Should be entertainment enough. Do let me suffer in peace this one morning."

Charlotte stamped her foot. "You brought your suffering on yourself. When we return to Bedfordshire, I shall tell Mama that you refused to take me to divine services because you drank too much and stayed out too late last night. What will she say to that?"

"Don't care what she would say. Had her chance to come along. Chose to stay behind to oversee the sewing of your wedding dress, and the banns not to be posted for two months. You'd think no one ever got married before."

"Don't change the subject, Father. I would not have agreed to accompany you had I thought you would treat me like a child. After all I am nearly twenty ... "

Sir Robert threw back the covers and raised himself on one elbow. "Agreed? You offered, remember? Anything to get away from your mother's nagging, you said. Besides, when did you become so devout? You're only hoping the bookstalls will be open outside the cathedral this morning."

Charlotte retreated to her adjoining room and slammed the door. With arms crossed she stared down into the High Holborn, wondering what new tactic to try on her father.

Even those who disliked Charlotte Foxley would have admitted that she made a striking sight with the morning sun turning her wavy chestnut hair almost auburn. Back in Bedfordshire opinions differed about her appearance. Rejected suitors wondered what they had seen in a girl with longish nose and little more bosom than a boy and who, more to the point, was possessed of too sharp a tongue to have made a proper wife, anyway. But others, especially her father and her fiancé, regarded her as lovely of face and form. And normally they delighted in her wit.

This visit to London would be her last before her marriage, and so far it had been disappointing. The stage from Bedford had been overladen with people and baggage. She had been squeezed in between Sir Robert and a fat old gentleman who stank of onions and tobacco, with her knees scraping against those of a distracted young mother holding a fretful baby. Then, arriving at Bishopsgate, they had found their favorite hostelry, The Four Swans, filled with others in town for the lord mayor's great annual show and been forced to take these tiny rooms at the Rose and Crown in High Holborn.

The wet, chilly weather had disappointed her too, but at least the lord mayor's show lived up to her expectations. With drums rattling and fifes shrilling away, the procession of the various guilds, led by Sir John Lawrence's own Worshipful Company of Haberdashers, had paraded in their splendid costumes from the Guildhall down to the Three Cranes Wharf. There, the official party boarded a barge that would have put Cleopatra's to shame and, to the accompaniment of great cannon booming from the banks of the Thames, was rowed up to Westminster Abbey for the swearing-in ceremony and thence back downstream again, to the thrilling bass chorus of still more cannon salutes.

All of London and half of England seemed to throng the parade route, everyone in a joyous mood despite the cold October rain. At first Charlotte had been miffed to see the bookstalls at Saint Paul's closed and the churchyard turned into a great fairground with tableaux and various exhibits demonstrating how hats and such things were made and sold. But soon her spirits had been lifted again by the sight of so many people merrily laughing and drinking.

Then, what a letdown, to be deposited back at the Rose and Crown like a piece of unwanted baggage. Well, no use repining over the previous evening. This was a new and glorious day in a city she loved. She had awakened with a strange feeling of expectancy. She would not remain there like a little mouse while the high and mighty Sir Robert snored away the morning.

After a few minutes of frowning and lip-biting, Charlotte played her trump card. With her fur-trimmed cape over her shoulders, she tied the ribbon of her bonnet under her chin, picked up her muff, and reopened the door to her father's room. Blue-gray eyes flashing, she shook the muff at Sir Robert.

"Very well, Father. You stay here and wallow in your selfishness. I shall ask our innkeeper to hail a coach for me. I shall proceed to Saint Paul's without you."

Foxley sat upright and swung his feet off the bed. "Venture forth alone into this wicked place? Never! I forbid it ... "

As their hired carriage rattled along the crowded Strand toward Ludgate, Charlotte concealed her pleasure at her latest triumph over male obduracy. Why did men force women to resort to guile? Would she be able to manipulate Marmaduke Harbinson as easily as she did her father? Or would it be necessary? 'Duke seemed pliable enough. He listened with respect to her opinions. And he claimed to love London and its theater as much as she.

"Look at that riffraff," her father said. "Wouldn't trade you an acre of good Bedford soil for this entire overcrowded fire trap of a town."

"I must not let him spoil my mood," Charlotte thought. To forestall another of his tirades, she pointed out the carriage window at the stubby tower of Saint Paul's looming in the brilliant sunshine. "There it is, Father, England's largest building."

"I call it her ugliest. Wish the Roundheads had torn the thing down. We could build a proper cathedral in its place."

Sir Robert's temper was not improved when the carriage halted and the driver announced: "There's a great press ahead, Sir, whereof I cannot pass through. I must wait upon you here."

With Charlotte in tow, Sir Robert shouldered his way through the promenading throng past Ludgate and up the rise leading to Saint Paul's. The father and daughter made an impressive pair, he wearing the high hat of a country squire, iron gray hair to his shoulders almost like a Puritan's, and she, nearly as tall, with a fine head of wavy locks and a chalky white complexion.

Most of London's 400,000 inhabitants seemed to have taken it into their heads to parade around the delapidated cathedral that morning, but Charlotte did not mind. It gave her the opportunity to examine the faces of the people. What a mixture they were: Bewigged gentlemen in velvet coats, ladies with rouged faces and wearing layers of lace, workmen in rough smocks, urchins in filthy rags, and prostitutes eyeing every unaccompanied male. Fascinated as she was by their faces, Charlotte could not resist gazing up at the cathedral. She wished she could have seen it in its old days, before its towering spire was destroyed by lightning and before Cromwell's officials allowed it to fall into such shocking disrepair.

"Don't stand gaping like a milkmaid, Charlotte," her father called back to her. "Now you've dragged me up here, let's not miss your precious service."

Sir Robert's mood received a further setback when they reached the steps of the west portico of the massive structure and found a pompous little verger blocking their path.

"No one else inside, please, until the king arrives. City marshal's orders."

"The king!" Charlotte exclaimed. "Oh, Father, the king is coming." She put her hand on his arm to interrupt his red-faced protest to the verger. "Please. You saw him and Queen Catherine last night at the banquet. I have always wanted to see the king at close hand. I felt in my heart this morning that something out of the ordinary would happen today."

As she stood with her head inclined against her father's shoulder, clutching his arm, Charlotte congratulated herself on her persistence. What if she had not got her way that morning? Or what if she had decided against coming with her father to London? She would be chafing back at Foxley Manor, counting the days until she would become Mistress Marmaduke Harbinson, free at last of her mother's long tyranny. She would not be experiencing this thrill of studying the hive of people who swarmed about the steps of Saint Paul's as news of the king's plans spread.

Later Charlotte would convince herself that even then she took particular notice of a curious little man and a boy standing just beyond the path the city marshal's men cleared up the steps and across the porch to the great doors of the cathedral. Actually, however, her eyes swept right past the man, even though he held an old-fashioned shepherd's crook and wore a low-crowned black hat with broad brim, even though the brown-haired, dark-eyed boy beside him was uncommonly handsome.

"'Ere 'e comes," someone shouted from the cathedral yard.

Standing on tiptoes, Charlotte watched in fascination as the royal coach, drawn by six fine gray geldings and surrounded by horsemen armed with halberds, rolled up Ludgate Hill, across the plaza and directly to the cathedral steps.

The crowd fell silent as the verger ran down the steps and opened the door of the coach. Charlotte caught her breath at the sight of King Charles himself stepping down from his coach. For a long moment, his dark-wigged head held high, he gazed with luminous eyes upon the crowd, like the masterful politician he was, knowing full well that each person would think his sovereign had looked directly into his face.

If she had not known him to be the king, would Charlotte have paid this man any more attention than some other foppish London gentleman? Yes, she decided, there was an unmistakable aura of power and authority about him. He bore himself like a king. As she squeezed her father's arm in her excitement, Charlotte thought at first that it was only her imagination. But those bold eyes did seem to rest on her face.

Then it happened, the encounter she would carry in her memory to her grave—one might say, the two encounters.

"Sir Robert," the king called out. "How good to see you."

Foxley's face turned pale, then flushed. Headache forgotten, beaming like a bumpkin, he removed his hat. The king put an elegantly shod foot on the first step and flashed a broad smile.

"And who is this beauty with you?"

Charlotte released her father's arm and gathered the hem of her gown. How would she find room on those close-packed steps to make a proper curtsy? Was she dreaming? Was King Charles actually approaching with hand outheld?

Then, while Sir Robert was making his bow, a shrill voice

cried out in a Somerset accent, piercing the respectful quiet of the cathedral plaza like an arrow.

"Cease, vain tyrant!"

Hand still outstretched, the king turned to seek out the person who hailed him so rudely.

"Cease thy oppressions against the children of the light!" the voice piped again.

Now the little man in the broad-brimmed hat raised his shepherd's crook high above his head. *"I bring this warning. All in sound of my voice, hear and beware what may befall thee if this Pharoah does not relent. Cease vain tyrant, I say, cease!"*

Suddenly an officer of his guard took the king's elbow. Without a further word to the Foxleys, a faint smile still on his face, Charles hurried across the porch and into the cathedral.

The strange little man continued his cries. *"Great are the tribulations that will fall upon thee all if this wicked leader changeth not his ways. See how he flees from the truth . . . "*

Soldiers and the city marshal's men thrust aside shocked onlookers to get at the little man. Still shouting, he went down under their onslaught. A fresh hubbub followed when the boy, who could not have been more than twelve, seized the arm of a soldier. Within seconds, the lad had been thrown down, and the pair were gagged and their wrists bound.

Mouth agape, Charlotte watched as the soldiers hauled the two to their feet and, with halberd butts, prodded them through the mob. It took only a few seconds for the people to recover from their shock. With angry shouts, they pressed so close that the king's men formed a phalanx to move their prisoners across the cathedral yard to Ludgate Road.

"Did you ever witness anything so disgraceful?" Sir Robert spluttered. "Oh, damn! They've shut the doors on us again."

"No matter, Father. Let's see what happens to that pair."

Ignoring Sir Robert's protests, Charlotte trotted after the crowd, which surged around the soldiers and their prisoners. In the midst of growing numbers of ruffians, the cortege moved down Ludgate Hill to Old Bailey and there turned right toward Newgate Prison.

His own curiosity now aroused, Sir Robert gave up ordering Charlotte to stop and tagged along after the mob with her. By the time the soldiers reached the doors of Newgate Prison, while they waited for the jailers to answer their pounding, rumors of an attempted assassination against the king spread. Cries for revenge arose. Barking dogs circled the crowd. Sharp-eyed pickpockets closed in on their victims. From the high, narrow windows of Newgate's upper floors, prisoners jeered at the mob. Two bold women of the streets yelled insults back at them. Someone shouted, "They tried to murder the king. Kill them!" Charlotte's "No, they only spoke to him" was lost in the uproar. "My purse! Stop—thief!" a man cried.

The city marshal, an acquaintance of Foxley's, was a large man with a great belly and a broad, red face. Alarmed by the increasing hostility, he drew his sword and led an advance by the soldiers. The ruffians in the forefront fell back before the halberd points, so that Charlotte got a clear view of the prisoners. The little man lifted his face toward the sky with an expression of triumph. The lad stared at his feet with scarlet face. Charlotte could not help admiring the man's gentle defiance. For the boy, she felt pity.

At last the doors swung open. The city marshal put his booted foot against the little man's backside and catapulted him into the arms of the jailers. Next he lifted the boy by the back of the neck and tossed him through the doors.

"Wait here and I will find out what's what," Sir Robert said.

As the unsatisfied crowd milled about, still crying for blood, prisoners at the upper windows singled out a disdainful Charlotte with shouts of admiration. Ignoring their crude compliments, Charlotte shielded her face with her bonnet. She wanted to remember every detail of this experience to tell to her fiancé when she got home.

Her father returned to report: "City marshal says it's two of those confounded Quakers. Says the place overflows with them already, all insisting on their right to a grand jury hearing. Most of them here for meeting illegally or for disrupting divine services or for refusing to swear in courts of law. Says he has known none to confront the king himself before this. Serve those two right to rot in Newgate."

"What will happen to them?" Charlotte asked.

"They could be transported to the Indies. That's what I would do with them."

Sir Robert continued his harangue against nonconformists in general and members of George Fox's Society of Friends in particular as they walked back along Old Bailey. "I support Clarendon in his measures to suppress this sort of thing. Transport them, every one if necessary. Imagine, insulting the king on the very steps of Saint Paul's, and just as he was greeting us. What a tale that would have been to carry back to your mother."

"What we saw will make a good enough story. Such a display of courage!"

Only half listening, her father replied: "Indeed. Never saw soldiers move so swiftly to their tasks, without thought for their own safety. After all, they had no idea of whether those two were armed, or part of a larger plot. And it was marvelous the way they held off the mob."

They found their hired carriage with the horses tied to a hitching post and the driver inside, asleep. As Sir Robert shook the man awake, Charlotte once more indulged her habit of studying the faces of people in the street, until she realized that her gaze was being returned.

Surely no one of any breeding would stare so boldly. Strongly built, with gray-streaked blond hair cut unfashionably short, the man bore himself with the cocky air of an estate foreman in the midst of his farm laborers. His clothing looked out of date. Charlotte glanced away, then back again. There was no doubt: deep blue eyes, contrasting with that tanned face, were directed at her. The rude fellow even grinned.

Charlotte turned her back and moved closer to her father.

"Pardon me." The man approached with broad-brimmed straw hat in hand. "Might you be Colonel Foxley?"

"I am Robert Foxley. What's it to you?"

"Were you not in the old king's service in the siege of Colchester?"

"Indeed I was. And other places as well. Who might you be, my good man?"

The fellow cut his eyes toward Charlotte and back toward her father. "Have I aged so much in just sixteen years, colonel? I am Richard Bolton. I commanded a company at Balkerne Gate in the town's defense."

"By God, so it is." Foxley took the man's hand and, putting his arm around his shoulders, said to Charlotte, "My dear, I present to you one of the bravest of the brave. Captain Bolton, my youngest child and only daughter, Charlotte. Ah, Bolton, you were wounded ... "

"No, rather injured. Was in hospital at the surrender and the Roundheads Barbadosed me."

"Stupid lot. Near ruined the country exiling so many good men."

"In the long run they did me and Barbados a good turn, though I would not have said so at the time."

"Done well, have you? One of them rich sugar magnates, I reckon."

"I do own a plantation and a few slaves." Bolton shivered. "Excuse me. I just arrived yesterday. Am unused to the chill."

"Where are you staying?"

"With a cousin near Gray's Inn. Meant to attend divine services at Saint Paul's but there was some disturbance, and they wouldn't let me in."

"We got shut out, too. Damned nuisance."

"Indeed, so. You see, I heard the king was to attend. My name being up for honors in January, I wanted to be sure of who it is I am to kneel to."

"Knighted, by God."

"No, Father," quipped Charlotte, "only by the king."

Bolton laughed, too long and too loud for Charlotte's taste. "Your daughter has wit."

"If not manners. Look here, Bolton. We have a carriage.

Come back to our lodgings, and break bread with us. Don't think of refusing. I speak as your old superior. Come along like a good soldier."

Charlotte felt like kicking her father. She had never cared for blond men, beginning with her older brother, who used to torment her. And she dreaded the prospect of hearing reminiscences of the Civil Wars. If only Marmaduke were here to take her walking along the Strand. She longed to discuss with him the strange encounter of the Quakers and King Charles.

Charlotte's impression of Richard Bolton did not improve during their ride down Fleet Street and the Strand to Drury Lane and thence along that twisting, narrow way to High Holborn. She expressed herself to her father when they went up to their rooms to change, while Bolton waited below.

"That fellow thinks well enough of himself. Imagine, announcing his knighthood to you almost in his first breath."

"He has reason to be proud. The man has endured much and has prevailed."

"Perhaps so, but I don't like the way he speaks to you. As though he were your equal. After all, you were a colonel."

"He is a colonel, too, now. You heard him."

"In the militia of an out-of-the-way island. I suppose he means that idiotic grin to be charming. And that horrible accent. One minute he sounds Irish and the next West Country."

"Look here, Charlotte, that man did heroic service for the crown. He is our guest. If you are rude to him, you can forget about that damned play tomorrow." Then, with a softer expression: "Come, be a good lass, and I will take you back to the bookstalls at Saint Paul's in the morning."

"And for a stroll this afternoon?"

"That, too."

In the common room below, the innkeeper drew them up a table near the fire and brought out a dinner of roast beef, potatoes, peas, and turnips, followed by pints of ale. Bolton ate with a wolfish appetite. Catching Charlotte's disapproving glance, he apologized. "First good hot English meal I've had in many a day."

He was older than she first thought, judging from the brown spots on the backs of his hands and the crow's-feet around his eyes. But, unlike many middle-aged blondes, he had a full thatch of hair. Maybe he had earned the right to be self-assured, but Charlotte was unused to hearing another man dominate a conversation with her father. Yet Foxley did not seem to mind. He even encouraged Bolton to enlarge upon his adventures.

Charlotte had to bite her tongue at the end of the meal when her father said, "Look here, Bolton, we've only begun to talk. I'll have a fire lit in our sitting room upstairs, and we can take our port there."

As a little girl, Charlotte liked to sit on her father's knee and hear his stories of the struggle to keep the old King Charles on the throne. One of her most vivid memories was of his weeping at the news of the king's beheading. But she had long ago grown weary of war stories and so, while the two men stretched their legs before the fire and talked, she sat with her book in the window seat overlooking High Holborn.

Of Charlotte's three brothers, two were married and living away from home, and one served in the navy, thank God. They and her mother were convinced that Sir Robert had spoiled the girl, turning her into a willful old maid, good for nothing but skulking in the library to avoid household duties.

As for Charlotte, she did not mind what anyone thought about her manners or appearance. She dressed in good fashion but took no special pride in her looks. Her intellect was another matter. Charlotte not only regarded her mind as superior to those of most people, she also considered herself far better read.

" . . . I didn't care who won when I came down from Cambridge in 1646," Bolton was saying. "Country in a turmoil, you know. No prospects in the law. Parents dead. So I enlisted with King Charles. Roundheads took me prisoner at Stow-on-the-Wold in that disaster. Released me on parole. Near went mad the next two years. Nothing to do but tramp my uncle's acres, read books, or play cards."

"I know how that was," Foxley broke in. "I was virtually a prisoner on my own land. My only occupation was the education of my children, for which Charlotte should be grateful. Wish my boys had learned as well as she. But how did you come to be at Colchester?"

"I heard of the new rising of the king's men in Kent that summer of '48, and with no thought of my parole, I joined Lucas and Lisle, and they gave me a command of a mixed company of musketeers and pikesmen."

"We made a mistake, allowing ourselves to get shut up in that town," Foxley said. "Only meant to stay there for a day or two and refresh ourselves, you know. The population favored the Roundheads, damn their eyes. Didn't want us there..."

Charlotte looked out on the street, teeming with life, and sighed. She had heard her father tell a hundred times of how he and his fellow Cavaliers were reduced to eating dog and cat meat as well as horseflesh during the siege of Colchester and how his men went around the town after each bombardment to pick up cannonballs to fire back at the enemy. Thank God for 'Duke Harbinson. He would not bore her with long-winded tales of old wars. Thank God, too, that she had not given in to her mother's pressure to wed sooner. Her mother would have married her off at fifteen or sixteen if Charlotte had let her. And now she would be saddled with brats and dominated by some buffoon. Strange to tell, both she and her mother were glad that she had waited, now. The Harbinsons were an old, landed family.

"...Then why did they banish you to Barbados?" her father asked.

"The Roundheads wrapped a demand to surrender around an arrow and shot it into our sector. One of my sergeants picked it up." Bolton lowered his voice so that Charlotte had to strain to hear what followed. "He did his natural business and thrust the arrow through a generous portion."

"I recall the incident now. Was that your men?" Foxley choked with laughter. "You fired it back at them."

"More than that, I wrote a reply on the back of their note and signed my name. That little joke cost me dear later. You see, soon after that I was injured by a falling stone in a bombardment. I lay barely conscious until the surrender. My men were concerned for my life. They assumed all officers would be executed or imprisoned."

"With good reason," Foxley interrupted. "I spent two months in the Tower, and it near ruined my family to pay the fines."

"To make a long story short, my men spirited me to a stable turned into a hospital for soldiers and disguised me as one of them, thinking in that way to save my life. But, as you know, they executed only Sir Charles Lucas . . . "

"And poor George Lisle. As an example to the rest of us, the bastards. Bad business."

All interest in her book gone, Charlotte listened closely as Bolton told of being robbed by the resentful citizens of Colchester and then, barely able to walk, of being driven with his soldiers like cattle across Essex through a cold rain to London, where the men were divided into parcels to be sold off to British plantations in the West Indies. Learning that their officers were not being executed wholesale after all and hoping to spare Bolton from exile, his men revealed his identity.

"Alas, one of the Roundhead majors had just come from Colchester. Not only had he seen me lead a sortie that cost them a cannon, he recognized my name as the one signed to that note. And then, when he further learned that I had violated my parole, he wanted to have me shot the next morning. But there was a London magistrate on hand, and he objected, saying there had been bloodshed enow. The major remarked that the magistrate had remained safely in London during the fighting at Colchester, and then he told him about the turd business."

"Sealed your fate, eh?" Foxley asked.

"Actually, the magistrate laughed so hard, for a moment I thought he would release me, but the major said, 'You may find that humorous, but we who served with Lord Fairfax did not find it so. What if this scapegrace's family raises the money for his release? Would you have that?' The magistrate sided with the major in the end. 'He wishes to share the fate of his soldiers. He shall have that wish and more. They will be sold off for five years. For violating his parole, his term of banishment shall be for life.' "

Charlotte gave up pretending that she was bored by the conversation. "You remained with your men, then?" she asked.

Bolton smiled. "No, the major feared I might lead them into what he called 'fresh mischief.' They were parceled out to Saint Christopher. As the magistrate said, 'We shall fire this bolt-on off to Barbados.' Witty fellow, that magistrate."

In spite of herself, Charlotte smiled at the pun.

"By God, what a good story," Foxley said. "Often wondered what had become of you, Bolton. Now tell us more about your life in Barbados. Hear it's a land of milk and honey out there."

"Alas, my cousin will be wondering where I am. Mistress Charlotte, I do hope all this talk of an old war has not wearied you."

He took her hand, squeezing it harder than she felt a gentleman should, and bowed.

That night, long after the cobblestones on the High Holborn had stopped ringing with hoof and wheel, after the crowds had thinned to the occasional gang of drunks still celebrating the lord mayor's inaugural or the odd team of panting sedan chair porters hauling gentlefolk to their homes, Charlotte still could not sleep. Her father snored away like a pond full of bullfrogs in his room, but she had seen and heard too much that day to drop off as easily as she did at home.

Her brain spinning with the memories, she arose, wrapped herself in a woolen cloak and replenished the wood on the fire. Then she drew a small table close to the flames, lit a candle and brought out pen and ink. She wrote in her diary for more than an hour, mostly about the confrontation of the little Quaker with King Charles and of her near-introduction to the monarch.

As for Richard Bolton, Charlotte described him as "a crude man who told the most vulgar story I think I ever did hear, one I would not repeat even in this diary. Very conceited, too. Father thought him a wonderful fellow; urged him to stay on talking through the afternoon, then charged me afterwards with treating his guest coldly. Sometimes Father taxes my patience as much as Mama. Give me strength to endure them both a little longer. How glad I am to have waited for a man like 'Duke. My life is just about to begin. I feel it in my bones."

In the next room, the snores of Robert Foxley ceased. Hearing the creak of his bed and the scrape of his chamberpot, Charlotte blew out her candle and sat quietly in the dark while he relieved himself. Biting her knuckles to suppress her giggles, she waited until the sound of urination stopped and snoring had begun again before she returned to her bed. Her last thoughts before falling asleep were of the Quaker and the handsome little boy being kicked and shoved by soldiers from Saint Paul's to Newgate. It was strange how she could not banish that scene from her mind.

On another midnight, three weeks later, in Newgate Prison's great central room, men thrashed in their sleep or moaned or shivered under their lice-ridden blankets. Some cried out from bad dreams or cursed. Only a few, mostly Quakers, slept with easy minds.

On one side of a huge oaken pillar in the middle of the room, a slattern, picked up on Cheapside for soliciting, copulated with a pickpocket, arrested for stealing a gentleman's silk handkerchief. On the other side of the pillar, Moses Martin sat cross-legged in his old tailor's way and stared up between the crisscross of hammocks above him at a narrow window in the stone wall. A half-moon cast a dim light on this window. Oblivious to the sounds of lovemaking a few feet away, and to the snores and moans of his fellow prisoners, Moses was transfixed by the images that appeared to him in the aperture. At first the scenes shone faintly, but soon they grew as clear as in one of the lantern shows he had seen back in Bristol.

First, children and, then, men and women fell ill before his eyes. Their splotchy faces swelled to fill the window, then faded and were replaced by an entire family weeping and praying around a bedside. Now he saw people being carried out of doors to pesthouses. Faster and faster flashed the images. Carts piled high with bodies creaked along London's narrow streets. As clearly as if he were standing nearby, Moses saw men with cloths over their noses digging burial pits for long rows of corpses.

The little Quaker tailor watched in horror, until he could bear no more. His head felt as though it would burst. A film of blood seemed to pour over his eyes. In a shrill voice heard throughout the prison, he cried out twice, then fell silent.

John Martin, his son, sleeping in a hammock on the topmost row, awakened at the cry. "Father, are thou all right?"

Another Quaker, an elderly man who occupied the hammock just below, spoke. "He is only having a nightmare, Johnny."

John lay quietly and, hearing nothing more than the usual Newgate noises, went back to sleep, to dream of home and school. The boy had become the pet of the prison. The other Quakers had been especially kind, but many of the criminals, the women in particular, enjoyed talking to him. Some even saved tidbits of food for him. He and his father were still bruised from the beating they had received on their arrival, but on the whole prison life had not been so bad. People told him stories of their own childhoods. And he had been asked a hundred times to describe the confrontation between his father and King Charles; Moses, refusing to answer their questions, spent most of his time in prayer. The pickpocket, who now slept off the exertions of lovemaking, liked to perform sleight-of-hand tricks for John and, to the disapproval of Moses, jokingly offered to make him his apprentice. Even the gaolers asked after the health of "the Quaker lad" when they brought in pots of stew and loaves of stale bread twice a day. For John Martin, being in Newgate seemed rather like taking part in a twenty-four-hour carnival.

The Quakers formed their own society in the prison, just as they did in England at that time. The same old man who slept just below John paid a jailer for the boy's hammock. A prosperous draper from Islington, he had been hauled in for opening his shop to fellow Quakers for meetings in violation of the new Clarendon Code. This draper had infleuntial friends who brought him small gifts (which he promptly distributed to other prisoners) and who gave him unheeded advice. As they pointed out, all he had to do to win his freedom was to promise not to repeat his offense.

"Ah, but I have committed no offense against anyone, whereas the authorities daily and hourly are guilty of the gravest of injustices by keeping me and others like me in this den of misery. Besides, there is much to be gained here. Every moment I work at comforting and ministering to others. I suspect that the Almighty wishes me to be here as his agent."

The old man had converted at least two criminals to his Quaker views, and many others had been moved by his tireless charity. Recognizing that Moses Martin was, if not demented, at least incompetent, he had taken John under his special protection, like a grandson. Without a word to Moses, he had sent news of their imprisonment back to the Martin household in Bristol.

So the wretches of Newgate passed the long night. Morning came in gray and cold, and the jailers drove away the remnants of peace by banging on pans and shouting, "Up, up ye worthies! Rise and shine. Take down your hammocks."

The draper helped John untie his hammock. As they folded it, they noticed Moses still sitting cross-legged against the pillar. He gazed without expression at the window. One side of his face drooped and saliva trickled from a corner of his mouth. He did not respond when John shook his shoulder.

"Father, why will thou not speak?"

"Ah, poor Johnny," the draper said. "I fear the poor man hath suffered a stroke of apoplexy."

Two days later, Jacob Martin, the twenty-one-year-old eldest son of Moses, arrived from Bristol riding a horse borrowed from a fellow Quaker and carrying a purse of several pounds donated by his local meeting. Jacob had inherited a streak of shrewdness from his mother. Upon arriving in London and obtaining free lodging at the Bull and Mouth Inn in Aldersgate, whose proprietor often aided Quakers, and after inquiring around the Inns of Court for a barrister in particular need of a case, Jacob appeared at Newgate in the company of a fat young lawyer who overawed the jailers into allowing an interview.

Moses gave no sign that he understood the questions, but John told what happened at Saint Paul's. Holding a handkerchief over his nose and trying to ignore the other prisoners who eavesdropped, the lawyer concluded, "It would require my best efforts."

"I thought I was paying for thy best," Jacob replied. "If thou don't want the money, just say so."

"You did not tell me that your father carried a cudgel and that he shouted at the king while a church service was in progress."

"It was only a shepherd's crook. He always carries it. And he did not actually disrupt the service. Look, let's strike a bargain. Get them both off, and I'll pay thy fee twice over. Fail and thou get nothing."

The lawyer closed his eyes for a moment, then opened them to say, "We'd have to plead him guilty. Would have to waive his rights to a grand jury hearing."

"Plead him any way thou wish. Thou see that he cannot speak for himself."

The lawyer turned his back to the other prisoners and whispered, "If we went straight to the lord mayor with a guilty plea, and if your father behaves himself . . ."

Moses and John were conveyed in a cart along Cheapside from Newgate to the residence of the new lord mayor. As they rattled over the cobbled pavement of that broad, fashionable street, Moses experienced a fresh vision, more awesome than the one that had appeared to him in prison. In this one, he saw all the grand shops along Cheapside engulfed by fire. People ran through the smoke, screaming. Beyond the row of burning buildings, the stubby, multi-buttressed tower of Saint Paul's flamed like an enormous torch.

His groan both alarmed and pleased John, for it was the first sound Moses had uttered since his seizure. The boy put his hand on his father's arm and smiled. " 'Tis all right."

Long a prominent Parliamentarian, Sir John Lawrence had turned rabid Royalist upon Cromwell's death. Indeed, it was he who had led a delegation of Londoners out of the city to greet King Charles upon his return from exile. His improved fortunes under the Restoration were reflected in his new residence, which faced Saint Helen's Place, just off Bishopsgate. A four-storied structure, its front was emblazoned with the arms of the City of London and his own family's. While still an alderman, he had built a low gallery across the end of his hall so that it could double as a courtroom. Sir John sat on that gallery now, looking down in amused contempt at the three Martins as their lawyer explained how he despised "these deluded people as much as your honor."

"Yet, whose heart is so hard that it cannot feel pity for the family of this madman?" he added.

"The boy," Sir John asked. "Do you deny his presence at the disgraceful affront to our majesty?"

"He was not a party to the action, your honor. He was only sent along by his poor mother to keep his father from harm. He did not participate . . ."

"Nor prevent the act. And he laid hands on the guards." The lord mayor waved his hand to stop the lawyer's attempt to reply. "Who is this other fellow?"

"His eldest son, a law-abiding, honest tailor of Bristol, who assures me that he loves our gracious majesty and is much distressed by his father's conduct."

"What of the miscreant himself? I have never known one of his religious ilk not to speak. Is he senseless?"

"Nay, your honor, only speechless." The lawyer explained Moses' condition.

"Too bad he did not suffer his stroke before he came to London. He has been twice arrested for outrages against the established religion in his own district. As this is his third offense, he should be transported to some foreign plantation. I cannot think a jury would find otherwise."

Jacob's shrewd bargain began its work. The voice of the lawyer trembled. "Oh, your honor, this is a man of fifty. He has a wife and three children. Speechless as he is, he can do no further harm. I do not presume to advise your honor, but it seems to me that, if you consider both mercy and economy . . ."

"But you do presume. Come close, young man, and let us consult."

Wig drooping over the railing, the lord mayor leaned down from his gallery and whispered to the lawyer for several minutes. Meanwhile, Jacob prayed that Moses would not suddenly recover his speech. His father long had been an embarrassment to him. Perhaps it would be no bad thing for him to remain mute, if at the same time he gave up his wandering and did his share of the work in the family tailoring shop.

"You there, fellow." The lord mayor addressed him. "You may thank the Almighty for your father's seizure." Rolling his eyes at his clerk and bailiff, he added, "Some might regard it as a stroke of good fortune."

After the laughter subsided, he asked, "How do the defendants wish to plead?"

"Guilty, your honor," boomed the young lawyer.

Jacob glanced at Moses with dread, fearing he might protest in some nonverbal way. But Moses' mind still lay under the spell of his vision of a great fire. Tears ran down his face at the recollection.

The lord mayor fixed the Martins with a long stare, as though debating what verdict to hand down. At last he spoke. "Guilty? Then I find it will not be necessary to bind them over for a formal trial. I dismiss the charges against the boy. As for his father, I shall not order his exile to a foreign plantation. I shall only banish him to Bristol, which some might regard as punishment enough."

He waited for the obligatory laughter to stop.

"But should this Moses Martin, tailor of Bristol, make any further disturbance against the order of the realm in any way, he shall be placed on the next ship leaving Bristol for the New World. That is my judgment, and I am so notifying the lord mayor of Bristol. Now begone, the lot of you. Next case."

Outside the house, Jacob forced himself to pay the lawyer his double fee. With John's help, he lifted Moses into the saddle of the borrowed horse. Eyes closed, Moses rode back along Threadneedle Street and past Ludgate. He did not open them until they neared Westminster, where the Thames curved so that one could see a stretch of the bank clear down to the Tower of London. But where a mass of buildings and church spires appeared to his sons, Moses saw only blackened ruins dominated by the charred hulk of Saint Paul's.

His vision ended with Jacob's slapping the horse's rump and saying, "Don't lag behind gawking, John. I mean to reach Slough by nightfall. Father's foolishness hath cost us enough time and money. This whole business is done and over with now."

... Back home in Bedfordshire, I thought often of the Quaker man and lad and of my nearly meeting King Charles. As for the Barbadian planter, I quickly put him out of my mind, although Father told all

who would listen of his encountering an old comrade from the siege of Colchester.

Mama drove the servants and attempted to drive me at a furious rate to make all ready at Foxley Manor for a grand Christmas.

In looking back, I regard that First Day of Christmas, 1664, as a last interlude of contentment before the initial storm of my great life's voyage broke. Despite Mama's summons to help clear away the debris from the Christmas Eve festivities, I spent most of the morning in my room, reading a life of Queen Elizabeth, given me by my fiancé, the kind and patient Marmaduke Harbinson, who understood my fascination for the good Queen Bess. Some women have told me how, in growing up, they sometimes longed to have been born male rather than female. I never harbored such an idle wish. No, rather I preferred to remain a woman, but yearned to wield the power and influence of a Queen Elizabeth. My three brothers used to mock me as "Princess Charlotte" because they felt Father spoilt me so. Actually, the name did not displease me, although I pretended otherwise. But, no, I never wished to be anything but a woman, only not some simpering, submissive wife, nor yet someone like my mother, who, though as strong of will as I, cared for naught save household affairs and local gossip. I was determined to make my existence on this earth—as a woman—count for something. I was not sure just what. I simply resolved early in life that, while I did not expect the adventure and excitement of a man's life, at least I would keep control of my own existence. And, if ever I did marry, it would be only to a man who would not try to curb my own ambitions. My brothers warned Father and Mama that they would be burdened in their old age with a willful old maid, and perhaps it came close to that.

My dear, dear brothers. Cuthbert was the eldest, twelve years my senior. He married the only child of a neighboring family that did not go back as far as the Foxleys but did possess more land. And Cuthbert, by siring three little towheaded replicas of himself in unseemly haste, stood to collect his father-in-law's lands as his considerable stud fee. Cuthbert never deigned to waste his time on me, and I shall give him no more space in my memoir. He was a lout.

Then there was Francis, who was ten when I was born. Bullied unmercifully by Cuthbert, he paid me rather more attention than I wished to receive. Francis was too good for this world. He plagued me with criticisms of my behavior and unwanted advice about my spiritual development. Father was disappointed in Francis for his physical cowardice. But my saintly brother found his vocation in the Church. Upon the Restoration of the Monarchy, Francis accepted a living at a parish nearby and married the daughter of a merchant of means, who took up in bullying him where Cuthbert had left off.

My brothers and their wives were on hand that Christmas Eve, but, to my satisfaction, left the next morning to visit their in-laws. To my even greater pleasure, the youngest of my brothers, Charles, was not present at all.

Charles's absence, at Christmas or any other time, was present enough for me. He had been the baby of the Foxley family for six years, until my arrival late in my parents' lives dethroned him. I could fill this logbook with a recitation of the torments he visited upon me as his revenge: surreptitious slaps and pinches, broken toys, stories of ghosts in the attic calculated to terrify me, and sly taunts. But I evened the score when, in my sixth year, it was discovered that I could read and write and do sums as well as he could at 12. Thereafter, I learned a hundred ways to make him look the fool in Father's sight. I would be amazed if he did not hate me still, as I did him, at the time. The day that Charles left home to join the navy was one of the happiest in my childhood.

'Duke Harbinson was nothing like my brothers, or I would have sent him packing as I did the others who came sniffing about with their eyes as much on my father's fortune as on me. He was a most gracious, considerate young man, and I really do not understand what he saw in me. Instead of taking offense at my sometimes abrasive remarks, he found—or pretended to find—them amusing. At any rate, he refused to be put off by the same behavior that had sent many another suitor slinking off with his tail between his legs. And, to tell the truth, after my nineteenth birthday, it dawned on me that, if I did not marry within the year, the best I might expect would be some widower of middle years, looking for a mother to his brats. To shorten a long tale, I could find nothing to criticize in Marmaduke and much to admire. So finally, on his third proposal, I gave him permission to speak to Father.

*I mentioned 'Duke's gift of a biography of Queen Elizabeth.
Father gave me another that Christmas Day, one that I cherish to this
day, and which, I am happy to say, survived our late calamity as the
life of Elizabeth did not.*

*In a tone I found overbearing, Father ordered me to quit my
room and answer the door. I bristled, wondering why we employed a
butler, but I dared not disobey so direct a command. There, mounted
on his horse, sat 'Duke, and beside him stood our groom, Old Hadley,
holding the reins of a beautiful little bay mare.*

*"I done named her, Mistress Charlotte," Old Hadley said. "'Er
name be Nutmeg."*

*Father and 'Duke had been in league to surprise me. Nutmeg had
been secreted in the Harbinson stable for the past week.*

*What a happy day! 'Duke and I rode for miles. Nutmeg was a
superb little steed, friskier than now, of course. So was I, for that
matter.*

*Upon our return, 'Duke accepted Mama's invitation to sup with
us, and afterwards we sat in the library, talking of our future. It was
a time of tranquility, and yet I quivered with expectation . . .*

A three-storied house with wings protruding at either end,
Foxley Manor had been built by Sir Robert's grandfather in the
reign of James I. Designed by a student of Inigo Jones, it was
noted for its ornate interior. Foxley's grandfather nearly bank-
rupted the family paying one small army of craftsmen to carve
the woodwork in the library and another to fashion the exqui-
site plaster ceiling of the great entrance hall.

Charlotte sat on a bench in front of the fire in the library,
her head against Marmaduke Harbinson's shoulder, while the
ancient family nurse, who was supposed to be chaperoning the
couple, slept in a corner chair.

"Mama is driving us all quite mad. She is determined to
make this Christmas memorable, because . . . " Her voice rose to
a whine. " . . . 'after all, this will be daughter's last under our
roof.' "

Harbinson laughed at her mimicry. "Be patient. We shall
spend next Christmas exactly as we wish."

She smiled and took his hand. "In London, perhaps?"

"Why not?"

With his long face and dark eyes catching the reflection of the fire, 'Duke came near to being handsome, Charlotte thought. More important, he made her feel comfortable. She admired his lively, if conventional, sense of humor and the inquiring mind that lay just below his quiet surface.

"Patience," Charlotte said with disdain. "I am weary of being patient. I wish we had held to our first plan and posted our banns today. But no, this Sunday falls on the first day of Christmas. Mama can keep but one thing in her head at a time."

Harbinson looked about at the candles in the library window and the bowls of greenery on the tables. "I'd say she has done it in good style. This all reminds me of the old Christmases before Cromwell. You don't recall them, do you?"

Charlotte withdrew her hand from his. "You sound like an old man. I am only five years younger than you." But seeing the hurt look on his face, she laughed. "It *was* dreary with all the Puritans in the village spying to see if there were any unseemly festivities. Well, we are having it all this year. Boar's head and yule log last night. And she has something planned for nearly every one of the next twelve days."

Listening to Charlotte complain, mock, and speculate about their future in her animated way, Harbinson wondered why his mother did not think her beautiful as he did. He could have married any one of many conventionally pretty girls of good families, but none of them appealed to him as did Charlotte. Oh, well, his mother would come to appreciate her grace and wit as he did. Give her time.

"Let us celebrate this first day of Christmas with a kiss," he said. Making sure the nanny still dozed, he put his arm around her waist.

She leaned away when he attempted a second kiss. "Only one a day. No more."

"Not so. One the first day, two the second, and so on."

They were interrupted by a hammering on the great door of the entrance hall and Sir Robert's shouts for someone to see who was there. Charlotte and Harbinson continued talking until the library door opened and Foxley announced, "In here. Warm yourself whilst I have your horse put away and summon my wife. You remember Charlotte. This is her intended, 'Duke Harbinson. Charlotte, see who's come."

During the six weeks since she had met the Barbadian planter, much of his tan had faded. Well-tailored woolen trousers and a bright waistcoat showed beneath a new cloak. He held a plumed hat that would have done justice to a London dandy.

"How could I forget your lovely daughter? Fact is, I've brought her a gift." He stopped to cough. "Damp English weather disagrees with my lungs." He bowed to Harbinson and held out a package to Charlotte. "Your father mentioned your love of books. Here is one about Barbados."

Charlotte curtsied and took the book. "Most generous of you," she said, but when the planter turned to warm himself by the fire, she made a face and shrugged at her fiancé.

Bolton explained that he had been in Birmingham to order machinery for his sugar mill and was on his way to spend the rest of Christmas with friends in Cambridge.

"Glad we are you stopped by," Foxley boomed. "Have you et? Here's my wife. Catherine, this is the old comrade I told you about. Here, now, we must give you something for that ugly cough."

After her parents led Bolton away, Charlotte told Harbinson of their meeting. "Such a bore. Talks always of himself."

"Before I go, let's see the book."

Charlotte untied the parcel and drew out a long, thin volume bound in green cloth. "*A True and Exact History of the Island of Barbados,*" she read, "by Richard Ligon."

Harbinson donned his cloak. "May I read it when you have finished?"

"If ever I read it at all," she replied. "At the moment I much prefer your gift of the book about good Queen Bess."

At the door, he surprised her with a quick kiss, then pointed to the mistletoe.

"That makes two from your allotment. At this rate, 'Duke, there will be none left for you on the last day of Christmas, and you shall have to wait until we are man and wife for more."

Charlotte heard her parents quarreling as she came down the stairs the next morning. She paused outside the door to eavesdrop.

"It can't be helped, Catherine. The man is too sick to travel on today."

Lady Bolton was a short woman with reddish blond hair gathered into a huge bun that appeared to draw back her head with its weight. Normally pale, now her cheeks glowed with anger.

"We are not running a pesthouse here. You don't know how much this Christmas means to me."

"And you don't know how much it means to me to show an old comrade hospitality when he is ill. Come, my dear, let us not contest the matter further. Up there in Charles's old room, he will be out of the way. I'll send for the doctor this morning."

"Don't tell me Colonel Bolton is still here," Charlotte said as she entered the dining hall.

"Yes, and likely to be for several days, despite what your father says. Look, Robert, the fellow knew he was ill when he appeared on our doorstep yesterday."

Foxley arose and threw his napkin on the table. "Damn it, I have assured him he is welcome until he feels like traveling, and, by God, he will stay. I am weary of discussing it."

The doctor, declaring the planter had "lung congestion," bled him and prescribed several days of rest in a warm room with frequent draughts of hot brandy punch. The Foxleys assigned the cook's son to attend him. Charlotte went about those household duties she could not avoid without thinking of the sick man. The next morning, the doctor found Bolton much worse.

"There you are, Robert," Lady Bolton said with narrowed eyes and tight lips. "I hope you are satisfied. Our Christmas is ruined. How can I look after a sick man and run this house? The doctor says someone must attend him even at night."

"To keep the fire going. The lad can sleep in his room and do that."

"But during the day, when all my girls are busy . . . "

"Charlotte can sit with him, and so can I."

Charlotte had never liked the little dormer room on the top floor of Foxley Manor, perhaps because she had got on so badly with its former occupant, her brother Charles. In that room, Bolton now lay propped up on the narrow bed, looking at her with glazed eyes.

"Sorry to make this trouble for you. Never been this ill in my life."

"It is all right. We would do as much for anyone."

"I am glad you are here."

Charlotte did not reply. When she glanced at him again, he was asleep.

When she entered the room the next morning, his eyes were half closed, and he turned his head wildly from side to side between attacks of coughing. By noon he was delirious.

"The cannon, men, the cannon. Take it . . . "

Charlotte wiped the sweat from his face with a damp cloth.

"You shan't strike me with that. I am an Englishman."

"It is all right, Colonel."

"Mandze? Where have you been?"

"Who? Have no fear, sir. You are in good hands."

The sweat streamed down his face afresh, and Charlotte, seeing that his sleeping shirt was soaked, called her father. She waited in the hall while Sir Robert and the serving lad sponged Bolton and changed his bed linens.

"Here, take this stinking shirt to be washed while I fetch one of mine. He'll be alright under the covers a bit. Poor chap, body's like a forge. Watch him a moment, Charlotte."

Covers drawn up about his chin, Bolton lay on his back while Charlotte gazed down at the strong-jawed face with mixed feelings of pity and annoyance. She had hoped to spend the morning riding her new mare. Suddenly Bolton coughed and flung up his arm as though warding off a blow. The movement cast back the covers and, for the first time in her life, Charlotte found herself looking upon the body of a completely naked, mature man. The clean-muscled torso and the contrast between his milky white hips and bronzed throat and face amazed her. And there it lay, protruding from a mass of blond, wiry hair, the thing she had never looked upon before. Confused but fascinated, she could not take her eyes away. She was disappointed when he turned onto his belly and then shocked when she saw the crisscross of long welts across his broad back.

"Charlotte! For shame!" Her mother stood in the doorway, aghast.

"Oh, Mama, he kicked off his covers. You can put them back if it bothers you so."

They did not hear the footsteps of Sir Robert in the hall.

"Here's a shirt. Stand aside, Catherine." He raised his eyebrows. "Would you look at that back? Must be a story behind those scars. Quite a man. Got yourselves an eyeful, you two, what?"

"Father, you are disgusting."

That night Bolton went through a crisis so severe that the Foxleys summoned the vicar as well as the doctor, so severe that Charlotte felt impelled to pray for the recovery of this strange man whom she first despised and now pitied. The next morning she was embarrassed by the dreams she had experienced, dreams of a blond, naked man.

Whether in answer to her prayers or because of his strong constitution, Bolton's fever broke the next day, but his voice remained weak and his complexion looked waxen when Charlotte offered him a draught of brandy.

"You are all the medicine I need," he said with a faint smile.

The following day, with the help of Charlotte and her father, Bolton was able to sit by the fire for a while. He mentioned the book he gave Charlotte but confessed that he had never read it himself. "I met the chap who wrote it: Ligon. He came out a year before me and returned after only three years. Had a better time than I. But he ended up in debtor's prison all the same."

Charlotte hated her father for saying, "Not read the thing? Then Charlotte will read it to you."

Before she could respond, Bolton accepted. Charlotte hated him as well. There seemed to be a conspiracy to prevent her from enjoying her new little mare or completing her biography of Queen Elizabeth.

Deciding to get the chore over with quickly, each morning and afternoon Charlotte drew up a stool by the window to read from the green book by the feeble winter sunlight, while Bolton lay propped up in her brother's bed like a sickly boy being entertained by his mother, his eyes never leaving Charlotte's face. Did he have to stare so?

In spite of herself, Charlotte enjoyed the book's descriptions of a prosperous island, abounding with succulent fruits and governed by wise and good planters. Her interest faded, however, during a long account of how cane was grown and sugar refined. Bolton urged her to skip to the end.

"Barbados must be a pleasant, happy land," Charlotte said at the conclusion.

"Dear Charlotte," Bolton began.

Charlotte glared at him for this use of her given name, but he continued without apology.

"Ligon was a fool. He came out as a privileged lackey and returned to write his pretty little book, which is full of errors."

Offended by his mocking tone, Charlotte arose.

"It sounds convincing enough. Why did you let me read it then?"

"You could read the Book of Lamentations, and I would hang on every word."

"You make light of me." She started toward the door.

"Please stay. Look, Charlotte, the Barbados I knew was a tropical hell. No feasts and pleasant conversations for me. I never saw the island until we anchored in Carlisle Bay and they finally allowed us to come up from that dark, stinking hold and make us take off our filthy rags to be doused with sea water. There they left us, like so many naked animals, so the planters could come aboard and inspect us for physical defects. They sold me to a Roundhead, one Peter Simpson, as one of his white slaves to finish clearing the forest from his lands northwest of Holetown. Fifty men and women on three hundred acres. We made our own huts out of tree limbs and plantain leaves. Slept on the bare earth, like cattle. The labor was worse than you can imagine. Hour after hour of hacking away at stone-hard tree trunks in a constant, damp heat, wearing only a linsey-woolsey shirt and wool cap. All the while an overseer watched on horseback with a whip that cut through our clothing at every lash. You should see my back."

"I know . . . " Charlotte caught herself and added quickly, hoping she was not blushing, "What happened to you?"

"I endured that first year, but a good third of my fellow white slaves, or Christian servants as they were called, died. My owner discovered, as did other planters, that black slaves cost no more than white servants and, moreover, could work longer and harder in the sun. So he set his white workers to constructing a sugar mill. I was assigned to dig the foundation for a plantation house to replace their cabin of mastic logs. Seeing the man's difficulty with his plantation records, I asked if I might help. His overseer knew I was at Cambridge and had abused me the more for it, but had kept this knowledge to himself. To make a long story short, I became Simpson's secretary. Thereafter my life was more tolerable, but I shall never forget the hell I endured under the lash of that overseer's whip."

Awed by the passion of his speech, Charlotte looked at the planter with fresh respect. "How then did you come to own a plantation?"

"Simpson understood buying and selling, and his overseer knew how to drive slaves, white or black. The man wanted to build a three-storied house with tiny glass windows, low ceilings and a fireplace, entirely wrong for that climate. I designed him a long, two-floor dwelling with high ceilings and deep windows to let in the breezes. I am glad he heeded me, for it is now my house."

"Indeed? What happened to the Simpsons?"

"The planters tried to ignore the Civil War at first. They were glad to be free of interference, but Cromwell shipped out so many Royalist prisoners like me that they tipped the balance. The king's men gained influence over the aged governor and placed themselves in control of his council. They even proclaimed Charles to be their true sovereign and persecuted the Roundhead planters like Simpson. Poor man took to drink. I discovered the overseer had been cheating him for some time. When I confronted the fellow, he cursed me and tried to strike me with his whip. I knocked him down and beat him senseless, then sent him packing. That whip hangs over my doorway today. No slave of mine is flogged without my permission and only in private with a leather strap. Am I wearying you, Charlotte?"

"On the contrary. It is fascinating. How did you come to own the plantation?"

"Our crops were poor in 1650 and '51. Mistress Simpson grew homesick. She felt out of place with the new gentry of the island. Poor Simpson offered me a half interest in the plantation for five thousand pounds. Left me in charge and gave me fifteen years to pay the principal. I promptly sold off part of the land and the remaining terms of the white servants and invested the proceeds in more Africans and refining equipment."

"You have been successful, then?"

"In general, but it has not been easy. There were times I would have returned to England gladly but could not while the Roundheads ruled. Also, it takes much investment to make a sugar plantation go. Slaves cost twelve pounds these days, plus their food and clothing. You are at the mercy of the weather on one hand and the whims of Parliament and the king on another. Yet for all my troubles, I would not trade places with King Charles himself, had I but a queen of my own."

He paused, then smiling, asked, "Tell me, how did you know about my back?"

Caught off guard, Charlotte flushed and stammered. "Father said it was badly scarred."

She smoothed her skirt nervously before rising. "Well, we have finished the book, and you are mending. I must go."

"Mama was right about Colonel Bolton," Charlotte confided to her diary that night. "The man is a boor. He asked me a question that never would have passed the lips of a gentleman, an arrant breach of good manners. I was beginning to develop a measure of sympathy for the man. Now I wish I had not bothered to show him any kindness. I shall be glad when he recovers and we are rid of him. 'Tis time I concentrated on my wedding."

The next day Bolton dressed and took a few steps about the house, but Charlotte avoided him. By the end of the week he was able to stroll the grounds. Except for a drawn look about his eyes, he appeared to have recovered enough to depart, but Sir Robert persuaded him to remain for a gathering of neighborhood friends.

That evening, Marmaduke noticed how Bolton fastened his eyes on Charlotte. "Tell me I have no cause to be jealous," he jested.

"Don't be ridiculous. The man is twice my age."

In the hall with her parents, bidding guests good night, Charlotte could not avoid Bolton. Waiting in the background, he watched her give Marmaduke a discreet kiss, then fell in beside her as she turned to go upstairs.

"Charlotte, may I ask a question of you?"

"It is late, and I am rather tired."

"Do you really mean to marry that Harbinson boy?"

She drew in her breath at his impertinence and did not reply.

"Don't be angry. I have a confession. That Sunday morning at Ludgate, I first noticed you and only later recognized your father. Every night since, I have dreamed of you."

He took her hand, but she jerked it away. "You are insuffer-able, sir. If I were to tell my father, he would turn you out of the house this moment. Good night."

In her room, Charlotte sat on her bed, trembling. The man had insulted her. Perhaps she should report him to her father. Why had he come here to upset the household at such an important time? Damn him and his cocky manners and his sloppy accent. And damn his Barbados.

When sleep finally came, it was fitful, broken by the sort of dreams that had caused her such shame in recent days. She dreamed his arms were around her and her hands were thrust under his shirt against his bare back, feeling the old marks of the whip. Now she held his head against her breast, comforting him. His blond thatch down there was pressed against her own patch of dark hairs. Then, suddenly, she awakened.

"Charlotte, oh, Charlotte. Don't be afraid."

"How dare you enter my chamber?" she whispered.

"I cannot leave without telling you that I love you. Do you understand?"

Before she could answer, he leaned down and kissed her on the lips. She tried to pull away, but with one of his hands on her shoulder and the other on the small of her back, she could not move. Never had anyone, even the most ardent of her suitors, kissed her like this.

"You don't know what you are doing," Charlotte gasped.

"But I do . . . "

Quickly, before she could reply, he drew her closer and, without willing to, she put her arms around him and began returning his kisses as fervently as in her recent, troubling dreams.

When Charlotte came to the breakfast table, her mother said sharply, "You took long enough. We shall be late for church."

"Where is Colonel Bolton?" Charlotte asked hesitantly, trying to sound matter-of-fact.

"That rude man. He left at dawn without thanking me for all the inconvenience."

"He asked me to express his gratitude to both of you," Foxley said.

"Well, let us hasten, or we will be late for church."

"I am not going," Charlotte announced. "I feel feverish."

"You look well enough."

"If Charlotte says she is ill, Catherine, she is ill ... "

" 'Tis no wonder. Should not have spent so much time with that Bolton. He has spoiled everything. If she has caught this thing from him, I shall never forgive you, Robert."

The Charlotte Foxley who had mounted the stairs the previous night had been a proud young woman, definite about her hopes for the future, sure of her place in the world, outwardly self-possessed but actually naive. A very different person came down the stairs that morning. Although confused by what had happened to her during the night, she felt physically more alive than ever before and not in the least ashamed. Her only thought had been to see Richard Bolton again.

The Charlotte Foxley who returned to her room that Sunday morning was a wretched creature by comparison.

The realization of what had happened struck her as she watched her parents' coach disappear from view. Throwing herself across her bed, she wept until exhausted.

How could she have been so stupid? In spite of his talk of love, she had been nothing but a conquest for Bolton, probably just one of a long string. What would 'Duke do if he learned that his fiancée has been seduced by another man on the eve of their wedding? She must live the rest of her life with the knowledge of what she had done, or rather had permitted to be done to her, yes, and with the sense of having been callously betrayed in a manner calculated to humiliate her.

Charlotte wept until no more tears would come. By the time her parents returned from church, her eyes were so puffy and her face so red, that her mother ordered her to bed and her father sent for Doctor Goodfellow.

Finding no fever or lung congestion, the doctor diagnosed her trouble as "exhaustion and overexcitement of the nerves." He said he had observed many such cases in the Civil Wars and prescribed a week of rest.

But rest would not come for Charlotte. She passed the long hours brooding over what she saw variously as her shame, her deep sin, or her foolishness. She looked in vain for solace in the pages of her books of essays by Bacon and Montaigne, and poems by Donne. The Bible gave her no comfort, either, nor did Shakespeare.

Harbinson was allowed in her room briefly without a chaperone, but the sight of his earnest face only made her feel worse. Besides, his conversation now seemed banal to her. If he discovered her secret, surely he would reject her as a damaged piece of goods. He might even humiliate her in the privileged circle in which their families moved. But what if he were to forgive her? Charlotte suspected that she then would despise him for letting himself be so used. And even if she kept her guilty secret, she had herself to live with. Damn Richard Bolton and all men like him.

Charlotte really did not understand what had happened between her and Bolton. She had not wanted to involve herself with the planter. She had taken pains to avoid him, had been rude to him. How could she have made it more plain that her hand was spoken for?

Although there was not a more intellectually sophisticated woman in Bedfordshire, although she had been courted by many young men bent on marrying the only daughter of Robert Foxley, Charlotte had remained strangely innocent about sex. Her father joked about such things, without imparting any real knowledge. Her mother had never permitted the subject to be discussed in Charlotte's presence. In protecting her innocence, her parents had made her easy prey for the predatory Bolton. At least that was the way it appeared to Charlotte as she tried to sort out what she regarded as her humiliation.

The more she brooded, the more it seemed that her world

had come apart and could never be mended. That man had used her like a tavern bawd. He had made a mocking game out of conquering the haughty miss who had treated him with disdain. She could picture him boasting of his exploit over a pint of ale in a public house.

Charlotte wished desperately for someone in whom to confide. If she were a Papist, she could confess her conduct to a priestling, and while she might be given an onerous penance, at least she could feel forgiven. The minister of the village church would faint at her confession, surely. Such things only happened to serving maids. Prayer brought her no relief; it only caused her knees to ache.

Charlotte's morale was not helped when she overheard her mother say to her father: "Can it be that she has gone mad? I tell you, Robert, the girl acts demented, keeping to her room, speaking to no one. What has upset her so, I do wonder."

After a spell of loathing herself, Charlotte turned to hating Bolton. She burned the book he had given her about Barbados. She toyed with the idea of sending an anonymous letter to Whitehall to prevent his being knighted. But, occasionally, between these bouts of plotting revenge, she let her mind slip back to that brief time in which they had lain together in her bed and she had learned the secret that had been kept from her. How could she ever do that with anyone else?

At other times she considered calling in 'Duke and telling him that upon reflection she had decided against marriage to anyone, ever. She would devote her life to study and doing good works for the poor of the community. Thus would she expiate her sin. But then she considered what little patience she had for the humble folk of their estate and nearby village. And besides, that course would mean remaining under the rule of her mother.

The nearer the time drew to the day that she and 'Duke were to post their banns, the more distraught Charlotte grew, the more she felt trapped. The next time 'Duke came to Foxley Manor, she refused to see him. As she looked out her window at him riding away, slumped in his saddle, it came to Charlotte how, at a single stroke, she could escape from her situation and take revenge upon the man who had misused her. For the first time since her seduction, she wrote in her diary.

"The Prince of Denmark rejected self-destruction in favor of slaying the man who debauched his mother. If I could put a dagger in the heart of a certain wicked man, I would. But I am not Hamlet. Nor will I permit myself to turn Ophelia and take refuge in madness to escape my sorrow. I hate that vile man, but in all honesty, I loathe myself as well. Perhaps there is a way to take my revenge upon us both. It is something to think about. Oh, dear God, is Mama right? Am I losing my mind after all? Yet I must do something. Time is running out for me. No, the more I think about it, the more the thing makes sense . . . "

With an odd half-smile distorting her face, Charlotte put down her pen and stared into the fire.

"Father would hunt him down like a mad dog and kill him," she murmured.

. . . With the point of his knife at my throat, I was helpless to resist him. He said he would kill me if I cried out, or if I ever told another living soul. I wish now that I had resisted him and died. Forgive me, dear Father and Mother, for what I am about to do . . .

Charlotte sat in her room composing this, her third suicide note of the morning. Her hair hung over her face in a tangle. Her face had lost its normal self-possessed expression. Her eyes had grown dull. Although it was long past her normal time for dressing, she remained in her night clothes.

"Charlotte, I must talk to you." Her father stood in the doorway.

"Please leave me alone."

"No, we must talk. This is something I cannot discuss with your mother."

Charlotte turned her note face down. "Can't it wait?"

"No. You must pull yourself together and listen carefully. I made a mistake in opening our home to Richard Bolton. How was I to know he would get notions?"

My God, Charlotte thought, how did he find out? Then aloud, "Notions about what?"

Foxley cleared his throat in embarrassment. "About you. I received a message day before yesterday by post, from London. From Colonel Bolton. Been debating with myself ever since whether to mention it to you."

It took a moment for Charlotte to grasp his words. "Since the day before yesterday. I don't understand . . . "

"The fellow says it plain enough. Wants to marry you. Says he thinks you love him but that you are afraid to break your engagement. Says you don't care for Marmaduke at all. What about all this?"

Still Charlotte did not comprehend. "About what?"

"Damn it, girl, have you gone mad after all? Do you love 'Duke? Do you still want to go ahead with the marriage?"

"I thought I did . . . "

Foxley frowned, waiting for her to finish her sentence. Finally, he asked, "Well then, do you love Bolton?"

Charlotte arose and, with her arms about her father, leaned her head against his chest. "I don't know."

"Oh, my God, what will we tell your mother?" he said when her sobs finally subsided.

Catherine Foxley reacted more drastically than they had feared. Flying into hysterics, she raged at both her daughter and her husband and then gave way to tears out of their sight, in her room. She emerged an hour later, outwardly composed at last but with eyes full of anger.

"The banns tomorrow. What about them?"

"I suppose we will have to call them off," Foxley said.

"Surely, Robert, you don't wish her to marry that colonial adventurer?"

"No, but neither do I want her to marry young Harbinson. Not against her will."

"She should be forced to proceed. It is time she showed some sense of duty to her family."

"No one can force me, Mama," Charlotte said. "You are wasting your time to speak of it."

"What about poor Marmaduke? Oh, you are making such a mistake."

"I will tell him."

At first Harbinson took it better than Charlotte expected. His eyes brimmed with tears, but he did not berate her. She would have respected him more if he had.

"You never really loved me, then?"

"I was terribly fond of you, 'Duke. Fonder than of anyone."

"Was?" The look of pain on his face made Charlotte want to get this over with. She merely nodded.

"And you don't think you could become ... " His voice broke.

"Why take such a chance? I am sorry, 'Duke. That is all I can say. I don't like to be cruel, but it would be more cruel to go ahead. Forgive me if you can."

His face hardened. "Just now, Charlotte, I rather hate you. Mother tried to tell me that you were too selfish and headstrong to make a good wife. I see that she was right. You say we could not be happy together. Now that I understand for the first time the kind of person you really are, I wonder if you ever will be happy with anyone. Or that you will make him happy."

Two days later, Richard Bolton returned, freshly knighted by King Charles and looking full of expectation. Her outraged mother sent Charlotte to her room, where she remained for two hours, chafing, while Bolton and her father talked in the library. Coming down the stairs at Foxley's summons at last, she passed her mother, who said through tight lips, "Just remember, it is your life. If you make a mess of it, don't come crying on my shoulder."

Bolton arose and bowed when she entered the library but did not move toward her.

"My dear Charlotte."

Charlotte neither curtsied nor spoke to him.

"He has something to say to you, Charlotte."

"Quite," Bolton said. "Your father and I have been speak-

AN AUTHOR'S PARTY TO CELEBRATE PUBLICATION
OF ROBERT H. FOWLER'S SPOILS OF EDEN

To honor this outstanding work and to show
our appreciation for the Reagan Administration's
surplus cheese program, a Wine and Cheese
reception will be held on Saturday, May 4,
from 5 to 7 p.m., at Hilltop House,
240 Gettysburg Road, Shepherdstown.
(Directions on opposite page.)

The SPOILS OF EDEN is already out-selling
Fowler's previous work.

Listen to what the critics have to say...

Clifton Fadiman..."This is a book."

Robert Cromie..."I read it."
Norman Mailer..."I especially liked the
                   naughty bits."
Samuel Beckett..."Has anyone seen Godot?"

This book is about raising cane, a
favorite Fowler past time.

"Researching this book was fun."

                      Fowler quote.

"No! No use begging. The
royalties are mine, do you
hear! All mine!"

DIRECTIONS TO HILLTOP HOUSE: Rte. 15 South to
Rte. 114, the Mechanicsburg-Bowmansdale exit.
Turn right off exit, then take first left on
Old Gettysburg Rd. House is on top of hill on
right. Park in Methodist Church lot, around
corner. Fete is on third floor of hotel. Just
walk in. For those coming from Rte. 81 or
Mechanicsburg: take Rte. 114 (Market St.) to
Shepherdstown, then turn right onto Old Gettys-
burg Rd. As before, hotel is at the top of hill.

            THIS OCCASION IS A PRODUCTION OF

                    Wade Fowler
                      (hort)
                    Jack Davis
                      (cohort)

WILLIAM SHAKESPEARE, NATHANIEL HAWTHORNE, HERMAN
MELVILLE, GEOFFREY CHAUCER, CLIFFORD IRVING, AND
THE LITERARY ESTATE OF ANONYMOUS, CORDIALLY INVITE
YOU TO ATTEND A LITERARY EVENT.

Robert H. Fowler is the author of two highly acclaimed
historical novels—*Jim Mundy* and *Jason McGee*. When he
first visited Barbados as a tourist, he was impressed with its
long, rich history and intrigued with the possibility of using
the island as the setting for a new novel. Later, he and his wife
spent weeks in the country's archives, traveling the back-
roads, and talking to local historians to insure that the
background for *The Spoils of Eden* be completely accurate. Mr.
Fowler, a former newspaper reporter and editor, is the
founder and chairman of the board of Historical Times, Inc.,
publisher of magazines and books of popular history.

A WINE AND CHEESE FETE TO HONOR THE

PUBLICATION OF ROBERT FOWLER'S NEW BOOK:

THE SPOILS OF EDEN

(A SEQUEL TO HIS ACCLAIMED MEDICAL SUSPENSE
NOVEL, THE BOILS OF SWEDEN.)

ing with great frankness. I have asked him for permission to seek for your hand in marriage. He is concerned by the difference in our ages and by the fact that I would be taking you three thousand miles to a strange land. I gather that your mother does not have the highest opinion of me, but Sir Robert says it is you who must decide. And I would have it no other way. What say ye?"

Charlotte raised her eyes and stared at him until she saw a look of concern replace his confident expression.

"I would devote myself to your happiness," he said.

Still she made no reply.

"You would be Lady Bolton," her father intervened. "Richard assures me that you would want for nothing. It is up to you."

"Please, Father, would you leave us alone?"

After he had left, Bolton started to speak, but she held up her hand to silence him.

"There is something you must understand. I do not intend to spend my life knuckling under to any man. I will not be dictated to by anyone just because he wears trousers or is older than I."

Her chin trembled, but she met his gaze and did not blink.

"Another thing," she continued, and now her eyes danced. "You must swear to be faithful to me. I am not going halfway around the world with an unfaithful husband."

He ran to her and picked her off her feet, kissing her throat and laughing. "Oh, you minx. I would have shot myself if you had turned me down."

That night, Charlotte and Richard stood in the garden with her father to watch a comet blaze across the eastern horizon. Numb with happiness, she huddled under Richard's cloak as the strange light moved to the southwest.

"I wonder what it portends," she said.

"Great and lasting happiness, my dearest, what else?"

That night, after barring her door, Charlotte ripped out her most recent diary entries and burned them. Her despair now seemed like a bad dream. On a fresh page she wrote: "He is not like anyone I ever knew. I don't think he would be afraid of the devil himself. He possesses a tremendous strength that both frightens and attracts me. He has charmed all the servants, even old Nanny who thought there was no one like 'Duke. Father likes him enormously. Only mother cannot see what a wonderful man he is. He reminds me of Father's sorrel stallion. He undoubtedly will take some taming, but Father has taught me well in horsemanship. Richard says I will live like a queen in Barbados. Imagine, nearly a hundred slaves, all doing just as we tell them. And Richard promises in time to build me a house finer than Foxley Manor, with a library just for me. What did I ever see in Marmaduke Harbinson? I am to marry a real man."

Throughout England for several nights, people marveled at the great comet in the eastern skies, wondering what it meant. In the rear of their little cottage on the outskirts of Bristol, Moses Martin mutely watched with his wife and children. Tears ran down his cheeks, and he trembled in the dark, as his family pointed at the strange light and speculated about it with their neighbors.

3

... My marriage to Richard Bolton scandalized Bedforshire. Despite her mistrust and dislike of Richard, Mama, having made so many arrangements for my wedding to Marmaduke in our village church,

agreed simply to postpone the ceremony for a fortnight and carry on with a switch in grooms.

The church was packed with people who came as much out of curiousity, to see "this planter fellow Charlotte Foxley is marrying," as out of friendship for our family. The Harbinsons were the only people of any note who did not attend.

To this day, I cannot say exactly why I married Richard. I loved him, as I never dreamed I could love a man, yet he held for me an attraction that went deeper than that all-too-common emotion. I needed him in ways I cannot easily express. It was almost as though we were fated to wed, for better or for worse.

Nor can I say just why Richard married me. Some thought it was for my dowry. Others, such as Mama, thought it was for the prestige of relating himself to the famous Foxleys of Bedford, which, incidentally, I believe to be the real reason she married Father. My brother, the saintly Francis, insinuated that it was a matter of age seeking out youth. Only Cuthbert raised no objections. I think he had feared a merger of our lands with those of the Harbinsons, which would have spoiled his ambition to combine our estate with that of his wife's father. As for Charles, he was on duty at sea and did not learn of the marriage for months.

Richard was a handsome fellow, for sure, and with his new title he could have found himself any number of girls who would have made him a better wife than I. Truth to tell, I think he considered me a challenge. He was for me, as well.

Our union, although peaceful at first, was not always placid. There was to be much happiness for us, but also occasional heartbreak, and many a clash of wills. He was no less strong-minded than I, but far more skillful in hiding it. Where I too often spoke out plainly in those early days, he knew when to keep silent, when to take charge masterfully, and when and to whom to be deferential. Yet, he kept his eye ever on the main chance. At the precise moment of decision in some vital matter, he could act with alacrity and sometimes appalling ruthlessness.

Later, I discovered that some considered him overly ambitious and self-serving. And there sometimes appeared in him a streak of deviousness that I hated. He was to hurt me deeply, more than once.

But never have I known a man of greater charm. He swept me off my feet, and it took a while for me to regain my footing and stand up for myself. There was never another like him. I was overjoyed to become his wife.

What of my girlish dreams of becoming another Queen Elizabeth? I felt that, in marrying Richard, I would experience the sort of adventure and excitement that could never come my way as the wife of Marmaduke Harbinson. It seemed to me that, as mistress of a plantation with a hundred slaves, a title as Lady Bolton, and great wealth, I would come nearer to being a queen in Barbados than in old England.

So, we were wed. We spent our honeymoon in Birmingham, of all places, so that the ever practical Richard could order more equipment for his plantation's sugar works. Then we paid our final visit to Foxley Manor.

We considered taking Nanny Graham to Barbados with us, but she wisely refused. "I'm too old. Ye'd ha to bury me at sea."

When he heard we meant to take Nutmeg, Old Hadley offered to accompany us "ter look arfter yer horses and gardens," but Richard declined with a grace that saved our old groom's pride.

Dear Mama had been nagging Father for a year to let her follow the new fashion and replace our old, heavy oaken furniture with new pieces made of walnut. She seized on the opportunity to foist off on us many of her old articles. Although Richard winced at the cost of transporting them, he thought it politick to accept and did so with a courteousness that quite undid her.

We said goodbye to the servants and Mama on the porch at dawn the day after we dispatched the wagons with our furniture and wedding gifts. I held my tears through those of Nanny and Old Hadley, but broke down when I saw that Mama was weeping. We clung to each other as we had not since I was a little girl.

"Oh, I am so concerned for you," she said.

"It will be all right, Mama," I assured her. And I promised to write regularly.

Father insisted on riding his own horse with us to the crossroads at Wolverton. I did not realize how much I loved that dear old man until we said goodbye. Richard and I turned our steeds west toward

Bristol, free at last of my family. A decade older and wiser, I know now that one is never free of one's past.

It was a chilly morning in March. Bristol's narrow harbor was so close packed with ships that it took a while for Richard Bolton to locate the *Mary Leigh*. With no space available alongside any wharf, she had to be boarded across the deck of an adjacent vessel. Riding high above the narrow tidal waters of the Avon, to Bolton's critical eye, she looked both clumsy and untidy. Had he been less eager to return to Barbados, he would have walked back to King Street to the comfortable new inn where Charlotte still lay abed and suggested that they extend their honeymoon to wait for a more presentable ship.

But then, his costly machinery for a new windmill was crated and ready for loading along with the oaken furniture donated by the Foxleys. And he had arranged for the delivery of a six-week supply of oats and hay for Charlotte's little mare, Nutmeg. More important, a new war had broken out with the Dutch, and there was talk of requiring convoys to the Indies. Bolton preferred sailing on a dilapidated ship to delays and further expenses.

Having confirmed his decision, he borrowed a light for his pipe from a sailor and strolled along the docks bordering Bristol's Marsh district between the Avon and its tributary, the Froome. He marveled at the number and variety of ships tied up in this, England's second busiest port and her chief outlet to the West Indies and North America. The masts clustered thickly, like the naked trees of a great forest in winter.

As he knocked the ashes from his pipe, it occurred to Bolton that, if he were a young man again, he might seek his fortune in this prosperous town of twenty thousand. Instead of producing raw sugar under a tropical sun, he could be refining and selling it to the English masses, yes, and living most agreeably in one of the merchants' fine mansions north of the Froome. Ah, well, he hadn't done so badly in the sixteen years since he was shipped off to virtual slavery. And his situation had been considerably improved just in the past four months back in England. Besides being knighted, he had found and married a most suitable girl, not perfect perhaps, but certainly younger and more attractive than he had hoped for. Charlotte wanted some maturing, but he could hardly wait to show off this only daughter of Sir Robert Foxley to his friends in Barbados. What a prize he had won.

He smiled at the recollection of what Foxley had said about Charlotte. "Not like other girls at all, you know. Got more sense than the rest of the family put together. Bit hard to handle at times, I warn you. Got a strong mind, take that as you will. But you keep her respect, and you'll not want a better wife. Afraid she suffers fools badly. She'll learn to moderate her tendency to speak her mind so bluntly. I'll miss having someone about the house to talk to on equal terms. Don't you go squelching her intellect, or I'll never forgive you."

Then Foxley had mentioned a dowry figure so large that Bolton could only respond with "most generous, indeed."

He looked forward to seeing the faces of certain greedy merchants in Barbados when they came around to demand payments on their loans. The world had suddenly become his oyster, and it contained a pearl named Charlotte. Caught up in a joyous mood, he ran back to the Llandoger Trow as eagerly as a boy racing home from school.

"What is the matter?" Charlotte demanded at his breathless entrance.

"Out of that bed, you lazy wench. Let's make the best of our last day in Bristol, or for that matter in England."

They spent the rest of the morning and early afternoon walking about the town, admiring its Custom House, Guildhall, and several beautiful churches. Avoiding the waterfront, Richard later left Charlotte to browse in a booksellers on High Street while he oversaw the loading of their equipment and goods. The *Mary Leigh* now squatted low in the water. Richard wondered what Charlotte would think about the smell of all the barrels of salt fish going aboard the vessel. It was nearly dark before the man from the livery stable arrived with Nutmeg and a sled laden with feed for the mare. Forgetting his promise that

Charlotte could watch, he blindfolded Nutmeg and led her gently across the boards and down to her narrow pen on the main deck.

He returned to the Llandoger Trow to find Charlotte fuming at his long absence. "No time to fetch you," he explained. "They wanted to move the ship from the wharf and have her ready to sail upon the midmorning tide. Don't sulk, and I'll buy you a memorable feast for your supper."

By the next morning, the *Mary Leigh* lay anchored in midstream below the juncture of the two rivers. Muffled against the cold and filled with apprehensions, Charlotte waited for a boat to take them and their trunks to the vessel. They were met at the gangplank by a dapper little man with a dark beard, who said with a reproachful Welsh lilt, "Name's Williams. I'm the captain. Understand they've sold you me own cabin for the voyage. Quartermaster'll show you the way."

Between Nutmeg's pen and a longboat, little room remained for the score of passengers who enviously watched the well-dressed couple come aboard. Just forward of the main deck, there rose a steep forecastle, from which protruded the short, forward mast. Just aft lay a low half-deck, which housed the tiller, and behind it a high poop containing the captain's cabin and a smaller one for his mates.

Concealing her dismay at the ill-furnished, low-ceilinged space, Charlotte joined Richard on the half-deck to watch the approach of another boat carrying a score of passengers with bound hands, under the guard of two constables. After these people had been marched up the gangplank and exchanged for receipts from the captain, the constables returned to the boat and, with a sailor's help, carried up a barely conscious middle-aged man in worn-out clothing.

The captain counted out several coins, while his bosun's mate hauled the man below decks.

"What is going on there, Richard?" Charlotte asked.

"They are being Barbadosed, transported."

"But the ragged fellow was drunk."

"I expect the constables collected him on their way. Not strictly legal, but they have rid Bristol of a public nuisance and picked up a bit of coin. The captain will make his money back several times over in Bridgetown."

"And the others?"

"Judging from their dress, I'd say several are Quakers."

"How sad. They look so innocent. Did you note the older man, the one being helped by the lad? He has the face of a saint."

Suddenly it came to her. "Richard, you remember the Sunday we met? We could not get into Saint Paul's because of a disturbance."

"I thank the Almighty we could not. I might have missed meeting you."

"That is not what I mean. The two Quakers who accosted the king. It is they! The old man and the boy."

Charlotte might have questioned the two Quakers then had not Captain Williams ordered his crew to shut the ordinary passengers in the forward hold and haul up the anchor. Then, just as the sailors began to crank the capstan, a signal gun sounded from the shore, and a cockleboat carrying a single passenger drew alongside. Charlotte looked down into the face of a stout, sandy-haired man of about thirty.

"What the hell do you want?" the captain demanded.

"I am David Higganbotham, a physician ... "

"I don't give a damn about your name or your occupation. The tide is ready to turn, and you are wasting valuable time. State your business and begone."

"Your company sold me passage this morning." The man waved papers at the captain. "They said you would find me cabin space."

"Lord save me. Where's your blasted baggage?"

"I have only this small trunk."

On deck, out of breath and sweating despite the cold, the man handed his papers to the captain.

"The fools did sell you cabin space, and I have none left

except my first mate's. Here bosun, take his stuff to the mate's cabin. Bring up the anchor!"

The *Mary Leigh* shuddered as the anchor broke free of the Avon's muddy bottom. Like a horse reluctant to leave its stable, the heavy laden vessel remained in place briefly until the current turned her sideways. Then the captain began yelling orders and rushing from one side of the half-deck to the other. Brushing against Richard, he growled, "Either stay in your cabin or go up on the poop deck."

They were joined above by the new passenger. "Our captain does not mince words," he said to Richard.

"Aye, and I expect we'll have the smoother voyage for it. How do you do? I am Richard Bolton, and this is my wife, Charlotte."

The man took off his hat and bowed. "My pleasure. It seems I am to share a cabin with the captain. He is none too happy and the first mate even less, for he is to be shunted to the forecastle. I feel badly about that."

"Don't," Richard replied. "I overheard you say you had paid good money. A doctor of medicine, eh? You'll find work aplenty in Barbados, believe me."

" 'Tis not my plan to practice medicine there, Mister Bolton. I just got word that my brother has died out on the island. I am hastening to close out his estate. Did you know James Higganbotham?"

"Why, yes, but only slightly. Grew cotton in Saint George Parish. Sorry to hear of his death."

As they chatted in the cautious way of strangers getting acquainted, the tide started its strong seaward run. All sails still furled except for one, the *Mary Leigh* soon moved briskly down the Avon, through a spectacular gorge and then past low hills and deep-grassed meadows, six miles to where the river emptied into the broad Severn.

Charlotte was glad the men were talking. She needed the privacy to sort out her emotions at the sight of her homeland, her beloved England, sweeping past. Surely she would miss her native land. Also she had never been to sea. The ship smelled of fish; her cabin was cramped; and the captain's language appalled her. Besides these apprehensions, she was consumed with curiosity about the man and boy.

With the other transportees, the Martins remained in the hold until the Somerset coast lay too far off the port bow for even the strongest swimmer to reach. When John Martin stumbled up to the deck, he broke into tears and Moses silently took his hand. Others groaned or cursed. The drunken fellow who had been carried aboard came up last, hands shielding his eyes, weaving to keep his footing against the rise and fall of the deck. He made such an uproar that the sailors bound and gagged him and lashed him to the mainmast.

After satisfying himself that the worn sails of the *Mary Leigh* were set properly and the helmsman understood his course, the captain struck a pose on the rail of the half-deck and took up a megaphone.

"I will brook no disorder on my ship," he announced. "Newgate will seem like a paradise if you steal so much as a crust. Strike or threaten another, and in a twinkling I will have you whipped. There, that's the only warning you will get. Now, these are the rules you will obey on this passage ... "

While the captain hectored his passengers, Richard asked Doctor Higganbotham why he looked so pale.

"I am having some difficulty with the motion of the sea."

Richard laughed. "Never fear. You'll get your sea legs."

"It is my stomach that concerns me. By the way, I meant no offense when I addressed you as Mister Bolton earlier, Sir Richard. The mate set me straight. My apologies to you and Lady Bolton."

"Nonsense," Richard replied. "I'm not used to the title anyway, Doctor. We will be seeing each other a good deal the next few weeks. Hope you play cards."

"Fear I must disappoint you, but I did bring along a good supply of books, both medical and otherwise."

Richard groaned. "Another bookworm. Hear that, Charlotte? My wife stripped her poor father's library. Well, the two of you will have something to talk about at any rate."

At first, Charlotte had thought the doctor too dull to bother with, but now she smiled at him. "Yes, we might well wish to exchange volumes after we have grown used to shipboard life."

Higganbotham forgot his queasiness for a moment to watch with envy how Charlotte leaned on her husband's arm and bent her head close to his. He already had noted her slender waist and fair complexion. And to think she was a woman of learning. What a lucky man was this Richard Bolton, to have such a wife and a new title.

The *Mary Leigh* encountered heavy weather while still in sight of Lands End. Although Richard dismissed it as "just a bit of a blow," both Charlotte and Doctor Higganbotham grew seasick, and the captain ordered all the other passengers to remain in the hold, out of the way of his sailors, who were kept busy taking in or letting out sail. Charlotte put on her bravest face, but she was terrified by the violent pitching of the vessel as it dived down one slope of the foam-capped waves and plunged her bow into the next. The ship shuddered under the punishment, and her ancient timbers cried out in constant complaint. While Richard saw to providing Nutmeg with a harness to keep her from falling in her sea-drenched pen, Charlotte put her hands over her ears to shut out the sound of the wind shrilling through the rigging and of Higganbotham's retching next door. She forced herself to fight against the desperate wish to be back at Foxley Manor. She could not recall having ever been so sick.

Her peace of mind was not helped by overhearing Captain Williams confide to Richard that the *Mary Leigh* was leaking faster than his decrepit pumps could keep up. "I don't have hands enough to handle the sails and man the pumps properly. If this don't let up, we may have to turn back."

"Why not press some of your passengers into service?" Richard asked.

"Easier said than done. That would be like commanding a second crew, and I have enough trouble with this lot."

"I would command it for you."

As her husband outlined how the transportees could be made to help ("If they don't work, they don't eat"), Charlotte saw what her father had meant when he praised Richard's knack for organizing things. Quickly, he explained a plan under which all pumping duties would be performed by passengers, leaving the understaffed crew to handle tasks requiring greater skills.

The storm turned out well for the voyage. The winds drove the *Mary Leigh* southerly at a good clip. By the time the weather improved several days later, Richard had forged the able-bodied passengers into an efficient work force. Younger and nimbler ones drew lookout duty. Others were set to helping the ship's cook, but most took turns at working the canvas pumps in the bilge. At noon on the first clear day, Captain Williams took a sighting of the sun and declared himself well ahead of schedule.

With the return of good weather and the departure of her seasickness, Charlotte mentioned to the captain and Richard her desire to interview the Quaker man and boy. Both men opposed the idea. "Every one of them has some sad tale of woe," Captain Williams said. "Start letting them play on your sympathy, and they will pester the life out of you."

"He is right," Richard said.

But Charlotte was not to be put off so easily. "We have paid a handsome price for this cabin," she said. "I fail to see why we need anyone's permission to invite others here. But, if necessary, I will go down into the hold to see them."

After breakfast next day, Richard, with an air of resignation, escorted Moses and John Martin to the cabin and left.

Hats firmly in place on their heads, the pair declined Charlotte's invitation to sit.

"Forgive the inconvenience, but were you not at Saint Paul's the day after the Lord Mayor's last show?"

"Yes, ma'am," John replied.

"And did you not address the king?"

"My father did."

"Why does he not speak for himself?"

"He cannot. He suffered a stroke. In Newgate Prison . . . " John's voice broke.

Charlotte arose and took his hand. "I did not mean to upset you. Please sit and tell me about it."

Facing the lad across the table, while his father remained standing, Charlotte gradually drew from him the story of how they had come to be on the steps of Saint Paul's, what had happened to them after their arrest, and more.

Natives of Taunton, Moses Martin and his wife had been converted to Quakerism several years earlier, when George Fox preached to a crowd of serveral thousand in an orchard near their new home on the outskirts of Bristol. Ernestine Martin thereafter had devoted herself to simple good works amongst the poor of the district, but Moses had grown increasingly zealous, going so far as to preach to parishioners outside established churches. The lord mayor of Bristol, who hated Quakers, had had him flogged out of the gates and instructed the sheriff to crop his ears if he returned. Next, Moses had been thrown into jail for similar offenses in Bath. After a respite at home, he had betaken himself to Taunton with the intent to save his native town from its sins. An indignant housewife had doused him with the contents of her chamberpot. And among those who had ridden the hapless prophet out of town on a rail had been some of his boyhood friends. Later, near Ilminster, a country squire had set his hunting dogs on him.

Torn between sympathy for John and amusement, Charlotte asked, "What did your father say that so angered folk?"

"He told them their churches are vain, empty steeple houses. And he called King Charles a tyrant."

"Was not this painful to you?"

"Me mother worried herself sick. Didn't bother me so much. At dame's school most students be Friends. Worst part was my brother Jacob ordering me about when Father was away and my sister Sarah nagging at me."

"What impelled your father to confront the king?"

"Thee see, he calmed down after the pack of dogs had at

him. Stayed home and prayed and read his Bible, until they passed them new laws against our meetings. One morning he tells us he is off to London. Wouldn't say why. Sarah and me mother begged him not to go, but when they seen 'twas no use, they asked Jacob to go, too. Jacob said he had to work to feed us, and I should go, as I was of little use to anyone anyway."

Charlotte felt uncomfortable, talking about Moses Martin while he stood before her as mute and unmoving as a statue, but she had got too caught up in the boy's story to stop now.

Sleeping in haystacks and hedgerows, they had reached London within a week, a few days before the lord mayor's show. The proprietor of the Bull and Mouth, true to his reputation, had allowed them free lodging in the stable behind his Aldersgate hostelry.

Charlotte smiled at the lad's enthusiastic account of how he and his father had wandered through London's streets and of his awe at the lord mayor's parade. "Did you ever see so many fine boats? And all them cannon booming away. I thought I should never want to go home."

"It was a grand occasion. Tell me, did you not know your father's intentions?"

"Nay. I was standing there thinking the king was just a man when my father raised his staff and began shouting."

"I know. I stood not twenty feet away at the time," Charlotte replied. "And I followed you to Newgate. What happened after that?"

Charlotte was fascinated by his description of life in prison and of their appearance before the lord mayor.

"And Sir John Lawrence ordered your banishment? How cruel and unjust."

John explained about the suspended sentence.

"Then why were you exiled?"

"Thou see, Father could not speak, so we thought there would be no more trouble. Then Bristol got a new lord mayor, and he said Father could enter the city again. By now the tailor shop was busier than ever. Friends thought Father a hero for what he done. Brought us their trade. Father took up the needle

again. Jacob married and brought his wife home. We got care-
less, I fear. Didn't watch Father proper. One night, as we sat
down to our supper, two constables came for Father. He had
written out a prophecy and nailed it to the door of Bristol
Cathedral."

"What kind of prophecy?"

"They read it in court. He said England was another
Babylon and that God would punish the land if King Charles
and Parliament did not stop persecuting us. He warned a great
sickness will come upon England and carry off whole families
at once. And he wrote that London itself would be destroyed by
fire."

"And what happened?"

"They banished him."

"But you committed no offense, John. Why did they exile
you?"

"I am not exiled. We could not let Father come alone. Jacob
sold my bond for three pounds. I think he was glad to get rid of
Father and me. I don't mind. Will have me freedom in five
years, when I am eighteen. Some says Barbados be a pleasant
land where folks never needs a coat and can live on fruit."

"Much will depend, I suppose, on who buys your term of
service."

"I do worry about Father. Some says they be more tolerant
of Friends in Barbados. Anyway, he lives in his own world.
Some thinks him mad, but mayhap them that beat us and
imprisoned us is mad. Father may be the sanest man on this
ship. But mad or sane, he be me father, and I must look after
him."

Charlotte could not help hugging the boy.

"My husband and I will do as much as we can for you,
John. Thank you for telling me your story. You are a brave
lad."

Charlotte spent the afternoon recording John's story in her
diary. "And to think that Richard objected to my questioning
the pair. *Sir* Richard might as well learn now that he cannot

dominate me like a child. What makes men think they can ride roughshod over women in such matters? It would serve him right if I told only Doctor Higganbotham what I have learned. There is a gentleman who respects a good mind, whether it be in male or female form. We had a grand talk last night about Shakespeare and Bacon while Richard played cards with that trite little Captain Williams."

Under Richard's scheme for augmenting Captain William's crew, few passengers escaped assignments. He pressed Moses Martin into service as a sailmender and gave John a daily watch as a lookout in the crow's-nest. Agile as a monkey, John outdid any sailor in climbing to his post. He enjoyed a sense of freedom sitting high above the crowded center deck, rocking with the rhythm of the sea, while below him his father sat cross-legged against Nutmeg's pen, with his lap full of mending for the crew.

John also liked to watch Charlotte as she and Doctor Higganbotham promenaded about the poop deck, talking. He wondered if there were other women as lovely as she on Barbados. Nothing so pleased him as for her to smile and wave at him.

Having found her sea legs, Charlotte began to enjoy the voyage. She found it exhilarating to brace herself against the rail with the deck slanted beneath her, just letting the wind blow through her hair. Now the sight of whitecaps stimulated rather than frightened her. She did not like the toilet arrangements on the *Mary Leigh,* however. An amused Richard stood guard to make certain no one approached when she used the little railed platform on the stern. She objected to his jokes about her modesty. "I fear I have not married a gentleman."

"And you were no lady until you married me and gained the title."

All in all, those few weeks on the sea were happy ones for Charlotte Foxley Bolton. She grew to like the snugness of the cabin. The creaking of the masts and the sighing of the wind through the rigging became comforting sounds. David Higganbotham could always be depended on for a good conversation, despite his shyness. When she grew bored, she amused herself with daydreams of her pending new life on Barbados. But best of all were the nights.

From the moment he had taken her under her father's roof, Richard Bolton had become her Adam and she, in her mind, his Eve. Although she would never tell him, she almost believed, had he not sent his letter to her father, she just might have killed herself. On the ocean, in the privacy of their little cabin, she discovered night after night the magic that exists between a man and a woman in love. Her first climax, soon after her bout with seasickness, took her unawares, for no one had ever explained such things to her. Richard put his hand over her mouth, lest the captain and Higganbotham hear her moans.

Afterwards, she asked him the question that had bothered her since their wedding: "Why did you come to my room that night? Were you so sure of me?"

"I was desperate. There was not time to win you by a gradual approach, by a siege, if you will. It was all at once or not at all. A bold sortie."

"It was a knavish thing to do. Father would have killed you. But I am glad you had the courage."

During their preparations for bed one night, Charlotte asked Richard another question that had been bothering her: "What will happen to the old man and the boy when they reach Barbados?"

"Someone will buy their indentures, I expect."

"Things could go hard for them, then, if they got the wrong sort of master?"

"They could hardly expect to be rewarded for what he did."

"Yet the old man is so frail. And the boy is so sensitive. I do worry about them."

"They are not our concern."

"Have you any white slaves?"

"My only slaves are Africans. I used to have a family of white tenants, but I got rid of them. Except for my overseer, Wilkens, and I, everyone at Bolton Hall is black."

Charlotte waited until they were in their bunks and the lantern was extinguished to ask, "Those two Quakers . . . Why don't you purchase their bonds?"

"I have no use for a mad tailor or a snot-nosed boy. I would rather apply their cost toward a sturdy black field hand."

"Then could I not pay the price and set them free? Use my own funds?"

"Look you, Charlotte, I indulged you in bringing them up here to tell their story, but I must put my foot down on further involvement."

Charlotte, resisting the impulse to flare up, forced herself to reply in a calm tone, "He is such a bright, winsome boy. And, however much we may deplore what his father did, still one must admire his courage."

"I have no such difficulty."

"It would be my own money," she persisted.

What he next said and his tone shocked her.

"Understand me well, Charlotte. You are going to a strange country, and you do not know the conditions there. I will not argue this point with you further. I forbid what you propose, and I will not hear another word about it."

It required all of her willpower not to respond. Long after he had fallen asleep, she lay awake, choking back angry tears. But she did not mention the subject to him again.

None of the things Captain Williams dreaded on leaving Bristol actually happened. The *Mary Leigh* did not encounter a hurricane. Her pumps did not break down. She met no hostile Dutch ships. The criminals among his passengers were not too much for his shorthanded crew to handle. He did not run out of fresh water; in fact, he made such swift progress on the southerly leg of his voyage that he did not have to stop at the Azores to refill his kegs as usual. True, the *Mary Leigh* had continued to leak at a distressing rate, but, under the direction of Sir Richard Bolton, the passengers had kept his bilge pumped dry.

Fine fellow, that Sir Richard. Good company, too. Although he contributed little, the captain liked the talk between the Boltons and Doctor Higganbotham. He found Lady Bolton's condescending air a bit hard to take, but damn, she was a fine-looking young woman. All in all, Captain Williams could not have asked for better company nor for a smoother voyage. Now that they had changed course to catch the ever-helpful trade winds, now that passengers and crewmen no longer had to bundle themselves against the weather, well, he almost hated for the voyage to end.

John Martin, on duty in the crow's-nest, first thought he saw a bank of blue clouds on the western horizon. He waited for a few minutes and then squinted again through cupped hands. Finally he shouted down to the quarterdeck, "Land ho!"

The captain drew out his spyglass, then handed the instrument to Richard.

"There she lies, Sir Richard."

"Yes, I can make out Mount Hillaby. Here, Charlotte. Take your first look at your new homeland."

By afternoon, with a strong breeze from the southeast, the *Mary Leigh* had sailed near enough to the island for them to make out its rocky windward shore with the naked eye.

"We call that district Scotland because it is so rugged compared to the westward or lee shore," Richard explained.

"And your house?"

"*Our* house overlooks the upper west coast. We won't see it from the ship. The normal route into Carlisle Bay from England goes around the lower part of the island."

Captain Williams interrupted. "Actually, I am changing course. We are north of my intended landfall anyway, and with this wind 'twill be easier to skirt the northern headland."

"There you are, Charlotte. 'Tis a good omen. By morning we may see our house after all."

The sun went down in a sky rimmed with colors Charlotte

had not known existed. The captain shortened his sails as night fell, and he stationed special lookouts in the bow with lead lines. The next morning, Richard awakened Charlotte early to show her the sun rising out of a delicate, light blue sky over Mount Hillaby.

"That town there is Speightstown, or Little Bristol, as some call it. Look down the coast and then raise the glass a bit. See the stone tower about a mile inland? That is the housing for our new windmill. Just below it in the grove, see the house with the long porch? That is home."

Charlotte could tell little about the house at such a distance, but she was captivated by the series of long terraces that led up like giant steps from curving white beaches.

"Sir Richard, Lady Bolton," Higganbotham said. "At long last we are here."

"Yes," Richard replied, "And now that we are, let's hear no more of this Sir Richard and Lady Bolton. Richard and Charlotte will do very nicely. You'll find us a democratic lot on Barbados. Gentlemen treat each other as equals."

Richard excused himself to arrange for his transportee crew to help him prepare his millworks and household furniture for quick unloading. Seeing that Higganbotham wanted to speak, Charlotte smiled at him sweetly to encourage him.

"I do hope that you will be happy here, Charlotte."

"Why thank you, David. There is every reason for us to be so. Isn't this an exciting day?"

"But a sad one, too, at least for me. I shall miss your company and Richard's."

"No reason for that. We hope you will visit us. And Richard says 'twould not surprise him were some rich planter's widow to end your bachelorhood and keep you on Barbados."

It amused her to see the earnest physician blush. Although she had sometimes found the man boring, she had come to respect him, and it was plain that he admired her. She looked into his face, until he stammered, "That would be most unlikely. I only wanted to say how much I appreciate your kindness and to assure you that, if ever I may be of service ... "

"If you are truly sincere, there is a matter I would like to discuss with you in strictest confidence."

She motioned for him to follow her to the stern rail, out of hearing of the helmsman or Captain Williams.

The *Mary Leigh* laboriously tacked back and forth against stubborn headwinds through most of the day before she reached a point far down the lee coast for her final run into Carlisle Bay. Charlotte, who had pictured Bridgetown as a dreamy village of log huts, was amazed at the two-story buildings and the many ships gathered close to a shore lined with wharves and warehouses.

Richard came up from the hold to point out landmarks.

"To our right, that is Needham's Fort, our chief defense for the harbor. Over beside the mouth of that little river, just below the town, you see Willoughby's Fort. That steep thatched roof is Saint Michael Church. Over there, to your right, that is the new parish church still under construction. 'Twill be the finest and largest in the Indies."

He frowned. "Damned odd. The ships normally anchor all about. I wonder why they have drawn in so close. And why would the militia be out in such force on a Thursday?"

Their attention was diverted by a red-uniformed militia officer approaching the ship in a boat rowed by several half-naked black slaves. As the boat drew alongside, Richard called to the officer, "Hey there, Wainwright. What is going on?"

"Why, Bolton, you devil. You've come back at a good time. We've got a fresh alert against a Dutch fleet. Lord Willoughby has been laid up with injuries in Surinam since February. He's left his nephew, Henry, behind as deputy governor, and the young puppy is afraid of his shadow. I say, who is that with you?"

4

From the Diary of Charlotte Foxley

The Bow Bells Tavern
Bridgetown, Barbados,
April 20, 1665

Arrived at last. I take up my pen at first light, while Richard still sleeps, to record my impressions of this strange but lovely land. I slept but little last night. Our bed seemed to rise and fall as though we were still at sea, and I could not erase from my mind reports of a Dutch fleet under their famous admiral de Ruyter, which has been ravaging English slaving stations in West Africa. One of our warships is freshly arrived here from Africa with verification of these seizures. And King Charles himself has dispatched warnings that this Dutch fleet might cross the ocean and swoop down on Barbados itself.

Richard's friends scoff at these fears. They are more concerned about losing valuable sugar harvest time reporting for militia musters than any Dutch threat. In point of fact, we landed yesterday afternoon in the midst of a fresh alarm. Lookouts had reported several sails on the southern horizon. Richard says they probably were only a convoy on its way to Surinam and not to worry. This morning, with a breeze blowing through our room and the sky full of gorgeous colors, my fears seem foolish.

This place will take some getting used to, however. The afternoon

heat is beyond description, like a steaming hot blanket over everything. Richard says I will find it cooler at the plantation because of
the higher elevation there. And I wonder if I ever will learn the names
of the peculiar trees on this island. Barbados, many do believe, takes
its name from one of these. Called "The Bearded Fig Tree," it is a
grotesque thing, which is distinguished by aerial roots or filiaments
that sprout downward from the branches. When these "beards" get a
footing in the earth, they grow into additional supports for the main
trunk. It is not known what the original Indian inhabitants called
this island. They disappeared long before the first English settlers
landed 38 years ago. Spanish explorers referred to the island as "Los
Barbudos," or "The Bearded Ones," apprently in reference to the
Bearded Fig Trees. Hence, Barbados. Richard has warned me about
another strange tree, the manchineel, whose leaves contain a caustic
substance, which makes it dangerous for humans or animals to stand
under them during a rain. And there are many other equally exotic
trees and flowers.

Yet, strangest of all are the people. I have seen Negroes in London
and even in Bristol but never in such profusion as here, where they
now outnumber the white population two to one. They move about
with a sort of sullen grace, faces like ebony masks, naked from the
waist up, women as well as men.

The white people are quite different from folk back home, too.
They thronged the docks as we came ashore, all demanding the latest
news and asking what cargo we carried. Richard appears to be
acquainted with everyone. One hears proper English spoken very little
here. Not only are the accents atrocious, but they are uttered in voices
far too loud for my ears.

Half the men are clad in a new sort of red militia uniform. The
others wear long linen jackets over shirts open at the neck. About their
waists one usually sees a wide belt, and in that belt is often carried a
pistol. Imagine him further sporting long boots, despite the heat, his
face shaded by a broad-brimmed straw hat, his right hand occupied
with a short-lashed whip, and you have a picture of the typical
Barbadian male.

Their manners are as appalling as their accents. They ask such
blunt questions. No one seems to know his place, not even the keeper of

this otherwise excellent inn. A presumptuous Cockney, to whom my father would give the back of his hand, he winked and smirked as he offered us his "bridal suite."

Before Richard left to see to bringing our goods ashore, he had a large tub in our rooms filled with delicious fresh water. What a joy to bathe away the salt and grime of our long voyage. Then, near sundown, he escorted me about the town. I am amazed at the supply of goods to be purchased here, and at prices far lower than in London. Richard says they use receipts from sugar warehouses as currency. He likes to point out that, while Barbados is smaller than most English counties, measuring only 21 miles in length and 14 in width, it produces more wealth than the largest. I suppose in time I shall become used to the Barbadian habit of boasting.

During our promenade, we came upon a sort of square called Eggington's Green, where, penned like animals, we espied our hapless fellow passengers from the Mary Leigh, *the poor Martins among them. Richard refused my request to speak to them, and I let sleeping dogs lie. However, I am troubled by the report that the exiles, or anyway their terms of indenture, will be auctioned off early today. Usually, says Richard, the buyers go out to the ships to inspect their human wares but, because of the Dutch scare, this lot was brought ashore immediately.*

I only hope that David Higganbotham has heard this report and will follow my instructions. The proprietor of another tavern, The Roebuck, was a friend of his brother, and he insisted that David lodge with him last night. More I shall not say, except that we shall see who has the last word in the matter of the Martins, Richard or I. Friend Husband will have to learn that I am not got around as easily as he may think. He and his "I forbid what you propose," indeed!

I can hardly wait to see my new home. It sounds like a garden spot. Mistress of my own grand estate, imagine. I am delighted to be safely ashore in this Land of Eden, with all our dangers far behind us and a prosperous, peaceful future before us. Why ever did I think I might miss tiresome old England?

The militiaman on watch in the tower of Christ Church over-looking the coast below Bridgetown did not want to be accused of crying wolf. There had been too many false alarms of late. He simply called for his sergeant to bring his spyglass and join him.

"There, beyond Oistin's Bay. Watch the edge of the mist."

The sergeant raised the glass to his eye. "Mist, hell, I call it a proper old fog. You sure it weren't your imagination? Wait!"

He focused on a break in the mist, as a ship with towering poop and three gun decks glided across his view like an enormous ghost.

"Great God Almighty! Never saw such a vessel. Can't make out the flag, damn it."

He held his glass steady as a smaller ship, then another and another passed through the clear space and disappeared back into the fog.

"Dutch or English, they are men-of-war. Better safe than sorry."

"Hey down there," he shouted to the rest of his squad in the churchyard. "Get your fingers out of your arses. Prepare your pieces for firing. Ready now. Not all at once. You first, Corporal. Fire!"

The reports of the ten muskets, one after the other, echoed over the vast canefields along the Christ Church ridge. An answering shot rang out from the next lookout post. Soon the squad heard still others in the distance.

"God help us if we are wrong," the sergeant said to the lookout. "You saw them first, Higgins. Ride to Bridgetown and tell them what you have seen. Take my horse, and hurry."

Even his English enemies counted Michel de Ruyter, the fifty-eight-year-old commander of the Dutch fleet, as the most able admiral in any navy. And for de Ruyter, this was a day he had long dreamed of. Barbados! He knew the island well from his early days as a merchant captain, during the long period in which his countrymen had enjoyed free trade with this English colony, during England's Civil War, when Barbadian planters had practically governed themselves, before they had got back their king and with him their stupid laws curbing free trade.

The Dutch had long memories. Without their help, there would be no sugar industry in the island. Who had sold the ingrates slaves at low rates with long terms of credit? Who had bought their sugar at fair prices? Who had lent them money to buy equipment? And how had his countrymen been repaid? Not only had the English shut Dutch goods and ships out of their colonial markets, they were now horning in on the slave trade, with a monopoly requiring their West Indian planters to pay twice the normal price per head.

A smile spread over de Ruyter's weathered face as he thought of how he had played havoc with the English slavers in his recent sweep of the Guinea coast. But that pleasure could not compare with the joy he had felt the day before, when he had caught sight of Barbados looking like a bluish lump on the horizon. And now, leaning on his heavy cane on the quarterdeck of his new flagship, the mighty *De Spiegel*, he could glimpse the familiar terraces rising one after another from the coast. The windmills he saw here and there made him think of home.

His reverie was broken by the captain of *De Spiegel*.

"It is a beautiful land, my Lord Vice-Admiral."

"Too beautiful for the English, van Meppelen. And thanks to our investors, the richest land in the New World."

"Well, sir, we shall punish them for their perfidy this day, I assure you."

"If you, Sweers, and the other captains can silence their forts, and if we can get our soldiers ashore quickly at Bridge-town, we can do more than merely punish them."

"We discussed that at our council of war yesterday, sir. I thought we had concluded that, since their militia outnumbers our soldiers several times over . . . " He stopped at de Ruyter's frown.

"I asked my captains for advice, not orders. Timidity never accomplished anything, van Meppelen. With our fleet anchored close in and their forts out of action, it would be a risk well worth taking. And the rewards would be beyond imagination. Enough speculation. Is all in order?"

"Indeed, sir. Our cannon are loaded and primed. As you can see, our musketeers stand ready there on the main deck to mount the rigging. Surgeons and their helpers are at their stations below, prepared to receive any wounded. We are in good battle trim, I assure you. To effect a landing is another matter."

"Enough, enough. We draw too near. Change your course, and sail parallel to the coast until we clear Needham's Point."

At one order from the captain, gangs of sailors began hauling in lines and resetting the ship's enormous sails; at another, the helmsman turned his wheel hard to the left. *De Spiegel* paused and then, with the wind more squarely behind her, seemed to leap ahead.

De Ruyter did not blame his captain for his skepticism about a landing on Barbados. How could a few hundred soldiers overcome a population that, including slaves, must now exceed fifty thousand? It all depended on timing.

On the trip from Africa, the admiral had studied his charts well enough to draw an accurate map of Carlisle Bay from memory. Opening into the usually placid Caribbean, this broad anchorage measured more than a mile from north to south and about a half mile from west to east. He knew its fortifications well, too. Needham's Fort, mounting forty guns, guarded the bay on the south. And next to Bridgetown itself stood Willoughby's Fort. Dutch spies had reported the erection of smaller batteries here and there about the shoreline, as well.

De Ruyter did not delude himself about the hazards. There was good reason why Barbados had remained English since its settlement in 1627. The prevailing trade winds made it easy for ships to reach the vicinity from Europe and Africa. But the reef-rimmed eastern and southern coasts, pounded by the Atlantic surf and lacking good beaches or harbors, shielded the island from a direct approach. The hospitable western shore, lined with sandy beaches and washed by the gentle Caribbean, normally could not be taken by surprise. To enter Carlisle Bay, ships had to tack back and forth against the trade winds, giving a watchful defender time to prepare. Thank the Good Lord for this morning mist. De Ruyter struck his cane against the deck and danced a quick jig. Barbados, the English call this island. What would his government back home choose as its new name?

David Higganbotham had heard about the premature auction of the *Mary Leigh*'s human cargo but nonetheless slept right past the hour set for the "public outcry." Richard Bolton had warned him of the warm hospitality of Barbadians but had failed to mention the strength of the island's rum. His brother's old friends had thought it a great joke to get the stuffy English physician drunk.

Higganbotham might have slept until noon, had it not been for the outbreak of guns firing in the vicinity of The Roebuck. He could not remember being carried up to his room, but the pain jabbing in his brain reminded him of the rum. Did those fools have to fire their confounded guns? He put his hands over his ears and turned his face away from the sun shining through the tiny window.

Then he remembered his promise to Charlotte. Fighting back the impulse to throw up, barely able to stand, he dressed and ran shakily down the stairs and out the tavern toward Eggington's Green.

He found Moses and John Martin tearfully embracing each other while a tall man with a whip and a gray-bearded old fellow, dressed in rags and holding the reins of a donkey, waited for them to finish their good-byes.

The boy's face brightened at the sight of Higganbotham.

"They sold me to him," he said, pointing to the tall planter. "And the old man bought Father."

"The boy speaks true," the planter said. "They put up the culls first and Crazy Tom here bought the old man's bond for a pound. Nobody else wanted him. I paid five pounds for the boy. He says he can read and write. He'll make a handy chap around the sugar works. Dry your tears, boy. I won't eat you."

"I was commissioned to buy them both. I was detained . . . " Higganbotham began.

"Should have got here early. They don't bring in so many white servants anymore."

He must not get sick here, Higganbotham thought. If only his brain were clear of that wicked rum.

"Look, my good man, you paid five pounds. Suppose I just add a pound to that . . . "

"Nay, I need a bright, handy lad more than a quick profit. And I am not your good man."

He turned his back, and Higganbotham caught his sleeve.

"Two pounds then."

The planter jerked his arm free of the physician's grasp.

"What do you want with the boy?"

"I am a physician. I came out on the same ship with him and his father."

"Oh? And you have formed a special affection for the lad, is that it? The answer is still no."

Tormented by his headache and his sense of failure, Higganbotham felt an urge to strike the man. He had given Charlotte his solemn promise. What would she say if he failed her? He could never handle strong drink. Why did he take even the first glass?

The planter had put his hand on John's shoulder and was pointing to his horse when the idea occurred to Higganbotham. He must not let John become the bond servant of this obnoxious man.

"Wait. It is not that at all. You see . . . " Damn it, Richard Bolton could have brought this off without stuttering so. "You s . . . see, the poor lad has aroused my scientific, my medical curiosity. That's it. I am a specialist in epilepsy."

The planter removed his hand from John's shoulder.

"What is that?"

"The falling sickness. Did the lad not tell you?"

Higganbotham narrowed his eyes at John and winked. He prayed that the boy would not expose his subterfuge. John suddenly smiled.

"I am not troubled as much as before you treated me, sir."

"Yes, but I mind how you nearly fell overboard twice." He

looked into the planter's now concerned face. "The disease runs in families you know." He turned to the old man in rags. "That is why the father cannot speak."

"Makes no difference to me," the old man replied.

"Ah, well, it is a shame that no one warned either of you. Caveat emptor. I'll bid you both good-bye then."

Now the planter plucked at Higganbotham's sleeve.

"Over here a moment, sir," he said in a confidential tone. "Don't think me hardhearted, but my wife gave me stern instructions to buy us a white servant."

"Quite so," Higganbotham said. "And she will not be disappointed, I hope. After all, when he is well, the boy is not entirely stupid. Besides the fits, the only problem they had with him aboard ship was his bed-wetting. But, if you wouldn't mind my dropping around to see him from time to time, I'd be pleased to study his case. You could keep a record of the frequency and length of his seizures. And I would not charge you full price for my medical attention."

The planter looked down at the ground and Higganbotham turned his back.

"Wait. I am not a harsh man. I wouldn't want to stand between you and your studies. I'll take the two pounds profit, if it be in gold."

The old man who bought Moses Martin's term was made of stronger stuff. He refused Higganbotham's offer of first two, then three and finally five pounds without wavering, until the exasperated doctor said, "Look, he is feeble, a victim of a stroke. Fieldwork will kill him."

"Don't want him for that."

"Come, sir, he and his son have suffered enough. Surely you are not so cruel . . . "

"You got your servant, and I got mine. Now begone. I want to clear out of this place before somebody gets shot with all these damn guns going off."

At that Higganbotham could not resist his sick stomach any longer. He wished John were not standing by to see him vomiting up the rum and with it the supper to which the proprietor of The Roebuck had treated him.

When at last he had stopped throwing up and had recovered a measure of his dignity, a mob of militiamen and others raced through the square. Amid the hubbub, Moses had disappeared with the bearded man and the donkey.

Charlotte and Richard were eating their breakfast at the Bow Bells when they heard gunshots in the street.

"It could be an alarm," he said. "Wait here. I will venture out and inquire."

During his absence, Charlotte became more and more anxious at the sight of militiamen running past the tavern door toward the harbor.

Richard galloped up Cheapside and leapt from the saddle. "Horseman just rode in from Christ Church. They have sighted more than a dozen sail off Oistin's Bay. Now look, Charlotte, I want you to ride on to the plantation where you will be safe. Wilkens is here now. He will escort you, and Caesar will follow with our trunks."

He pointed to a dishevelled chap slouching outside with a huge Negro beside an ox-drawn cart.

"What about you?"

"I am an old soldier, remember? Besides, they may not be Dutch after all."

While Wilkens saddled Nutmeg, Charlotte dressed in a riding costume and closed her trunks to be hauled downstairs.

"This is my overseer, Wilkens, my dear," Richard said when she came down. "He has been with me five years."

"Madame." The man made a half bow. Charlotte merely nodded in response.

"Can she ride?" Wilkens asked Richard in a tone that made Charlotte bristle.

"She is an accomplished horsewoman, but the mare should be given time to get used to dry land. Don't go too fast."

While Wilkens oversaw the loading of their trunks on the

ox cart, Richard tried to reassure Charlotte, but he angered her by saying that she looked like "a frightened schoolgirl."

"I am frightened for you, you fool."

At the sound of the first cannon blast from Needham's Fort echoing through the streets of Bridgetown, the color drained from Richard's face. He kissed Charlotte and lifted her to the sidesaddle.

"Don't dawdle, Wilkens. Take my wife away immediately."

Walking stick in one hand, a cutlass in the other, de Ruyter watched his musketeers lug their cumbersome pieces up to the three crow's-nests of *De Spiegel*. His gunners, who already had opened their ports and run out their loaded cannon, sat about quietly, tensely, waiting for his command. Closely followed by the rest of the fleet, his great flagship approached Carlisle Bay with Needham's Fort on her starboard bow. From the red blur of scurrying militiamen on the shore and the sound of small arms fire, the admiral knew that the alarm had been given. He did not mind. In fact, he liked to picture the shock the people of Bridgetown must feel at the sight of his fleet bearing down upon them, and the panic of the merchantmen's officers, too. Without putting spyglass to eye, he could make out the masts of at least thirty vessels, all drawn in close to shore. How exhilarating. De Ruyter felt like the leader of a pack of wolves about to descend on a herd of helpless sheep.

"Steady on course until we pass the fort," he commanded.

The same first cannon blast that caused such an uproar in Bridgetown had no effect on de Ruyter. The shot threw up a spout of water far short of the ship. Nor did he so much as duck when a second cannonball whistled over his rigging and splashed into the water off his port beam. Soon missiles whirred all about him, and still the admiral ignored them. His eye remained fixed on Bridgetown and the ships clustered near its waterfront.

"Now, sir?" the captain asked.

"Hold your fire."

In majestic disdain, *De Spiegel* glided into Carlisle Bay, past Needham's Fort, whose gunners turned their attention to the next Dutch ship. Now de Ruyter took a closer look at the ships in the harbor.

"Damn me for a fool," he exclaimed. "Van Meppelen, one of those vessels is that confounded British frigate we paroled at Goree, *The Gift*."

He pondered over this hitch in his plans; he had not reckoned on the presence of a 40-gun warship in Carlisle Bay. But then he shrugged and said, "No matter. Continue dead ahead, and we'll deal with her first."

With *De Spiegel* still several cable lengths away, the guns of *The Gift* suddenly flashed into action, sending a hail of cannonballs skipping across the water. De Ruyter held his fire until it appeared his flagship would ram the frigate, until one shot from a second English broadside had ripped through a sail and another had smacked into the side of *De Spiegel*.

At last he raised his cutlass. "Fire!" he called out, and brought down the blade.

De Spiegel, ponderous as she was, shuddered and seemed to slide sideways from the recoil of her own broadside. A powder monkey's cap flew off his head from the concussion; musketeers winced and put their hands over their ears; a fog bank of white smoke rolled over the deck as the cannon lurched against their restraining ropes like startled horses.

"Now bring her about and put the other broadside into the town," de Ruyter ordered. "Musketeers open fire!"

He raised his chin and took a deep breath. There was nothing like the smell of gunpowder smoke, nothing like the sound of men shouting and swearing as they swabbed the bores of their cannon, nothing like the crash of a broadside or the sputter of musketry. Indeed, there was nothing like war.

At the outbreak of firing from the fort, the same people who had run toward the harbor now scampered back to their houses and shops. Charlotte found herself caught up in a mob of screaming women and shouting men. The skittish Nutmeg, her legs unused to dry land, staggered about in the crowd so that Charlotte could barely keep her seat. Then, just as she and the overseer got free of that mob, several companies of red-coated militiamen hurried toward the waterfront, causing Nutmeg to rear and nearly throw Charlotte. Numbly, mutely fighting to keep control of herself and her mare, Charlotte followed the overseer's horse up into the countryside. Leaving the ox cart stranded in the traffic, they did not pause until they reached a hill from which they could gaze down upon the broad, greenish waters of Carlisle Bay.

Sweating from the unaccustomed heat and anxiety, legs and arms trembling with the exertion of controlling her mare, Charlotte looked in disbelief at the spectacle of the enormous Dutch flagship advancing with ponderous dignity, as if oblivious to the puffs of smoke from the forts and the plumes of water spouting up all around her.

Like ducklings swimming behind their mother, the other, smaller Dutch ships followed their flagship. Charlotte was interrupted in her count of the vessels in the fleet by Wilkens.

"We ought to be moving on."

She shook her head in irritation.

"No, I can't miss this."

When, far beneath them, *The Gift* loosed her first broadside, Charlotte was amazed by the interval between the bursts of smoke and the sound of the blasts. She watched in awe as the great Dutch flagship finally replied, the blasts from her fifty-gun broadside flattening the rippled surface of the water in curious coned shapes quickly obscured by billows of white smoke. The port broadside, directed toward the town, was even more spectacular, for now Charlotte could see the sheets of red fire spouting from the muzzles.

"There comes Caesar with the cart," Wilkens said.

Charlotte did not reply. One part of her was near panic, but another was filled with a sort of wild joy and excitement. The violence of the battle both terrified and fascinated her. Her father's accounts of Civil War fighting, gripping as they were, had not conveyed the awful reality of an actual battle.

"Madam . . . "

Charlotte held up her hand to silence the man. Where is Richard, she wondered. Would she ever see him alive again?

At Willoughby's Fort, on the edge of Bridgetown next to the mouth of Saint Michael River, Richard had been pressed into service as commander of a section of culverins. Laying aside his jacket and rolling up his sleeves, he quickly organized the militiamen into gun crews and oversaw the preparation of the long-barrelled weapons.

Now, all around him, cannonballs from first *De Spiegel* and then the other Dutch ships shrieked and sang. Peering over the earthen ramparts, he and his crews marveled at the sight of a towering mass of white canvas blotting out their view of the harbor. This huge engine of war appeared headed straight for them, as though its captain meant to ride right into the walls of the fort.

Although Richard was as awed as his soldiers by the scores of cannon barrels bristling from the great hull, he forced his voice to remain calm. "Steady, men. The bigger she is, the harder it is to miss." Before he could give the order to fire, *De Spiegel* delivered her second starboard broadside. The blast staggered the gunners, but the balls overshot the fort and ricocheted across the wharves and into the buildings facing the bay, all except one, which struck the muzzle of one of Richard's culverins and hurled the mass of tangled metal across the terreplein.

"Back to your positions!" Richard yelled at the cowering militiamen. "Fire at will."

One after the other, the guns of Willoughby's Fort rang out in a ragged salvo. As the smoke cleared, Richard raised his head to observe the Dutch ship veering just in time to avoid running aground. Part of her rail had been shot away, and the remains of a shattered longboat were strewn about the main deck, but, as if unmindful of this damage, a strange figure stood on the quarterdeck, leaning on a cane and waving a cutlass as though it were a concertmaster's violin bow. A burst of small arms fire from the ship's crow's-nests caused Richard to duck his head.

Again and again, the Dutch fleet circled Carlisle Bay, hammering away at ships and forts. They sailed as close to their targets as the depth of the water would allow, then drew off to reload their cannon and get back into the queue. *The Gift* had been reduced to a battered wreck. Her captain had been gravely wounded, and only a few of her guns were still in operation. Several merchant ships had been severely damaged as well. But despite the punishment they were taking, the forts dotted about the bay remained in the fray. At first their guns had been largely ineffective, but now the crews were settling down and doing some good shooting. Here and there among the Dutch ships could be seen broken spars and hulls with holes in them.

Despite the damage he was taking, de Ruyter continued to push his ships to almost point-blank range. His captains thought him mad to take such chances, but they dared not question his judgment; indeed, they could not, now that the battle was joined.

De Ruyter would have pressed his attack even harder had he known the condition of the defenders' supply of ammunition. Although they had been drilled for several weeks, few of the militiamen had ever been in battle before. Most were so-called "poor whites"—small landowners, tradesmen, carters, artisans—but their officers came largely from the ranks of the island's planters. They made lavish use of their gunpowder, firing off shots without properly aiming their guns.

Just as their ammunition was depleted, so was their energy. Exhausted by so much exertion and excitement, scores of them had fainted or fallen out to rest in the shade.

The commander of Willoughby's Fort had been in bed with a fever at the first alarm that morning. The longer the fight continued the worse he felt; by midday, he no longer could stand. He huddled in a corner, alternately shivering and sweating. During a lull in the fighting, Henry Willoughby, the deputy governor, arrived to inspect the fort. Already alarmed by the shortage of gunpowder at Needham's Fort, he was further upset to find the commander of Willoughby's Fort near collapse. He confided his concern to Richard, who volunteered to take command.

The deputy governor recalled that his uncle, Lord Francis Willoughby, had described Bolton as "not altogether trustworthy," but, damn it, that was in politics. This was war, and his uncle languished six hundred miles away, in Surinam.

"What would you do if I gave you temporary command?"

"Oh, I lernt a trick or two in the Civil War ... "

The deputy governor looked at the other officers in the fort and nodded. "Just don't waste any more of our gunpowder."

From her vantage point under a palm tree on the hill, Charlotte got so caught up in the excitement of the battle that she forgot her fear. By now the gunsmoke lay so thick over the harbor that at times she could see only the masts of the larger Dutch vessels above the artificial fog. Red and orange flashes lit up the white smoke, creating the effect of a violent thunderstorm viewed from high above the clouds. Charlotte shuddered at the sheer magnificence of the scene.

Wilkins annoyed her with, "Madam, there are a hundred slaves back at the plantation, and there is no one to direct them except their foremen. It is the height of our harvest here ... "

"In a moment ... "

Charlotte smiled at the recollection of something her mother had said just before her wedding: "You will be stuck in a backwater where nothing of interest ever happens." No matter who won the battle raging below, she would enjoy writing home about this, her first full day on Barbados.

"Caesar has nearly caught up with us now," Wilkens said. "Please, madam, my instructions were to hurry you back to Bolton Hall."

Richard held his fire at the next approach of the Dutch flagship, hoping her captain would think him out of ammunition. Well before *De Spiegel* began yet another sweep, Richard showed his gunners how to lay their guns. He took into account the receding tide in aiming all the cannon at one point a few score of yards from the fort. Then he ordered the militiamen to sit down, out of sight behind the ramparts, and wait.

Three of his guns were out of action. He had very little powder left for his remaining cannon.

"She's coming again, Colonel Bolton. Great God, she's headed right for us," the lookout announced.

"Stay down. And keep quiet."

The wind had slacked off now, and the tide was waning. *De Spiegel* approached at a maddeningly slow pace. Every eye in the fort was turned on Richard as the gun crews waited.

Richard was relieved when the crash of a broadside shook the fort once more, and he felt even better when he realized that this one had been aimed into the town. Now he raised his head cautiously. Minutes passed with agonizing slowness.

"Now." Richard arose, held up his hand, and then brought it down. "Fire!"

All his guns erupted in a single ear-splitting roar, and his men crowded the ramparts to see the effect of their salvo.

"Looky there," one shouted. "Holy mother, would you look?"

The main topmast of *De Spiegel*, as large as the mainmast of an ordinary ship, was gone, and its sail lay in a heap over the side. His men cheered. Richard climbed atop the rampart and shook his fist at the stern of the vessel.

"I knew we could do it. She looks like a fat-assed old Dutch housewife with her drawers down about her ankles. Isn't that a grand sight?"

Aboard the flagship, de Ruyter took personal command, issuing orders directly to the bosuns and quartermaster. Turning her remaining sails to catch the slight breeze astern, he drew *De Spiegel* out of range of the forts and hoisted a pennant to signal the rest of the fleet to join him for a council of war.

Henry Willoughby took advantage of this lull to call the commanders of the forts for a dockside conference.

"You should have warned us earlier to ration our powder," the commander of Needham's Fort complained. "Anyway, look there, we have stood them off. Forced them to break off the engagement."

Willoughby shook his head. "The fact remains that our powder will be gone in another round of fighting. *The Gift* is out of action. And the Dutch decks are crowded with soldiers. God knows how many more are aboard their transports lying to outside the bay. God help us if they return."

"They will have to replace that topmast, I should think," Richard said. "We have broken their mirror; perhaps they will take that as a sign of bad luck and decide to call it a day."

Willoughby looked puzzled.

"Did you not see the name of his flagship? It means 'the mirror.'"

"This is no time for joking, Bolton. The fate of Barbados is being decided aboard that flagship. If they elect to effect a landing, we may have to learn more than a few words of Dutch, we and our children. Are you not concerned?"

"Indeed, I am, Mister Deputy Governor. But I, for one, do not intend to surrender until they come ashore and fight it out, man to man. I am too old to learn Dutch."

"But not too old to take a young wife, what, Richard?" a man wearing the insignia of a major said.

"What's that?" Willoughby asked.

"Richard has brought home a bride. And have you heard of his knighthood?"

"Why, no. Congratulations on both counts, Bolton, or should I say 'Sir Richard.'"

Richard stretched out and put his hat over his face. "Just wake me when the Dutch come our way again."

Cannon fire ringing in her ears, Charlotte followed Wilkens past cane fields stretching in all directions, their expanse broken here and there by windmills, sugar works, the homes of plantation owners, and slave huts.

In the fields, lines of Negroes, male and female alike, bare to the waist, their skins gleaming black with sweat, labored away under the eyes of men with whips. And to Charlotte's horror, more than once she saw those whips laid across the back of a man or flicked at the buttocks of a female.

The road, good at first, became little more than a cart track as it climbed steadily to the top of an escarpment and thence to a parish church with a tower that made Charlotte think of the one in which she and Richard had been married. Without bothering to explain or to introduce Charlotte, Wilkens dismounted there to talk to the captain of a company of militiamen lounging in the shade, apparently as a reserve against a Dutch landing. The stop afforded Charlotte the opportunity to look out over the plains and slopes that led down to the dazzlingly blue sea. Although Carlisle Bay lay out of sight, cannon fire still pounded in her ears like the throbbing of a headache.

Once the ox cart lumbered into view, Wilkens mounted his horse and nodded for Charlotte to follow. Swallowing her growing dislike of the little man, she guided Nutmeg alongside his horse and asked about the daily schedule of the slaves.

"Why, they rise at dawn and eat their breakfast first thing. Get two hours off in the middle of the day. Quit work at sundown. Time off? All day Sunday. Some gives them Saturday afternoon, too."

Charlotte hated his calling her "madam" and was offended by his offhand way of answering her questions, but there would be time enough to put him in his place.

"Where do they attend church?"

"Church?" He laughed. "Oh, madam, we don't convert them. They believe in their own mumbo jumbo. Spirits and such. Worship their dead. Bury them right under their own huts if you lets them. No, madam, I don't know their African talk. They can't understand each other unless they come from the same tribe. Oh, they's several tribes, and each one different. Worst is the Coromantees, from the Gold Coast. Strong fellows, but too proud for their own good. I've told the colonel I don't want no more of that lot. Run away?" He laughed again. "Ah, madam, where would they run to?"

"I had hoped you might tell *me*," Charlotte said coolly.

"Well, the plantations to the south had some trouble with slaves and Irish servants. Section in Saint Phillips Parish called 'the Thickets.' Militia has to go in with dogs and catch a runaway now and then. Irishmen has been known to sneak aboard a ship or steal a boat. Yes, 'tis a hard life, but you must remember many of the blacks was slaves back in Africa. Don't mean to criticize Colonel Bolton but to my way of thinking . . . What, madam?"

"Sir Richard," Charlotte repeated. "My husband was knighted by King Charles. Perhaps you had not heard."

"Sir Richard, yes. Well, as I was saying, he shows 'em too much kindness. Don't allow me to flog them in the fields. And it takes a touch of the lash now and then to get your best work out of an African."

With the cannon fire sounding like distant thunder, they continued along the rutted road until they came to a lane lined with palms. Charlotte recognized the windmill and then the house, her house.

Its rude appearance shocked her. Made of cedar wood, two-storied with a shingled roof, it lacked the graceful lines she had assumed from Richard's description. A cookhouse with chimney was attached to the rear wall. The yard looked like a jungle. And shading the kitchen grew one of those grotesque trees that sprouted aerial roots. Aboard the *Mary Leigh* Charlotte had daydreamed of arriving in a carriage at a magnificent plantation house surrounded by exotic tropical flowers. In her imagination, Richard had carried her across the threshold while a line of smiling servants waited to be introduced.

"Mandze," Wilkens called. "You there?"

A stout, barefooted Negro woman with tribal scars on each broad cheek appeared in the open doorway.

"This is the master's new wife. You understand? She is from England. Across the water. This is Mistress Bolton. Excuse me, this is Lady Bolton."

The woman stared at Charlotte with no expression in her black, cold eyes, then nodded and stood aside.

Charlotte experienced a fresh shock when she stepped into the front room. The atmosphere was stifling, and it was dark. She was even more upset, when she pushed open the rotting blinds, to see chests and chairs so crude they might have come from the cottage of one of her father's tenants. And they, as well as the stark bare walls, were coated with thick mildew.

The dining room table was a makeshift affair consisting of three broad planks laid across two sawhorses, with benches rather than chairs along each side and a stool at either end. Earthenware dishes were stacked on a warped chest.

The lean-to kitchen at the rear offended both her sense of smell and order. Long-unwashed pots and pans stood about on a grease-spattered hearth. Utensils were piled on a table that had been constructed from two halves of a split log. A bed of straw had been piled in the corner beside the fireplace.

Richard had never described his furnishings. She had assumed they would be at least as fine as those of Foxley Manor, perhaps even finer. And here she found he had been living in a veritable pigsty.

Upstairs she found the same sort of appalling disorder. Richard's narrow bed was covered with a musty straw tick. Although pegs lined one wall and a large chest stood in a corner, his clothing lay about in piles. It was even hotter up here under the roof, but she lay face down on the stinking mattress and longed for her home in England.

Upon the arrival of the ox cart, Charlotte found some comfort in unloading the trunks and boxes and handling their familiar contents. Although she understood Charlotte's instructions well enough to help her unpack the clothing, Mandze seemed unable to speak much English, which was just as well. Charlotte was too depressed for conversation.

At midday, Mandze brought her a soggy kind of bread made of cassava root and bran, roasted yams, and a bittersweet brew she called "mobby." Alone at the rude table in the dining room, Charlotte ate in silence, determined not to display her despair to this sullen black woman and wishing that she had never heard of Richard Bolton, yet at the same time half-sick with fear for his safety. After she had eaten, the rumble of the cannon halted. Surely those awesome Dutch ships had smashed the forts. Any minute now, the Dutch might come tramping along the road to this very plantation. Thus Charlotte's imagination tormented her through the long afternoon.

The swiftness of nightfall took her by surprise. It seemed that one moment she was on the porch watching the sun's lower edge just touch a gold-and-blue horizon and the next that she was groping her way upstairs to the bedroom. With a trunk wedged against the door and the blinds shut tight, she spent a long, lonely, fretful night listening to the unfamiliar screech of insects and strange rustlings on the roof.

Her brain spun with the memory of the day's events and with apprehensions both for herself and Richard. That noise on the roof—was it some huge poisonous reptile or perhaps a bloodthirsty animal? The house creaked as it lost some of its daytime heat, but to Charlotte's ears the sounds became footsteps. She could barely get her breath, yet she dared not open the blinds to catch the coolness Richard had told her night usually brought at this altitude.

Compounding her fears was the unthinking way Richard had packed her off with that offensive little overseer, so that he could join in the battle with the Dutch fleet. It seemed to her that he loved war more than he did her. What if he had been killed or carried off as a prisoner by the Dutch? How would she ever find her way back to England? And what kind of life would she have there after the way she had scandalized all of Bedfordshire with her hasty marriage? Would Marmaduke take her back? What if she were pregnant?

Finally, when out of exhaustion she fell asleep, she was wracked by nightmares more terrifying than her real fears. Never had Charlotte ever spent such a night of horror. It would be a long time before she could bear to spend a night alone.

That sickening feeling of dread was waiting for her at dawn. It followed her down the narrow stairs to the kitchen, where she found Mandze still asleep on her pile of straw. Charlotte forgot her fears for a moment as she gazed at the strong ebony face, wondering what the woman had looked like in her youth.

Mandze awakened with a look of alarm that quickly gave way to her usual sullen stare.

"Let us begin the day," Charlotte said.

She was just sitting down to eat a lonely breakfast when she heard the hooves of a horse in the yard and then Richard's voice calling her name. She leapt up and ran past a surprised Mandze and out into his arms.

"Thank God. You are alive."

"Of course, I am."

"I was sure you were dead in that awful battle."

Drawing back to look into his haggard face, she held her nose. "You smell like a stable hand."

"I smell like a soldier. Sweat and gunpowder. Ah, Charlotte, it was a glorious fight. Better than Colchester. The Dutch fired everything they had, and we gave it right back to them. Damnified them something terrible."

"The little I saw of the battle made me think otherwise. What happened?"

"We shot away their masts and generally battered them so they broke off the attack. Lay to all afternoon, then set their sails and moved off. We stood by our guns throughout the night. At daybreak they were gone. Good thing for us they did not try again. Our gunpowder was nearly gone. Dutch blockheads. I tell you, Charlotte, it was wonderful to be in battle again after so many years. And to think I nearly missed getting back in time. Were you frightened, my dear?"

How could this supposedly mature man rattle on about war like an eager youth? What made men such fools?

"I was merely terrified. My first day in a new land, and I get caught up in a bombardment ... " Later, as they were seated in the dining room: "I really feared I might never see you again."

"You'll not get rid of this husband so easily as that. Well, what do you think of your new home?"

Partly to keep from replying, Charlotte arose and put her

arms about his neck. As they kissed, she opened her eyes to see Mandze start into the room and then turn away.

The hut, an open-sided affair with a steep thatched roof, stood in a patch of hard-packed earth on the western slope of Mount Hillaby. The close-crowding trees and bushes had been cleared on one side to allow a view of the coast and the sea. A hammock stretched between two corner posts. Several chickens pecked in the yard. In a tree growing from the side of a nearby ravine, a pair of monkeys chattered and swung crazily.

The bearded old man tied his donkey to a tree and turned to Moses. "You will live here. Understand?"

Moses nodded.

"My name is Tom."

Moses bent and scratched his name in the dirt.

"No use. Can't read. No matter. I'll find out your name or give you one myself. You take my hammock. I'll make me a bed later. Understand? Here, I'll show you around."

As proudly as though he were a planter with two hundred acres of prime sugar fields, Tom Cochran pointed out his vegetable garden and tobacco plot.

"Come down here in the ravine and see my palm and fig trees."

After the tour, Tom squatted on his haunches and motioned Moses to his only stool.

"Takes a while to get used to this place. Me, I been here nearly forty years. Oh, yes, I came out on the second boat, with old John Powell hisself, I did. Came as a boy for the promise of wages and a chance to buy land later. Found this place hunting wild pigs. Yes, great creatures they were, descended from a herd turned loose by Portugee sailors, God knows how long ago. Marked the spot and when my indenture was up and I had saved a bit of money, got me a wife, and they sold me ten acres for ten shillings. Nobody else wanted the land. You wonder about my wife, don't ye? She was Injun. They brought her here from Surinam that first year and made a slave of her. I paid a pound for her, just like I did for you. My mates mocked me for taking up with an Injun woman. To hell with them. I called her Sadie. Gentle as a dove and faithful as a dog, she were. Never learned no English, but she taught me enough Arawak so we could talk a bit. We had a son ... "

Tom wiped his nose and stood up.

"Named the boy Powell. But him and Sadie both died in '47. Yellow fever hit the island that year. Killed thousands. I mean thousands. So many they just threw the bodies in the swamp t'other side of Bridgetown ... "

He turned his back to Moses and brushed his sleeve over his eyes.

"Powell died in the morning. I buried him up there beside that big cedar. Came back and, Lord God, Sadie had give up the ghost too. Here, now, I'll show you how to roast sweet potatoes."

Near dusk, Tom drew the potatoes from the coals of his cook fire and gave one to Moses with a corn cake.

"Mobby's the drink for me. Try it. Cools the blood. Guess you heard 'em call me Crazy Tom. Never called me that before '47. Before then I were a sergeant in the militia, a sergeant, mind you. And, with Sadie's help, I growed lots more tobacco. That was afore the big dogs came over and started buying out the little man what started this colony. Before the Dutch hauled in all them black fellows and cut down the trees. Now everything is sugar, sugar. Feel that breeze. Down in Bridgetown they can hardly get their breath. They call me crazy, but you don't see me breaking my back, toiling in the sun. I don't lay awake in a big house worrying my blacks may cut my throat or the merchants will foreclose. And you don't see me selling out and moving off to Jamaica or the Carolinas, neither. Like the mobby?"

Moses nodded and smiled.

"Auctioneer said you was a tailor. That's good. And that boy. He your son?"

Moses blinked back tears.

"Not to worry. After we get settled in, we'll look him up. Maybe I'll show you around the island. Would you like that?"

Having finished their simple supper, the two men watched

the sun sink toward the rim of the sea. After dark, Tom spoke again.

"Up here I have time to think. Know what I decided is wrong with mankind?"

Moses shook his head.

"You'll see signs of it all around. Look, there was ninety of us boys and young fellows on the boat. Eighty settlers was here already. Nearly every one of us has either been worked to death or has died off from some plague or has been squeezed out by the big dogs. And they lured us out here on the promises of finding a new life in a promised land. Just look around you. Man takes from his neighbors. Must have a grander house. More land. Then slaves. More money. More slaves and land. Never satisfied . . . "

Tom stared into the fire as if he had lost his train of thought. Then, feeling Moses' expectant eyes on him, he continued.

"Greed. That is what is wrong with mankind. That is what is wrong with this island. You'll see for yourself soon enough. Ah, Great God, I've missed having someone to talk to all these years."

5

. . . Had there been any easy or graceful way to depart Barbados and escape my hasty marriage during those first few weeks, I might have taken it.

My house, its furnishing and grounds, appalled me. I was

confused by the strange plants and frightened by the lizards that came and went as they pleased in the house.

Foolishly, I had assumed the weather would be no warmer than that of an English summer. My clothing proved entirely too heavy for the dreadful heat of the island.

I was too proud to admit my inability to deal with the sullen Mandze, who only feigned, so I suspected, not to understand my simplest instructions, with the result that I ended up doing many chores myself.

I was further constrained from complaining to Richard because we had arrived during the peak of the cane harvest, the very busiest period of the year, and he spent nearly every minute either in the fields making sure the ripe cane was being cut properly or at the sugar works to see after the intricate process of extracting the juice and boiling it down into sugar. So he was too tired and busy to note signs of my discontent.

I missed the familiar sounds, smells, foods, and climate of England. Lacking anyone to converse with, I was so lonely I even missed my mother. But, trapped by my own foolhardiness, I forced myself to make the best of my lot.

The only bearable time was during the coolness of early morning, when I lay abed talking with Richard. Often in my childhood I had wondered at the quiet pleasure my parents took in these talks before rising to meet a new day. Now this communication with my husband was all that enabled me to endure my misery.

Writing to my parents provided me a pastime, but not only was I too proud to admit my unhappiness to them, but also I wanted neither to cause my father any anxiety nor to give my mother the satisfaction of saying "did I not warn Charlotte?" My first letter back to Foxley Manor, an exceedingly long one, dealt with the voyage over from Bristol, my meeting the two Quakers who confronted the King, and the Dutch attack on Bridgetown. I waited until the worst of my homesickness and disappointment in my house had abated to compose my second epistle.

Much of that abatement came one afternoon when Richard, announcing that he had reached a breathing space in his own frantic work, ordered Nutmeg and his horse saddled and brought round so that we could "inspect our plantation."

Knowing that my parents were hungry for reports of my new life in Barbados, I wrote at great length and in considerable detail of what Richard showed and explained to me. Richard was pleased at my grasp of plantation life when I showed what I had written to him. And I learned later that my father proudly displayed my letter all around Bedfordshire and then gave it permanent place in our family archives with his letters to Mama from the Civil Wars...

... I did not appreciate the intricacies of running a plantation until Richard escorted me about our two hundred acres, which he says are worth far more than a like number in England. He keeps about half his land in the principal crop of the island, namely sugar cane. About thirty acres are set aside for the growing of provisions, most of which are imported from North America. Wood is very scarce here, and so about thirty acres are kept in a variety of strange-looking trees. The rest of the land is taken up with buildings, garden plots for the slaves, and cattle pens. (They save every animal dropping for fertilizer. Richard says some planters even husband the excrement of their slaves.)

Growing cane is a far cry from farming in England, Father. The work is hard and requires meticulous management. The cane is planted during the rainy autumn months, spaced so that the stalks ripen in stages about fifteen months later during the driest time, February through May. The slaves dig long trenches in which are placed joints of cane. Constant cultivation is required until the following summer to prevent weeds from overgrowing the cane. The stalks eventually grow thick against each other and as high as the head of a man on horseback.

We are in the midst of the harvest now, and I am amazed by the toil required of our slaves to chop down the stalks, strip them of their leaves and tops, and transport them on ox carts to the mill, or *ignineo,* as it is called. The strongest males cut the cane while women and small boys do the stripping and loading. For extracting the juice from the stalks, Richard has a cattle mill, which consists of two long, horizontal sweeps connected to a set of vertical rollers. Two oxen are yoked to the end of each sweep. Round and round the beasts plod, while bare-bosomed women and naked boys feed the stalks through the rollers.

Richard can hardly wait to complete this harvest so that he

can install his windmill machinery in a stone tower built in his absence. As he explains it, the cane must be cut before it overripens and then be promptly crushed, or the juice goes bad. They save the bagasse or crushed cane to help feed the furnaces of the boiling room. Father, there is nothing this side of Dante's Inferno to compare with the boiling room. The frantic pace of the cane-cutting crews and those around the grinding mill is leisurely by comparison. The juice runs through a leaden pipe into a cistern in a stone building and inside that building, amidst stifling heat from several furnaces, slaves feverishly ladle the sweet liquid into a series of copper vats of diminishing size. The overheated atmosphere is made to seem even closer by the odor of African sweat and boiling juice, the effect of a Hades on earth heightened by the glow of the furnaces and by the anxious way the slaves dart back and forth between the vats, as though driven by devils. The juice is brought to a boil, but no more, in the first vat. The slaves skim off the scum, saving it for our new rum still, and then ladle the juice into the next vat, and so on until in the last and smallest receptacle, grown thicker at each stage, it forms a substance full of sugar crystals called "sling." Richard employs the most skilled and intelligent of his slaves as boilers. I watched one of these, a wiry little graying man with a horrible burn scar across his chest, at work with great interest. He never rests. His name is Cromwell, and Richard says he is worth his weight in gold.

Beyond the boiling room, we have the filling shed wherein reside hundreds of conical clay pots in rows, with a hole in the bottom of each. Two red-haired white youths, whom Richard hires for the harvest only, plug the holes and fill the pots with the sling after it has cooled. Two days later, they extract the plugs and allow the molasses to drip into collecting pans. A month later, the sugar is tapped from the cones, spread out to dry, and later packed into hogsheads to be hauled down to a warehouse in Speightstown. There, Mama, never again would you take your sweetened tea for granted if you knew how much trouble it is to produce. And, Father, I told Richard what you said about rich planters who sit in the shade whilst their blackamoors do all the work. In truth, I never saw the owner of an estate back home exert himself half as much as does my dear husband.

By the bye, Richard has given me a present. 'Tis a slave boy they call Toby, not more than thirteen or fourteen. He is to be my little gardener. Because of a club foot, he is of little use in the cane fields or around the sugar mills but, says Richard, he hath a marvelous gift for growing vegetables and tending animals. He is alert and eager to please. Richard has told me to plan my garden and, when the sugar harvest is over, he will bring up his prime field hands to clear the soil around the house so that Toby and I can put in flowers and herbs. The flowers here are so much more colorful than those back home but they want putting into good English order. Mama, I hope you are enjoying your new walnut furniture as much as we do the oaken pieces you gave us. They make this house seem more like home, although you would be amused by the way we have set the legs of the old bed in clay bowls of water to prevent ourselves from being joined in the night by various crawling things.

I think of you both and of home often. With the cane harvest nearing an end, Richard will have more time to introduce me to his friends. In fact, we are invited Sunday afternoon to dinner at the next plantation, called Fulham. The owners, Harold and Esther Lawnton, are old friends of Richard's. This will be my first social occasion, and I must admit to some anxiety ...

Interrupted by bouts of punch drinking, the dinner at Fulham Plantation lasted from 2:00 P.M. until nearly 5:00. Charlotte was amazed by the amount of wine and burnt brandy punch consumed and by the boisterousness of the conversation. Around a great cedar table in a long dining hall, she heard practically every shade of accent in the English language and observed a variety of table manners, as well.

The women wore layered gowns of lawn and linen with lacework finer than any she had seen in London. And the food outdid any feast Charlotte had ever enjoyed in Bedford: roast turkey, sugar-fed mutton, shellfish, pineapple, pomegranates, baked yams, corn puddings, and several sorts of breads, jams, and jellies.

Charlotte hated acting like a prig but could not help feeling shy amid all this exuberance. And her thick dress made her even more uncomfortable in the tropic heat. Nor could she easily follow the conversations whirling about the table. The men talked about the Dutch attack and the likely damper this new war would put on trade; they complained about the growing cost of slaves, the unfairness of a new 4½ percent royal tax on exports, the difficulty of getting firewood for boiling sugar, and the shiftlessness of the island's considerable population of poor whites.

The women complained and, Charlotte thought, boasted about their house servants and bemoaned delays in the delivery of furniture and fine cloth or silver from London.

When the men finally staggered from the table to light their pipes, the mistress of Fulham, a well-bred little woman with a soft voice, drew Charlotte aside and asked if she would like to see her garden.

Mistress Lawnton took pride in showing off her hedges of croton and frangipani and her windbreak of lime trees. Yes, she would be glad to visit Bolton Hall and advise Charlotte on what to plant.

"By the way, my dear, you must be miserable in that gown. Did Richard not advise you about our climate?"

"He did, but he said nothing about clothing. If I weren't such a goose..."

"Make him buy you a quantity of lawn and linen and other lightweight fabrics in Bridgetown. Do you sew?"

"Rather badly, I fear."

"Get yourself a clever Negro girl and train her. My woman could instruct her. I noticed you were very quiet at dinner. Do you miss England very much?"

Not trusting herself to speak, Charlotte nodded.

"We're a mixed lot here on Barbados, but you will get used to us in time. Everyone likes your husband, or nearly everyone. When I heard he had brought back a wife, I thought lucky woman, but now I see that he is the lucky one. I hope you will be happy here."

"With a garden and cooler clothing, there is no reason I should not be happy, Mistress Lawnton. There are always my books for companionship."

"Call me Esther, please. Let us not allow age to stand between our being friends."

*

After their guests had departed, Esther and Harold Lawnton sat in the growing dark of their veranda, talking about the dinner and Charlotte.

"Well, what did you think of her?" Esther asked.

"Pretty enough for any man, I'd say. Seems a bit stand-offish, as if she is too good for us colonials. Got the idea she sits in judgment on everything a man says."

"I think you misjudge her. She is a well-brought-up girl. Has lived in a world of books, protected by her family, which incidentally is a good one. Also, I think she may be rather overwhelmed by Richard and Barbados."

"I daresay she'll loosen up in time. Not act so stiff. Expect Richard will break her to the saddle soon enough."

"Now, Harold, you are speaking of a very well-bred English girl, not a mare. And let me tell you something else. That girl has a mind of her own. Shouldn't be surprised if Richard Bolton doesn't have to do some adjusting of his own to that one. Curious young woman. I hope she will be happy here."

"Can't think why she wouldn't be."

"I felt sorry for her when she showed up in that silly woolen dress, looking like a shy English rose set down in tropical soil. But you know something, Harold? I envy her. She is so young and bright. Her whole life lies before her. You have always charged Richard with being ambitious. Let me tell you something. I think his Charlotte may match him ambition for ambition."

"Ambition for what?"

" 'Twill be most interesting to discover that. Meanwhile, I intend to be a good friend and neighbor to her."

"No harm in that. Richard and I have always looked out for each other. Only right to extend the same courtesy to his wife, but I still say she holds too high an opinion of herself."

"And I say she is simply a bright young woman with a will of her own."

For their next dinner the following Sunday at a plantation down on the coast near Saint James Church, Charlotte wore a gown of soft blue lawn acquired in Bridgetown and laboriously sewn by herself. She wore a broad-brimmed bonnet as well. Comfortably clothed, she was determined not to sit about like a backward schoolgirl. Her resolve was strengthened by the unexpected appearance of David Higganbotham. She was struck by his loss of weight and by lines of worry around his eyes. But his face brightened when he saw the Boltons.

Out of Richard's hearing Charlotte drew the physician aside and asked, "Did you buy their freedom?"

"Alas, I have been dreading this moment."

He told her of the auction.

"What happened to the boy, then?"

"John is with me. He misses his father, but he is adjusting. Clever lad. I am becoming quite fond of him. Do you want him at your place?"

"Impossible. Richard is adamant about taking on no more indentured servants."

"I can't very well turn the lad free with no one to look after him."

"Then keep him as long as you remain here. Consider him a gift from me."

Richard interrupted with questions about Higganbotham's plantation. Charlotte then discovered why the doctor looked so careworn.

"The bad news began at the lawyer's office. My brother had borrowed a thousand pounds for a sugar mill, and unless I can begin repaying the money, his creditors will foreclose. The place is in shocking condition. The yard is littered with piles of lumber and shingles for a veranda that was begun a year ago. The overseer and his wife are mean, slovenly people. Took it upon themselves to move into the house when Brother James died. The slaves are in terrible condition. They cringe before him like beaten dogs. Two have died since James himself passed away."

"How much land is there?" Richard asked.

"A hundred and ten acres, mostly in cotton, and twenty-eight slaves, of whom several are very feeble. The overseer has been starving them, I rather think."

"I should like to meet this overseer."

"He was astounded when John and I showed up. Said James promised them they could have the land and pay rents to our family back in England. Didn't like it a bit when I required them to move back into their cottage near the Negro yard."

"Who is this John?"

Higganbotham avoided Charlotte's eyes as he replied, "The Quaker boy who was on our ship. I picked up his indenture..."

"Foolish thing to do. Now you are saddled with a rundown plantation, a pile of debts, a bad overseer, and a snot-nosed boy."

"Really, Richard," Charlotte said. "You are uncharitable."

Richard clapped Higganbotham on the shoulder.

"What if we ride over one day next week and have a look at things?"

Leaving Charlotte in the yard with John, Richard had the overseer, a beefy Yorkshireman, show them about the plantation with David. He dismounted to inspect signs of erosion in the fields. He inquired closely about the number of cattle and why they were so sickly. The slaves looked like invalids. Richard spoke to several in a low voice, out of hearing of the overseer. Back at the house, he asked to see the plantation records.

By now the sullen expression on the overseer's face had turned to one of concern. "Records, Sir Richard?"

"Come, man, you know what records are. Where is your ledger? Where are your account books? The lawyer told Doctor Higganbotham that his brother kept excellent records."

"Ah, those." The overseer brought out several ledgers, and Richard spent half an hour reading them, stopping now and then to ask sharp questions.

During all this time, Charlotte enjoyed talking to John, or rather listening to his enthusiastic account of his first few days. "It be a strange and wonderful land. Nothing like England, at all. I goes a'roaming as I pleases. Just looking about. Doctor says I may go a'swimming in the sea, sometime, too. Have you seen the monkeys? Yes, he has set me to reading his books, but the poor man is that worried about this place. 'Tis dreadful the way they treat the poor blackamoors here, like as if they weren't human beings. Yes, ma'am, I does miss me father, but I reckon the Good Lord will look after him."

"Don't interrupt me!" Richard's voice startled them. "And don't tell me any more of your damned lies."

At the sound of this commanding tone from the plantation office, Charlotte and John fell silent.

"You have exactly thirty days to get this place back in good order. Begin by feeding the slaves their full rations. No more floggings without the doctor's permission. There will be no more hiring out the slaves next door and pocketing the proceeds, and don't deny you've been doing that during the sugar harvest. Your wife can do her own housework henceforth. Keep all the slaves in the fields where they belong."

The overseer began to protest, but Richard cut him off.

"I've seen enough to convince a judge you should be put in stocks at Egginton's Green and then shipped off the island as an example to other dishonest overseers. I will be back in a few days. You will not know when to expect me. I want to see progress. Now go and get started."

Charlotte listened with awe. Richard's voice frightened her but also gave her a feeling of security.

"Your husband knows how to gain one's attention," Higganbotham said wryly as the overseer rode away.

"Now I must speak some plain words to you, David," Richard said. "With the best of overseers, you stand to lose this place unless you can bring in fresh capital. No, I don't mean borrow it. Earn it. I have been talking to other planters, and they all are showing more concern for the health of their slaves. Back when the Dutch would sell you an African for seven pounds, they used to say, 'It's cheaper to buy them than to breed them,' but today a good saltwater Negro will run you twelve pounds or more."

"What are you getting at?"

"Your practicing medicine on a contract basis. Barbados has too many quacksalvers and barbers calling themselves surgeons. A real physician such as yourself could do very well making regular visits to plantations, examining the slaves, even instructing the planters' wives, who do some creditable doctoring of their own. I can have you a dozen contracts in a week."

"That would mean my remaining on Barbados."

"Would that be so awful?" Charlotte asked. "John can help you with the plantation records. I have been catechizing him about his reading and writing. He says he is good at sums, and Richard himself could take lessons from him in handwriting."

"There you are, David," Richard said. "Might as well get your money's worth from the boy."

Higganbotham frowned. "Is there a proper book on diseases peculiar to this climate?"

"Not that I know of. There is another job for you."

Charlotte squeezed Richard's arm and exclaimed, "Wouldn't that be wonderful? *Higganbotham on Diseases of the Tropics*. Oh, David, do stay on here and make a new life for yourself."

Venturing from their jungle retreat into Bridgetown for the first time, Tom Cochran and Moses Martin quickly became the objects of much curiosity and fun-poking for the sunburned, barefooted white ruffians who frequented the waterfront.

"Who you got there, Tom?"

"He is my servant. I bought him."

"If he is your servant, how come he is riding and you are walking?"

"If it is any of your business, he has not been well. Besides, he is a man of education."

"Educated, eh? Well, la te da. What's his name?"

"I don't know. He can't talk."

"If he can't talk, how do you know he is educated? Somebody has sold you a dummy, Tom."

"I have seen him write. He writes in the dirt sometimes."

"In the dirt? Let's see him write his name."

Tom helped Moses dismount and handed him the donkey goad.

"Show them."

Moses bent and scratched in the earth. The men in the front rank looked at each other and shrugged. Then one in the rear of the crowd came forward and examined the letters.

"Moses. Moses Martin. That is what he has written."

"God in heaven, I thought he might have been Jesus Christ hisself, riding his ass into Jerusalem. But it is only Moses."

Tom grabbed the goad and brandished it at his tormentors. "Get out of my way, or I'll break your heads."

"Aw, Tom, don't be cross. Here, I'll buy some of that tobacco off you."

Others crowded close to purchase twists of tobacco from the hermit, until his stock was exhausted. At last, tired of their sport, they left the two eccentrics alone. Tom helped Moses back on the donkey.

"So, your name is Moses. I like it. Say, you seen how that lot bought up my tobacco. Usually have to go about peddling it. Anyway, they have give me a idea. Are you a good tailor, Moses? Yes, of course you are."

Tom led the donkey to Swan Street, to a small shop owned by a Portuguese Jew, and there purchased a pen, bottle of ink, and supply of paper. He spent the rest of his coins at another shop for several yards of cloth, scissors, needles, thread, and a new hammock. Back at their hut that evening, he gave the writing materials to Moses.

"Teach me to write."

Moses pointed to the sinking sun.

"Tomorrow, then. And you seen the smocks the carters and such wears in Bridgetown. Could you make some of them while I work in our tobacco patch? If you will, we can sell them until we get enough money to buy your son's time from that doctor fellow. How would you like that, Moses?"

Moses scratched "T O M" in the dirt and then pointed to his owner.

"That's my name?"

Moses smiled. Tom inspected the letters from every side, caught up by the magic secret he felt opening to him. Moses put the stick in his hand and guided him until, using both hands, he could trace the letters.

Early the next morning, Moses awakened and looked in alarm at the hermit's empty hammock. He found him beside their fire pit, scratching out the same three letters in the dirt over and over.

"Hurry and eat your breakfast. I am ready for the rest of my name. You know how to write Cochran?"

"John, John, see who is here."

Higganbotham called from his newly completed veranda into the plantation house, where John was copying in a ledger. The boy came to the door to see his father, wearing a smock and hat made of palm leaves, sitting on a donkey. He ran into the yard and Moses slid off the donkey to embrace him.

"Thou cannot speak yet? No matter. Thou look well, Father. Better than ever I can recall."

"Of course he is well," Tom said. "Him and me has a rare old good time. He's my partner now. Is teaching me my letters, he is, and I have give him employment at his old trade."

"Tailoring again, Father?"

"He is that, and a damned fine tailor he is. I sells his work fast as he can turn it out. Say, lad, we've come to take you with us."

Higganbotham cleared his throat. "Not so fast here..."

"We've been working hard these past few weeks and saving our money. I am prepared to make you an offer for the lad's freedom."

Amused, but mildly alarmed, Higganbotham replied, "But you told me that I had my servant and you had yours. And you told me to begone."

"I spoke in haste. Look, I don't mind the boy has fits. I want him for Moses' sake."

"He does not have fits, and you are not buying him. John is my accounts keeper. I can't spare him."

"I'd throw my donkey into the bargain."

"You are wasting your breath, Mister Cochran. Please, let us speak of other matters while they visit. You left so quickly during the Dutch attack that you did not learn something you should know about this Moses Martin."

When Higganbotham finished the story of Moses' confrontation with King Charles, Tom whistled in amazement. "He done that? Coo, what a one. Wish more than ever he could talk now. The king hisself, and on the steps of Saint Paul's . . ."

Higganbotham enjoyed the visit of the two old men. And Charlotte would be eager to hear about Moses and his new life.

Charlotte. It pleased him to think of her listening with her head inclined, her clear eyes fixed on his face as he spoke. He would be embarrassed for her to know how much she had influenced his decision to remain on Barbados. And Richard had proved a friend indeed. The overseer had turned to and completed the porch, filled in and terraced the eroded patches in the fields, and increased the rations of the Negroes, all without prodding from Higganbotham, whose time was taken up with establishing his medical practice. Bearing in mind Richard's observation that he had too little land for successful sugar production, Higganbotham had sold off the machinery and boiling equipment his brother had foolishly bought and planned to revert to growing cotton and indigo on the land.

Charlotte's estimate of John's intelligence had been accurate; the boy was a natural with figures and bookkeeping. Higganbotham liked having him about so much he considered buying him a pony so that John could accompany him on his medical rounds.

It delighted the physician to overhear John saying to Tom Cochran, "But I likes it here. And Father seems content with thee. Mayhap I might visit thee, mighten I, Doctor?"

Higganbotham looked at Tom. "You live off the road to the Bolton plantation?"

"Aye, about two mile from there, this side."

"Draw me a map in the dirt here. The Boltons have invited us to spend a day or so with them. There should be time to visit you as well."

Thereafter, Tom and Moses became familiar figures up and down the lee coast of Barbados. Tom stopped referring to the Quaker as "my servant." In fact, he treated him as an honored visitor and told all who would listen about the incident with the king. The pair traveled as far north as Speightstown and as far south as Oistin's Bay and inland to the deep-soiled land of Saint George Valley, where the richest plantations lay. More for Moses' benefit than his own, Tom stopped often to talk to small landowners and peddlers and hear their complaints about the increasing ownership of the island's land by well-financed planters. They saw white emigrants with defeated expressions waiting in Bridgetown for ships to take them to other islands or North America. At Needham's Point late one afternoon, they observed a slaver stop just outside Carlisle Bay while the crew cast overboard the bodies of several dead or dying Africans and watched in horror as sharks raced in from the sea to feast on the carcasses.

At a plantation in the shadow of Christ Church, they witnessed an overseer whipping a pregnant black woman. And one Sunday, they met a troop of elegantly dressed planters riding fine horses to church services, while beside the road a bit further on, slaves danced and sang around one of their burial grounds. The sight of the two odd-looking white men, one wearing a robe and riding a donkey led by the other, excited the Negroes' mirth. They halted their revelry to point and laugh at the ludicrous pair.

"Look at 'em, Moses," Tom said in disgust. "To think this was a white man's country until they started bringing them in. Hear their monkey chatter. They think they fly back to Africa when they die. I'd like to see every one of them fly back to

Africa and let us have our island back. This land is ruint, I tell you, Moses, and it's greed as has done it. But you and me, we got our place. None of this has aught to do with us."

Charlotte had little in common with most of the planters' wives she met from that immediate area of Barbados. She was younger and more attractive. And both she and they were conscious of her position as the daughter of one titled gentleman and the wife of another. So, during her early days on Barbados, she established no real friendships with other wives, except for Esther Lawnton. Yet her standoffishness did not diminish the invitations she and Richard received in that gregarious society.

After several dinners at nearby plantations, Charlotte found her homesickness fading. She began to enjoy the secure place she was making for herself in Barbadian society. And, now that she had sensible clothing, she had adjusted to the heat. She had only to avoid the midday sun and pace her activities. Her garden provided a pleasant occupation for the early and late parts of the day. And she enjoyed reading during the hotter hours.

With the end of harvest, Richard spent more time with her. Charlotte wondered what he would say if he learned of her conspiracy with David Higganbotham to look after the Martins. How adroitly she had got around him on that point.

Her friendship with Esther Lawnton also helped relieve her homesickness. This well-bred neighbor had become like an older sister or favorite aunt. So it was to Esther rather than Richard that Charlotte confessed her concern about Mandze's continued sullenness.

"Toby is a jewel. He lives to do my wishes. But Mandze seems to resent me so. I suppose she grew too used to working without supervision while Richard was in England."

"Have you mentioned this to Richard?"

"I hesitate to do so. I prefer to handle such matters myself."

Without replying, Esther looked down at her hands, and

Charlotte changed the subject to the visit she expected the next day from David Higganbotham and John.

"We plan to ride up Apes Hill to see John's father, the old Quaker I told you about. His indenture was purchased by a hermit who lives up there."

"That would be Tom Cochran. Everyone knows Crazy Tom."

Upon returning to Bolton Hall, Charlotte found that Mandze had completed none of her chores. And she merely turned down the corners of her mouth at Charlotte's reprimand. So, reluctantly, Charlotte told Richard of her dissatisfaction late that afternoon as they sat on the veranda.

"Leave the matter to me," Richard said.

Later, in the kitchen, Charlotte found Mandze in tears, but the Negress's only response to her inquiries was to turn her back as if to tend the fire. That night, as they settled in their bed, Charlotte mentioned the incident to Richard. He merely shrugged.

"Well, did you speak to her?"

"I did."

"Is that why she was crying?"

"I suppose so. Don't fret about her. You will have no more trouble with her."

"I do not like anyone in my household to be unhappy. What did you say to her?"

"Oh, Charlotte, let us not dwell on the matter. I am dealing with it in my own way."

"Why does she resent me so? I don't understand it."

"Don't try to understand them. Only make certain that they understand you and what you expect of them. That is the only way to deal with Negroes."

"You speak of them with so little feeling. David says they are as human as you or I. He has begun to make notes on their various languages and to ask them about their way of life back in Africa."

"So he has told me, at rather weary length. I have neither

time nor interest to inquire into how they feel. Rather let me feel your lovely arms about my neck."

Charlotte put her hands against his chest.

"Of what tribe is Mandze?"

"Cormontine, I think."

"And how did you come by her?"

"For God's sake, Charlotte, why all this interest of a sudden in a black wench? I bought her off a boat twelve years ago. Now please may we change the subject?"

In a different way, Charlotte enjoyed her friendship, or her's and Richard's, with David Higganbotham almost as much as that with Esther Lawnton. The physician's earnest goodwill and boyish curiosity about his new surroundings were appealing. He lacked Richard's often vulgar sense of humor and masculine dash but showed a greater depth of mind. Charlotte found him easy to talk to. Their secret about John Martin gave them an extra bond of understanding.

When David and John came for their visit, they brought along their plantation books for Richard to examine. While he reviewed the precise entries with the lad, Charlotte showed off her garden to David. He admired the walks of crushed coral and the stone borders of the flower beds.

"But you must save a bed for medicinal herbs. One could operate a pharmaceutical business right here on Barbados, using our own leaves and plants. Aloes for purgatives. Or, if one wished to poison an enemy, the juice from machineel leaves."

"You said 'our' plants. You sound like a Barbadian, David."

"I suppose I am one. I am enjoying myself vastly out here. And there is nothing in England to draw me back there. Here I am needed. The slaves fascinate me. I make notes on their speech. Examining them closely as I do and talking to them, I see how different they are from each other, and how human. It sickens me when brutish overseers treat them like animals. They respond to kindness. Of course the owners who employ me already accept the wisdom of good care, but I further emphasize the importance of improved diets and time off for rest and recreation. Two weeks ago, I refunded my retainer to a man who refused to feed his slaves properly. He called me a fool and a meddler."

"Richard says that firmness is necessary in dealing with them, but he will allow no brutality here. He says the way to deal with chronic misbehavior is to sell the offending Negro to a slaver on its way to Jamaica. As he puts it, 'That way you get rid of the problem, take in revenue, and make an example for the others.' "

"Richard is a very practical man."

Upon completing his examination of John's ledger, Richard begged off taking part in the search for Tom Cochran's retreat, but he insisted that Charlotte ride along. After he kissed her and lifted her onto Nutmeg's back, she paused to instruct Toby to dig a new section for a flower bed, and then said to Mandze, who stood in the doorway, "Don't forget to air the bedding. You know, the mattress. Hang it in the window."

"On your way. I'll see she does it," Richard said.

Charlotte, David, and John missed the path to Tom Cochran's hideaway, but the old man stepped onto the road from a thicket and called them back.

"We been watching you. Follow me."

Charlotte marveled at the beauty of the overgrown lair and at the self-sufficiency of the pair. Noticing a patch of herbs, Higganbotham questioned Tom closely about each plant. At first, Tom affected an air of annoyance, but he soon warmed to the doctor's interest. John and Moses stood under the eaves of the hut, beaming at each other.

"Here," Tom said. "We have forgot our manners. You must all have some of Moses' mobby. Taught him how to make it meself."

Charlotte settled herself on a log as the drink was passed.

"Mister Martin, you should be proud of John." Then, after describing his work on the plantation accounts, she added, "So, you need have no fears about him. He is in good hands."

Moses scratched in the earth, "In God's hands."

Having learned that Tom obtained his medicinal lore from

an Indian wife, David brought out his notebook and pressed him for more information. With John rattling away to his father, Charlotte wandered about the plot, admiring the view, and then walked down into the ravine. Here she felt a new kind of peace. This place that no one but Tom Cochran had wanted was a haven. At Bolton Hall, Charlotte had missed her privacy, with Mandze padding resentfully through the house or Toby waiting for her in the garden like an anxious puppy. And she could never forget that a hundred slaves lived and worked nearby. How comforting it was to be truly alone with her thoughts. Just eight months ago she had taken that fateful journey to London. What if her mother had decided to accompany Sir Robert, after all? Charlotte would not have met Richard Bolton. She would be Mistress Marmaduke Harbinson. Or suppose her father had not escorted her to Saint Paul's? How different her life would be. Or suppose that Moses had not posted his broadside on the door of the Bristol cathedral. He and John would still be at home, and she would not have discovered this oasis of tranquility.

She remained in the cool shade of the ravine, savoring her thoughts, until David, alarmed by her disappearance, called.

"Mister Cochran should be a doctor himself. And I was fascinated by his recollections of the early days here."

Charlotte held out her hand to Tom.

"I hope that I may visit you again."

"Anytime at all, ma'am."

Bidding good-bye to David and John at the lane to Bolton Hall, Charlotte was relieved that they declined her invitation to stay the night. Having a guest, even one as agreeable as the amiable physician, was rather a strain, since Mandze did only those routine tasks that she had learned when the housekeeping was her responsibility.

Richard came galloping up from the sugar works as she rode into the yard. "Here," she said after he hugged and kissed her vigorously, "I've only been away a few hours."

"Come in the kitchen and see what I have for you."

On the stool where Mandze usually sat was perched a slender mulatto girl.

"Stand up, Clemmie. Charlotte, this is your new girl. She can cook and sew. Esther Lawnton taught her. Clemmie, this is Lady Bolton, Mistress Charlotte to you."

The girl arose, smiling, and curtsied.

"Where is Mandze?" Charlotte asked.

"I traded her off to the Lawntons. They have a gang foreman whose woman died, and they wanted him to have a good wife. Esther knew you needed a seamstress, so we struck a bargain. She assures me Clemmie has a good disposition. And she is only fifteen."

Charlotte was incredulous. "Just like that, you traded two human beings? Was that why Mandze cried last night?"

"That is all behind us. The Lawntons say her new husband is a good man. And Clemmie is eager to come here."

"But you did not even consult me."

"I wanted to surprise you. Why are you not pleased?"

"In the future, Richard, I would be grateful if you would let me make my own choices in running the household."

He looked crestfallen. "I did what I thought best. I was thinking of your happiness."

"Let us speak no more of it."

But that night, when he wanted to make love, Charlotte turned her back. And the next morning, after eating an excellent breakfast cheerfully served by Clemmie, she asked Richard to saddle Nutmeg.

"Where are you going?"

"To visit Esther Lawnton."

"What for? Do you wish me to escort you?"

"I do not."

So Charlotte saved her tears until she reached Fulham Plantation, until she was alone in the drawing room with her gray-haired neighbor.

"To think that he would make such a change without consulting me. I could have brought Mandze around in time.

And you were a party to this, Esther. I thought we were to be friends."

Esther made no comment, merely shaking her head until Charlotte stopped to blow her nose.

"You are much younger and less experienced than Richard. You know that."

"I don't see what that has to do . . ."

"And you are but newly come here. Barbados is not England, my dear. And Negroes are not English. They are very different, and I fear their presence makes us different, especially our men folk. Really, I was trying to be kind. Don't blame Richard. It was my idea."

"Yours?" Charlotte felt her anger rising. "How dare you interfere!"

"There is something you do not understand, Charlotte. We have known Richard for a long time. Both Harold and I admire him. But he is a man, and men do not have our sense of delicacy or sensitivity."

"What are you implying?"

"Richard should have replaced Mandze before he brought you here. It was not good to have her in the same house with you. She is human, too, just as you say."

"You mean she was spoiled by her long lack of supervision?"

Esther turned and stared out the window. Her face still averted, she continued. "Mandze was quite attractive before she became so stout."

The room grew very quiet. Charlotte felt a tightness spread through her chest. Esther now looked at her with a pained expression.

"These things happen out here. Until recent years there were never enough white women, not the sort to make suitable wives for gentlemen. Be glad there are no half-breed children to complicate your life."

Charlotte sat down and put her face in her hands. Esther stood beside her.

"Look at me, Charlotte." Her soft, usually tranquil face

now appeared as anguished as Charlotte's. "Be as thankful that you do not have Mandze about as that I no longer have Clemmie daily reminding me. You see, Harold came out here alone just after we married and did not send for me for three years. One cannot blame him, I suppose. I was bitter at first, but I have adjusted, and so must you. Don't you see, my dear?"

For a moment, with her hand over her mouth, Esther seemed at the point of breaking down.

Charlotte arose and, fighting to control her voice, said, "We shall be very kind to Clemmie."

"Then let us never again speak of this painful matter. Count your blessings, Charlotte. You are a most fortunate young woman in so many ways. Come, I want you to see my garden now that my new frangipani is in bloom."

6

... Ten years have passed since my discovery that my husband, whom I had come to adore, had kept a black concubine. Never had I been so crushed, so hurt. Had this occurred in England, I could have renounced him and returned to my parents. But here I was trapped in what suddenly seemed a tropical hell, a place of despair, doomed to life with a man whom suddenly I loathed as much as previously I had loved, doomed, so I thought, never again to lie in his arms without thinking, not just of her, but also of his duplicity and callousness.

Esther Lawnton said many white men had black concubines, but that knowledge brought me no comfort. It happened before he met me, true. Yet the fact that he kept the relationship from me, that he brought me to Bolton Hall with her still in the house, that he did nothing about her until he saw that she could not accept me, and then, when he did take action, he did so in a sly manner, without consulting me ... all this disturbed me more than I could bear.

Toward Mandze herself, I felt pity rather than jealousy. In her own way, she must have loved him, too, else why would she have resented me so? I was shocked that he could ruthlessly trade her off like an animal he no longer needed. And I hated his treating me as though I were a simple-minded girl who could be easily duped. If I had not loved him so unreservedly, it would not have mattered as much. But he shattered my trust. What other secrets did he harbor behind that facade of charm?

Today, although the memory still pains me, I can understand and even excuse that old relationship. At the time it began Richard was deeply in debt, trying to pay the Simpsons for Bolton Hall, and in no position to win the hand of a suitable white woman. Indeed, working as hard as he did in those days, he hardly had time to pay court to a woman of his own social level. Besides, he was out of favor on the island politically. He was lonely. And he was a man of lusty appetites.

All this Esther offered in his defense. She pointed out, also, that the Dutch attack had made it impossible for Richard to remove Mandze from the house before I came out from Bridgetown. Then once back, he got caught up in the sugar harvest. There was more to it than that, however. In my opinion, he observed that I, in my innocence, saw nothing askance in the presence of a slave woman in the house. So he let matters slide. It was only after Mandze became difficult that he took action. He was quite taken aback when his scheme to substitute Clemmie went awry.

I kept my word to Esther that I would not berate Richard. But, while I could hide my feelings, I could not control them. They had changed, not just toward Richard, but toward Barbados as well. Just as I was beginning to grow fond of the place, I found myself longing to be back in England, where human beings were not bought and sold like cattle.

We did not talk about the incident. Had I not been so stubborn and proud, I might have raged at him, purging myself in a storm of tears. He surely would have begged my forgiveness, and perhaps my hurt would have healed faster. Instead, I treated him with a cool civility, and he responded with a dogged solicitude, being not quite certain whether I knew the entire story.

I was glad he could not discern my thoughts, for I resolved that as soon as the war with the Dutch permitted safe passage home, I would leave Barbados and never return.

Meanwhile, I found Clemmie a welcome change from Mandze. She spoke excellent English and was anxious to please. I tried to keep a formal distance, but her sunny disposition melted my reserve, and I came to regard her as a trusted personal maid rather than a slave. With relations between Richard and me so distant, she offered pleasant company as we sat through the torrid afternoons sewing and talking.

Clemmie loved hearing about England. She took me aback once by asking whether I missed my home. When I admitted that I did, she made a penetrating remark.

"My mother came from Africa, you know. She used to wish to be back there. I do not know whether to wish for Africa or England. I am like a mule, neither horse nor donkey."

"If you were set down in either place, I expect you would be homesick for Barbados," I replied and then suggested that we keep our minds on our sewing. But it occurred to me that I might be equally homesick for the island, or at least its beauty.

Soon thereafter, Richard asked my permission to purchase an older African woman at the sale of a plantation near Speightstown. She was named Mirabel, after the ship that had brought her from Gambia. Her owners had trained her well in cooking and cleaning, and she had a good disposition.

Did I wish still more help? At that time my mind was more on returning to England than on creating a household staff. "No," I told him. "We have no need for so many servants as one sees at Fulham and Westover."

He grinned in that way I had once found charming and said, "That is because we have not started to entertain yet. That will change soon."

I asked what he meant, observing that it seemed to me nothing ever changed on this island.

"Lord Willoughby has returned from Surinam at last. Friends in Bridgetown have informed him of my knighthood and my wife."

"You might have reversed the order," I replied.

That was my first jest since the Mandze-Clemmie affair, and he laughed rather too heartily, then added, "And they have taken pains to tell him of my part in repelling the Dutch attack, not to mention the beauty of my wife."

"Why say you 'pains'? Do your friends find it so hard to speak well of you?"

Ignoring my shrewish remark, he explained to me, for the first time, that Willoughby bore him an old grudge. In 1651, when Parliament sent a fleet to regain control of the island from the Royalists, Richard had deserted the governor.

"The Roundheads kicked him off the island. One of his first acts upon returning three years ago was to remove me from command of my old militia regiment."

"You have been slow to tell me this story," I said frostily.

"No matter. I stole a march on him by having old friends at home quietly put my name before the king for my services on his father's behalf at Colchester. Now London is asking Willoughby when there will be a new Assembly. The high-handed old goat adjourned the last one two years ago after ramming through the royal export tax everyone complains of. Now, he needs my support. He has sent me a sign he would like to repair the breach between us."

I had been listening to him with an air of disdain, but now my interest quickened. "A sign?" I asked.

He held up an envelope and announced that Sir Richard and Lady Bolton had received an invitation from the governor to attend a dinner the next Sunday at Parham Park, his country residence in Saint Thomas Parish . . .

"He looks more like the king than the king himself," Charlotte whispered to Richard as they waited at the entrance to the grand country home of Francis, Lord Willoughby, governor and royal proprietor of Barbados.

"Hush. You will give him notions. He thinks well enough of himself already."

A large man in his mid-fifties, Willoughby bore himself with an air of self-assurance befitting the chief official of England's richest and most populous colony. As he greeted his guests at the doorway, Charlotte studied his face. She had heard the story of how a demented acquaintance in Surinam had attacked Willoughby with a cutlass. A deep, barely healed gash ran across his forehead, and two fingers were missing from his left hand.

"Where is his wife?"

"Dead. Died soon after King Charles restored him here, before he could send back for her."

Willoughby kissed Charlotte's hand and, after gazing into her eyes an embarrassingly long while, said, "What a beauty you have brought back from England, Bolton. Or should I say, Sir Richard? By Jove, after we have eaten, you must tell me how you brought off such a coup."

Except for the high windows, now open to admit the breeze, and a small army of liveried black servants padding about barefooted, Parham Park reminded Charlotte of Foxley Manor on a grander scale. And the guests were better dressed than any who had ever visited her old home. Richard identified them for her.

"There is Colonel Codrington and Newton. Over there we have old Hawley, who was governor during the thirties, the unscrupulous old tyrant. Look about you, Charlotte. More wealth is present in this reception hall than you'd find at a royal dinner at Windsor, leaving out the king, of course."

Richard moved her from couple to couple, making sure she got each name right and adding sotto voce comments such as "five hundred acres in Saint George's Valley. Two hundred slaves. He was a vicar's son in Bucks. Knighted by Cromwell."

On entering the dining hall, Charlotte was amazed when Lord Willoughby placed her on his right and pleased beyond measure when he proposed a toast to "Charlotte, Lady Bolton, may she have a long and happy life in Barbados."

Flattered by this attention and warmed by the excellent wine, Charlotte momentarily forgot her unhappiness at home. She spoke easily with those around her, answering questions about her family and recent conditions in England. When one of her jests set Lord Willoughby to laughing, she noticed Richard looking down the table at her with approval.

The meal continued, course after course, until Charlotte felt ready to burst. Withdrawing with the other women after dinner, she found their conversation boring. Many of them still longed for England and hoped their husbands would retire there someday. She could not, would not, spend the rest of her days like this, listening to shallow, spoiled women talk about trivial matters, married to what her mother so aptly called a "colonial adventurer." Well, the evening had not been a loss. She had enjoyed the attention paid her by Lord Willoughby and the other men. This had been far better than sitting back at Bolton Hall with a man for whom she had lost her respect. A planter, dear God, a planter. The word had sounded so romantic back in England. But all he did, all he seemed to be interested in was the raising of cane and the manufacture of sugar. Why could he not be like Lord Willoughby? Wouldn't that be something, to be the wife of a peer, no, more than that, the ruler of a virtual kingdom.

Only later did it dawn on Charlotte that, while Richard knew most of the guests, this was the first time he had ever been received at Parham Park and that he had been far more apprehensive than he had showed. He was nearly drunk when time came to say their good-byes. Again Lord Willoughby kissed Charlotte's hand and congratulated Richard on his good fortune and good taste. As they rode down the palm-lined lane, Richard broke into a bawdy song, and, when she tried to shush him, said, "Oh, don't act such a turnip. Here, I'll race you back to Saint Thomas Church."

"Don't be a fool. It is nearly dark, and you are drunk."

"A fool? You dare speak so to a member of the governor's council?"

"What did you say?"

He struck Nutmeg's rump with his hat and set off at a canter. Within seconds both horses were galloping along the road. Getting caught up in his spirit, Charlotte lashed the mare until she drew even with Richard. A band of poor whites scrambled off the road to avoid the flashing hooves. Charlotte's bonnet blew off her head but was saved by the ribbon round her neck. Slaves around their supper cookfires pointed at this apparently mad couple. It had been a long time since Charlotte had raced a horse like this. Nearly drunk herself from Willoughby's wine and his compliments, Charlotte stayed even with him until they reached Saint Thomas. There Richard reined in his horse and smiled knowingly while she caught her breath.

"What did you mean about the council?"

"Willoughby wants me to serve on his governor's council."

"What is that?"

"That is a group of twelve men who act as a kind of upper house to the Assembly. It is a great honor and a considerable responsibility."

"I thought Willoughby mistrusted you."

"He needs my political support and my military skill. Anyway I told him I would accept only if my wife gave her permission."

"Don't be ridiculous. Since when have you consulted me about anything?"

When they got home, Charlotte, still intoxicated, threw open the windows and tossed off her clothes. For the first time in weeks, she allowed Richard to make love to her.

Although there had never been a more eager pupil than Tom Cochran, Moses' inability to speak made it difficult to teach him quickly. Tom had learned to write the letters of the alphabet but could not sound them. He developed a wide writing vocabulary by calling out words to Moses who then scratched them in the dirt.

Arriving on his new pony one day while they were in the midst of a lesson, John taught Tom the sounds of the letters through a rhyme he had learned in dame's school. All the next week, digging in his vegetable patch or walking on the road to and from Bridgetown, the old man chanted the letters, to the amusement of Moses.

Higganbotham had developed a social life of his own as a pleasant extra man at Sunday dinners. This gave John the opportunity to ride abroad on his pony. On his next visit to his father, John brought along a copy of Bacon's essays that Charlotte had given him and, from it, showed Tom some of the words Moses had taught him to write.

"And you say your doctor has more books?"

"He has many. Most concern medicine. Lady Bolton has even more. She says I may borrow others."

Tom held the book wonderingly, as though it were a fragile treasure, turning the pages with great care as he sought words he knew, looking for them as one would for familiar faces in a crowd, and mumbling to himself. "Coo, all them words. All meaning something. There's 'he' and 'it.' To think one man knowed all them words and writ them down like this."

"Art thou well, Father?" John asked.

Moses nodded.

"Do you need anything?"

He shook his head.

"Do you mind Barbados so much now that you are here?"

Moses' eyes narrowed at John's lapse into non-Quaker speech.

"Isn't it a grand country? Doctor Higganbotham is getting on well here. He likes it so he don't want to sell his plantation anymore. I miss Mama and home, but I don't think I would go back to England if I could. Doctor says if I keeps up my reading and learns all about planting, there is no reason I can't have my own plantation someday. Imagine owning my own land and slaves. Wouldn't that be something?"

Moses shook his head, a look of distress on his face.

"What's wrong, Father?"

Moses wrote in the dirt.

John felt a chill as he made out the word. "Why say you

'wicked'? There are many kind and good people here, Father. It be a better place than England. They be not so ready to throw folk into jail for their beliefs. Did you know there be Friends' meetings here and there about the island? Why do you write down such a word about Barbados?"

Moses wrote another single word: "Slavery."

"Why, Father, many Friends owns slaves here, and they treats them with great kindness. Some gets in trouble with the law for converting them."

Moses turned his gaze away, toward Bridgetown. John was grateful to Tom for interrupting to ask him the meaning of a word in the essays. The boy considered warning the hermit to keep a close watch on Moses but decided it was not necessary.

... I did not regain my former happiness all at once, but my heartache did diminish after that dinner at Parham Park. My social success restored my damaged self-esteem, and my spirits were further buoyed by the news that, not only was Richard back in political favor, he had gained a higher position than ever before. Not that I forgot his deception about Mandze, or even that I forgave him; I simply allowed the matter to be crowded from my consciousness by my ambition for myself, socially, and for him, politically. So, I gave up my daydreams of returning to England and faced up to the reality of my life on Barbados.

At Richard's insistence, I accompanied him on several trips to make speeches on Willoughby's behalf at political gatherings around

Speightstown and over in the rugged Scotland district. These excursions gave me a fresh appreciation both for Richard's powers of persuasion and for the colorful beauty of the Barbadian back country. It became clear to me that I had married a natural leader of men. But I was dismayed by the anti–Willoughby views of some of the planters whose hospitality we enjoyed, and by their reluctance to pay taxes to rebuild the island's depleted defenses, war or no war. One of our hosts, a Colonel Farmer, accused the governor of trying to turn Barbados from a largely self-ruled proprietorship into "a colony of the Crown, by the Crown, and for the Crown" and called Richard "Willoughby's cat's-paw."

I picked up much interesting local gossip, also. At a plantation called Berringers, we were entertained by a Sir John Yeamans, a pushy, dislikeable man who tried to persuade Richard to join him in a land scheme in the Carolinas, where a few Barbadian planters had already moved with their slaves.

"We'll all have to emigrate there if the Assembly does not provide for the defense of Barbados," Richard replied.

The house, a three-story affair built of coral stone, struck me as better suited to Gloucestershire than a tropical climate, but it did renew my determination for Richard to make good on his promise to build me a proper mansion.

On our ride back from a political rally at Berringers, Richard laughed at my description of Yeamans as "rough cut."

"That is putting it mildly. Mistress Yeamans's first husband and John were partners in land speculation. Although a court inquiry found otherwise, many still think John killed Berringer in a duel over the lady's affection."

At another plantation overlooking the Atlantic shore, I was charmed by the spectacular view and by the stories the venerable owner told me about life on Barbados in the 1630s and 1640s, before sugar and slaves were widely introduced, while much of the land was still forested and life was hard for everyone. Such stories deepened my affection for my new homeland.

The new Assembly lasted for several weeks, and during that time Richard spent much time in Bridgetown. At home he seemed distracted and out of sorts. Willoughby's request for defense appropria-

tions got rough treatment from the Assemblymen, especially Colonel Farmer, whom they named their Speaker.

The summer heat and frequent rains made my loneliness all the more irksome. At times I found it impossible to do more than sit quietly and read or watch the sails of a becalmed ship headed down the coast to Bridgetown. I wondered at the endurance of the slaves as they weeded the long rows of knee-high cane under the vigilant eye of our overseer, Wilkens. Richard had labored under the same relentless sun and sudden, drenching rains. One might think the experience would have made him too sympathetic to require others to endure the same conditions, but, no, it seemed to have rendered him callous.

Even after a half year of marriage, Richard still baffled me. He had hurt me deeply more than once. He had harshly refused to let me buy the freedom of the Martins, but I had got around him nicely enough in the end. As for Mandze, well, what was done was done. Only, I could not help resenting his getting away with such a thing. What would his reaction be if he were to learn that I had kept a lover of any color back in England? My grudging acceptance of male freedom was made easier, however, by my increased appreciation of Richard as a political leader. If I had to play a subservient role to anyone, thank God it was to a man of importance.

Then, too, damn him, I needed him, emotionally. There was no more joyous sound than that of his horse's hooves in the lane. It did not matter that he usually was too weary those nights to do more than eat and fall asleep. I loved to lie quietly and listen to his breathing and then, at daylight, while our room was cool, to nestle in his arms and hear the news from Bridgetown.

Despite the best efforts of Richard and others of the Governor's Council, Samuel Farmer would not stop his protesting the defense appropriation. He even went so far as to draw up a list of formal grievances against the arbitrary rule of Lord Willoughby, who thereupon dissolved the Assembly and placed Farmer under house arrest at his plantation.

Still, Colonel Farmer continued to speak out. Finally, in exasperation, Willoughby sent Richard and the Provost Marshal with a troop of mounted militiamen to haul the stubborn Farmer to Bridge-

town and there placed him on a ship bound for England to be taken before the King on charges of treason.

"It was a sad thing, but what choice did I have?" a weary Richard asked me after the deportation.

"Sad, indeed," I replied. "Was Colonel Farmer not elected to speak his mind? Is that treason?"

Richard was so annoyed by my questions he refused to discuss the matter further. But I lay long awake that night thinking of how a defiant Moses Martin had been shipped off to Barbados for confronting the King, and now Samuel Farmer was being shipped back to England to confront that same King for a different kind of defiance. How could Richard fall asleep so quickly after being a party to such an injustice? Farmer had called him "Willoughby's cat's-paw," and he may have had a point after all.

On his weekly visits to our Negro yard, David Higganbotham always stopped to pay his respects. I enjoyed the gossip he brought from other plantations. He also brought us our first news of the dreadful plague that had broken out back home . . .

"When will these rains let up?" Charlotte asked Richard. "My clothing and books are mildewed."

"Every extra inch of rain means that much more sugar in next year's crop."

"And that much less time for me in the garden."

"And that much better growth for your flowers. Now quit your complaining. What is the matter with you, Charlotte? Do you miss your mother so much?"

Ignoring his sarcasm, she replied, "No, but I wish sometimes for London, just long enough to see a play or walk about the city."

"Be glad you are not in London these days, my dear. According to a ship's captain with whom I spoke yesterday, they have closed the theaters and the churches because of the plague."

"While here there are no theaters to begin with . . ."

He put his hand on her head, a gesture she found annoying, and said, "My dear Charlotte, I know you feel cooped up.

Look, we owe hospitality to many people who have entertained us. The rains ease up in December, and by that time the new crop of cane will have been planted. Why don't we plan a dinner to repay our obligations?"

"A dinner? All people do in this place is eat and drink and talk of politics."

"Not so fast. You and Higganbotham talked much of Shakespeare on our voyage out. Why not present a program of his plays?"

"A play? Here at Bolton Hall?"

"Not an entire play. Rather a collection of your favorite scenes."

"You really think we could? Yes, David and I could take parts, and John, too. And Esther Lawnton. And you, too."

"Now don't drag me into this. I only want you to have a diversion. You know I am too old for such foolishness."

"Why then, you poor old man, you can play Lear and I, Cordelia."

"Lord," he groaned. "What have I got myself into?" But he was pleased to see how animated she had become. And when he further suggested that they invite Lord Willoughby, she threw her arms around his neck and kissed him.

Charlotte could hardly wait to ask David to help with her program, but first had to suffer through his recitation of his interviews with passengers and ships' companies about the plague back in London.

"It broke out last spring in the City's Saint Giles Parish. Awful illness. Comes without warning as a rash all over the body, followed by the most painful swellings in the groin and armpits."

Charlotte smiled to see him blush. "And is it always fatal?"

"Nearly always. Some die quickly and easily, they say, but most suffer so dreadfully from fever and delirium that death comes as a blessing to victim and loved ones alike."

At last, weary of so much talk of death and sickness,

Charlotte interrupted to ask if David and John would help her present her Shakespearian program.

Thereafter, at least once a week during the rest of the rainy autumn, the doctor and his young ward showed up at Bolton Hall, frequently soaking wet, to practice their readings. They were joined by Esther Lawnton who agreed to do the "out, out, damned spot" speech of Lady Macbeth. Although Richard refused to take a part, he did condescend to act as master of ceremonies. Clemmie got so caught up in the excitement that Charlotte had to order her to stop hanging about and return to her household work.

"Still missing London?" Richard asked her at supper one evening late in October after a rehearsal.

"From what David how hears, there are few left there. Six thousand people died in one week, he said. Nearly everyone has fled to the countryside. Six thousand in a week! Imagine."

"I don't have to imagine. We lost four thousand here in little more time just before I arrived. There was a ghastly stench in Bridgetown. Too many had died to bury, so they had dumped the bodies in that great swamp outside the town."

"So you have told me more than once."

"Do you know what day this is?"

"Why, 'tis October 30, I believe."

"And do you remember what you were doing exactly a year ago?"

She thought for a moment, then smiled. "I was sitting in a window seat listening to you talk about the past, just as I am doing now."

"And what were you thinking?"

"I thought: There sits the most conceited man I have ever met. When will he go about his business and leave my father to take me strolling? And then, when you told that crude story about the siege . . ."

Richard laughed. "And I was thinking: Now there is a cold young woman, or rather one trying to appear so. And I was thinking how I would like to take away your book and give you a rousing kiss." He paused. "Are you not happy here, Charlotte?"

"Happy enough now, I suppose, but there have been times I wished I had never laid eyes on you or Barbados, I must admit. You may be too busy with your new windmill and politics to notice, but I have rather grown up in the past year, Richard. Am I happy? In a more mature way, yes. And I shall be even happier when you build me the grand house you promised."

"In time, my dear."

"And you, Richard, are you happy?"

"More so than ever before in my life, thanks to you."

During the hectic week before the dinner, Charlotte reminded herself of her mother as she ordered Mirabel and Clemmie about like a tyrant. Clemmie sewed a bright red smock for Toby and drafted the bewildered lad as a waiter. It amused Charlotte to hear Clemmie threaten him with a beating if he should spill anything while serving, and Mirabel with banishment to the cane fields if she broke any of "our china."

At noon on a December Sunday, a weary, apprehensive Charlotte sat on the veranda with an infuriatingly calm Richard, awaiting the arrival of their guests. At his insistence, she drank a glass of madeira and, by the time David arrived with John, felt more relaxed. Richard greeted the guests with ease, although Charlotte thought him almost obsequious when he welcomed Lord Willoughby.

Their mutton, from a sheep fattened on cane pulp, was declared by all to be sweet and tender. Mirabel hung about the kitchen door, beaming at the compliments to her cooking. Seeing how successfully her dinner was going, Charlotte began to enjoy herself.

Later, over dessert, one of their neighbors asked Willoughby what he intended doing about raising money to repair Barbados's system of forts and replenish its ammunition.

"Why, now that Farmer is out of the way, I'll call a new Assembly. Here, Charlotte, excuse us so we may discuss this out of the hearing of delicate ears."

Despite her awe of the governor, Charlotte took a deep breath and said firmly, "No, My Lord. You can ship Colonel Farmer out of your way, but I am not so easily got rid of."

An embarrassed Richard hurriedly explained that she was only joking. "She and Doctor Higganbotham have prepared an entertainment, you see, My Lord."

Their program turned out even better than the dinner. Concealing his ignorance of Shakespeare, Richard introduced the various scenes with a delightful wit. Charlotte was amazed at the transformation of the shy, bumbling Higganbotham into first a vehement Shylock and then an eloquent Mark Antony and finally a sensitive Hamlet. Esther played Lady Macbeth so skillfully that she drew applause. And Charlotte was pleased by her own delivery of "the quality of mercy" speech from *The Merchant of Venice.*

As the guests crowded around to congratulate her, it occurred to Charlotte how profoundly her life had changed since the last Christmas. Then she had shared her mother's annoyance at the unannounced arrival of a forward Barbadian planter, and here she was, a year later, his wife, at the center of a group far wealthier and more powerful than had ever gathered in her father's house.

She was further flattered when Lord Willoughby excused himself from a political conversation and requested her to show him her garden.

"How lovely," he said when they were outside. "My dear wife loved her gardens back in England."

"Did she not have one out here?"

"Alas, she never saw Barbados," Willoughby replied. "I dared not bring her out. The times were turbulent back in the fifties."

"Richard mentioned the great civil strife out here."

"Well he might. Like many, I supported Parliament until I sickened of the Roundheads' excesses. Fleeing England, I obtained from the Earl of Carlisle a twenty-one-year proprietorship of Barbados for my family. Came out here to find the political situation the reverse of that in England. The local fire-eating Cavees were oppressing the Roundheads. Well, I assumed the governorship and tried to calm down things. But so many Roundheads had betaken themselves to England with stories of persecution, that Parliament sent out an expedition under Sir Charles Ayscue. In October of 1651, two warships and other vessels carrying over eight hundred soldiers sailed into Carlisle Bay and captured or sank all the Dutch ships anchored there, just as de Ruyter tried to do last April. Ayscue lacked the strength to come ashore. I had eight thousand militiamen under arms. But Ayscue blockaded us and raided up and down the lee coast. Put agents ashore to undermine my authority. Several influential planters, your Richard among them, went over to Ayscue, taking a considerable part of my militia with them. Did you know that?"

"I was not aware Richard had played so large a role."

"He did. And thus Ayscue was able to establish a base down at Oistin's Bay. I was ready for a pitched battle between my loyal militiamen and those who had gone over to Ayscue, but capitulated to avoid bloodshed. To make a long story short, articles of agreement were signed, which recognized our Assembly as a permanent lawmaking body, a fact that causes me some grief these days. The island elected a new Assembly, and it banished the chief troublemakers for one year and restored the estates of the Roundheads."

"And you, sir?"

"They banished me. Me, the legal proprietor of this island. They kicked me out and I was not able to return until three years ago."

"Whereupon you relieved Richard of his colonelcy?"

Willoughby laughed, "My, you are sharp. But then he got around me with this knighthood. For services to the king at Colchester. At Colchester in '48. If I had been consulted, I might have informed the king of Richard's service to his enemies and mine in '51."

"Surely, My Lord, you do not begrudge him that honor."

"No, I admire boldness. And now that I have met you, I

envy him, too. His trip to England paid off rather handsomely, I should say."

"You flatter me, My Lord."

"Richard is ambitious, is he not?"

"I would rather say determined."

"Then yourself? Are you not ambitious for him? I find that ambition in a clever wife can carry a man farther than the same sentiment in his own heart."

"Well, sir, what wife would not wish her husband success?"

Willoughby took her hand. "Ah, sweet Charlotte, Richard has all that any man could wish. I am glad to have him on my council. And I am thinking of another mission for him."

"What is that, My Lord?"

"It is not to be repeated, but I am considering an expedition against the Dutch at Tobago. As you know, the king has ordered me to repair our forts and replenish our ammunition, endeavors that depend on our infernal Assembly for revenues. Meantime, the Dutch go unpunished for their attack on Bridgetown, not to mention their depredations along the African coast and elsewhere. I mean to recruit a force of several hundred from the militia, impress some visiting ships, and swoop down on Tobago."

Concealing her ignorance of the location of Tobago, Charlotte replied, "That seems a bold action, My Lord."

"It is, and I need a bold lieutenant to help me carry it out. I am thinking of Richard."

Charlotte's heart raced at the memories of her fears and confusion that hot, lonely night after the Dutch attack on Bridgetown. Never did she want to repeat such an experience.

She blurted out, "I wish you would not, My Lord."

"I thought you were ambitious for him."

"It is just that I cannot bear . . ." She removed her hand from Willoughby's and put it to her face. "Oh, please do not send him off."

"My dear girl. My sweet child." Willoughby removed a perfumed handkerchief from his sleeve and offered it to her.

Seeing how concerned Willoughby looked, Charlotte pressed her advantage. "I could not bear to have him leave me. Please, are there not others for your expedition?"

"Oh, there are dozens who would be honored. But Richard has long military experience. And he performed magnificently in repulsing the Dutch fleet."

"I would be greatly in your debt if you were to ask someone else to accompany you." She dabbed his handkerchief to her eyes.

"I had thought you might be pleased at this offer of military preferment."

"Will you ask another to go in Richard's place, then?"

"If I say yes, how will you reward me?" He clasped her hand again.

"With my gratitude, of course."

"Expressed in what way?"

"Why, sir, I do not follow your meaning."

"Bargains must be sealed. A kiss is not too much for an old man to expect, is it? There are wives who would grant me more than a mere kiss should I choose their husbands for the very duty you wish yours to be spared."

Charlotte disliked the course the conversation was taking but did not know how to end it. She raised her face to Willoughby, expecting a genteel kiss on the cheek. Instead, he pressed his lips hard against hers. She struggled to free herself.

"Really, sir, you misjudge me. I think we should return to my guests."

She did allow Willoughby to hold her hand as they walked back toward the great house, however. Just as they reached the door, Charlotte paused to say in her most demure tone, "One thing more, My Lord. I would prefer you did not speak of this to Richard. He would not like my interfering."

"You don't wish him to know his innocent young bride is capable of machinations?" Then, with a disarming smile, he added, "Seriously, it shall remain our secret. I hope that in time we may have other secrets to keep between us." And before she could react, he had kissed her again.

8

. . . I did not know whether to be flattered or offended. Many women might have had their heads turned by the attentions of so rich and influential a man, but really, he was a good ten years older even than Richard and besides I was not that sort of person. I knew otherwise respectable married women sometimes engaged in playful flirtations, but I had no experience in such things and did not wish to gain any. Lord Willoughby was a man of great charm, even handsome, but was as old as my father. I wondered what Richard would say or do if he learned of the old fox's advances. I did not tell him, of course, for it would only have made difficulties. I did want Richard to get on politically. And I could not very well complain of the governor's liberties without disclosing my maneuver to keep my husband at home. Richard would have been furious with me had he known. But I was desperate at the thought of his leaving.

Hearing naught of an expedition, I thought that perhaps Willoughby had changed his mind about Tobago. Meanwhile, Richard was working night and day to complete his grand new windmill. Finally, one morning in January, he called me to the sugar works to watch Wilkens and a crew of mechanics lash canvas sails on the great arms of the machine and shift the contraption around to catch the wind. Gears groaned and clanked into action, and Richard clapped his hands like an excited boy. He said the thing would reduce the need for so many oxen and would speed up the harvest. It pleased me to see him so enthusiastic.

Richard's mood was shattered a few days later, when David, on one of his weekly health inspections, offhandedly mentioned that Willoughby had just departed in personal command of an expedition of three hundred fifty men on six commandeered ships, bound for Tobago.

"You did not know of this?" David asked. "I would have thought he would have consulted with you."

"I am puzzled that he did not," Richard said. "I would like to have gone along."

I felt guilty at his crestfallen look, but never divulged my part in his exclusion from the plan, anymore than I revealed my role in David's purchase of John Martin's indenture. Toward the end of the month, I felt less guilty. Willoughby returned from Tobago in what Richard called "a terrible temper." He and his expedition had sailed the two hundred miles to the Dutch island, only to find the English flag already flying there. A band of eighty freebooters from Jamaica had ousted the Dutch with little effort.

Willoughby's mood grew worse in February with the alarming news that the French had joined the war as allies of the Dutch. The Dutch had come nearer than they knew to overcoming the defenses of Barbados the previous April. How could the island possibly withstand an attack by a combined French and Dutch force? Convening a new Assembly, Willoughby asked an immediate appropriation of half a million pounds of sugar to get on with the refitting of the Barbadian defenses. The Assembly had not learned from the example of Colonel Farmer; instead of passing the appropriation, a majority voted that the cost be paid from the Royal export tax Willoughby had forced upon Barbados in 1663. This planter mentality continues to baffle me to this day; most of them can see no further than their narrow self-interests.

With the French in the war against England, shipping from the homeland practically halted, and, since the Navigation Act prohibited Barbadians from buying anything brought over in foreign ships, the island began to suffer a shortage of goods.

The crisis inflicted a further hardship on us at Bolton Hall. Just as our cane was ripening, Richard was kept busy riding back and forth to Bridgetown or Parham Park to meet with the Governor and other members of the Council. Not only did I miss him, for the first *time since our marriage, I thought he looked his age. His face was drawn with fatigue, and he did not hold his shoulders so erectly.*

"You were late again last night," I said to him one morning late in February, after one of these late night sessions.

"I tried not to disturb you."

"I find it lonely without you. How much longer will this go on?"

"It has ended for the time. Willoughby adjourned the Assembly."

"I am relieved. They passed his appropriation then?"

"In a most unacceptable manner. They proposed a committee of three planters to spend the money. They want to use two hundred thousand pounds of sugar for ammunition and the other three hundred thousand to purchase firearms in England. But mark this, Charlotte. They would sell the weapons, sell them, mind you, to our white inhabitants at fixed prices and place those proceeds in the hands of the parish vestries for our defense. Did you ever hear of anything so harebrained? I thought Willoughby would suffer a stroke of apoplexy at this affront to his authority. He had no choice but to send the fools home."

"I hope that you will remain at home for a while. I have missed you terribly."

"I hope so, too. We'll go bankrupt if we do not get in a good crop this year."

"I thought the new windmill solved all our problems."

"If we don't make a good crop, the windmill could become a problem itself. I have to produce enough sugar to finish paying for the damn machinery."

Willoughby convened the Assembly again in April after receiving a report that the French were organizing an expedition to attack English islands in the West Indies. Richard joined him in presenting a grim prospect of Barbados's fate in case of a combined French and Dutch attack. Willoughby got his appropriation at last, but the Assembly accompanied its passage with a formal complaint to the King about the Governor's high-handed methods.

Willoughby was too busy pressing for revenge against the Dutch to fret over his unpopularity. He commandeered thirty sugar-laden English ships hovering in Carlisle Bay, loaded them with six hundred militiamen, and sent them off to Antigua under the command of his nephew Henry. Richard's disappointment at once more being over-looked turned to relief when he and other Council members received a worrisome dispatch from Henry. At Antigua, the Governor's nephew learned that a large force of French and Dutch ships had seized the English island of Saint Christopher just three hundred fifty miles from Barbados. Antigua stood in immediate threat, as did the thirty commandeered merchant ships and their rich cargoes. So our mili-tiamen went ashore at Antigua to secure that island, and the fleet hurried on its way to England.

This news alarmed us all, and with good reason. Barbados might well suffer the same fate as Saint Christopher. Willoughby sent off a dispatch to King Charles begging for immediate military reinforce-ments. He also risked Royal disfavor by asking for permission to trade with other nations.

During all this uproar I assumed that Lord Willoughby's seem-ing infatuation for me had been either a pretense or else forgotten. I put from my mind his unwanted kisses and suggestive remarks. Perhaps, I thought, I had exaggerated the import of his words and actions. Thus I was shaken when Richard reported that the Governor had selected him to make a two-day inspection of the defenses of Oistin's Bay. I questioned why a council member from that region could not have done the job.

"It is a tribute to me that he trusts my judgment. Look, the crop is in, and a damned good one, too. I have the time."

"You know I do not like being left alone at night."

"How can I say to the Governor, 'Oh, My Lord, I would be happy to comply, but alas, my wife will not permit me'?"

There was nothing I could do but accept the situation. Actually, with Clemmie sleeping outside my door on a pallet, I got through that first night better than I had expected. Near noon the next day, while I was resting from my morning's gardening, a messenger arrived on horseback with a letter bearing the seal of the Governor. He was instructed to wait for my reply, he said.

I sat on the veranda and read the letter with astonishment. Lord Willoughby apologized for "my long neglect due to official duties of the most pressing nature" and alluded to "our pact made last Christ-mas in your lovely garden." He protested a "deep affection" for me and claimed that I had been in his thoughts constantly during the trying weeks since he had been our guest.

His letter went on to remind me that he had twice passed over Richard in selecting officers for military expeditions "in accord with your wishes" and added, "Now, while your husband is away on his inspection tour, while I have a brief respite from the press of official business, I am ready to seek my reward..."

The letter closed with the proposition that I visit him at Parham Park that very evening, "or, should that prove impossible, pray grant me the honor of receiving me at your home..."

At first I thought the letter might have been written in jest. Only on second reading did the enormity of the proposition strike me. The messenger was waiting in the yard for my reply. I was angry, yet in truth slightly flattered; I was embarrassed yet mildly amused; and I was shocked, yet touched by the old man's almost boyish protestation of love.

For a moment, but a moment only, I considered granting him the privilege of paying me a visit, so that I could inform him face to face of my feeling, but quickly rejected that notion. Instead, I went into the house and hurriedly wrote my reply, saying in part:

"... What you suggest is out of the question. I am shocked that a man of your position would send one of his most loyal lieutenants away on a military mission in the expectation of taking advantage of his wife during his absence. I have no intention of playing Bathsheba to your King David, sir. Nor would Richard wish to be your Uriah.

"Really, your Lordship, I would have been more flattered by your expressions of affection were they accompanied by greater evidence of respect for my character. You must have a low opinion of me even to dream that I would permit such a thing.

"As you have discerned, I am ambitious for my husband, but I will not play the harlot to advance his career. Now, sir, I will close with a firm rejection of your insulting suggestion and the assurance that I will make no mention of your action to Richard, so long as it is never repeated. Bear that in mind. I make it not as a threat, but as a fair warning."

I was just turned twenty-one and, as I say, had no experience in these matters. An older woman might have refused him more grace-

fully but just as definitely. I had much still to learn in diplomacy, I fear.

Even as I watched the messenger ride down our lane with my answer to Willoughby, I wished that I had taken the time to draft a more carefully considered reply, but on the whole I felt rather self-satisfied, even self-righteous at having put the imperious Lord Willoughby in his place. After all, what could he do? He had placed himself in a compromising situaton by sending me such a letter. Yes, I really felt rather smug with the way I had handled the matter. I wished there were someone in whom I could safely confide my little triumph of virtue.

Despite the war with the Dutch and French, the month of May 1666 proved a pleasant interlude for Richard and me. Bolton Hall's sugar crop lived up to his hopes. Under Toby's sure hand and my direction, our garden thrived; the house was surrounded by a blaze of colors. Clemmie and Mirabel vied for my approval. With his political tensions eased, Richard found time to enjoy a glass of wine and watch the sun set with me. We began to take our morning coffee in bed from a tray brought up by Clemmie. Twice we rode down to the shore with a packed lunch and lolled at the water's edge. The loss of a few imported luxuries caused us no great distress. I pushed Lord Willoughby's clumsy seduction attempt from my mind, along with memories of Mandze.

That same month brought the death of Cleo, Toby's grandmother and the oldest slave on the plantation. Richard allowed all the Negroes to take the afternoon off to bury the poor old woman. He set his best carpenters to fashion a coffin from scraps of his precious lumber. Richard had inherited Cleo from the Simpsons, the previous owners. As he explained it, her funeral was a sort of belated reward for loyalty.

Wilkens was on hand in the Negro yard with a little keg of rum from which he meted out small portions. One of the men produced a fifelike instrument and another a kind of mandolin made from a gourd, with horsehair strings. To the accompaniment of this discordant music, some clapped their hands and danced while others sat about wailing. The empty coffin rested in front of Cleo's little mud and wattle hut. Upon our arrival, several women brought out the wasted corpse. Once it was in the coffin, they put in her beads, clay pipe, a bowl and spoon.

We followed the chanting, moaning mourners to the slave cemetery in a grove of cedar trees beside the road. I asked Richard why there was no rector or at least someone to read the Bible, and he said he never interfered. After the coffin had been lowered and covered with dirt, we returned to our house, but the sounds of laughter and music continued long into the night.

I told David Higganbotham of my shock at the way old Cleo was buried like a dog. "After all, they are human beings," I told him.

"But different human beings," he said. "With different beliefs. They believe in God, but they look upon him as a good man who gives them life and food and so on. To their way of thinking, that is His nature, and they need not pray to Him. They also believe in a sort of Satan, a being who will cause them harm if they do not cajole and humor him. So to ward off evil luck, they save their prayers for their devil god."

David also said they beleived in an afterlife and that Richard was right to allow them to make a festival of death. It helped them bear their harsh lives with a measure of hope, he said, and after a decade on this island I quite agree, although at the time I was too priggish to understand.

Richard returned from the sugar works while I was engaged in this conversation, and he scoffed at my reaction to Cleo's funeral.

"For God's sake, Charlotte, I don't treat my blacks so very different than your father treats the tenants on your lands back home," he said. "I noted quite a disparity between the manner of their living and yours."

"I disagree there, Richard," David replied. "The English poor at least belong to the same race as the rich. And they have the same Christian religion. More important, they cannot be bought and sold like animals."

"The same religion? Look at the ranks of the nonconformists, especially the idiotic Quakers, back home, and see how many of them are from the lower classes."

Thinking of dear little John, who was listening, I winced. I

*guided the conversation to another subject, but it struck me how
callous Richard could be.*

*On the whole, however, I felt good about my marriage and my
life on Barbados. I was mistress of my own household, and while
dissatisfied with the house itself, I felt certain we would replace it with
a finer structure. I had established myself as a hostess and now moved
with ease in the higher social circles of the island. I had developed at
least three confidantes in David Higganbotham, Esther Lawnton, and
Clemmie. As for Richard, was there anything the man could not do,
could not become, if he set his mind to it, or had it set for him subtly,
surreptitiously even, by a clever, determined wife?*

*While I would not have committed murder (or adultery) to
advance Richard, I was becoming almost as ambitious for my husband as was Lady Macbeth for hers . . .*

"I have tremendous news for you, Charlotte. For all of Barbados." Richard made his announcement while still seated on his
horse, having ridden back from Bridgetown.

"I am eager for news of any sort," she replied. "This has
been a tedious day. And a lonely one, too. What is your news?"

"Two frigates arrived at Carlisle Bay this morning. Stout
men-of-war, they are. And they brought a royal order for Lord
Willoughby forthwith to organize an expedition to retake Saint
Christopher."

"That sounds like a dangerous undertaking. Expensive,
too."

"The king's order gives us no choice. Willoughby has
called an emergency session of the Assembly for tomorrow. He
will ask for an additional appropriation, and I think he will get
it. As for the danger, we have the two frigates. We shall borrow
several other ships and recruit a thousand men. A thousand,
mind you. That should be a large enough force to demolish the
French and raise the rightful flag once more on Saint Kitts."

"What about the safety of Barbados? Is it wise to send off
so many of our white males on such a dangerous adventure?
Who will protect us?"

"Don't you see, instead of waiting to be struck, we shall

strike them with overwhelming force. I'd much prefer to fight on other soil and with surprise on our side."

Charlotte sighed. "Well, you have told me your news. Do you propose to sit on your horse all afternoon? Clemmie and I have our sewing to complete before dark."

"You don't mind then?"

"Mind? I was not aware that my opinion mattered to the government of this island."

"Not that, you goose. I mean my going on the expedition." He dismounted and tied his horse to the hitching post. "And that's not all. Willoughby wants me to be his second in command... Why are you looking at me like that?"

"The governor asked you to go?"

"He announced his decision to the entire council, said he would head the expedition, and then asked all present with any military experience to go with him."

"And you . . ."

"I was the first to volunteer."

"And Lord Willoughby accepted?"

"Actually, he said, 'Are you certain your dear Charlotte will allow you to go?' But of course he was jesting. Anyway, I told him you were hardly the sort of woman to keep her husband tied to her apron strings when duty called. The other council members enjoyed the jest. Several others offered their services. But he named me his chief lieutenant on the spot."

"You mentioned duty. Have you no duty to me and the others here at Bolton Hall who depend on you?"

"Oh, my dear girl, of course, I do. But Barbados and the king need me. Don't spoil this for me. I want to go."

"I would prefer that you do not go."

A hard look came into his eyes. "You disappoint me, Charlotte. I want to go. It is my duty to go. I have given my word, and I will go."

So did Charlotte find herself outmaneuvered. The knowledge that Willoughby had got the better of her was galling, but she kept a bitter silence, which was lost on Richard as he went about with great zest to help recruit the men and equip the vessels for the expedition. It would not do for him to learn how she had headed off his selection to go to Tobago. Had Willoughby not announced that he would lead the expedition in person, she might have shown Richard the governor's incriminating letter propositioning her, but she did not see how that would help. Only one thought comforted her. A major role in the recovery of Saint Christopher could hardly damage Richard's political career; it might even make him independent of Lord Willoughby.

Anyway, Charlotte resolved not to act like a selfish, frightened schoolgirl. Although she squelched her impulse to lash out at Richard and accuse him of playing the willful, irresponsible boy, she longed to point out his hypocrisy in promoting enlistments among what he had been wont to speak of contemptuously as "our surplus white population." No longer did he complain of their insolence and lack of initiative. And they responded in great numbers.

Another inhabitant of Barbados shared Charlotte's attitude about the expedition, but from a different perspective. Tom Cochran freely and loudly expressed his disgust at the sight of throngs of sun-scorched, mostly barefooted recruits lined up to receive their firearms and swords and sweating through their awkward drills in the oppressive mid July heat.

"Look at the fools," Tom said to the still speechless Moses. "Tools for old Willoughby. Going off to save a lot of planters on another island as what don't give a damn for them. I see out there many a one as has sold his land to some big dog and now is ready to sell his life as well."

Later Tom would recall that, while he and Moses had watched the recruits drill, other spectators had spoken of the special service of blessing Willoughby had announced for the next day, Sunday, July 15, in the new Saint Michael Church in Bridgetown. Upon their return to their hut, Tom remembered also that Moses "weren't acting his usual self." In his words, "He wouldn't look at me. Just sat and stared back toward Bridgetown. Wouldn't eat no supper, neither."

At the time, however, Tom had seen no reason to worry. He did not expect Moses to behave like other men. And while he scoffed at the military review, at least the recruits had been eager customers for his tobacco and Moses' smocks. So, weary from the walk to and from Bridgetown and satisfied with the day's trading, Tom went to sleep quickly and soundly. He did not see Moses rise from his own hammock and kneel in the light of the half-moon and, with clasped hands and face turned to the sky, pray so intensely that sweat soaked his clothing.

Tom slept well past dawn. It took him a while to realize that Moses was not in his hammock. But he did not grow alarmed until he had searched the ravine and nearby thickets and found no sign of his companion.

That Sunday morning on the road to Bridgetown, a keyed-up Richard and a resigned Charlotte encountered John Martin riding his pony in the other direction. To Richard's annoyance, Charlotte reined in Nutmeg and chatted with the boy.

"You're going to Saint Michael Church, are you?" John asked. "Doctor's a'going there too. I shall spend the day with my father."

"And how is he these days?"

"I worries about him. He broods more than usual. For a time he was trying hard to speak. Could almost say his words, but last week he seemed to have give up."

"Charlotte," Richard said. "You can visit another time. Lord Willoughby did ask me to be there early."

At Tom's hideaway, John found the hermit deeply distressed, pacing about and blaming himself for Moses' absence. Equally disturbed, John asked what they did the day before. He frowned at Tom's account of the militia gathering.

"He hasn't been writing anything, has he?"

"Nothing this past week. Before that, just to help me with me reading."

"Did he know of the church service at Saint Michael today?"

"Why, there was some talk of it in the crowd yesterday. Someone was saying the governor and all his crew was to be there."

"And Father heard it? What did he do?"

"He stared at the people that was talking, and I seen he had tears in his eyes."

The church was filled long before 11:00 A.M., the time set for the service. The front pews were reserved for Lord Willoughby, members of his council, leaders of his expedition, and their wives. Charlotte sat beside Richard, savoring the sea breeze blowing through the deep windows, praying that no harm would befall him on this adventure, for which, despite all his explanations, she still saw no good reason. She prayed also that Richard's real reason for volunteering was not from boredom with her or their marriage.

She looked scornfully at Lord Willoughby sitting in the next pew, like a battle-scarred old lion. He had only nodded to her when they entered the church. She did not mind, but she wondered what part her rejection of his advances played in his choice of Richard as his right-hand man. Was the selection one of spite, or did he really depend that heavily on Richard?

Then, as she heard the comforting words of the Twenty-third Psalm, she thought how wrong it was to harbor such thoughts. And perhaps it was wrong of her to want to deny Richard the thrill of taking part in the expedition. To be honest, her fears were more for herself than for him. Dangerous? Look at the formidable force Willoughby had put together: besides the two men-of-war, six large merchant vessels, a ketch, and a fire ship, and, of course, one thousand eager Barbadian men. If she were a man, surely she would want to go along. As Richard had put it, "Lifetime reputations will be made. This is a crusade." Like it or not, he was going. She could survive a few weeks of loneliness.

Feeling her eyes on him, Richard smiled at her and took her hand.

The minister, who had been brought to Barbados by Willoughby as his personal chaplain, preached a fervent sermon praising the courage of the men of Barbados and urging them to victory over the French interlopers on Saint Christopher. He owned a mighty voice, which he employed fully so that his exhortations would carry outside the crowded church to the militiamen who stood around the doors and windows.

The space behind the church was deserted. On a branch of a bearded fig tree that overhung the roof, Moses Martin waited until the minister finished his sermon and the closing hymn had been sung. Then, during the benediction, he lowered himself onto the steep, shingled roof and, bent over like a monkey, scrambled to the front of the church. He perched on the peak of the roof, looking down at the church entrance when Lord Willoughby came out with Richard and Charlotte just behind him.

Moses' voice was so weak from long disuse that only those nearest the church could hear him at first.

"Hypocrites! Liars! Thieves! Murderers!" he piped with slurred speech. "Wicked exploiters of your fellow humans! Pay heed to what I have to say!"

Willoughby broke off his compliments to the minister to look up at the strange little man in the white smock who sat atop the church roof.

"This land is marked for destruction by God if it does not swerve from its evil course. I have come to warn thee all." He pointed his finger at Willoughby, and his voice grew stronger. "And thou in particular, oh thou Pontius Pilate. Barbados is bringing itself under a curse."

"Get that lunatic down from there," Willoughby said to a militia captain. "Who is he, anyway?"

"I know him, My Lord," Charlotte said. "He is a Quaker. A kind of prophet."

Richard gripped Charlotte's elbow and said, "He came out on the same ship with us. He was exiled for creating just such disturbances as this."

Willoughby looked up at Moses. "What is troubling you, my good man?"

"Greed! Inhumanity! Pride! Slavery! These things and more trouble me. This island stinketh with them all."

Willoughby laughed. "My good man, you exaggerate. We are not so bad as all that. Come down, and stop making a fool of yourself."

"Thou are nothing to me," Moses continued. "I have confronted the man thou call king, and I do not fear to defy thee. I thought England a place steeped in sin, but it is a paradise compared with what men like thee hath made of this island."

Out of the side of his mouth, Willoughby said to the captain, "Can't you get him down from there?"

"All of thee pay heed," Moses cried. "This island might have been a new Garden of Eden. But love of profit hath despoiled it. The rich oppress the poor. And all treat the unoffending Africans like animals. I have seen women with child beaten with whips. I have seen slave ships throw their dead to sharks. I see men and women, fashioned in the image of God, bought and sold like oxen. You rip them from their natural homes, bring them here as chattel, and then deny them the solace of the knowledge of our Savior. All for gain, gain, gain." He paused to look into the faces of the militiamen close gathered in front of the church. "All of thee in one way or another hath sold thy souls as thou sellest thy sugar. Oh, this wicked Barbados will be punished. This town with its slave sales and its money grubbing will be laid waste; not one stone shall be left standing on another."

The militiamen were laughing and shouting taunts at Moses, as John, near exhaustion, arrived on foot, his pony having collapsed on the edge of the town. Seeing his father, he shouted for him to come down, but Moses seemed not to hear.

"I will be heard," he continued. "I may be too old to see it, but more will come. God will send a great wind to purge this place as he did ancient Sodom. And fires. I see this wicked town in ashes . . . "

Now three militiamen were shinnying up the fig tree at the rear of the church. Those on the ground in front were shouting questions at Moses.

"How are we to escape this wrath of which you warn?"

"Return the African to his homeland. Bring no more here as slaves. Restore the land to the yeoman farmer. And thou, oh so-called governor, call off your foolish expedition. It will end in disaster. I have seen it all happening."

"Please, Father," John called. "Please come down."

"Who is the lad?" Willoughby asked Richard.

"His son. The boy is apprenticed to Doctor Higganbotham."

"Well, I have heard enough of his prating. I suppose someone will deal with the lunatic." Willoughby tipped his hat to Charlotte and headed away from the church as the three militiamen crawled the last few feet along the rooftop.

"Come, Charlotte . . ." Richard said.

She pulled her arm free of his grasp. "No, I want to see this."

"Please don't hurt him," John cried out.

Moses stood up shakily and raised his face to the sky. "All will perish. You are doomed if you go."

He tried to fight free of the militiamen's hands and in doing so lost his footing. Before the horrified eyes of John and Charlotte, he fell on his side and then rolled over the edge of the roof and plunged headfirst onto the church steps.

9

. . . Over Richard's objections, I attended the funeral the Quakers of Bridgetown conducted for Moses Martin in their tiny meetinghouse on Tudor Street the next morning. David Higganbotham and I sat with little John on a log bench in the plain little building, in silence with a score of Quakers, all staring at the box resting on two sawhorses. It was a strange, almost mystical experience.

At first, the only sounds were John's sobs and the rattle of carts in the street. Then a plump, red-haired woman, wearing a bonnet, arose to say, "We pray for the soul of our brother who died while speaking the truth. May he rest in peace."

Next, a middle-aged man dressed in dark suit and hat got up to say, "We know little of this Moses Martin except that he was a brave Friend and that somehow God spoke through him."

The red-haired woman spoke again. "And we pray that this lad, his son, may be comforted by the Holy Spirit of God."

During the subsequent silence, I reflected on how I first saw Moses Martin on the steps of St. Paul's, and of how, when he came aboard the Mary Leigh, *I had been impressed by the saintliness of his face even before I recognized him. I wished I had learned more about him, had not dismissed him just as an eccentric. It seemed a shame to let him be put in the ground in a strange land with so little ceremony. Without knowing what I was doing exactly, I, too, arose and said:*

"Moses Martin was a tailor of Bristol. While I did not know him long or well, I have learned enough about him to say that there never

was a more courageous man on this earth. Let me tell you how he first came to my notice . . ."

The Quakers listened closely as I related the story of his confrontation with King Charles, his imprisonment in Newgate, his loss of speech, and his exile.

"I apologize for speaking out when I am not of your faith. Women keep silent in the Church of England . . ."

The red-haired woman interrupted. "In the Society of Friends, we are all brothers and sisters in Christ and therefore equals. Speak on, sister."

And so I did, concluding with, "I have little more to say. Many regarded Moses Martin as a lunatic. But his son John said to me once that he thought the men that persecuted his father were mad and that he was saner than most of us. Perhaps John was correct. Right now a thousand men of this island prepare to sail away to make war. They consider themselves brave men. But what Moses Martin did and said yesterday took greater courage. I just thought it would be a pity if he were laid to rest without someone paying him that tribute."

While I still had my composure, I sat down. After a few more minutes of silence, the men of the meeting carried the box out into the graveyard and lowered it into the hole two slaves had dug.

I don't know what possessed me that day, but I am glad I spoke out. I came away from that meeting profoundly moved. Until then, I had thought, like everyone else, that Moses Martin was a near-lunatic, certainly not a person to be taken seriously. His words of warning spoken from the church roof, followed by his death and his simple but touching funeral, gave me much to reflect upon during my ride back to Bolton Hall. This had been no ordinary man, for sure. While I was not superstitious, there was something about his message that stirred deep misgivings within me. I recalled John's account of how his father had nailed predictions of dire events on the door of the Cathedral at Bristol. England would be struck by a great plague which would kill tens of thousands. And London would be destroyed by fire. The plague of the previous year back home? Could he have foreseen that? So far as we knew in Barbados at that time, London had suffered no calamitous fire. As for the plague, in Richard's words, "England is full of wild-eyed fanatics who predict earthquakes, fire from heaven, plagues and anything they may dream of whilst suffering from indigestion." And my own father, certainly no prophet, often predicted an outbreak of disease in London because of the filth and overcrowding. Still the little Quaker's prediction of a disaster for the expedition to Saint Kitts troubled me more than I could bear. His funeral renewed my old doubts. Only now my fears were for Richard rather than myself. Although I could not stop Willoughby's military juggernaut, I had to prevent Richard from going on that expedition. But how?

Tom Cochran had been half mad with grief since arriving at Saint Michael and finding a mob standing around the broken body of his friend. After hearing of what Moses had said from the church roof, he asked bitterly, "What did he want to do that for? Now who will finish teaching me to read? Who will I talk to anymore?" During the funeral, he had stood outside the meetinghouse, holding his donkey's reins, tears soaking his moustache and beard. Before anyone could speak to him, he departed for his hermitage. He would not be seen again for many weeks.

To Richard, the death of Moses Martin was a sad end to a meaningless life. In his view, religious fanatics were nuisances, not to be taken seriously, because "Nobody of any significance here pays them much notice." He was irked with Charlotte, for there were many things they should discuss before he left the next day to help Willoughby prepare for Wednesday's embarkation. And she was spending nearly the entire day at the burial of a madman who practically committed suicide. He did hope that girl would finish growing up and start behaving as a proper wife.

Charlotte puzzled him by riding past the sugar mill without returning his wave. He was further confused when he came to the house at dusk to hear Clemmie say, "Mistress Charlotte went to bed early. Said to give you your supper."

When he went up to their room, he found the bed empty. The door to the guest room was locked, and she did not respond to his knock. Resisting the impulse to break open the door, Richard spent the night alone, both angry and mystified.

So the confrontation was delayed until the next morning. Arising early and finding her door still locked, Richard packed his own knapsack. He went out for a final conference with Wilkens, then ordered his horse to be saddled, and came into the dining room to find a red-eyed Charlotte waiting with tight lips and stiff back.

"You shut yourself away from me last night. Were you ill?"

"I am well enough."

"Then pray explain your strange behavior."

"Pray explain yours."

"What do you mean?"

"You are leaving on a fool's errand."

"Let's not go over that old ground again. Look, Charlotte, I will return before you know it. Our victory will be swift and sure. And then all will be well for us and for Barbados. I do not wish to part with hard feelings between us."

He held out his arms. "Come, show me some tenderness."

She stepped away from him. "Did you hear what that poor old man said when he sat atop the church roof?"

"That bloody fool. Pretending to be mute when all the time he was just waiting for an audience. He brought his death upon himself."

"But did you hear him?"

"Your precious Shakespeare said it better than I can. 'A tale told by an idiot. Full of sound and fury, signifying nothing.' "

"You have not replied to my question of whether you heard what he predicted for this expedition, and so I will tell you. He warned that it will meet with doom. I do not wish you to go."

"He also predicted that great calamities will befall Barbados if we don't return our slaves to Africa and give the land back to our poor whites. Now *there* would be a calamity. Do you suggest that we follow that advice as well?"

"I only know that you must not go on this adventure."

"And I only know that I am going. Once more, let us not part with hard words."

Again he held out his arms, and again she stepped away, standing now in the doorway of the dining room, aware from the cessation of kitchen noises that Clemmie and Mirabel were eavesdropping.

"Doom awaits this adventure," Charlotte said.

"Not 'adventure'. Rather, this expedition ordered by King Charles and necessary for our survival as an English colony."

Charlotte had never engaged in a quarrel as serious as this one was fast becoming, nor one in which the stakes were so high. One part of her wished there were a safe way to avoid her next words, but another was determined to bring the matter to a head.

"Very well. What I am about to say is not a prophecy, not a prediction, but rather a pledge, an oath, if you will."

"You are not on a stage, Charlotte. Please desist from dramatics."

She closed her eyes for a moment to blot out the sight of his grim expression and took a deep breath.

"If you sail tomorrow, you may or may not meet with some calamity. But this you may count upon. Should you return to Bolton Hall, I will not be here to greet you."

"What?" His voice rang as it had when he laid down the law to Higganbotham's overseer.

"I mean that I shall pack my clothing and book passage on the next ship home."

"Great God Almighty," he roared. "I thought I had married a young woman of good sense, and I have taken to wife a foolish girl."

"Do not raise your voice to me, and do not swear. If you say good-bye to me this morning, it shall be good-bye forever."

"Don't threaten me, Charlotte." His tone grew low and ugly. "Does our marriage mean so little to you?"

"Perhaps as little, or much, as it does to you, to run off just to puff up your own vanity with a military exploit, yes, and to curry favor with Lord Willoughby."

She was unprepared for the rage that followed. "Damn you for a selfish, spoilt little bitch," he shouted. "You haven't grown up, Charlotte. All you know is your sheltered life in Bedford, a few visits to London, and book learning. Out here you have had your head turned by all the attention paid you because you are the young wife of an established planter. To think I deceived myself in thinking you loved me. You only love yourself."

Charlotte nearly fainted, and later would wish that she had. The wails of Clemmie from the kitchen—"Oh, please, they mustn't talk like that to each other . . ."—and Mirabel's frightened moans somehow helped her fight off her faintness. She moved behind a chair and gripped the back until her knuckles whitened. She gasped with fear and unbelief. Then she trembled and felt a curious kind of relief from her mounting anger.

"My mother warned me you were an opportunist. You deserted Willoughby back in '51. He told me about that. Now that he is back in power, you curry his favor. His esteem means more to you than my concern or happiness. It is that simple. I could tell you something about Lord Willoughby if I chose . . ."

But he was beyond hearing her. For a moment, she feared he would strike her, but instead he picked up the cut glass decanter that had been left to her by her grandmother and hurled it against the wall.

"Enjoy your voyage to England. I shall enjoy mine to Saint Kitts."

He raged out of the house, leaving Charlotte still standing behind the chair.

She sat down with her face in her hands, too shocked for tears, until he had ridden out of the yard and down the lane. Clemmie tiptoed from the kitchen. Putting her arms around Charlotte, the girl uttered the soothing African words with which her own mother had used to comfort her.

The remainder of that day dragged on like a bad dream for Charlotte. She had hoped desperately for her threat to deter Richard, but, now that it had failed, her pride would not let her relent. Never in all her twenty-one years had anyone spoken so to her. To remain at Bolton Hall like a ninny, waiting for the conquering hero to return, would be to surrender forever to the will of a man she now regarded as flawed. She would rather accept the failure of her marriage than endure a lifelong indignity. Damn Richard Bolton, and damn Lord Willoughby. They were cut out of the same domineering, overbearing cloth.

Damn the island of Barbados, too. It had brought her nothing but misery. First, the shock and humiliation of discovering that her husband had kept an African concubine, his callous disposal of the poor creature, his role in the suppression of Colonel Farmer, and now, his willingness to abandon her for this stupid expedition. But the hardest thing to take was his cruel, hateful words.

Had he not been such a cold and ruthless man, he would have recognized how upset she was at the death of the harmless old Quaker. He would at least have shown some sympathy for her fears, too.

Yes, damn Richard Bolton, and damn Barbados. She had come out here naively expecting a wonderland and had found nothing more than a dumping ground for the offscourings of England and a preserve of the greedy. The men drank and gambled and whored and died too early. The women lived showy lives of indolence. She could not think of a single family such as her own, with a father and mother and sons and daughters, living a normal kind of English life. It was all sugar and rum, and grab, grab, grab.

How had she ever imagined that she was happy in the midst of this misery? The slaves believed that when they died they would fly back to Africa. She would like to fly back to England, to be, in a twinkling, under her father's roof again.

By noon, she had done with crying. She spent the rest of the day numbly making lists of which possessions she would pack for shipment back to England. Richard could keep her old oak furniture. She would take only her clothing, the silverware, and her books.

During the afternoon, Clemmie ventured to suggest that she ought not to leave so hastily, only to be told to mind her own business. When Toby asked what she wanted done in the garden, she ordered the bewildered boy to report to Wilkens henceforth for his instructions.

The night was even worse. She spent it on the upholstered chaise in the bedroom, alternately catnapping and planning how to reorder her life in England. It was a bleak prospect of dependence on her father again, with no hope of remarriage as long as Richard lived. Fantasies swirled through her brain. King Charles was known to maintain several mistresses. Wouldn't that be something, to become a favorite of the king? What would Richard say to that? Or what if he returned from his expedition not only to find her gone but also his ugly wooden house burned to the ground?

Many hateful thoughts passed through Charlotte's waking mind. And nightmares spoiled her brief periods of sleep. In one, she dreamed of seeing a ship engulfed by enormous waves and of hearing Richard's cries for her to save him. In another, Willoughby mocked her, saying, "See, you wench? This will teach you to spurn me. I have bested you."

Unrefreshed, she arose at dawn and began packing her trunks. She was annoyed to be interrupted by Clemmie with the news that Esther Lawnton was calling.

"I don't want to see her."

"But, mistress, she is downstairs."

"I don't care. Tell her I am not able to receive her."

A few minutes later, she heard footsteps in the hall. Esther entered the bedroom.

"I told Clemmie I was not receiving guests."

"So she said. Now don't be rude to me, Charlotte. What's this I hear about your leaving Barbados?"

"How do you know that?"

"Never mind. You are acting like a goose, Charlotte. You are cutting off your nose to spite your face, just because you can't dominate your husband as if he were a little boy."

"Clemmie has been talking out of turn, has she? Well, you can have her back. Knowing Richard, I would not think her chastity would remain long intact in this house after I go."

"Clemmie adores you. She cared enough to run to Fulham in the dark to tell me."

Charlotte felt a stab of pity for this older woman trying to play trusted adviser in a hopeless situation. Esther was trapped by her own life in Barbados. Yet, Charlotte did not wish to hurt her, and so she stopped packing long enough to explain.

"So this is serious between you?"

"If you call the end of a marriage serious."

"Is there anything I can do to bring you to your senses?"

"No, Esther, and I would be offended if you tried. Thank you for your kindness to me. You have been a good neighbor."

Esther paused and would have said more, but Charlotte looked at her too uncompromisingly. "Then while we are still friends, good-bye, dear Charlotte. I hope you may find back in England the happiness that eluded you in Barbados."

Once rid of Esther, Charlotte wanted nothing more than to be on her way to Bridgetown and to find a ship ready to sail. Wilkens was under orders to bring a cart and Nutmeg around at 2:00 p.m. She could be at the Bow Bells well before dark. By noon she had packed and was toying with the idea of departing early, without her midday meal, when Clemmie timidly called her to the veranda.

"Look there." She pointed to the sea.

The sails of Willoughby's fleet shone white in the afternoon sun. Charlotte watched with a sense of utter hopelessness as the ten vessels tacked away from Barbados, with the ketch in the lead, the frigates on the flanks, the fire ship lumbering in the rear, and the six transports massed in the center. She wondered on which ship Richard might be a passenger, if he might be gazing across the water at his plantation, speculating himself over whether she was carrying out her threat to leave.

"You want something to eat?" Clemmie asked

"Yes. Out here, please."

She spent the next hour pecking away at her food as the fleet completed its long tack and turned back toward the north-northeast and Saint Christopher. She watched until the last ship passed from view, then arose and brushed the crumbs from her dress.

Partly to pass the time and partly to have a last spiteful word, Charlotte went upstairs and wrote Richard a letter.

... Whether the old Quaker's prophecy be wrong or right, I shall never see you again. Doubtless my voyage back shall be long and unhappy. I was a gullible girl when we met. The events of the past year and a half have shown me to have been a foolish one, as well. I am not the same person I was when we met and you are not the same I thought you to be, then or now. You have inflicted many hurts upon me, Richard, but none like your abandoning me and with such cruel expressions of contempt. True, there have been some happy times for me on this unnatural island but others so painful that I pray time will erase their memory.

The saddest thing of all has been my realization that the man I thought I loved is, as my mother warned, "an opportunist and an adventurer." Well, Richard, you got a dowry and the favor of Lord Willoughby through me. Like the original owners of these acres, I am returning to sweet England, defeated and disappointed, and also like them, I leave you enriched at my expense. So I make no apologies for what some might regard as a desertion, for it was you who deserted me, and I can never forgive you for that.

In the end, you chose the esteem of Willoughby over the desires of your wife. Had you not departed so hastily, I would have shown you something that might have dissuaded you from committing yourself further to that high-handed old tyrant. The attached letter from his Lordship is self-explanatory. I leave it to you how you shall deal with the knowledge that your beloved leader tried to seduce your wife...

Finally she wrote, "Should you not return from Saint Kitts," but, thinking how pointless the words were, scratched them out and began again, "Besides the furniture, I am leaving you Nutmeg..."

Hearing the sound of wheels in the yard, she paused, annoyed by what she interpreted as the effrontery of Wilkens in bringing the cart around half an hour early. Well, no matter how much the little man wished to see her leave, she would depart only when she was ready.

"Charlotte, are you there?" Higganbotham's voice sounded from the veranda.

"Dear God, must I endure another tiresome visit?" Charlotte thought. "More explanations and meddling pleas for reconciliation?"

"David," she called down. "I am rather busy at the moment."

"Please come down. We need your help."

Higganbotham stood just inside the door, with a tall man she recognized as a popular Bridgetown carter.

"Really, David, you have come at a most awkward time."

"You better go see, Mistress," Clemmie said with an idiotic look of glee.

A large cart drawn by two horses stood by the veranda steps.

"See what we have brought you," David said.

"There is nothing I need at this point, unless it might be to hire that cart to take me and my trunks to Bridgetown."

"At least look."

At first Charlotte did not recognize the figure lying on its back in the cart with hat protecting the face from the fierce sun. But there could only be one such set of sun-browned hands, and she knew only one such pair of boots as hung over the end of the cart.

"Oh, God, he is dead."

"Not dead. Not quite."

"Sick then. He is sick?"

"In a way, very sick. I fear he has drunk rather too much. Enough for a dozen men. We brought him home before he came to harm."

Suddenly the sun seemed to circle over her head. Then the blue drained from the sky and the sea. The earth spun under her feet and rose up to meet her as she collapsed.

Higganbotham and the carter, with Toby's help, carried Richard to the bedroom, undressed him, and lay him across the great bed, still unconscious.

When Charlotte came to, Clemmie was holding her head and frantically fanning her with Richard's hat.

"Nothing to worry about no more, Mistress. Master's home."

Higganbotham helped her into a chair and sent Clemmie for coffee.

"Why did he not sail with Willoughby? Did he miss the departure only because he was drunk?"

Higganbotham told how he had met Richard "in a dreadful state" at the Bow Bells the previous afternoon. "He told me of your quarrel and of his determination not to remain behind despite your threat to leave."

"Indeed? I thought he had more discretion."

"The more he blustered, however, the more I saw that he feared you were serious. When he asked my advice, I told him I thought you would carry out your threat, judging from what I know of your character. That was not what he wanted to hear."

"And what was your advice?"

Higganbotham coughed nervously and flushed. "I told him that if I had a wife like you, I would not take the risk. He called me a damned fool. But then he promised he would take up the matter with Willoughby. I saw him no more until this morning, when the proprietor called me to the Bow Bells to help rouse him. A man of weaker constitution would have died from drinking so much rum."

"What should be done for him now?"

"Let him sleep as long as he will. Then be prepared with more coffee. And do not rebuke him. He has suffered enough and will suffer more upon awakening. Richard does love you, you know."

"I would not have thought so from his parting words."

"He can tell you himself when he sobers up. Look you, Charlotte. It alarms me that you meant to leave Barbados. I . . . I don't think I should care to remain here myself, should anything happen to you and Richard . . . "

Charlotte put her hand on his. "David, I am touched. And I am most grateful for your attention to Richard. There comes

Wilkens with the cart and my horse. Be a dear and tell him I shan't be needing them, at least not before tomorrow."

Then she went into the kitchen and broke up a conversation between Clemmie and Mirabel to order them to prepare food for the doctor.

Just before leaving, David checked once more on Richard. "His pulse is steady and his breathing easier. He'll likely awake tomorrow with a splitting head and a huge appetite."

At first light the next morning, Charlotte went to the foot of Richard's bed and looked at his naked body. She returned later with a pot of strong coffee to find him lying on his back with one arm over his face. He raised his head and opened one eye.

"Great Jehovah, I am home."

He propped himself up and reached with trembling hands for the coffee cup. "What day is it?"

"Thursday morning."

"The fleet has left?"

Charlotte had considered putting him through a cross-examination and lecture, but she found it disconcerting to speak sternly to a stark-naked man in such obvious distress. In fact, it was difficult not to laugh.

He made a face at the heat of the coffee and groaned. "Why was I ever born?"

"I suppose so that you could ruin my life."

"Show me a little mercy, Charlotte. I have been through torment."

"David Higganbotham delivered you here yesterday afternoon in a disgusting condition, just as I was leaving. He said you meant to talk to Willoughby."

Richard groaned again. "Don't remind me. I told Willoughby I might lose you if I accompanied him."

"And what did his high and mighty lordship say to that?"

"He was outraged. Called me a milksop and a coward who hid behind his wife's skirts. Dragged up my going over to the Roundheads fifteen years ago. Said his first act on returning from Saint Kitts would be to remove me from his council, that I was of no further use to him anyway. He said all this at the top of his voice in the presence of the others. It was humiliating."

"And you really told him you put me ahead of the expedition?"

"That is about the size of it."

"And he told you that meant the end of your political career?"

"On Barbados, yes."

"And instead of returning home to tell me so, you spent the night getting drunk?"

"Did you say 'home'?" He was grinning at her again.

"Yes, damn your eyes, I said 'home'."

She went to her desk and tore up both her letter to Richard and the old one from Willoughby. Then, before she burst out either laughing or crying, she left him alone.

No climactic reconciliation occurred between them, either that morning or any other. Charlotte could not easily forget his bitter accusations or her torment the night before the fleet sailed. And Richard still harbored a resentment over her readiness to return to England and the apparent end of his friendship with Willoughby. Nor did he recover from his bout of rum-drinking as quickly as Higganbotham had hoped. For several days, he could barely stand, and his limbs were palsied. Charlotte continued to sleep alone in the guest room, and Richard, even after he was able to leave the house, was both too proud and too weak to ask her to share his bed.

David diagnosed his ailment as "the dry bellyache" and forbid him to drink any more rum. "I see much of this complaint, and I have noticed that Quakers and other teetotalers do not suffer from it. Nor do those who drink less potent beverages."

"I was not aware there were any teetotalers here," Richard replied. But he took the doctor's advice, and within the month the symptoms disappeared.

In retrospect, it seemed to Charlotte that this period marked a turning point in the growth of her own maturity and in her relationship with Richard. She sympathized with him for his physical distress, but she sensed that his spirits suffered even more. She recognized that all this had been her fault. Sometimes she wished she had not interfered with his going on the expedition. At least she had a new assurance that she mattered to him more than military reputation or adventure. And it was comforting to have him with her. So from the experience there emerged a new Charlotte, less self-centered, more understanding toward her husband, and yet a woman of greater confidence as well as compassion.

Without consulting the still-ailing Richard, Charlotte decided to take a more active interest in the well-being of Bolton Hall's slaves. She forced a resentful Wilkens to introduce more variety into their diets. And she cajoled David Higganbotham into teaching her enough basic medicine to deal with minor illnesses. She even took pains to learn the names of each slave, especially the women and the children, thereby winning their trust as Wilkens or Richard could never have done.

A year earlier, she reflected, Richard probably would have forbidden her to visit the Negro yard alone, and she would have obeyed. But a year ago she had been too wrapped up in herself to take an interest in them as human beings and too unsure of herself to disobey a direct order from him in an overt way. Perhaps Richard had been right to call her "a spoiled little bitch." She wondered what he would say when she urged him to buy cloth for lightweight smocks to cover the upper bodies of the females, and to give mothers of newborn children three weeks rather than two before returning to fieldwork.

Even after he had recovered from the dry bellyache, Richard did not venture down to Bridgetown. It pained Charlotte to see him moping about the plantation. She did not realize just how deeply humiliated he felt until one evening, as they watched the sun going down, he asked, "What do you think of my selling out here and our going back to England to live out our days?"

"What would you do there?"

"Try to make you happy, I suppose."

"I am not unhappy here, Richard. Not anymore. What about yourself?"

"I helped grub the trees off this land. I built this house. I have put in sixteen crops of cane here. Is that to be the story of the rest of my life, merely to plant and harvest cane and make sugar from the juice?"

"How much would Bolton Hall bring?"

"With the sugar equipment and the slaves, I calculate we could clear several thousand pounds after all debts are paid."

"It is rather late in your life to start anew in England. Somehow I cannot picture you doing nothing."

"It is early to end my political life in Barbados," he said as he rose from his chair. "But believe me, my dear, it is over."

Before she could reply, he walked away into the dusk to smoke his pipe.

Just as Richard was embarrassed to go to Bridgetown, so Charlotte avoided Esther Lawnton after her rebuff of the kindly neighbor. There would be time enough to make amends for her rudeness. Meanwhile, she did something to repair a more serious wrong. Without Richard's knowledge, she wrote a long letter to Colonel Farmer in London, asking the outspoken planter's forgiveness for her husband's part in his summary exile. Also she related the news of the island, especially the expedition to Saint Christopher, and mentioned casually that Richard found himself out of favor with Lord Willoughby for his refusal to go.

In closing, she wished him vindication in the eyes of the king and a speedy return to Barbados.

Without asking awkward questions, David agreed to dispatch the letter with the captain of a ship about to sail for London.

That month or so after Richard's drunken return was a time both of triumph and melancholy for Charlotte. He had put her above either military or political success, but what had she won if her victory meant the defeat of his sense of manhood?

She, too, was disappointed because she had enjoyed being on the fringes of power. She did not mind that failure as much as her failure to make him happy. She wondered how to put her feelings into words without his misunderstanding them. The last thing he would want from her was pity.

She did not have to say the words. Near noon, one day later in July, a rider galloped his horse into their yard with a sealed message from Bridgetown. Charlotte sent Toby to summon Richard from the sugar mill. The look of annoyance on his face turned to one of concern when she handed him the letter and he saw the seal of Lord Willoughby.

"I suppose this is it."

"It? What do you mean?"

"Notice of my dismissal from the governor's council. Willoughby has had time enough to have taken Saint Kitts and returned."

"We have not seen the fleet."

"He might have sent back an order."

Richard broke the seal and drew out the message. Charlotte grew impatient for him to finish reading and tell her the contents. A look first of disbelief and then shock came over his face.

"I can't believe this."

"For heaven's sake, what is it? Are you to be arrested?"

"They never reached Saint Kitts. They took two prizes at Saint Lucia and anchored off Guadeloupe on June 23 while the frigates sailed into the harbor and brought out several French prizes. But then a violent hurricane came up without warning and scattered our ships."

"Scattered? But they weathered the storm, surely?"

"Only three survived, and they are severely damaged."

"What about Lord Willoughby?"

"Missing. He and all but a handful of the militiamen are presumed to have perished. They found his chair floating off the coast of Guadeloupe. Dreadful. Nearly a thousand men lost. Some of my best friends. Here, read it for yourself."

He gave her the letter and sat on the edge of the veranda with his hands over his face.

Charlotte's eyes raced over the account of the disaster to the final paragraph.

"Please join me and the other members of the council in Bridgetown tomorrow morning at eleven to consider what actions to take in response to this catastrophe."

And the letter was signed by Willoughby's nephew Henry.

Saccharum officinarum

(sugar cane)

Book Two

. . . Few persons in the Saint Michael Churchyard that July Sunday in 1666 had heard Moses' slurred speech well enough to know all that he predicted, and most of them could not remember his exact words or lived long enough to repeat them anyway. Willoughby and his chief aides perished in the hurricane, of course. Richard had been too annoyed to pay close attention; John had arrived too late. Even though David and I heard and remembered, we did not discuss the prophecies with each other. I feared that speaking of them might hasten their coming true. But come true they did.

Hard on the heels of the Saint Kitts disaster came the news that in September the worst fire in London's history had burnt out 367 acres of the City's crowded area, destroying Saint Paul's and eighty-six other churches, as well as scores of buildings such as the Guildhall and more than 13,000 houses. But Barbados was more concerned at the time and for many months thereafter about the war with the French and the Dutch that seesawed back and forth through the New World, ending in the uneasy Peace of Breda in 1667, which awarded New Amsterdam to the English but left the Barbadian economy in distress with the local government deep in debt, and our white population much diminished from war losses and a hastened emigration to other islands and South Carolina. During a long drought, many planters lost their crops to ruinous cane field fires, which some believed were set by resentful slaves. An epidemic of "shipboard fever" began in Bridgetown and swept across the island, costing both us and the Lawntons several slaves. But the most spectacular calamity occurred the evening of April 18, 1668, a Saturday, when the clerks in a Bridgetown countinghouse, working over the week's receipts, upset a candle and started a fire in their offices. Next door to the countinghouse stood the chief magazine of the island, finally restocked after the Dutch attack, and what began as a fire which the townsmen might have contained spread quickly to the ammunition storehouse. One hundred and seventy barrels of gunpowder exploded. The shock waves flattened buildings for several blocks and brought startled people out of their houses all up and down the lee coast.

Richard and I ran out to our windmill and watched the sky

above Bridgetown glow long into the night. It was only after I heard the next day how the explosion and resulting fires had destroyed some 800 buildings that I remembered with a chill Moses Martin's grim warning: "Not one stone will remain standing on another."

Bridgetown had only begun to rebuild with lumber brought in by enterprising New Englanders when a second catastrophe struck Barbados in the form of rains that fell longer and heavier than any inhabitant could remember. For four days and nights in November 1669, the rains deluged the island, washing out roads, cutting deep gullies in the fields, causing mud slides and flooding out the long-suffering inhabitants of Bridgetown. Perhaps in earlier days, when the land was covered with forests and thickets, the rain would have been absorbed, but it wrought havoc to our cleared fields. The damage was particularly severe in the southern part of the island. There a torrent rushing off Christ Church ridge cleaved a gully 50 feet wide and 150 long through the loosened earth of a cemetery and swept 1,500 coffined bodies out into Oistin's Bay.

In the midst of war and rumors of war, fires, drought, and flood, political jousting went on with only brief truces. Henry and William Willoughby, the nephews of Francis, formed an uneasy rump government with two prominent planters until the King selected their father, Francis's younger brother, William, Lord Willoughby, to come out from England and serve the three remaining years of the family proprietorship.

Near the end of the Dutch war, on April 23, 1667, William arrived at Barbados with a fleet carrying large stores of ammunition and, to the amazement of many, Samuel Farmer. William Willoughby, wiser than his brother in statecraft, had rescued Farmer from imprisonment and quickly set out to win over other rebellious planters by distributing offices among them.

Richard was surprised at the cordiality with which Samuel Farmer greeted him when they encountered each other on a Bridgetown Street and puzzled by his reference to "your thoughtful letter," until I confessed my authorship.

"You meddlesome wench," he said.

"Why call ye me meddlesome, dear heart?" I replied. "Is it meddlesome for a wife to look after the best interest of her husband? At

the time it was not politick for you to apologize to Colonel Farmer. So I did it for you. And hath it not turned out well?"

He laughed and embraced me.

Older and wiser, Richard kept clear of active military and political involvements and concentrated on making Bolton Hall more prosperous, but, with my eye on the future, I worked behind the scenes to help him form new friendships and repair old ones with influential Barbadians. Bolton Hall became famous for my dinners. At these, representatives of rival political factions more and more asked Richard's advice. While he gave it sparingly, he did listen to all sides. I was pleased to observe how, with my help, his reputation for sagacity grew. I twitted him for becoming "the wise old man of Barbados," until one morning I saw him woriedly looking in a mirror at the gray hair spreading along his temples.

Although I still harbored unfulfilled ambitions for us both, in general I came to terms with my life on Barbados, my marriage, and our circle of friends. My longing for London was a thing of my girlish past. After all, the great fire of which Moses Martin warned had destroyed the heart of the city.

The relationship between Richard and me deepened as we treated each other with more consideration. I no longer spoke my mind so rashly. He showed greater respect for my opinion. I think we both dreaded another such confrontation as had followed the death of Moses Martin. While our physical passion slackened, our sense of friendship and mutual respect increased. I thought of him not as a man, but Man. Mine. I could view him realistically, admit his flaws, and still love him. I regretted that the child I longed for did not come. I was tempted to ask David's opinion as to whether I ever could have children but feared it would embarrass us both.

Another of my regrets was Richard's failure to build me the grand house he had promised.

"We need another good crop or two before I would feel secure enough to build you the sort of place a woman of your quality deserves." That is what he said.

Reminding myself that anticipation was half the pleasure of such a project, I accepted that excuse.

This was a period of great contentment in my life. I was

learning one of the great secrets of happiness, and that is to ease the lot of one's fellow human beings. With David's help, I improved the well-being of our slaves, despite Richard's grumbling and Wilken's downright disgust. Richard also grumbled about the cost of entertaining so often but I noticed that he seemed to enjoy our dinners and parties as much as any of our guests.

It bothered me that David remained a bachelor, despite so many well-off and attractive enough widows, but, as Richard rather crudely put it, "You can lead the horse to the mare . . . " Still, I worried about David, and young John, too. About their futures, that is to say . . .

1

Under the terms of his indenture, John Martin was to remain in the service of David Higganbotham for five years, and at the end of that time was to be set free with a suit and ten shillings. Since from the first the physician had treated the boy more like a nephew than an indentured servant, this was only a technicality. So it was as a kind of ceremonial joke that Higganbotham took John down to Bridgetown to have a Jewish tailor on Swan Street measure him for two suits early in April 1670.

Now going on eighteen, John was fully grown to just above average height, with his mother's stocky build and his father's brown hair and eyes. Thanks to Higganbotham's good food and medical attention, John's healthy appearance contrasted with the usual sickly look of young white bondsmen on Barbados.

As he watched the tailor measure the lad, Higganbotham

felt a glow of satisfaction and a glimmer of regret. There were times he wished John had been younger when he acquired him. He might then have taken advantage of one of his opportunities to marry a planter's widow, just so the boy would have a mother. And John might have got over Moses' death easier if he had been younger. Ever since that tragic Sunday in July 1666, John, formerly so open and trusting, had kept to himself more and sometimes treated Higganbotham with a baffling aloofness.

"Your son? You are sending him back to England to study, maybe?" the tailor said.

Before Higganbotham could reply, John said, "I am not his son."

Too bad, the doctor thought. Because of John's lowly origins, it was awkward for a bachelor to introduce him into the society of the island's elite, especially at his age. Yet John had more poise and better manners than many a rough-cut planter who lived in a mansion and owned a hundred or more slaves. And thanks to Charlotte's books, there were few Barbadians as well read as this quiet, strapping youth.

Charlotte had thought he was doing her a service when he bought John's term with her money, but it was he who had benefitted from the boy's company and from his very real help on the plantation. Neither he nor Charlotte had ever told anyone of the arrangement. Higganbotham had taken five years of pleasure from sharing this secret with the woman he so much admired.

"We ought to have a celebration on April 20, John," Higganbotham said as they left the tailor shop. "What would you like? How about a dinner at the new Bow Bells?"

"I would just as soon eat at home."

"We have never entertained at home, have we? Who would we invite to come and help you mark your escape from my terrible bondage?"

"Lady Bolton."

"Charlotte, quite. And of course, Sir Richard."

Knowing that she could not persuade Richard to take a

day off from the harvest season to travel several miles just to attend a dinner marking the end of a young bondsman's indenture, Charlotte insisted they come to Bolton Hall for the occasion and also the Lawntons, who had grown fond of John.

Clad in a new linen suit, wearing a wide-brimmed hat, and riding the horse that had recently replaced his worn-out pony, John looked more like a rising young planter than the son of a visionary Quaker tailor. Like a very handsome young planter, Charlotte thought, as he and Higganbotham dismounted.

"Sorry to be late," the doctor said. "I wanted to look in on old Tom Cochran."

"And how is he? I never see him out with his donkey anymore."

"He is rather feeble now and grown more eccentric, if that were possible. But he was so pleased to see us, it was pathetic. Poor old man."

The dinner went well enough at first. John did not drink even wine, but Richard, making little effort to hide his boredom, drank enough for both and then embarrassed Charlotte by asking the youth, "Thought of opening a tailor shop now that you are a free man? Carry on the family tradition, perhaps?"

Charlotte glared down the length of the table at him. She was grateful to Higganbotham for speaking up.

"John can do a number of things. He has proven himself a good bookkeeper and clerk. I think he would make someone a fine overseer. The Negroes all respect him; some call him young master, already. Or, if he applied himself hard for the next year and a half, I could teach him enough medicine to make a passable physician."

"There you are, John boy, no tailor shop for you after all," Richard persisted.

John raised his eyes from his plate, to say with a pained expression, "I have never meant for one minute to become a tailor, Sir Richard. But I am grateful to Doctor Higganbotham for giving me a choice. I hope I may have some time to think it over."

Charlotte was further annoyed at Clemmie's behavior. The

girl kept peering out of the kitchen at John, and when she came in to serve the plates she paused overlong at his place. Charlotte felt like slapping her. Perhaps it was time she did as Richard suggested and married her off to Toby, even though the girl scorned the clubfooted gardener.

After dinner, Richard took Lawnton and the doctor away from the table to smoke and talk of current events, leaving John with the two women. Charlotte felt sorry for him to be thus stranded and set out to put him at his ease, not realizing that he was glad just to be near her or that he ached to be able to chat with her as unreservedly as he had often done before his father's death. So he answered their questions politely and listened to their small talk, but he did not reveal himself.

She is even more beautiful than when I first saw her aboard the *Mary Leigh*, he thought. What would she think or say if she knew how I feel about her? He wondered whether she would laugh or be angry if she knew how his dreams about her awakened him deep in the night and how he lay there imagining, longing to have been better born, earlier born, and fortunate enough to have met her in different circumstances.

Thus John sat, concealing his feelings and speaking just enough not to be thought backward, as he stored up memories of how she held her head, the intent look in her eyes when others spoke, the way she moved her hands, the sound of her voice, and her manner of brushing back the lock of hair from her excellent white forehead—memories to be brought out when he was alone, like jewels from a secret place to be fondled over and over.

When they said their good-byes, Charlotte had an impulse to kiss the lad, but seeing Richard glowering nearby, impatient to get back to the sugar mill, she took his hand instead. "Dear John, you have become a man. I wish great success for you, no matter what course you may choose." Then looking archly at Higganbotham, "The doctor made a good investment when he bought your bond five years ago, I should say."

On the ride back to their plantation, John thought hard about what he should do with his freedom. Without any capital, he would be just another freedman at loose ends on an island where there was virtually no middle class to aspire to. He did not enjoy driving Negroes as many young whites did; there was too much of the Quaker in him, and he carried too many memories of brutality from Newgate and the early days at Barbados before Bolton set the old overseer straight. One of the merchants in Bridgetown would gladly make a place for him, he felt certain, but then that would remove him from further contact with Lady Bolton. She would hardly receive visits from a shipping clerk, anymore than from a tailor.

Higganbotham was surprised when he broke their long silence.

"Did you mean it when you said you thought you could make me a doctor within a year or so?"

Higganbotham was so startled and pleased that he halted his horse in the middle of the dark road.

"I could, John. I could if you would apply yourself. Yes, and a very fine doctor, too."

"And I would not have to leave then?"

"My soul, no. You need never leave me."

David Higganbotham had experienced few times of joy such as he felt on the rest of the ride back to the cotton plantation he had inherited from his brother. He might have felt so even had he known that his easy social acceptance by the Boltons and others had been noted by John as an asset of great value. A good doctor would be treated with respect, even one whose father had plunged to his death while making a futile gesture that hardly anyone, including John, had understood.

All John had understood was that the gentle little man who had never spoken harshly to him had died a shocking death and that, as the frail body lay there on the church steps with the head turned at an unnatural angle and the clear brown eyes staring up into the stark blue tropical sky, he, John, had felt a rage not at the rude, uncaring crowd, but at Moses Martin himself, and not for bringing death upon himself but for the embarrassment he caused him. For a long moment before grief consumed him, while he was still in shock, John appreciated the emotion that had shown on his brother Jacob's face when the constables had come that evening in Bristol, resignation if not relief. But the grief had come, and it had remained long after people stopped joking about the incident on the streets and in the taverns of Bridgetown.

There were times during the next eighteen months when John wished he had not so readily taken up Higganbotham's offer to teach him medicine. Actually the youth knew enough from observing the physician on his plantation rounds to have passed himself off as a chirurgeon and made a living from sewing up wounds, setting bones, applying salves to sores while appearing wiser than he was, but Higganbotham was determined to teach him all he could learn outside London or Edinburgh or some European university. Upon deciding to remain in Barbados, the doctor had sent back for his entire medical library and ordered other books as well, and he immediately set John to reading those printed in English.

He began him with Burton's *The Anatomy of Melancholy*, "not for the medicine but the philosophy," and followed this with various books on anatomy and surgery. He required him practically to memorize Harvey's *Anatomical Treatise on the Movement of the Heart and Blood in Animals*, taking time from his own affairs to catechize him carefully on what he had read and to translate orally other works written in Latin.

Higganbotham was a disciple of regular exercise.

"The limbs in particular should be moved about vigorously. Nothing better for health. You can see it for yourself when you observe planters who never exert themselves beyond riding down to Bridgetown and there overeating and drinking. How many such gouty, self-indulgent fellows in their forties have we seen die these past five years? It is a pity the climate here is not conducive to games such as we play back in England. Observe those former indentured servants who lay about peddling and begging. Contrast their sickly complexions and slack muscles with the ruddy look of a workman back home who can hardly wait for a Sunday to tramp about the country or play football and wrestle on the village common. I have not had a sick day since I arrived on Barbados, and do you know to what I attribute it?"

"Riding horseback so much," John said. He had heard this story many times.

"Exactly. The act of posting and general jogging about of the body are what does it. And have you noticed, I have lost much of my fat?"

"And it is good for the horse as well, I suppose," John said slyly.

Higganbotham looked at him sharply and then laughed. "Jest if you like. Horses soon sicken and die if not exercised."

"Our slave patients get enough exercise and see how they die."

"From poor diets and mistreatment. And lack of hope. This slavery is a cruel business, John."

"It is indeed. I don't know what is the cure for the evil, but I know that I never mean to buy one."

"And I never mean to sell one of mine. But enough of moralizing. Your next assignment is Sydenham on acute diseases. Read with care what he says about the value of moderate exercise. It is based on many cases which he treated and noted in his practice."

"Have I not read enough for one day?"

"If you were to read and observe every day for the next hundred years, it would not be enough. The sum of what we do not know about this human frame so far exceeds the little we do know that it behooves those of us who call ourselves physicians to waste not a moment in our pursuit of knowledge."

With a sigh, John took the book. "At least might I not wait until tomorrow's light? I have a headache. Perhaps I should take a turn about the plantation to set my own limbs in motion."

"Go, go. But remember that I mean to teach you all I know. I will not have it said that I set yet another ignorant quacksalver upon this island to add to the miseries of the ailing."

*

Although he had affected to be stern with John, Higganbotham actually was pleased by his quick grasp of the principles of medicine. He regretted the lad's inability to read Latin or other languages, and also the lack of opportunity to teach him anatomy by dissecting cadavers. There were plenty of white paupers and slaves dying every week, but the climate caused such quick decay that there was not time for a meticulous dissection, and besides, his own practice did not allow him the leisure even to complete his own treatise on diseases in the tropics. That, he persuaded himself, might come after the end of John's training, when the young man could take over part of his practice.

Higganbotham often reflected on the turn his life had taken when he came out to Barbados, expecting to liquidate his brother's estate in a few months and return to his practice in Norfolk. Well, he had no responsibilities back there. His father, a country vicar, and his mother dead, his sisters securely married, the girl he had loved wed to another, why should he go back even if he did not have this investment in a plantation, a platonic love for Charlotte Bolton, and this surrogate son-nephew, John Martin?

David Higganbotham was a better physician than he realized. Aside from the advantage of an Edinburgh training, he looked upon his patients, black and white, as persons, taking into account their emotions, and he recognized that he, like the rest of his profession, had much to learn.

Higganbotham did not talk about it, but, curiously, he learned much from the Negroes he treated, especially some of the older ones who knew Obeah or who had had this kind of African witchcraft practiced on them. He discovered it early when a strapping Gambian field hand fell sick, and the owner, who had invested twenty pounds in him just a year before, sent for the doctor. Higganbotham could find nothing wrong with the slave, no fever, no skin eruptions or dysentery. The man was reasonably well nourished; yet he was nearly comatose.

Persistent questioning of the slave's mate elicited the word "Obeah."

"Oh, my God, not that again," the overseer groaned. "It is Leah. She wanted him for her man, and I thought the other woman, being younger, would breed better."

Through threats of beating and branding, the overseer forced Leah to go to the hut of the afflicted slave and, through incantations and manipulations of bones and beads, convince him that she had lifted her curse. The "cure" was like a miracle. Within a few minutes the man had arisen and asked for water and "loblob" and by that afternoon was back in the cane field with his hoe in hand.

"You know they think that nobody dies except through some kind of spell," the overseer explained.

Thereafter, Higganbotham, when he came across a slave illness arising from no apparent medical cause, inquired until he discovered which African was the Obeah man or woman on the plantation. They were reluctant to acknowledge their identity and even slower to reveal to a white man just how they exercised their power, but gradually, through a piece of information here and there, he gained enough knowledge so that he could someday write an entire chapter on the subject for his diseases-of-the-tropics book. And, though for fear of ridicule he would never admit it, he practiced a form of Obeah himself. When all else failed, after determining the bewitched slave's native tongue, he would enter the hut alone, bring from his bag certain feathers and bones, and then repeat the magic words, accompanying them with violent gestures and grimaces. After that he would close his eyes in silent Christian prayer and, opening them, smile upon the puzzled patient brightly and say, again in the slave's own tongue, "There, the evil man has departed. You saw him leap out the window, didn't you?" And generally, the slave would smile just as brightly and nod, then return to work convinced that the strange white doctor was a sort of super-Obeah man.

As Higganbotham often told John, "Remember that we are

more than machines and more than animals. Hope and confidence are the best medicine of all."

Just as John was unprepared for the strenuous study demanded of him by Higganbotham, so he was frustrated in his design to see Charlotte more often and on a new footing.

Although Higganbotham visited Bolton Hall as he had always done, he required John to remain at home with his medical books. The youth hated the earnest physician when he watched him ride away on a Sunday afternoon to dine with the Boltons. There were times when he was ready to announce that becoming a doctor did not mean that much to him, but he persisted and gradually came to take a grim pleasure in his study and a sly pride in turning the tables on Higganbotham during their catechism by asking him questions that he could not answer.

"How is it that we command our legs to move, our tongues to form words?"

"It is a mystery waiting to be solved."

Higganbotham did not keep John strictly to book learning about medicine. When an unusual case came up, he took him along to help and observe. Thus they were called out at midnight to attend a prominent planter shot in the leg by his rival for the affections of a Bridgetown demimondaine. They found him in agony, laid out on the kitchen table of a tavern, his shinbone shattered beyond repair by a pistol ball.

"Give him brandy. Let him drink all he wants," Higganbotham said as he laid out his scalpel and saw. "Bring him a piece of wood to bite on."

"You're not about to take off my leg?" the planter groaned.

"You'll die if I don't. Off with his trousers."

This was a new Higganbotham. No longer the quiet-spoken, bumbling, father confessor, he ordered more candles brought in and the room cleared of all except John and three strong men to hold down the reluctant patient.

John could not believe the skill and speed with which

Higganbotham performed the amputation. First a tourniquet in place above the knee, then with a "hold him tight, lads," the curved knife slashed through skin, muscles, tendons, and nerves all the way around the leg, clear to the bones, and it was done so swiftly the man did not feel anything until John handed the doctor the saw. Once, twice, and thrice, the saw rasped and the bones just above the knee parted. The planter screamed and passed out.

Some doctors still cauterized stumps with boiling oil or red-hot irons, but Higganbotham painstakingly tied the blood vessels and sewed a flap of skin over the exposed flesh.

It all took less than half an hour. Afterwards, resting his elbows on the bloody table, his face dripping with sweat, Higganbotham asked, "Any of that brandy left?" Then, to John, "You can put that leg down now, lad."

John set the severed limb on the table and went out into the alley to throw up.

Higganbotham agonized over the myriad diseases in his practice for which he could find neither cause nor cure. Some Africans arrived already infected with sleeping sickness. He learned to distinguish the symptoms from the effect of an Obeah curse, but could do no more than isolate the slave with plenty of water and rest. Other Africans, fresh from the wretched slave ships, developed elephantiasis. Their feet and legs swelled to thrice their normal size, and there was nothing Higganbotham could do except let the disease run its course.

The worst and most common of the black man's infirmities was called yaws. Lumps and lesions appeared on the face and, in extreme cases, ate away the nose and lips. Like other doctors, Higganbotham was convinced this was a venereal disease, which called for the patients to be quarantined.

He did his greatest good, however, in persuading slave owners to give their Negroes adequate food and water and to allow them more time for rest and play. "They like to swim. By all means take them to the shore and let them have their sport. They'll be the better workers for it." Or, "Look you, sir, what did you pay for your last strong Guinea buck? Twenty pounds? Now if he dies, you have lost that money and must pay out as much or more for a replacement. By being cheeseparing with your expenditure on the food for your slaves you might save twenty pounds a year. But spend that much and more on proper nourishment for them, and you might prevent more than one from dying. And, mark this well, I warrant you'll get more efficient labor from all. Be not penny-wise and pound-foolish."

Those planters who took his advice found it to be sound. He had less success with his counsel regarding their own health. "You complain, sir, of your potbelly and pains in your bowels. Well, is it any wonder? When did you last walk as much as a mile? And I note that you have taken to riding about in a coach as though you had forgot your horsemanship. The body is meant to be exercised, sir. And how much strong drink do you consume in a week? Yes, yes, including madeira. Well, sir, I would eliminate the rum altogether, and allow myself no more than two glasses of wine with dinner. And you might curb your appetite for pastries and breads and partake of more fruits. Then lastly, might I suggest that each morning and evening, when it is cool, you walk about your boundaries at a moderate pace to speed the sluggish flow of blood. Besides aiding your health, it will have a good effect on your slaves and servants to see you looking about. You'll sleep better for it, I promise you. Now then, let us examine a specimen of your urine. What? Yes, in this glass flask."

The pasty-faced planter buttoned his trousers while Higganbotham held up the flask to the light, sniffed the contents, and made a face. The planter, who usually presided over his acres with the confidence of a bantam rooster, looked like a worried schoolboy.

"Not good. Cloudy and pale. And the odor bespeaks your dissipation."

"Foolish, foolish man, able to command a hundred black humans in matters of life or death, but unable to say no to his own selfish appetites." This to John, after they had left the plantation house. "He did not tell me, but I know that he keeps an Irish girl in Bridgetown, and he has got several of his slave women with child. He would not have consulted me had he not lost his lust, and he expects me to regain that for him with some medicinal potion. John, I tell you the Scriptures are faithful to the truth when they say that he that controlleth himself is mightier than the man who conquers a city. The white women of this island are healthier and live longer because they are more moderate; 'tis a pity their husbands do not follow their examples."

By the end of his year of instruction, John could answer Higganbotham's sharpest questions regarding anatomy, surgery, and physick. He was allowed to take off the arm of a slave who had caught his hand in the rollers of a sugar mill. He lost count of the number of persons he bled or to whom he administered enemas with Higganbotham's great syringe. Higganbotham knew it would be several years before the lad would have the experience or grave manner to enjoy the full trust of planters and their families, but he had no qualms about sending him out on his own to look after part of his slave practice.

For his part, John had grown weary of his mentor's voice and the deliberate way he consulted with his patients. It seemed to John that most ailments they encountered could be diagnosed at a glance and treated as quickly, and he found the ponderous consultations of Higganbotham tiresome and unnecessary.

During the five years after his father's death, John had avoided contact with the Quakers of the island. A few of those who had attended the funeral and had been moved by Charlotte's tribute tried to converse with him when he appeared in Bridgetown with Higganbotham, but he refused their invitations to attend their meetings, and they finally gave up, thinking that the lad had been infected with the Anglicanism of his master. For his part, John had experienced nothing but imprisonment, exile, and shame from his association with the religion, and he wished nothing more to do with it. And yet Quakerism had left its mark on him, causing him to abhor violence and injustice.

But the zeal of Friends in Barbados was not to be diminished by the apostasy of a green lad. They remained in constant disfavor with the elite of the island for their refusal to serve in the militia or to pay taxes earmarked for arms and fortifications. The Assembly passed laws making it a crime punishable by heavy fines for allowing one's slaves to attend religious services, and still some Quakers brought their Negroes to sit in silence at meeting. On at least one occasion, the authorities invaded the Bridgetown meetinghouse and removed the benches; without murmur, the congregation stood for their next service. Another time, constables sealed shut the doors, but their determination and prejudices did not run as deep as back in England. The meetinghouse was reopened.

News that George Fox, the founder of Quakerism himself, would visit Barbados caused great excitement on the island. He arrived in October 1671 aboard the *Industry*, and the Quakers of Barbados received him as though he were King Charles, vying for the privilege of entertaining him in their homes. It was Higganbotham's rather than John's idea to go and see the arrival of the little man who had set loose this powerful spiritual force in an empire more comfortable with an established church that made few demands except that of conformity. John remembered Fox as a dynamic speaker whose voice had pierced to the outer edge of the orchard near Bristol the day his parents were converted, a decade earlier. Now the man seemed shrunken. He was in fact suffering from a rheumatic heart condition, brought on by long imprisonments, but after a brief rest he began a series of meetings with the island's Quakers.

Many persons, Quaker or not, heard him speak and among these were Charlotte and a reluctant Richard. Charlotte wondered if Fox might do as Moses Martin had done and condemn slavery or threaten doom to the island if the Africans were not returned to their homelands. She was relieved to hear him counsel his followers who owned slaves to be kind to them and allow for them to be set free after a period of indenture. She had expected to hear stronger stuff from the man who had inspired the zeal of Moses Martin.

Fox remained on Barbados for three months. John was glad to see him depart for North America. His presence on the island brought back too many unpleasant memories.

Near the end of John's year and a half of medical instruction, he and Higganbotham answered an emergency call from a midwife in Saint James Parish who found herself unable to deliver the baby of the young wife of a white plantation mechanic. It was the woman's first baby, and she had been in labor for thirty-six hours. They could hear her moans as they approached the tiny house that stood between the Negro yard and the home of the planter. The midwife, a fat, gray woman with a Cornish accent, waited with the worried wife of the planter in the doorway.

The planter's wife said, "Mistress Gwinter here has done all she knows to do . . . "

"Indeed, I have. It's a breech baby, no doubt of it, and I can't turn it."

"The poor girl. She is too weak to strain anymore. We fear for her life now."

"Where is the father?"

"My husband took him away. The fellow is beside himself. They so want a child."

Inside the low-ceilinged house, it was stifling hot. Higganbotham ordered the windows of the little bedroom opened and then bent over the frail, wearied girl who lay there feebly turning her head from side to side and groaning. John watched as Higganbotham drew back the cover and deftly made his pelvic examination.

"Midwife is right. I feel its buttocks. Why did you not send for me sooner?"

"I've never had to call a doctor before, and I've delivered hundreds."

He felt the woman's pulse and bent his head down against her thin chest to listen to her heart and breathing. "I fear you waited too late. Now it is a question of which to save."

"Dear God," the midwife sobbed.

"Are you sure, Doctor Higganbotham?"

"I would not have said so if I were not. John, lay out my instruments, then send word for the husband to come at once."

"Doctor, the poor fellow is distraught."

"He'll just have to pull himself together and tell me which he values more, the life of his wife or the child. I can only save one. Wait much longer arguing, and they'll both be lost."

Higganbotham set about making the woman as comfortable as he could. "John, I have noted an air of impatience about you lately as though you deceived yourself that you had learned all there is to know."

"I wouldn't say that, Doctor Higganbotham."

"Perhaps it is only my imagination, then. But should you ever become puffed up with your knowledge, just remember this scene. We should be able to save both mother and child, but I am no more able to do so than an African witch doctor. Poor thing. I wonder what she would decide?" Then, hearing the sound of men's voices outside, "Go out, and put the question to him straight. Make him stay there, and come tell me forthwith."

Never had John had to do so hard a thing as approach the mechanic, a thin former bond servant not much older than himself. It took a moment for the question to sink in, and then the husband replied simply, "My wife. Save her. To hell with the baby."

John reentered the bedroom to find Higganbotham leaning over the woman, and the midwife sobbing louder than ever.

"He says to save his wife."

"Too late. She is gone. No, no, don't tell him. We've work to do. Scalpel, quickly. Another sheet. There will be much blood. Be ready."

In amputating the planter's mangled leg, Higganbotham

had been brutally swift, more like a skillful butcher than a surgeon, but now he worked with delicacy as first he deftly split the skin of the dead woman's abdomen from navel to pubis and then, as gently as though to spare her pain, he slid the scalpel through the underlying muscles and finally, with the point of the instrument, carefully opened the womb itself to expose the baby with its rump jammed down into the birth canal.

"Keep silent, Mistress Gwinter, do, and be prepared to take the child."

With hands and arms bloodied to the elbows, unmindful of the splotches on his vest, he held up the child like a skinned rabbit by the feet with one hand. "No, no. Let's get him started on his own before we cut the cord. Here." He whacked the baby three times smartly across the back and was rewarded by a shrill cry.

"Now, Mistress Gwinter," he said, "Now you may cut the cord and take him away. John, you'll have to tell the father."

John hated his benefactor for making him do such a thing. The mechanic looked up with hopeful face. "He saved them both after all?"

"You have a son," John said.

"And my wife came through all right?"

And then John had to tell him, and in that instant he realized that being a doctor was more than enjoying the respect of the gentry and the awe of simple folk. And he wondered if he ever would be half the physician that David Higganbotham was.

John had never done more than take an occasional glass of wine before, but when they returned home, he joined Higganbotham in finishing off a bottle of French brandy.

"The father cursed me and called me a butcher," he said thickly.

"You cannot expect him to appreciate what we did. We are not doctors for the sake of praise. That planter called me a butcher for taking off his leg, even though it saved his life."

"But there should be a way to save the mother, too."

"Perhaps someday there will, but we dare not cut into the chest or belly."

"The midwife was the guilty one. That was a job for a doctor."

"She did the best she knew. She is highly esteemed as a midwife.

"But the suffering of childbirth. Is that so common?"

"Curious thing. You have noted how slave women deliver more quickly and with less pain. With them it is a few fast cries and grunts much like an animal, and out the baby shoots. And the woman is generally back on her feet quickly. You'll not find this in a book, but I think it is because the African is closer to nature. He does not tie himself into knots over theology or thoughts of profit or loss or politics or any of the wearisome concerns of the white man. He accepts childbirth as a part of nature rather than an unnatural event."

"Don't you mean she?"

"What?"

"We were talking about women and childbirth."

"So we were."

"Speaking of that, Lady Bolton has been married six years. Shouldn't she have had a child by now?"

John would never have asked the question if he had not been drinking, and perhaps Higganbotham would not have answered as he did had he been sober. John had never seen the physician react so angrily.

"How presumptuous of you to discuss such a thing! It is none of your business, you young puppy. Never discuss her in those terms in my presence or indeed in anyone's! You take liberties. There are limits, you know."

John did not know how to reply to this outburst. He hung his head, miserably looking at the floor, feeling crushed, until Higganbotham broke the painful silence.

"You must forgive me, John. I should not let my feelings show like that. I loved another woman once. Thought her a goddess, but I lost her to another man. Adored her, I did, but she was common clay compared to Charlotte Bolton. I have never known a woman like her."

"Neither have I," John mumbled. Then, taking a deep breath, he added, "I meant no offense. It is just that I would hate to think she should suffer so."

"Oh, was that it? Even so, it is not to be mentioned again. Come, John, our nerves are overwrought. Let us to our beds."

At the moment they were discussing her, Charlotte sat at a small candlelit table in her bedroom, writing her monthly letter to her parents while Richard slept. The house was quiet except for the normal sounds of insects, and the night air was cool. Charlotte sat in her nightdress with her hair flowing down over her shoulders, mouth slightly pursed as usual when she was thinking. She was writing about the peace that had come upon Barbados of late. No war anymore. There had been a dry spell in the southern parishes, but Bolton Hall was having a good harvest. Richard's fellow planters had their usual complaints about the scarcity and prices of African slaves and the difficulties of getting skilled white indentured servants. She was pleased at Higganbotham's reports of John's progress. She put her pen down to think about that pair. She and Esther Lawnton were about ready to give up their efforts at matchmaking for David. At thirty-five he was a mite too old for the short supply of well-off girls of marriageable age, but there was no lack of widows of all vintages.

"I'd marry him in a minute should anything happen to Harold," Esther had said recently.

"He is a pleasant, agreeable fellow but don't you think he would be rather, well, dull?" Charlotte had replied.

"I expect you would find any man dull after being married to Richard Bolton."

Charlotte looked at her husband, snoring away serenely. True, no one could call him or their marriage dull. Their early days together often had been stormy, but in looking back she could see that much of the trouble had arisen from her own immaturity and headstrongness. If Richard had tended in those days to treat her like a child, perhaps it was because she had behaved with willful childishness, quick to complain and inclined to blame others for her own mistakes. Well, she had learned a thing or two in the past few years about how to deal with a strong-willed man in a nonchallenging way while maintaining her own sense of independence. It was odd, she reflected, how one reaped rewards from making one's husband happy. He never returned from Bridgetown without some little gift for her. And he enjoyed making her laugh. They could hardly have been more different in their basic interests, yet she never tired of him or ceased to take pride in the great popularity he enjoyed among all classes of Barbadians, except for a handful of old enemies he had made during the conflicts between Cavalier and Roundhead back in the early 1650s. He was some man, her Richard was.

She thought, too, of John Martin. She and Esther would have to make a match for him once he became established as a doctor. Higganbotham, with his background and university degree, would be acceptable as a husband for the richest widow of the island, even though he was only a minor landowner. But John, the son of a tailor, with only a dame's school education and his lapses of accent, was different. She hated to think of him thrown away on some simpleminded servant girl or tradesman's daughter. Perhaps if he waited a few years until he was a full-fledged physician and a landowner, he might make a better match. By then his origins would be less important. Strange the pleasure it gave her to have been his patroness without his knowledge or her husband's, and even more so now that he was going further than she had imagined when he was only a sad, little winsome boy. She let her mind rest for a few minutes on thoughts of this full grown, handsome young man and then completed her letter and sealed it.

Then this woman, who was the object of near worship by the doctor and his apprentice, blew out the candle and did a thing that might have disillusioned them both. Crawling in bed, she put her hand on a certain part of her husband's body and whispered, "Richard?"

He stopped in mid-snore and mumbled sleepily, "What is the matter?"

"Don't be afraid. I won't harm you." She giggled.

Higganbotham made a ceremony of the completion of John's medical instruction. Without telling him, he arranged a dinner in the common room at the Bow Bells for nearly fifty guests. John, expecting only a small, private affair, was dumbfounded. He was embarrassed and thrilled to hear his benefactor say, "I am turning over my slave practice in the northern parishes to him. Have no fear. He has become a good diagnostician. Your Negroes will be in good hands."

Applause and cries of "Hear! Hear!" greeted the announcement.

"My medical library is his as well as mine, but we scarcely can use the same instruments. Some months ago, I sent to London for his tools of the trade."

Higganbotham set a small chest on the table and opened it to reveal scalpels, saws, trephine, forceps, syringe, tongs, probes, tourniquet, and other surgical appliances.

"There is all he will need for any situation. And in this other chest are his medicines. Ladies and gentlemen, this is a proud occasion for me. Now I would like you to witness a solemn event. At the completion of my studies at Edinburgh, I was required to repeat the ancient oath of Hippocrates, an oath as sacred as any sworn to by a priest. Indeed, medicine is a priestly art as well as a demanding science. John, stand before me and tell me if you are ready to swear this oath."

"I am ready."

Higganbotham handed him a copy of the traditional words.

"You may skip the opening bit about Apollo."

John hesitated. His father would have refused to take this or any other oath on the grounds that everything a man said should be taken as the truth.

"Whenever you are ready," Higganbotham said.

In an unnaturally loud voice, with only a trace of his old

accent, John read, "According to my ability and judgment, I will keep this oath and stipulation: To reckon him who taught me this art equally dear to me as my parents, to share my substance with him . . ."

At the end of the oath, cheers broke out and cries of "Speech! Speech!" sounded.

"I haven't much to say except that I am grateful to Doctor Higganbotham for all he has done for me. I will do my best to be a good doctor." And he sat down.

It would be many months before people stopped calling him "the boy doctor," but both slaves and planters liked John Martin. He was gentle with the slaves and courteous to the planters' wives. And he made his rounds with tireless zeal.

Higganbotham had meant his territory to begin just north of Bolton Hall, but John insisted that it be included. "I will ride right past there anyway. That will give you more time for your inquiries into tropical remedies."

2

. . . After the Willoughby family's proprietorship of Barbados expired in 1669, the canny Lord William returned to England, partly to plead for Barbadian interests, but also to divine the intentions of King Charles regarding his own future. He was still in England in 1672 when a new war broke out with the stubborn Dutch, and the King ordered him to return to Barbados as governor and tighten the Royal reins on our obstreperous island.

Yet another war! And this time poor Richard could not avoid either the military or political conflict. Long before Willoughby returned in October, Richard was practically dragooned into a more active role in the militia. I was proud of his success in persuading other planters to release slaves to rebuild the line of earthworks covering all likely landing spots along the lee coast and his winning command of a militia regiment again. Partly at my suggestion, he argued for arming a few of the most trustworthy slaves to augment our thinning ranks of white militia, but, alas, his pleas fell on unheeding ears.

Fortunately, a small regiment of English soldiers arrived ahead of Lord Willoughby to lend backbone to our forces, but more men and stronger fortifications could not protect the convoy that sailed for London in June carrying most of the 1672 crop of sugar. Dutch cruisers intercepted the fleet, dealing the Barbadian planters a costlier blow than de Ruyter's attack seven years before. Half of Bolton Hall's production was carried in the ill-fated convoy. Thus our plans for a new house were dashed again . . .

Lord Willoughby called the meeting to order in the large room at the rear of the Roebuck Tavern. All the members of his council were present, including Sir Tobias Bridge, the imperious and unpopular commander of the newly arrived English regiment. So were Richard Bolton and other prominent planters.

The governor looked so sickly and worried that Richard was surprised by his determined tone.

"His Majesty has given me instructions which cannot be ignored. He has ordered me to strike the Dutch and strike them hard. The question is when and where."

He paused to let his words sink in. "What advice do you have for me, gentlemen?"

Richard cleared his throat and arose. "My Lord, there is a further question: Strike with what? During your absence we prepared to defend ourselves. We are readier in some respects than in '65. But our militia is drastically short of men."

"Bolton is right," another planter spoke up. "Why did his majesty not send a fleet if he wishes to punish the Dutch?"

"He did send over Bridge and his regiment."

"Indeed, but they are only eight hundred men, and they arrived without any provision for food and lodging. And they were precious little good in preventing the seizure of our sugar fleet."

"I thirst for revenge as much as any man," Richard added. "We never repaid the Dutch for de Ruyter's little visit, but I ask again: What means do we have? Surely, My Lord, we shall not be expected to recruit another expedition such as the one in which we lost your brother and so many hundreds of our neighbors in '66. Then we would indeed be at the mercy of the Dutch."

Willoughby nodded. "We can spare six hundred men from Bridge's regiment. And we have at least one strong warship, the faithful *Saint David*."

"All respect to our soldier visitors and their commanding officer, that is far from a mighty army."

"One might have thought so from all the complaints I hear over the cost of feeding them," Willoughby said softly as he unrolled a map and spread it across the tavern table. "You have hearkened to August of '66, Bolton. I would remind you of what occurred earlier in that same year when Tobago fell to only eighty men."

The men crowded around the governor as he continued. "The Dutch have built up their colony there again since the last war. Tobago has several good harbors that would make attractive bases from which their navy could harass our shores or, God forbid, attempt an invasion of Barbados. As long as they control those harbors, we are in danger. But, if we move with dispatch, we strike the blow King Charles commands, and we end the danger."

He paused and sat down to hear their objections.

"Did they not rebuild their forts on Tobago?"

"True. But they are lightly manned at present."

"Tobago is a considerable island. Nearly as long as Barbados and half as wide."

"Yes, but the terrain works against the defenders. They are

sparsely settled and cannot shift their few men from point to point as we can on Barbados. This long ridge down the spine of the island separates one side from the other. And good landing beaches abound."

"Really, My Lord, should we go chasing off on a distant adventure when our own land may be in danger?"

"Tobago lies but two hundred miles away. With a good wind, we could reach it in two days. Three at the most."

"Still it would place us needlessly in danger at home."

"We shall be in a greater danger once a Dutch fleet arrives there," Willoughby replied. "You forget that I am under royal orders to take action. I have the *Saint David* standing by. We can impress enough of the merchantmen cowering in Carlisle Bay to transport Bridge and his men. We must strike while there is time. We will strike."

Richard broke the long silence. "Apparently your lordship has made up his mind. If you do not propose to draw upon our militia, what do you expect of us?"

"A modest appropriation to finance the provisioning of our troops and a garrison there. Perhaps seventy thousand pounds of sugar."

"And that is all?"

"A few Barbadians with military experience, if they wish to volunteer. Bridge would be glad to have you along, I expect, Bolton. But only if you wish to go."

"And a good doctor would be helpful," Bridge added.

Charlotte did not want Richard to accompany the expedition against Tobago, but neither did she want another dreadful scene and estrangement such as they had had six years ago over a similar issue. At least good, steady David Higganbotham had agreed to go with Richard. And, she reminded herself, here was a chance for her husband to advance his reputation, perhaps even with the king himself. So, swallowing her fears and putting on a brave face, she helped Richard pack, went down to Bridgetown to see him and Higganbotham go aboard the *Saint*

David, and then watched as the warship led five soldier-laden, commandeered merchantmen out of Carlisle Bay.

Richard stood at the rail waving until he no longer could distinguish Charlotte among the crowd along the dock. He turned his face to the open sea and squared his shoulders.

"Isn't this grand, David? I feel alive again."

"Let's hope you remain alive. You have much to live for."

"What about yourself?"

"I have my work. I suppose that is what I live for."

"Well, you'll have work enough on Tobago if there is a good fight. Now enough philosophizing. Let's stow our gear."

Richard did not like Sir Tobias Bridge. Like many other planters, he resented the king's appointment of an itinerant soldier to the governor's council. And he found the man's contemptuous attitude toward the colonial militia annoying. Captain Poole, commander of the *Saint David*, was a man more to his liking. The two men spent much time going over charts of Tobago. The only town of any size was Lampsinsburgh, which lay on a deep bay near the lower tip of the skinny island on the eastern side. The Dutch had erected forts at each end of the bay so that ships would have to run a gauntlet of cannon fire to get at the town. Fearful for the safety of his soldiers jammed aboard the merchant ships, Bridge favored making a landing on the western coast and marching five miles across the island to take Lampsinsburgh from the rear. "Then, Poole, you can come in close and engage the forts from the sea side while we attack from the town itself."

Richard, who had never visited Tobago, could find no fault with the plan, and neither did the commander of the *Saint David*. Higganbotham, who was seasick, volunteered to go ashore with the soldiers. "Anything to get on dry land," he said.

"If you go ashore, so do I," Richard replied. "I don't want to miss the fighting."

Although Richard's mission ostensibly was to report to Lord Willoughby on the expedition and the condition of

Tobago, no one aboard the *Saint David* objected when he announced he would join in the landing. "Just remember that you'll not be giving any orders," Bridge said.

The afternoon of the second day they sighted the northern tip of Tobago and by dusk had come within a cannon shot of the shore. The land was far more overgrown and rugged than Barbados. Rainclouds hung over the long central mountain range.

Fearful of reefs, Captain Poole led his convoy away from shore and they spent the night hove to, with sea anchors out and lookouts posted on all sides. The next morning they felt their way along the coast, watching for a landing site, until they found a curving beach with no offshore reef.

It thrilled Richard to see the longboats going over the sides of the merchantmen and then the red-coated soldiers, laden with knapsacks and muskets, climbing down the rope ladders. He and David waited until the soldiers were all ashore before they clambered down into a longboat. By the time all the men were on the palm-lined beach and their gear had been reassembled, it was too late to move into the jungled interior.

Richard could not put his finger on it, but he felt vaguely uneasy about the way in which they had been allowed to go ashore with no opposition. Indeed, they had seen no one, unfriendly or otherwise. Surely the Dutch would have some sort of lookout system; six ships lying offshore for an entire day must have attracted some notice. He voiced his alarm to Bridge.

"What is it that disturbs you so, Sir Richard?" the officer asked sarcastically.

"We don't know where the enemy is."

"We assume he is in Lampsinsburgh, looking out to sea."

"But what if he is not? My point is that we may be taking too much for granted to expect them to allow us to march across their island and grab the chief town just like that."

"And what do you propose?"

"Give me a squad, and I will scout the way to Lampsinsburgh. It will be tomorrow before you can move six hundred men and their equipment anyway. I can bring you information before then."

Under Richard's directions, the squad removed their red coats and exchanged their muskets for pairs of pistols. Remembering his pledge to Charlotte to look after Richard, David insisted on going, too. Dressed in a planter's hat and a linen jacket, Richard led the party away from the beach onto a narrow road that climbed up into the wooded hills toward Lampsinsburgh. Following his instructions, Higganbotham and the soldiers waited for him to walk ahead to the next bend in the road or clearing and to advance only after he whistled to them. The farther into the hills they climbed, the more Richard felt that Bridge had miscalculated in making a landing on the Caribbean side of Tobago. It was too quiet. Twice he and his men had to take shelter under a tree when a rainstorm swept down from the great central ridge. They passed a house in the midst of a large cleared area, but no one could be seen.

Near the crest of a hill they came to the edge of a large clearing, and Richard drew the squad off the road to reconnoiter the place. The plantation house was a long, ugly building. He saw several white women about the grounds and a gang of Negroes working in a nearby field, but no white men were in evidence. They crossed the road and made their way through the trees, out of sight of the house, until they were beyond the plantation.

"Wait, I hear someone."

They hid until they could make out the sound of cart wheels on the road and the voice of a slave singing an African song.

Higganbotham cocked his head and held up his hand for silence.

"He is singing in Ibo."

Richard drew his pistol. "Take him quietly," he said.

The young African, dressed in a ragged smock as well as the usual "arseabout", or loincloth, led a donkey that pulled a cart loaded with crates. The soldiers were on him before he

knew it, and in an instant he was gagged and bound. Once they
had him off the road, Richard put his pistol to the African's
head and nodded to Higganbotham. His face red and sweaty
from the heat and exertion, David knelt and removed the
youth's gag and began speaking. The Negro replied readily, his
words punctuated with nods toward Lampsinsburgh.

"He says most of the white men are assembled just down
the road overlooking Lampsinsburgh. Our soldiers would have
walked right into a trap."

Richard put his hand over his brow and peered through
the trees toward the setting sun. "Replace his gag and bring
him along. Leave his donkey."

It galled Sir Tobias Bridge to take advice from a mere
militia colonel, albeit a knighted one, but he quickly grasped
the information and acted upon it. It was out of the question to
reboard their ships after dark, so he posted a strong skirmish
line inland and gave strict orders against campfires or talking.
Early the next morning, he ordered his men up into columns
facing inland while Higganbotham led the captured Ibo into
the woods and after admonishing him, "You must not tell your
masters that we are marching to attack Lampsinsburgh,"
unbound his feet, but left his gag in place and his wrists tied
behind his back, as Richard had instructed him. The slave was
out of sight in an instant. Bridge immediately began herding
his soldiers aboard their longboats. By noon the fleet was round-
ing the southwestern tip of the island, and then, while the *Saint
David* made for the fort guarding the southern entrance to
Lampsins Bay, the five merchantmen dropped out of line to
anchor in close to a beach and begin putting soldiers ashore.

Richard was disappointed not to land with the troops, but
Captain Poole pointed out the foolishness of delaying their
attack even long enough to let a boat over the side. "And if our
calculations are correct, we will need Doctor Higganbotham
this afternoon more than will Sir Tobias."

"I don't understand something, Richard," David said as
they watched the fort loom off their port bow. "If that Ibo

wasn't supposed to tell about our presence, why did you wish his gag left in place and his hands bound? He would have to have help to free himself, and then wouldn't he have to explain?"

"Exactly, David. Exactly. And if he did as I calculated, there should be some very eager Dutchmen up in those hills waiting to ambush us. Isn't this wonderful? Now I know how de Ruyter felt when he came sailing ito Carlisle Bay."

Just as de Ruyter had done, Captain Poole waited for the fort to fire the first shot. His gun crews had double-loaded their cannon, and every man was straining to see their enemies in the squat fort when a gun flash and billow of smoke appeared from an embrasure, followed quickly by several more. Richard watched the projectiles arc up and splash in the water around the *Saint David*. Captain Poole ordered his gunnery officer to hold his broadside and reply only with his sakers. These long-barreled guns boomed one after the other, as though the *Saint David* were unconcernedly seeking the correct range.

"Keep it up," the captain shouted. "Keep them dodging our balls until we are close enough for a broadside."

Meanwhile, the guns of the fort were dropping their balls closer and closer. The first one to strike the *Saint David* smashed a longboat on deck, spraying a gun crew with deadly splinters. Three men went down, one of them the gunner's mate, and Higganbotham ran to help the ship's surgeon with the wounded. Seeing that the gun crew was leaderless, Richard took up the mate's lighted linstock and announced to the men, "Our soldiers wear red jackets so the blood won't show. The Dutch wear brown trousers very full in the seat. You'll soon see why. Stand to your gun, men, and we'll teach the bastards what English sailors are made of."

The sailors laughed so that Captain Poole frowned and commanded them to be quiet.

The *Saint David* took a shot through her foresail and another in her side before Captain Poole gave the order. It seemed to Richard that he might have thrown a stone into the fort by then. He touched the glowing end of the linstock to the tiny mound of fine powder atop the touch hole, and the cannon belched and lurched. The ship shook with the combined recoil of twenty cannon, and a cloud of white smoke drifted across the deck.

"Reload and fire at will," the captain ordered.

Richard's crew got in two more shots before the *Saint David* slid past the fort and turned to present her starboard broadside to the enemy.

Keeping out of the effective range of the fort at the northern entrance to the bay, Captain Poole concentrated on this one, moving back and forth, firing broadsides at close range and peppering the defenders with his long pieces as he made his turns. Richard lost all track of time. The constant slamming of the guns rendered him and his crew so deaf they could not hear each other's shouts, but as they fell into the rhythm of swabbing out the barrel, clearing the touch hole, ladling in the powder and ramming home the ball, then running the piece back in place, aiming it, pouring in the priming powder, and then standing aside for this blond-haired planter to touch off the charge, they became like machines, or rather like a series of machines working away on both sides of the main deck and below in the gun deck. Never did a captain get as much service out of a ship and a crew as did Captain Poole that afternoon of December 19, 1672. The *Saint David* lost her topmast, and her mainsail was riddled. Ropes, broken by cannonballs, dangled, and much of her railing was shot away, but the ship gave the Dutch defenders no rest. And while the *Saint David* kept that garrison occupied, the merchantmen, having disembarked Bridge's regiment a mile and a half away, sailed up and, although only lightly armed, engaged the attention of the other fort from a safe distance.

The battle raged on until late afternoon, by which time Bridge and his soldiers had approached the southernmost fort and were making a show of maneuvering past it and into the town.

The Dutch were noted for their reasonableness. The governor of the colony, whose residence was situated within the main fort, ordered the commander to signal for a cease-fire and then sent a message out to Sir Tobias that he was willing to discuss terms.

Richard learned of Willoughby's real reason for pressing the Tobago expedition only after he had returned to Barbados and a hero's welcome. The governor wished to make the Dutch island a Barbadian satellite and thereby add to his own sphere of power. Richard told him he did not think the place worth the investment it would require from an already overextended Barbadian economy.

"Besides that, Your Excellency, the last thing we need is another British possession competing with our plantations for a share of the sugar market. If I had known this was your intention, I would not so readily have agreed to accompany the expedition."

Invitations to the governor's house ceased after that, but as Richard said to Charlotte, "I have had nothing but bad luck letting myself be used by the Willoughby family."

"Anyway, you seem to have got your love of adventure out of your system for a while."

"For the present, yes."

To his great disappointment, Willoughby found little senti-ment for his scheme to extend Barbadian sovereignty to include Tobago. And he was not at all pleased by signs that Richard Bolton's popularity was growing because of his heroism and his forthright opposition. In fact Willoughby regretted his decision to send such an ungrateful fellow with Bridge and Poole.

" . . . And I say it is a damned outrage," Richard declared to Higganbotham and Harold Lawnton as Charlotte and Esther brought out tea to the veranda.

"What are you outraged about this time, dear?" Charlotte asked.

"David was telling us of a report just come to Bridgetown that the government is ending the monopoly of the Company of Royal Adventurers trading in Africa."

"Why does that outrage you? For years you have complained of the shortage of slaves and the price. I thought you pined for the good old days when you could buy them from the Dutch at seven pounds, when," and here her voice took on an edge of sarcasm, "it was cheaper to buy them than breed them."

"Oh, Charlotte, you don't understand. They have only formed a new monopoly."

"Yes," Higganbotham broke in. "This one is to be called the Royal African Company. It supposedly is better financed. It will have permanent agents on each of the islands, and the Royal Navy will protect its stations on the African coast..."

"And keep foreign slavers from our shores," Lawnton said.

"Ah, then," Charlotte replied. "There's the rub. No more smuggling slaves from the Dutch on Saint Eustatius."

"But Barbados will be assured of at least two thousand new slaves a year," Higganbotham said.

"Yes, but at seventeen pounds a head," Richard responded.

"This new arrangement may not be such a bad thing for Barbados," Higganbotham said. "The old African Adventurers were poorly financed and unable to deliver the Africans, with the war in '65 and now this one. But with the Navy's full protection and an assured price, we will have a dependable supply and..." He held up his hand to stop Lawnton from interrupting him, "Barbados will be the first stop for the slave ships."

"The first chance to be robbed of our money," Lawnton rejoined.

"No, the opportunity to take your pick of the Africans. You can choose the cleanest of limb, the freest of disease, the clearest of eye, the youngest and most nimble..." He very nearly said "the comeliest of female form" but, thinking of Clemmie's parentage, caught himself.

"And we can send the refuse to the other islands," Lawnton said.

"Won't that serve Modyford and the others right who deserted Barbados for new lands in Jamaica?" Richard laughed.

"Seriously, when will we see the fruits of this new scheme?" Lawnton asked.

"The report is that Edwin Stede is to be named agent for Bridgetown and that the first slaves will arrive under convoy sometime this year."

"If more people would listen to David and spend more on the care and feeding of their slaves, so many replacements would not be necessary," Charlotte said.

"Don't start on that theme again. You are bankrupting me with your smocks and additional time off for having babies. Yes, and running up bills with David's young protégé. That lad of yours is making hypochrondiacs of our slaves, David. If he spends that much time at every plantation, I wonder when he sleeps."

"John is very conscientious," David said.

"He is, indeed," Charlotte said. "I don't know why Richard likes to play the skinflint."

Lawnton laughed. "That is what some of Willoughby's men are calling him."

Richard's temper flared. "It will be years before we finish paying off the debts of the last war, and Willoughby wants to saddle us with even more just for the honor of saying Tobago is Barbadian territory."

"Calm down, Richard, I did not mean to upset you. There is also talk going about that Willoughby's health is none too good and that, when it is time to replace him, it should be done with a real Barbadian, a planter."

"Oh, anyone in particular?" Charlotte asked, with a feigned casualness.

"Several are being talked of. And one of them is the man you called a skinflint. Down Bridgetown way they are calling him the hero of Tobago these days. And with Willoughby looking so feeble, well, who knows?"

"Nonsense," Richard said, and switched the subject so quickly to the excellent prospects for the approaching sugar harvest that Charlotte could tell Lawnton's hint had struck home. She looked at her husband's face, so strong and still handsome, until his eyes met hers. She smiled.

3

... The last person I expected to have trouble with at Bolton Hall was Clemmie. I could not understand the change that came over her. Previously so cheerful and dutiful, she grew almost as sullen as Mandze, moping about and sometimes weeping for no good reason.

Being genuinely fond of the girl, I did not wish to take the matter up with Richard, for fear of what he might do. It was Esther Lawnton who suggested that I sound out Mirabel.

Mirabel was guarded at first, claiming not to comprehend. But after I praised her cooking and housework, she began to unbend.

Why did she think Clemmie was unhappy?

"She not right here." She pointed a finger to her heart. "You too kind. She think she too good for black man."

"I don't understand," I said.

And then Mirabel said something that astounded and shocked me. "The young doctor. She crazy for him."

"Oh, dear, what shall we do?" I said, rhetorically, to myself, but Mirabel took me literally.

"Beat her. Make her be Toby's woman. He plenty good enough for her. If she don't do it, sell her."

I debated long and hard over what to do ...

It was a Monday morning, John's favorite time of the week. He was rested after a languid Sunday of reading and talking to

Higganbotham about his cases. He had slept well and now, mounted on his roan gelding, with his saddlebags stuffed with instruments and medicines, was riding eagerly northward along the road to his first stop at Bolton Hall. Charlotte would receive him in the plantation office and tell him of the state of health of the slaves. He would listen gravely, asking an occasional question just to keep her talking. And then they would go together to the Negro yard to look after any ailing slaves.

One drawback to Bolton Hall's being his first stop was that he got there too soon to be invited to remain for dinner unless there was some very troublesome case or a large number of sick slaves. Charlotte talked to him with that easy grace she had learned from her father and with what he sometimes imagined to be just a touch of condescension. He longed to be able to sit across a table from her as an accepted equal, speaking his mind freely and teasing her as her husband did.

So that morning as he rode past Saint Thomas Church he let his mind go where it would, daydreaming of Charlotte. She was, he thought, nearly twenty-eight now and if anything more beautiful for the softening of her features and a wrinkle across her brow that had not been there aboard the *Mary Leigh*. She was only seven years older than he. Doctor Higganbotham often remarked on the relatively short lives of planters out here. Her husband must be nearing fifty now. What if he should die; it was not unheard of for a widow to marry a younger man. Newgate, exile, the shame of a lunatic father, and a year of excruciatingly hard study then would have proven a small price to pay.

"Hold there!"

John, who had been riding along with his hat brim over his eyes, lost in his guilty fantasies, nearly jumped out of the saddle. There by the intersection of the road to Apes Hill stood Tom Cochran and his donkey. John had seen the hermit only rarely and at a distance during the past few years. Both the man and the beast were far bonier and grayer than he remembered them. And Tom's voice was as feeble as his appearance.

"It is John Martin, is it not?"

"Yes, Mr. Cochran, it is I."

"I have seen you traveling this road often of late."

"I expect you have."

"But you don't look about you much, do you?"

"I have my mind on other things."

"Yes, I expect you do. It's a doctor you have become."

"Doctor Higganbotham trained me."

"And you've growed into a fine-looking, strapping fellow."

"How have you been, Mister Cochran?"

"Well enough. You never come to see me anymore."

"I did not want to be reminded."

"Of your father. Too bad. He is proud of you, you know."

John thought he had not heard correctly. "I hope he would be, if he knew."

"He does know, and he is."

"Is, did you say?"

"Yes, proud. He speaks of you often."

"Speaks, Mister Cochran?"

"Have you gone deaf, young fellow? Yes, speaks. At night, when the moon is dark, we talk by the hour. It all came to pass, you know."

"What?"

"His predictions. London burned. Plague. Bridgetown near blowed off the island. That expedition lost in a hurricane."

John wished desperately to escape from the old man. "Well, that is all behind us now."

"He says not. He says the worst is yet to come. This is only a pause in our calamities."

The old man had come out into the road and looked up with eyes that seemed to stare through John and with the smile of one with a deep secret. It was a warm morning, but John felt a chill creep down his spine and goosebumps on his arms. "You don't think you dream these things, Mister Cochran?"

"Dreams? I dreamed before your father came, and I know the difference."

"Why are you telling me this?"

"He says to warn you to beware of *her*. You'll bring destruction to ye both."

The tension was more than John could bear. Suddenly he could hear himself shouting: "You're lying! You're a dirty, bitter old man, and you've made this up to make me feel bad. I remember how you used to rant about the planters running Barbados, and you've heard that I look after their slaves, and this is your way of spoiling things for me. I have had a bellyful of crazy old men in my life. Get out of my path. I have better things to do than listen to your raving!"

He lashed his horse's flanks and cantered away from Tom, trying to get as far as he could from the old derelict.

At Bolton Hall, Charlotte wondered why John's horse was sweating and breathing so hard, and she thought him withdrawn and distracted. As she was to say to Esther Lawnton later, "I fear the lad is taking himself too seriously or that he is working too hard."

A month later, just after the dark of the moon, a militia company on its way to drill at Parey's Spring found the body of Tom Cochran lying beside the road with his decrepit old donkey standing by. There was little of apparent value on his person: a few twists of tobacco, a Spanish coin, and a piece of paper headed "Last Will and Testament of Thomas Cochran" and dated the previous day.

John was summoned to appear before the governor himself regarding the will. Standing before a bewigged Lord Willoughby, who sat as "Ordinary," the youth protested the inconvenience. "I have had naught to do with that old man, sir. He is not my responsibility."

"Well, now, *Doctor* Martin, I would not be so hasty, were I you. You are aware that Tom Cochran held title to ten acres up on Apes Hill."

"Yes, Your Lordship, I know the place."

"Could Cochran write?"

"My father taught him to write some, yes. I used to help him, too."

"So, you know his handwriting," the governor said with a smug smile.

"Such as it was," John replied.

"Is this a fair sample of his handwriting?"

He folded the paper so that only the heading and the first line showed.

"I, Thomas Cochran, resident of Apes Hill, Saint James Parish, Barbados, being of sound mind and body do make this, my last will and testament . . . "

The governor stopped him before he could read further. "Well, do you recognize the handwriting?"

John stood gaping, once again experiencing that strange chill going down his spine.

"Well, well, is it his handwriting?"

"Whose?"

"Damn it, young man. The handwriting of Thomas Cochran?"

"Yes," John said. He dared not tell the governor that the handwriting was his father's. He dreaded the ridicule he knew would follow.

"Very well, have you any interest in the provisions of the will?"

"No, Your Lordship. I have none. May I go now?"

"No, you may not. You do have an interest."

"Really, sir, I am due even now at the Negro yard of Nairn plantation. They are expecting me."

The governor burst out laughing. "You are a fool, though you call yourself a doctor. The will names you as Tom Cochran's heir. He has left you his ten acres, his donkey, and all his other earthly goods. He must have been on his way to town to file the will when he was stricken. Smile, lad, smile. You are about to become the owner of ten acres. That means you can vote in the Assembly elections."

"No, it doesn't," John said, recovering his composure.

Willoughby frowned. "You are the son of the unfortunate

Quaker who fell to his death from the roof of Saint Michael. Are you so eccentric as he? Are you saying you won't accept the land? Or that you hold the Quaker prejudice against the necessary oath?"

"Neither, Your Lordship. I only meant I cannot vote. I shan't be twenty-one until my next birthday."

Esther Lawnton was not surprised by Charlotte's report of what Mirabel said about Clemmie.

"What do you expect? They are nearly of the same age. And he is a fetching fellow, so solemn and handsome. Of course she finds him attractive. Don't you?"

"Oh, Esther, don't be ridiculous. You are no help at all."

With no improvement in Clemmie's disposition, Charlotte finally told Richard about the problem and instantly wished she had not. He laughed until she angrily demanded what was so humorous.

"That little prig. He wouldn't know what to do with her anyway, and she is mooning over him?"

"They cannot marry."

"Of course, they cannot marry. But if he were a different sort, she would make him a good enough ... " Seeing Charlotte's troubled expression, he stopped in mid-sentence. "I'm sorry. Yes, it is out of the question. Perhaps it would help if he confined his visits to the Negro yard in the future. Until she gets over it. And better yet, let's marry her off to Toby."

"But she scorns him."

"She would get over that once she had a taste of the old honey."

"You are a beast."

"All right, I am a beast. I leave it in your hands, madam."

Charlotte lay awake long into the night fretting over the problem. The next morning she called Clemmie out to the veranda where Mirabel could not hear and ordered the surprised girl to sit down.

"Clemmie, it is time for you to have a husband. The master and I have been thinking much about this, and we have considered several possibilities." She named three field hands of her age and Cromwell, whose wife had died recently.

Clemmie's face crumpled. "Oh, Mistress, please no."

"You don't like any of them?"

Clemmie was aghast. "They are field hands."

"Cromwell is not. He is a master boiler."

"He is too old, and he is black, too."

"Then that leaves Toby, who is not a field hand and is not too old. In fact he is two years younger than you."

"Him!"

"We would build you a little house at the edge of the garden. We would make Toby our butler and give him a new boy to work under his supervision in the garden. He would wear a red jacket."

"I don't want Toby."

"The master is determined. I fear he might sell you off the island if you refuse."

Charlotte hated herself for the threat, but she felt she had to resolve the matter.

"You going to force me then?"

"I see no other way."

"Our own house?"

"With two rooms. And you shall have a new dress."

"Is that what you want for me, Mistress?"

"I wish there were some other way."

Clemmie arose and ran into the house. Charlotte thought of what Esther had said long ago, "Negroes ... are very different and I fear their presence makes us different ... " If only the girl had kept to her place and not given herself notions about John Martin, or else had been able to keep her emotions hidden. It did not occur to Charlotte that she had treated Clemmie much as Richard had Mandze.

For Toby it was a dream come true to have as his own woman this girl with the smooth copper skin and quick speech. Richard gave him a week off from his gardening duties and the materials to build their hut, and he went about it with zeal from dawn to sundown until the structure was completed.

"I never saw him move with such alacrity in the garden," Charlotte commented to Richard.

"I told you he was a clever lad. He will be good for Clemmie, and he'll make us a better servant now, you watch."

Charlotte considered and rejected the idea of giving the couple a formal wedding ceremony. Instead, she let Richard handle the solemnities, which he did on a Saturday afternoon, late, calling Clemmie and Toby before them with Mirabel and ordering them to face him, holding hands. There under the fig tree he said, "Toby, I hereby give you this woman as your wife. You must be gentle with her. Leave other women alone. Look after her. She is yours. Clemmie, I give you this man to be your husband. Be kind to him. Stay away from other men. He is yours. You both understand?"

Beaming, Toby nodded vigorously. Clemmie, her eyes filled with tears, lowered her head in shame.

"Now we have some new clothes for you."

"And a blanket and bowls and two pillows from Bridgetown," Charlotte said brightly.

Toby held out his arms for the gifts, while Mirabel looked on with satisfaction.

"There, you are married," Richard said. "No work for either of you until Monday morning. Go now and put your things where they belong."

Thereafter, when John Martin stopped by Bolton Hall, Charlotte was careful to keep Clemmie from his presence. In a few months she assumed it was all over, this silly infatuation of a mulatto slave girl for her secret protégé. Certainly Toby seemed happy enough, and at least Clemmie was no longer moping about.

4

... *Bolton Hall had such a good cane crop in 1673 that my hopes for a new house were revived, and I resumed my pastime of redrawing the plans. Richard's spirits were buoyed by the prospects of a quick recovery from the loss of part of our previous crop in the Dutch attack on the convoy. But he complained of needing new slaves. "Why does my best crop in years come when I am shorthanded?" he asked.*

And so the now familiar process began again. Both the windmill and the old cattle mill remained in constant motion as the cutting crews labored through the long days in the fields, like a line of black ants, sending cartload after cartload of stalks creaking up to the mills. The furnaces glowed throughout the night. Richard's face became gray and drawn, for he often worked through half the night at the sugar mill, and on Sundays was required to drill his regiment so they would be prepared to repulse a Dutch attack. And still men would talk politics to him, and he would listen.

Then at the height of the harvest, William Lord Willoughby fell suddenly ill, so ill that he hastily named a deputy governor. And three days later, on April 10, he died.

The news had scarcely reached Bolton Hall before the first delegation of planters came to consult with Richard. They shut themselves up in the plantation office, and I could hear their voices just clearly enough to know they were arguing but not enough to make out what they were saying.

"Think about it, that's all we want," one of them said to Richard as the delegation mounted their horses.

"I'll put on my considering cap, but I think there are better men," he said.

I was appalled to see that Richard was about to ride off to the sugar works without telling me of his conversation. I ran out to the fig tree and grasped his horse's bridle.

"What did those men want?"

"Why do you ask?"

"Because I want to know, you lout."

"They swore me to secrecy." His grin was infuriating.

"Secrecy about what?"

"You prying wench. You don't want me to betray a sacred oath, do you?"

"Richard! I won't tell anyone. Now stop teasing me."

"No, just Esther Lawnton, and then . . . "

"Please. I swear I will tell no one. What is this all about?"

He turned serious. "Don't get excited about it. Probably only talk, and there would be many hurdles to overcome. But we have been hoping for years we could have a governor from our own ranks. A planter instead of some toady of the Court. They think I have a good chance since I fought for the King and hold a title."

"Do you want it?"

"I don't know yet."

"Don't know? What do you mean you don't know?"

"Codrington and Colleton are being touted, too, and they are formidable rivals. And the Walrond family hates my guts. They would be against me."

I felt like boxing his ears. "Nonsense. Don't be a fool, Richard Bolton," I said. "You'd be far the best of the lot. Come on, man, you can do anything you set your mind to . . . " I paused and laughed. "With the help of a clever determined wife, that is to say."

He made a face and tried to ride off, but I would not release the bridle.

" 'Hie thee hither, that I may pour my spirits in thine ear, and chastise with the valour of my tongue all that impedes thee from the golden round, which fate doth seem to have thee crowned withal.' "

"What?" he demanded. "Talk sensibly."

"Duncan is dead, you fool," I replied. "And we did not have to kill him. You will never have another such opportunity, my Lord Macbeth."

Willoughby's body was kept sealed in a lead coffin until late in May, after the cane harvest, and then the elite of the island gathered for the grandest funeral ever held in Barbados. I was amazed at the size of the crowd.

The ceremony was conducted with great pomp by the same minister who had preached the embarkation sermon for the ill-fated expedition to Guadeloupe. Afterward the mourners followed the heavy coffin past rank upon rank of the island's militia down to the wharf to go aboard the Saint David, the same ship on which Willoughby had arrived in 1667 to replace his brother and which now was to carry his body back to be buried in the family tomb in Lincolnshire, as his will specified.

As the cortege moved slowly away from the church, flags flew at half-mast over the forts protecting Bridgetown and ships anchored in Carlisle Bay. The minute gun at Charles Fort boomed at intervals. It occurred to me that I no longer felt English, that I had become a Barbadian. Perhaps that was why this solemn pageantry so thrilled me. My Richard would have such a funeral someday, many years hence, if he should become the island's first planter-governor. And, by all that was holy, I meant him to be just that.

I remained in Bridgetown with Richard over the weekend attending dinners and parties and listening to talk of politics until I was exasperated. Why couldn't they all see that Richard would make the ideal governor? He handled people so easily. The militiamen, in particular, respected him. And I assumed that he would be expected to travel to London to consult with the new Council for Trade and Plantations, the Committee of Gentlemen Planters, and likely, the King himself. I had been in Barbados for eight years by then, and while it had become home to me, I would have liked to return to England for a few months if I could have gone there as the wife of the governor of the richest colony under the English flag. Father wrote in a shaky hand that his health was failing, and Mama was crippled from rheumatism. I would have liked to see them and Foxley Manor again. Richard still doubted his chances, even if the King did heed Barbadian pleas to appoint one of their own as governor. But I could see a change in his bearing. His eyes were more alert than ever. Even as he protested that there were better men, I could discern behind this facade of modesty the churnings of a lust for power. He looked like a governor, even. Just as Esther Lawnton said, life was not fair for women. Men did as they pleased, and still they often, like Richard, became more handsome with age. True, his waist was thicker than when we married, his step a bit slower, and his hair had gone all gray along the temples, but he still exuded vigor and authority.

In the privacy of our room at the Bow Bells, Richard, with a perplexed look, asked, "What shall I do, Charlotte, about this matter of the governorship?"

I put my arms around him and said, "I think you would make the best governor this island ever had. And I think I might make a passable governor's wife."

He did not know, but letters from his friends supporting his appointment were already on their way back to London aboard the ship that bore Willoughby's body. Written to various influential men, they pointed out his military experience, his long residence on the island, his success as a planter, his knighthood and marriage to the only daughter of Sir Robert Foxley, and his support of the Royal tax on exports in 1663. The letters did not mention his going over to the Parliamentarians in 1651, his refusal to sail with Francis Willoughby in 1666, or his opposition to William Willoughby's annexation of Tobago more recently.

Nor did Richard know that I had posted my own letter to Father, urging him to use his influence with the king's ministers on behalf of his son-in-law.

Because the Assembly and the council were to meet Monday to consider how Barbados would be governed until the slow machinery of colonial rule would do its work in London, Richard remained in town, while a tired but excited Charlotte returned to Bolton Hall.

Richard was still there on Wednesday, dining with David Higganbotham and Harold Lawnton when a salute gun at Charles Fort announced the approach of a ship. Leaving their meal unfinished, they hurried down to the bay to watch a merchant ship and an English frigate beating their way up from the south.

The merchantman hove to at the entrance to Carlisle Bay and anchored there while the frigate drew closer to shore.

"Does she look familiar to you?" Richard asked David.

"She does indeed. But why would she be under escort?"

Richard borrowed the harbormaster's spyglass to confirm his identification.

"It's the *Mary Leigh* all right." Then to Lawnton. "That's the ship we came out on in April of '65."

A boat from the frigate soon brought the captain ashore, and he confirmed Richard's guess. "She is a slaver now. We escorted her over from the Gold Coast. She is in the service of the Royal African Company. Loaded to the gunwales, she is, with Africans."

"And is her captain still Thomas Williams?"

"You know the bloody little Welshman?"

"As a passenger, not as a friend."

"It is him, right enough. Little tyrant, he is. But a bloody good sailor for what they have given him to work with."

"I'd like to go aboard her. Wouldn't you, David, and you too, Harold?"

"They'll not want you aboard until they have cleaned up their cargo and thrown the dead and dying to the sharks. Hold your noses when you do go. I have tried to keep upwind of her all the way across."

Higganbotham was unenthusiastic about seeing the ship again, pointing out that he should be making his plantation rounds in Christ Church Parish, but Richard was insistent.

"The captain will remember us. Maybe he'll let us look over his cargo first. And, David, you are the best judge of black flesh I know. Furthermore, you know enough of their tongues to ask them questions. I need a few more hands, and so do you, Harold. This is a golden opportunity to get the cream."

"But the sugar harvest is over. They would only be to feed through the summer and fall."

"You will need that time to season and train them. You'll
do this for me, won't you, David?"

Without delaying for breakfast the next morning, Richard
hurried his friends to dockside to find that the *Mary Leigh* had
shifted anchorage closer to shore and that some of her sailors
were busy pulling buckets of water up by rope from the bay
while others were grouping black figures on the deck. Not
seeing any watermen up and about, Richard commandeered a
small boat and rowed his two friends out toward the *Mary Leigh.*

The odor of human excrement and sweat lay over the calm
waters of Carlisle Bay like an invisible fog. Higganbotham put
his handkerchief to his nose as they came alongside the *Mary
Leigh.*

"Boat ahoy! What do you want?"

Richard leaned on the oars and looked up. Captain Williams, who now displayed a potbelly and gray beard, glared
down at him.

"We want to come aboard."

"Well, you can't. Nobody allowed aboard until ten o'clock."

"Not even former passengers? Not even an old friend who
helped you bring your ship over in record time eight years
ago?" He took off his hat and grinned up at the captain. "It's
Richard Bolton. Don't you recognize me? And I have Doctor
Higganbotham with me."

"For the sake of sweet Jesus, Sir Richard! Of course, I
remember you. You really want to come aboard this stinking
tub?"

"We are determined to see our old seadog of a friend
again," said Richard.

On the quarterdeck they looked out over a black mass of
naked humanity, men and women, huddled in groups, eyes
blinking at the unaccustomed light, while the sailors doused
them with seawater.

"Smell bothers you, what?" Williams said. "You get used to
it. We lost only about twenty percent on the voyage. I understand that is lower than average. Some will die on you, no
matter what. Two of them jumped overboard early in the

voyage. Had my men watch them close after that. Nasty business, though, just so you planters can grow your sugar."

"This was your first trip then?"

"Aye, thirty years at sea, and I am reduced to commanding a slaver. I am a mind to retire when we get back to Bristol."

"The *Mary Leigh* looks quite different," Richard said absently, his eyes appraising the Africans.

"Oh, yes. More different than you see from outside. If you can stomach it, I'll show you about."

Richard did not really want to tour the hold, but he had to keep up the charade of interest in Williams and his ship. So with a wink to Higganbotham and Lawnton, he suffered the three of them to be shown below decks. In the place where his furniture and sugar equipment had been stored, in a space where only a short man could stand, now ran row after row of boards, five deep, only two feet wide, and sixteen inches between.

Higganbotham pressed his handkerchief closer to his nose. "They travel like this? There is hardly room to breathe."

"Oh, we bring them up twice a day and require them to jump about and dance. I would do it out of simple humanity even if the company rules did not require it. It's a bad business, I tell you, but someone has to do it, I suppose."

"How many did you bring over?"

"We began with two hundred. You will count on deck above, ninety-six males and sixty-four females. By the by, Sir Richard, you brought your wife out as I remember. How is she?"

"Very well, indeed, Captain. Thriving, in fact. She will be sorry to miss you."

"And you are doing well, I take it. Wouldn't you like to see your old cabin?"

"I am doing better than I deserve, and I *would* like to see our honeymoon cabin after I look over your cargo again."

Getting into the spirit of the occasion, Higganbotham waited until Richard and Lawnton had climbed the ladder back to the welcome fresh air topside and then put his hand on the captain's sleeve. "He is being modest. We just lost our governor. Yes, he died. There is serious talk here that Sir Richard will be named as his replacement."

"In truth? He is a real man, that one. I doubt not he would make a good 'un."

Even so, Williams was reluctant to allow them to select their slaves before the other planters had their chance. "There is supposed to be a scramble ashore later this afternoon. I violated the rules by letting you aboard before inspection time at ten o'clock."

Richard pressed his request as they were visiting the old cabin, now jammed with six bunks, since every square foot of space below had been converted for hauling Africans. He had almost persuaded the captain, he could tell, but when they returned to the deck and saw the newly appointed Bridgetown agent for the Royal African Company coming aboard, he whispered to Lawnton, "The game is up, damn it."

But the agent was a shrewd man, and he listened patiently as Williams told of his old friendship with Bolton. He had heard the talk of Richard Bolton for the governorship, and so far as he knew the other island candidates had slaves enough for their present needs.

"You know the price is seventeen pounds per head. No haggling."

"We do understand, Mister Stede, and you may be sure we will not disclose the matter. It is just that Mister Lawnton and I must return to our plantations, and it hardly seems fair that we should miss out on the scramble this afternoon."

"I don't think I could authorize credit under the circumstances."

"We can give you our letters of exchange on the spot."

"How many did you want?"

"Five each."

"They are grouped in lots of six. You can't go through the whole shipment taking your choice. No breaking up a parcel aboard ship."

"Fine with us, what, Harold? But we would like a few moments for Doctor Higganbotham here to examine the lots."

"Better make it fast, Sir Richard," the captain said. "Can't have you aboard when the others come at ten."

The sailors had tied the Africans with ropes. Each lot was a hasty mixture of sexes and physiques. Higganbotham looked them over quickly, stopping to require one to open his mouth and another to move his limbs. Where he saw early signs of yaws or an enlarged limb, he moved on to the next lot. Occasionally he stopped and ran through his repertoire of African tongues until he saw a face brighten, and when he did he asked a question or two. When he was done, he pointed to two lots. One included a robust male in his late twenties who, unlike the others, did not look down at his feet or appear terrified. In the other, the likeliest-looking African was a slender youth, dark brown in color rather than jet black, not yet fully grown, standing beside a potbellied boy of no more than seven who hugged a small drum as though afraid it would be taken from him.

"Those two are the best parcels," he said simply.

"Very well, Harold," Richard spoke up, "take your choice."

"No, no, Richard. You made this possible. And besides I want to stay on the good side of the next governor. If you don't choose, I shall buy none. I mean it."

Richard was not a man given to reflection, and it was a long time before he would understand what a crucial choice he made. He took only a moment to ask of Higganbotham, "That stout fellow who stares at us. Did you determine his tribe?"

"Fanti, one of the Coromantee tribes."

"Then the slender buck in that other parcel?"

"Whydaw."

Then to Lawnton. "You have any problems with Coromantees on your place?"

"No, I keep them apart and work them hard. I don't share the general prejudice about them."

"I'll take the second group. Let Harold have the Coromantee."

While the two planters made our their letters of credit and the agent their bills of sale, Higganbotham asked Williams if he might say something to all the slaves.

"You mean, make a speech?"

"Just a few words in their native tongues to reassure them."

"Can't see any harm in that."

So Richard, Lawnton, and the Royal African agent, as well as the crewmen of the *Mary Leigh* were amazed when the doctor mounted the half-deck with the captain's megaphone in hand and began shouting the same message over and over, in first one African language and then the other. As he began speaking a young Ibo girl looked across the deck at two of her fellow tribesmen and smiled, then three Pawpaws broke into wide grins, the stern faces of a dozen Coromantees relaxed, and when he was done, there was a hubbub of African speech arising from the deck, so loud that the alarmed sailors drew out their whips and belaying pins.

"What are you doing, Doctor?" Stede demanded.

"I just welcomed them to the island of Barbados. Told them it is a good place. That they will be well taken care of here, and they need have no fear if they behave themselves."

As Richard rowed them back to the dock, Lawnton looked suspiciously at Higganbotham.

"You seem awfully well pleased with yourself for one who did not want to go out with us in the first place."

"Yes, David," Richard said. "What did you really say to them to make them so happy?"

"Very simple. One of the Ga women told me they thought they were being brought over here as food for the white devils. They thought they were to be eaten. I told them we would not eat them if they promised not to eat us. Made a joke of it."

Richard roared with laughter. "I can't wait to tell that one to Charlotte."

Back at Cape Castle, Captain Williams had been shocked at the condition of the slaves brought out to his refitted *Mary*

Leigh. Their ankles and wrists were raw from shackles and their backs scabby from lashings by the middlemen—first black Denhyera and then white Englishmen—through whose brutal hands they had passed on their way to the mud-walled barracoon beside the sea. He had been appalled at the way agents of the Royal African Company crammed them down into the hold until they had filled not only every sleeping board but also the intervening walkways. Shocked as he was, Williams did not realize the full horror of his new business until he had spent a long, sleepless night listening to the moans and wails of his two hundred black passengers. He did not have to understand the languages of the laments to recognize the deep anguish they expressed. The next day, as the *Mary Leigh* drew away from the palm-lined coast, he allowed his black cargo to be brought on deck for a last look at their homeland. The women only wept, but a deep-throated groan arose from the first lot of males and, before the sailors could act, first one and then another leaped over the rail. With ankles and wrists shackled, they sank quickly. During subsequent exercise periods, the captain stationed his strongest crewmen along the rail with whips and clubs.

Quaco would have thrown himself into the sea had it not been for his son, Cudjoe. Not only did he feel a natural responsibility, but the boy was a comfort to him. In the dark, stinking hell below decks, he and Cudjoe talked about their life back in the village, speculating on the sex of the baby his wife carried in her womb and what the other children were doing. Back home, Quaco had held himself too aloof to be popular with his fellow villagers. Now he was glad to have the company of several who had been taken prisoner with him and Cudjoe. They joined in the conversations between father and son, offering the boy advice and telling him tales of old warring and hunting expeditions.

No one on that two-month voyage really got used to the horrible conditions, but at least there was more room as the weaker of body and spirit died and were thrown overboard. They were further relieved when Captain Williams began to allow his passengers to be brought on deck twice, rather than once, a day, to receive their gruel and water and dance to hornpipe music provided by a sailor.

At first, many of the Africans thought their captors to be not really men but some magical species without hearts or souls, able to make the wind carry their great craft where they wished and (after gunnery practice by the crew of the shepherding frigate) command the very lightning and thunder. But they revised this view after "the bloody flux" spread from hold to forecastle and six of the *Mary Leigh's* sailors died.

Then the little gray-bearded man the others obeyed did a thing that confused the Africans still more. He had purchased a small native drum at Cape Coast for his grandson in Bristol. Noting how Cudjoe hovered about Quaco, on impulse one day Williams handed the drum to the boy. The Africans were amazed at this, the first act of personal kindness they had experienced from a white devil. Tentatively at first and then with enthusiasm, Cudjoe beat out a rhythm on the drum with his fingers. In a few moments the deck flashed with dancing figures.

Williams had meant only to amuse the boy briefly, but when he observed his delight he allowed him to keep the drum for the rest of the voyage. Every night Cudjoe slept with his arms about the drum. And, instructed by the old Fantis, he learned not only a variety of ancestral dance rhythms but also how to send messages.

It annoyed Williams for the frigate's captain to leave him to anchor outside Carlisle Bay, as though ashamed to be seen in the company of a slaver. And it made him a bit nervous, too. After all, the *Mary Leigh's* hull was patched in two places where she had been struck by Dutch cannonballs eight years ago. But the rules of the Royal African Company were clear. He was to dispose of all dead and dying and to spruce up the living before entering the harbor.

Leaving the dirty work to his first mate, Williams oversaw the parceling of the living. He had noted how the Africans gathered in tribal groups on deck so he could separate them for sale. He placed Cudjoe and Quaco in different parcels.

"You want your drum back, don't you, Captain?" the bosun asked.

Seeing the tears in the boy's eyes, Williams shook his head. "It doesn't matter. Let him keep it."

Seemingly trivial at the time, certain such decisions— made quickly and arbitrarily—were to have enormous consequences: a captain's hasty groupings of his human cargo, his impulsive gift of a drum, a planter's selection of one parcel of slaves over another, and that same planter's waiting until the *Mary Leigh* had put her dazed, weakened passengers ashore, whereas his neighbor, Harold Lawnton, rode directly home and sent his overseer back to collect his parcel later in the day.

Quaco longed to be able to ask the strong man with the yellowish, graying hair what he meant to do with Cudjoe. The man bore himself as one used to being obeyed. See how the other whites hastened to follow his command to remove the chains from the three men, two women, and Cudjoe.

Quaco stood up in alarm as one of the whites lifted Cudjoe, drum and all, astride the horse in front of the yellow-haired one. The Fanti uttered a hoarse cry and took two steps before his weakened, shackled legs collapsed and he pitched flat upon his face. A group of whites with whips circled him, laughing.

Cudjoe, who had never seen a horse, wanted desperately to cry but feared the whites. He hugged his drum and closed his eyes. The white man smelled strange. He did not realize that Richard's own stomach could barely tolerate the stench of the slave ship that clung to the naked boy.

Richard was pleased with himself. The boy was not worth seventeen pounds but he would have paid even more for the other five in the parcel. They were just what Wilkens needed. He looked back to make sure they were keeping up behind his horse. Poor devils, there ought to be a way of bringing over more of them in good condition. He and Lawnton had often talked idly of leasing a sloop and sailing over to Africa to buy fifty or sixty direct from the slave pens at a third of the price they had to pay this damned monopoly. But that was illegal, just as it was to smuggle them in from Saint Eustatius. To have such a dealing on his record could hardly advance his chances to become governor.

Near Saint Thomas Church he encountered the Fulham Plantation overseer headed toward Bridgetown.

"Major Lawnton says he bought one particularly sturdy buck."

"He did that, Witherspoon. Gave me first chance but they said the fellow was a Coromantee, and I didn't like the look in his eye."

"I'll soon knock that out of him. Anyway, I'd take a parcel of gorillas, I am that shorthanded."

At Bolton Hall, Wilkens was delighted by the addition of five slaves to his work force. He walked around them, smiling.

"Look clean as a whistle to me."

"They should be. Doctor Higganbotham selected them."

"The women, did you inquire as to their tribe?"

"Both Whydahs, I believe."

"Shall I give one to Cromwell?"

"Yes. Let him take his pick."

"I'll wait a bit before mating up the other."

"Just don't get any ideas for yourself, Wilkens. Mistress Charlotte has strong opinions about that."

5

... Mirabel, Clemmie, Toby, and I gathered in the back yard under the bearded fig to witness the arrival of Richard holding in front of him a little African with a drum. The boy looked like a frightened animal, and he smelled to high heaven.

"A little something I picked up in Bridgetown. Toby, meet your new assistant. Start him in the garden. After we have tamed him, he can be Clemmie's houseboy. Make him an arseabout and start teaching him English."

He handed the child to Toby, who set him down disdainfully and asked, with wrinkled nose, "What tribe is he, master?"

"At his age, what does it matter?"

We must have looked very strange to the boy. He stared into our faces one after the other and then ran and buried his own in Mirabel's apron. She bent and spoke to him softly, then, taking his hand, announced, "His name is Cudjoe."

Richard repeated the name several times, each time altering the pronunciation until it came out "could you."

He grinned and said to me, "Madam, could you see that Cudjoe gets a bath? The smell of the slave ship is in his hair."

Although he was under the direct command of Toby, Cudjoe quickly became Mirabel's boy. I don't think he ever understood why we laughed when someone sent him on an errand with "Cudjoe, could you get the wine bottle?" but the joke lost its point when we adopted the diminutive "Joe," despite his timid efforts to correct us. I wish now that we had inquired further about him ...

A sense of peace came over John Martin as he turned his horse onto the path and dismounted to lead the animal through the overhanging bushes. Old Tom had kept the hut in good repair. His hammock still hung in its old place. John chased away the monkeys who trespassed now that the angry old man was not about.

It was a good place after all, John thought. Without Tom jabbering at him, it would make a retreat for the times when he grew weary of his medical practice and Doctor Higganbotham's company.

He tethered his horse and set his bottle of wine and packet of food on the ground, then leaned against a mastic tree to gaze out across the expanse of cane lands and groves that stretched down terrace by terrace to the vivid blue of the sea. He drank from the wine bottle, ate a banana, and took another swallow of wine. Despite the cruelties of slavery, some unavoidable, and the grasping natures of many planters, he reckoned this was a good enough land for those willing to apply themselves. Now that he was accepted as a doctor, he saw no reason to leave the place. What would he be now if Moses had not nailed his broadside to the cathedral door in Bristol? A tailor or, at best, a petty merchant. Curious thing, he thought as he drowsed off, he would have been more of a prisoner in England than in Barbados. There was freedom to rise above one's origins out here.

Later John could not be certain just what awakened him. He came to with the feeling of being watched, of there being a presence in the bushes nearby. Did he only imagine that he heard breathing? A chill crept down his spine, just as it had done when Tom claimed to have spoken with Moses. He reminded himself that he was a man of science, not an Obeah man. Yet he did hear the bushes moving. And it was unnatural how the monkeys had stopped chattering and the songs of the birds had halted.

He forced himself to face the bushes. "Father?"

No answer.

John could bear it no longer. He stood up. "Can't I be left

in peace? I have suffered enough. Why can't you leave me be to get on with my life?"

The bushes parted and out stepped a naked black man with his wrists shackled in front of him, holding a whip in his pinioned hands. His ankles were thick with scars and scabs; a fresh welt across one shoulder and arm oozed blood. Even though his ribs showed and his legs were thin, he was built as well as any black John had seen. And the wild look in his eye marked him as an untamed African.

"Who are you?"

John could not understand the man's mumbled reply. Suddenly he wished that he had heeded his clients who advised him to carry a brace of pistols on his rounds. The two men watched each other. John wondered if he had the strength to subdue this desperate Negro. There would be a reward for him, and it would help his reputation to return a runaway to his master. But the African made a gesture that dissipated John's gathering resolve. Whip tucked under one arm, he held out his shackled hands toward the parcel of food by the mastic tree.

John smiled and pointed to his mouth. Palms outstretched, the man nodded. John picked up both the food and wine and advanced gingerly toward the Negro, who took a half step backward. John set the bottle and food on the ground and slowly retreated.

Like a snake striking, the African scooped up the lunch and disappeared into the ravine.

John knew that he had behaved stupidly, perhaps even criminally in giving food to an escaped slave and making no move to capture him. But he did not regret what he had done. And he never told anyone of the encounter.

By Barbadian standards, Harold Lawnton was an easygoing man, but he did scorn slackness in others and hated losing something for which he had paid. He felt like murdering his overseer.

"Witherspoon, you are a fool. You actually let him pull you off the horse and ride it away?"

"He took me by surprise, and the horse shied just at that moment. Next thing I knew I was lying on the ground, stunned."

"And the others did not try to follow him?"

"Not after I fired my pistol at him. That frightened them. Major, you would have to a' been there to understand."

Once more the overseer explained how he had been escorting the parcel of slaves along the road, "with no sign of trouble until we got to the Apes Hill road and I seen the Coromantee was lagging. I rode over and laid the whip a good one across his shoulders and the whoreson grabbed it. Made the horse shy and jerked me out of the saddle while I was off balance."

"So I have got to pay out good money for slave catchers."

"I'll get him back, Major. When I get through with him, you won't have a more docile field hand."

"If you don't, I shall have to go looking myself."

"No need to trouble yourself, sir. I am quite capable ... "

"I meant for a new overseer."

Quaco would have gone along without resistance had he known he was being taken so near to Cudjoe. But he had no idea of the island's size or, for that matter, that it was an island. All along the way from Bridgetown, he had been studying the strange countryside so bare of forests with everything covered by the same tall grass. They were traveling north, and he felt in his bones that Africa lay just behind his right shoulder. He told himself that the mountain to his right would make a good vantage point. But he had not meant to try to escape so soon, while his legs were still weak. When the man on horseback struck him with the whip, he had reacted without thinking.

Quaco had never been astride a horse. It had been a fearful experience, clinging to the mane and bouncing wildly in the saddle. He was fortunate in passing no one on the road; indeed he might have ridden all the way to Hillaby's peak had a family of monkeys not frightened the horse. The animal reared, and it became Quaco's turn to lie stunned on the ground. The horse tossed its head and trotted back toward the Fulham stable.

Quaco had watched John Martin dozing against the tree for several minutes. Hearing him speak, he had thought there might be other white devils about. He did not step forth until the man arose and faced him as though aware of his presence.

Sleepy from the food and wine, Quaco slept until sundown in a thicket on the other side of the ravine. By the light of a full moon, he made his way across cane fields to a patch of virgin forest near a peak and there slept until after sunrise, awakening to the sound of African voices from the waist-high cane in an adjoining field. About thirty women and boys, watched by a white man on horseback, were digging out weeds with short-handled hoes. Quaco crept to the edge of the grove and listened. The women spoke pidgen English until the overseer rode to the shade of a cedar tree for water; then they lapsed into their native tongues. Quaco recognized a few words of the Akan language, which his tribe shared with other so-called Coromantees. They were spoken by two women, one of whom carried a baby strapped to her back.

At mid-morning, the slaves stopped work to receive gourds of water from a naked boy. The woman with the baby left the line to nurse the child beside a tree in the edge of the grove. Quaco sneaked to within a few feet of her and whispered, "Sister."

"Who is there?"

"My name is Quaco."

"What are you doing here?"

"They brought me here with my son. They took him from me, and I escaped. How long have you been their prisoner?"

"Ten summers, now. I am used to it. But I dream of our homeland every night."

"Sister, I am hungry. Have you anything to eat?"

"Wait." She called to the woman with whom she had been speaking. "Tell the boss I go into the forest to do my business."

Placing the baby on the ground, she slipped behind the tree

and sat down. "Come, brother, and I will give you what I have."

Had he not been so hungry, Quaco would have felt like a fool, a grown man sucking at the breast of a woman, like an unweaned toddler. The milk was thin but sweet. Her breasts were full and he drank greedily until the woman started at the call of the overseer.

"He want me back."

"Where can I go, sister?"

"My hut lies over there beyond the windmill, the tower with the great arms. Count five huts from this end. Come to the window at the rear. My husband is an Ibo, but he will not betray you. I will have food for you. Come when the moon is directly overhead."

The overseer called again and spurred his horse toward the grove.

"Coming, boss," the woman sang out.

As she picked up her baby, she said softly, "Brother, I will not tell my husband you suckled me. He is jealous."

The baby, its own hunger unsatisfied, began squalling as the woman took up her hoe again.

That night she was waiting for him at the window with roasted yams and cassava bread. As he wolfed down the food and drank water from the calabash gourd, she whispered, "My husband says you cannot escape from this island. There is a temporary hiding place they call the Thickets. White servants and Africans take refuge there as long as they can. Head just to the right of where the sun rises. Sooner or later they will catch you though. Africa?"

She said something in the bastard tongue learned from the white man. Her husband laughed and replied in a scornful tone.

"He says the Thickets lie in the direction of Africa, yes. He says if you were an Ibo, you would have the sense to know you cannot escape the white man. Now you must go. I can do nothing more except give you this bunch of plantain."

Reaching out in the darkness, Quaco took the fruit and touched her breast. "Thank you, sister. You are a true woman."

Quaco might have been even more grateful had he known that the woman had given him most of their week's rations.

Sleeping by day, it took him three moonlit nights to make his way the twelve miles from the shoulder of Hillaby across Saint John Parish to the underbrush that covered most of Barbados's southeast corner. He arrived near dawn, weaker and hungrier than ever. This part of the island reminded him of Africa. And he could smell the sea. He pressed on through the bushes until he could hear the surf. Finally he stopped at the brink of a cliff above a rocky, narrow beach and sat down to wait for a miracle.

There were two of them, and they were Irish. The dark one with the Galway accent had been shipped to Barbados for stealing bread from his landlord; the other, with a fair complexion and a saucy Cork lilt to his tongue, had pledged five years of his young life for passage to Barbados just to escape from his stepfather's tyranny. Now they had run away from their master's plantation in Saint George Parish. Working in this island's heat was bad enough, but their jobs around their English master's sugar mill were more than they could take. For weeks they had stockpiled food and laid knives and extra clothing in preparation for their escape.

"Look there, what's that?" Cork said.

"It's a Naygro, naked as the day his mother bore him," Galway replied.

They tiptoed, with knives in their hands, close to Quaco. "Is he breathing?"

The other winked and untied the rope that served him as a belt. Cork put his knife point against Quaco's throat while Galway gently bound his ankles together.

Quaco dreamed that he was back in his hut and that his wife was tickling his feet. He groaned and tried to move his legs. Now she was slapping his face, not playfully but sharply.

Quaco opened his eyes to see the knife. He tried to raise his arms, but the other man had his foot on the chain, pressing the links into his belly. He struggled for a moment and then fell back, exhausted and gasping.

"Must be starved. Glad he is. Expect it would take both of us to handle this one. What shall we do with him?"

"Slit his throat and roll him over the cliff," Galway said.

"I'll not be a party to a wanton murder. I don't want that on my conscience."

"Well, as he is not an Englishman, you may be right. What will we do with him?"

"Let's see if we can tame him. Might use him on the boat."

"Oh, yes, just what we need. Charges of helping a black-amoor escape."

"We are in for a sheep; might as well make it a Naygro."

The other youth laughed at this reference to the lamb they had filched from the last plantation they had passed before reaching the Thickets. That hapless creature was tethered to a bush beside the gulch where they had established their lair.

Quaco did not resist when they untied his legs and put the rope about his neck, nor when they led him the quarter mile to their camp. He was convinced they had been sent to catch him. He sat down, all hope gone, and watched numbly while the Irishmen cut the lamb's throat and caught the blood in a gourd dipper. He was amazed when they gave him the dipper.

He slept deeply that night, as his body restored itself from the strength of the lamb's blood, and awoke the next morning to smell meat roasting and to hear the Irish youths arguing good-naturedly over what to call their captive.

"King Charles."

"Nay, Cromwell."

"The island is full of Cromwells. How about Martin Luther?"

"Better yet, Henry, after their king of old."

Quaco wondered what was so funny. Seeing his eyes open, the fair one pointed to himself and said, "Kelly," then to his companion, "O'Halloran," and to Quaco, "You?" After several repetitions, Quaco understood. Pointing to himself he said, "Quaco. Fanti."

"Quaco Fantee? Well, it is plain he is no Irishman unless it is that he hails from Galway."

They laughed at the way "Quaco Fantee" devoured the roasted lamb. When it dawned on him that these young white men meant him no harm, that they were treating him as a kind of companion, he laughed too. They rolled about on the ground saying "Quaco Fantee can laugh," and "Come on, Quaco Fantee, let's see ye smile again."

Harold Lawnton's overseer, Witherspoon, did not intend to lose his job. The next morning he saw the slave catcher in Bridgetown, a swarthy fellow with the sad eyes of a hunting dog and bearing the scars of his trade: little finger of left hand bitten off by a black runaway and a knife scar across the other hand, inflicted by an Irishman who then had to be shot.

"A Coromantee? Headed for Apes Hill? Five pound reward?"

"Six pounds if you recover my whip."

The slave catcher looked at the overseer with contempt. "You let him take your whip?"

"It was an accident. Will you go after him?"

"I was about to go looking for a couple of Irish servants ran off the other day. After I catch them maybe."

"Look, I can't return without him. It would mean my job. Let me go with you. I'll help you find the Irishmen, and we'll press on after my African. I have a pistol and a horse."

"Expect you'll want me to break him for you as well."

"You help me get him back, and I'll take care of the breaking."

The whip might be considered their undoing. They were amusing themselves and Quaco by snapping it at lizards sunning themselves. Cork was ahead five lizards to three and was saying, "It's a pity Quaco Fantee can't try his hand. How will we get those irons off his wrists?"

"Oh, we'll find a way. Steal a file somewhere. See there, that makes four. Big one, too."

Quaco was puzzled by the pair. They no longer kept his feet bound. They acted like fugitives of some sort themselves. He recalled that the Akan-speaking woman referred to "white servants." He wished he could talk to them.

"Wait, Kelly, did you hear a dog?"

"It's only the hounds at the place where we took the lamb. Naught to worry about."

With no lizards in view, O'Halloran snapped the whip so that it kicked up the dust at Kelly's feet. "Here, let's show Quaco Fantee how an Irishman can dance."

"Look out there. Don't do that again."

"Oh, it's orders ye are giving now, like an Englishman."

He snapped the whip again, and Kelly set his foot on the lash and bent to seize the shaft.

"No, you don't." O'Halloran jerked at the whip but could not free it from Kelly's grasp. The game turned into a tug-of-war with neither able to break the other's grip.

Quaco understood they were not serious, but he wished they would stop. He, too, had heard the dogs.

Kelly released the whip abruptly, and as O'Halloran stumbled back he leaped upon him, trying with both hands to wrest the handle away. He got an elbow in the ribs and responded with a knee against a thigh.

Quaco stood up, trying to warn them to be quiet, but they ignored him, laughing and taunting each other. "Come at me again, Kelly, and I'll brain you, so help me God."

"Brave talk. You had the whip long enough. It's my turn."

"Look, you are upsetting Quaco Fantee."

And then it was too late. The dogs were upon them, and a shot flew over their heads. The Irishmen ran down the path toward the sea, but the slave catcher and two other men stood astride it with guns cocked and aimed. Quaco ran the other way, into the arms of Witherspoon, who knocked him down with his pistol butt.

*

Having learned his lesson about Quaco, the overseer bound the African's arms and noosed a rope about his neck with the other end tied to the saddle. In that fashion he led the warrior down to Bridgetown and thence back to the plantation. He saved the whipping until they reached the privacy of the curing shed.

"Don't kill him," Lawnton said. "He is no good to me dead."

"I won't kill him. Just make him wish he was dead."

"And I don't want his back cut to ribbons."

"I'll use a strap."

Once Lawnton left, the overseer drove his fist against Quaco's jaw, knocking him down. He did that three times and then, with the help of a white servant, tied the African's hands to an overhead beam. He flogged until his arm grew weary and he had to stop to catch his breath, but still Quaco showed no pain, did not once cry out.

The overseer sat down and wiped his face. "I wish I could use the whip on him or a hot poker. Here, you try it a while."

The servant remembered his own early floggings too well to have his heart in it, so the overseer took over the job again, until Quaco's back became a mass of broad, low welts. He whipped until Quaco passed out.

"Never saw such a stubborn one."

"Ain't he had enough?"

"I believe in whipping them until they cry and beg for mercy. Then you know they are ready for training. Until he cries out, I must keep on."

The overseer heated a poker to a red glow and held it close to Quaco's face, but still the warrior showed no fear. He tried flogging again, but his arm gave out.

"Damn it to hell. They want results, and they tie my hands. Could strap him on one of the windmill's sails and spin him around but no, that is too public. They don't want to be thought by the neighbors to be cruel. I wish it was curing season. I'd make him think we were going to throw him in the furnace or put his arm in the grinders. Or drop him into a boiling vat."

The man had got the petty spite out of his system; he had more than evened the score for being dragged off his horse, and now he wished he had left Quaco in the hands of the slave catcher, but it was too late for that. His reputation was at issue. What made this Coromantee so unyielding? He looked into Quaco's eyes. "Boss," he pointed to himself and motioned that Quaco was to repeat the word. Quaco looked at him with contempt.

"Boss," the overseer reiterated, and in response to his signal the white servant pointed at him and said the word, too.

"Boss." No reply. The overseer struck him across the face with the back of his left hand to spare the swollen knuckles of his right. "Boss."

"I don't think he understands," the servant said.

But Quaco understood very well. He himself had tortured prisoners in Africa. There one's captors did not care about him once the surrender of manhood was made. But these white people wanted more than a show of fear. They wanted to reduce him to laboring for them in their tall grass. Giving in would be only the beginning of his humiliation. And since he had no hope ever of seeing his homeland alive, or his son, let them kill him. Perhaps it might be true what some of those on the ship had said: If they died, they would fly back to Africa.

Lawnton came to the curing shed to find the overseer near exhaustion and Quaco hanging unconscious again.

"Can't break him?"

"Not yet. But I will. And if I fail, we can always have him gelded."

"Let's not be hasty. He will make good breeding stock. You are letting him get the better of you."

"Why, Major Lawnton, I have broke dozens. I know my job."

"Do you know the fable about the contest between the wind and the sun to see which could make the traveler remove his coat?"

"Can't say as I do, sir."

"I will explain it to you sometime. What other Coromantees do we have here?"

"That Mandze woman you got from Bolton Hall."

"Of course. Had any trouble with her?"

"No. Cicero keeps her in line. The other women don't like her, but she makes no trouble."

"Send her to me. Meanwhile, let our wild stallion hang there."

Mandze sat on a stool waiting for the African to regain consciousness. Here was a man, she thought. If they had to mate her like an animal, why could it not have been to this fine man, whom they said was of her tribe? They could have done worse than give her to Cicero, though. Since he had authority over the slaves, she received grudging deference from them as well. But nothing would ever be the same as it had been when she was the woman of the yellow-haired one, when she was practically the mistress of his great house. If only she had been able to bear him children, he might not have brought that anemic-looking one back from his own country. She had not yet borne him a child either. Mandze was glad of that.

Quaco awoke and stared at her for several minutes before she was aware of it. It had been a long time since she had spoken Akan.

"Brother, you want water?"

He nodded, and she filled a dipper from the pail at her feet. He drank it noisily, and then she poured another dipperful on his head, gently. Even more tenderly she ran her fingertips over his welted back.

"You are in pain?"

He looked at her, mistrustingly.

"Listen, brother, and let me tell you something. There is no end to their cruelty as long as you resist them. You may think that you can outlast them, but they are powerful, and they are cunning, and they will never give up. Do you know what they will do to you if you try to run away again?"

Quaco's eyes narrowed.

"They will tie you down, and with a sharp knife one of their doctors will take away your manhood. Never again will you enjoy a woman. And you will end up doing as they want anyway."

Quaco's lip curled. He did not like what she was saying or the fact that she was saying it. He suspected a trick.

"Some Africans think they will fly home if they die here. Let me tell you that, if you kill yourself, they will put your head on a stake so that the others will see and bury only your body. There is no escape from this place. I have been here since I was a girl, and I know. But there are ways to get around the white man. He is so puffed up that you can play on his self-importance and make your life more tolerable. There are many worse islands that would make you long to be back here. Listen, brother, and I will tell you how to survive here."

Mandze talked to him a long time. Besides offering advice on survival, she spoke of her memories of growing up in Africa and related the stories she had heard her father tell around their cook fire. She told how she came to be captured but said nothing about her long concubinage to Richard Bolton. At last, despairing of his replying to her, she arose and gave him another dipper of water.

"Remember what I have said, brother. It would be a shame if so fine a warrior as you were made a gelding."

"Well, Mandze?" Lawnton asked when she came out of the curing shed. "Any luck?"

"He listened, but he would not speak."

"Thank you for trying, Mandze. You shall have a new frock for this."

"I do not want a frock, master."

"Then what do you want?"

"I want you not to geld that man. I will speak to him again, as often as you wish."

"I will not say yes to that, Mandze. But I will not say no, either. Not yet."

*

The next morning when the arm-sore overseer and the servant opened the curing shed door they found Quaco standing flat-footed with his shoulders thrown back and his head erect, smiling.

"He's gone mad," the servant said.

"Let's see." The overseer walked closer to Quaco and blue eye stared into black with neither blinking.

"Who am I?" the overseer asked, pointing to himself.

"Boss," Quaco replied, and still smiling, looked down at the floor.

6

. . . The idea of Richard's going back to England to campaign for the governorship upset me at first. "Why, that would mean being apart for six months at least," I said when he proposed it.

But my ambition for him caused me to relent when he explained how it would help if he could lay his case directly before Lord Shaftesbury or even see the King himself.

Still, I did not like the idea. Besides missing Richard, I was dismayed by the prospects of my managing Bolton Hall throughout a planting and most of a harvest and curing season.

"You will be so busy it will help the time pass," he said.

"But, oh, Richard, I would so like to see a play in London once more. Would you really bring me back a trunkful of new books? And would you promise to ride up to Foxley Manor? You could bear one or two nights in the same house with Mother. Once she knows of the governorship she would welcome you."

I did not like the way he was grinning. "You don't want me to go with you, is that it? You must promise me you will have nothing to do with any woman in England."

"And I don't want to hear reports of your playing me false with a certain doctor of medicine."

"David? Don't be silly."

"Or, our tailor's son. Both of them are always mooning over you."

"I am not sure that a man who talks such rot is fit to be governor. If you can't tell how madly and faithfully I love you, then you really are a fool."

He turned serious. "Quite right, dear Charlotte. I do trust you there and in managing Bolton Hall, with Wilkens's help, of course. I would not dream of going to London without you if I could count on Wilkens to continue your good care of the health of the slaves."

Richard was never to know how much that offhand compliment meant to me. I looked at his face closely to see if he were being sarcastic. Then I kissed him. "I will permit you to go then, Your Excellency. And don't worry about Wilkens. I can deal with the little tyrant."

That Richard. What a one. He talked his way aboard a sloop-of-war leaving the very next week. I stood on the dock at Bridgetown waving to him until the craft cleared Carlisle Bay, and then I galloped Nutmeg back to Bolton Hall to watch the white sails headed north.

Clemmie brought down a large mirror from our bedroom and with that I flashed the sun's rays in the direction of the sloop. My answer came in the form of a salute from one of the vessel's aft guns. Richard had thought he could persuade the captain to let him do that. Persuasive man, my Richard Bolton. I prayed that the King and his advisors would react to him as most people did.

Those first few weeks were lonelier than Charlotte had expected. It was too early to begin planting the next crop, and the one that would be harvested early next year was advanced far enough so that it no longer needed weeding. She was afraid

Esther Lawnton would tire of her company. They had talked of everything, even their slaves.

"Our little Joe is priceless," Charlotte said. "Like a little wild creature that must be tamed, but Mirabel is working wonders with him. He seemed to think that tending garden was woman's work, but she has slapped that notion out of his head. And he is picking up English amazingly fast. Richard said Harold bought a parcel from the same ship. Is he as pleased with his lot as Richard is with ours?"

"Generally, yes. We had trouble with one buck. A Coromantee who escaped on the way here from Bridgetown. But they recovered him in the Thickets with two Irish runaways. And now Harold says there is not a more willing slave on the plantation."

"Is he the stalwart fellow who stares so boldly?"

"He is stalwart, all right. Why do you ask?"

"I noticed his eyes following me as I rode in."

"He will learn not to do that. It takes a while. At first Harold was afraid he would have to have him gelded he was so wild, but then . . ." She caught herself just in time from blurting out the role of Mandze in the taming of Quaco. "But then, Sambo came around when he saw we were not going to eat him."

"Sambo? Don't you have one of that name already?"

"We did, but he died last Easter and the title was vacant. Do you miss Richard very much?"

"It is as if half of me has been separated and sent off across the ocean."

"You two are very close, aren't you?"

"Very. Why?"

"Harold and I were close in England. But then he came out here without me, and when I joined him, it was never the same. Just now and then, almost. Anyway I am glad that Richard will be away only a few months."

"Not half as glad as I."

The afternoons were the worst time. Before the midday heat of the Barbadian summer closed in, she rode around the plantation to see and be seen by the slaves, and then spent an hour or so in the office with Wilkens, whom she kept off balance with sharp questions and reminders. "A regular monster, she is," he complained to the Lawnton overseer. "Treats the slaves with more respect than she does me. Hope Sir Richard does become governor. That will keep herself busy doing what she is suited for, giving teas and holding balls and such."

Charlotte welcomed John Martin's weekly visits. With Clemmie safely married, she saw no reason not to invite him to take dinner with her. It was difficult for her to stop thinking of him as the frightened lad she had first seen on the steps of Saint Paul's. Someday, perhaps she would reveal to him how she had paid for the purchase of his indenture. He acted so solemn and wise as he discussed this slave's case and that. She would like to make him laugh as he used to do before his father's death.

"What about your land, John?"

"Oh, it is still there, Lady Bolton. It is of little value, but I do enjoy riding up there to enjoy the view and think."

"John, we have known each other for nearly nine years. Now that you are grown into a man, you really need not call me Lady Bolton any longer. Charlotte will do."

"Oh, Lady Bolton, that would not be proper would it?"

"If we are to be entirely proper, I would have to call you Doctor Martin. Is that what you want?"

Charlotte enjoyed seeing him blush and hearing him stammer, "Not at all."

"Then say it. 'Charlotte.'"

"Charlotte." He broke into a smile to match hers.

He stopped by again near noon at the end of the week on his way back to Higganbotham's plantation.

"Why, John, what a pleasant surprise. It is good to see you."

He had rehearsed his speech a hundred times the past few days and he prayed his voice would not crack. "We were talking about my place up Apes Hill...Charlotte. You liked it when you came there before. I thought you might like to see it again."

Charlotte was about to decline when, as if reading her thoughts, he added, "There is a way to ride directly from here by path instead of taking the main road. A short cut."

Still she did not reply, and he began to wish he had kept the idea to himself. "I mean to go there anyway, and I thought to take a bit of lunch along. But if you think it not right to go, surely I would understand."

"I could not stay long."

His face brightened. "The short cut would save much time."

"Very well, John. I'll get a bottle of wine and some fruit."

John's heart sang as their horses picked their way along the rough trail that led from Bolton Hall's easternmost fields, along the border of the next plantation and to the Apes Hill Road. Alone with her at last. And on a new footing, more nearly as equals. He looked back to smile at the vision of grace she presented, holding her bonnet with one hand and balancing herself easily while riding sidesaddle.

"Not much farther."

"I remember."

He helped her dismount so they could walk along the overgrown path to the clearing. As John tied their horses, she removed her bonnet and gazed at the sea.

"What a grand place, John."

"I was not sure I wanted it at first."

"Because of your father?"

"Yes."

"Poor John, you miss him very much, I expect."

He was ashamed to tell her the truth, that he did not so much regret his father's death as he did the manner of it and the months of shame the man's mania had caused him.

"I hope you are hungry."

They ate the fruit and drank the wine as they sat beside the same tree where John had dozed when he heard Quaco laboring for breath in the bushes. Now he was alert, his heart pounding from the wine and the excitement of having her alone and so close. He wondered if he dared say the words, if he ever again would have the opportunity. Her overbearing husband was across the ocean. She had urged him to call her by her first name. She had accepted his invitation to come up here as readily as in his daydreams. Yet, he might spoil everything if he spoke out. She was so quiet now. He must say something. If he let his timidity put him off, he would despise himself for letting such a chance slip by.

He drank another swallow of wine and took a deep breath. "Charlotte."

She turned to look at him, startled in the midst of her own reverie.

"I can't keep this to myself any longer. Have you any idea how much I love you?"

"John!" She was frowning, but once started the words came tumbling out.

"For years now I have felt this way, and I was afraid you would laugh at me. I have told myself it was wrong, but then I see the way your husband treats you, the way he pokes fun and dominates you." He was concerned by the expression in her eyes and the way she had drawn herself erect, but he could not stop.

"I dream about you at night. I think about you all day long. I would do anything for you."

"John, please."

"Have I offended you? I will kill myself if I have."

"No, John, you have not offended me. You said you would do anything for me. Did you mean that?"

"Yes, anything."

She arose and tied on her bonnet. "What I want you to do is forget what you just said to me. Some women might be insulted, or at least pretend to be, but I know you meant no offense."

"I just told you honestly how I felt."

"I understand, but, John, one cannot always act on one's feelings. If everyone did so, our world would be a most disorderly place. Whatever gave you the notion that Richard mistreats me?"

"It is just the way he speaks to you sometimes, as though he thinks you are a fool."

"You don't hear some of the things I call him. No, John, I love my husband deeply, and he loves me. There can never be another man for me."

"What am I to do? I feel like a fool."

"What you can do is go on being a fine doctor. And get interested in some young lady. Perhaps more than one. You have never had a sweetheart, have you?"

"No."

"Then it is past time you did. With your new profession and your good looks, well, suppose we have a party sometime to help you broaden your circle of friends. Will you let me do that for you?"

"That would be very kind," John said. But actually he was thinking this would give him occasion to see Charlotte more often.

"You are not angry with me?" John asked, eyes downcast.

"No, John. I considered you my friend before this, and I still do. I just hope you understand that is all there can be between us. For a moment I regretted coming here with you, but now I am glad you told me so there can be no further misunderstanding. I really should return to Bolton Hall now, John."

She let him help her remount her horse, but when he offered to escort her back she declined, but with such grace that he felt relieved. He watched her ride away until she was lost from view.

It was a mark of Charlotte's maturity that she was not more flattered by John's declaration of love. At night the erotic intensity of her dreams sometimes awakened her, but the man was nearly always Richard, or someone very like him. Still she was fond of John. She and Esther gave two dinners in his honor, to which they invited the daughters of nearby planters or merchants in Speightstown, but to their knowledge no romantic sparks were struck.

"The lad is backward," Esther said.

"Give him time," Charlotte replied. "He had a bad boyhood."

"So attractive a young fellow should not go to waste."

"I don't call his fine work as a physician a waste."

"Oh, Charlotte, you know what I mean."

In retrospect, 1673 was a good year in Charlotte's view, what with a satisfactory harvest before Richard's departure and, under her nominal supervision, a successful planting for the crop that would mature in 1675. Meanwhile England made peace with the Dutch so that shipping could move freely again. And there was the prospect of the governorship for Richard.

In late November, Charlotte received a letter from Richard dispatched in September, two weeks after he had arrived in London. It told of his meetings with the Gentlemen Planters of London and the Council for Trade and Plantations and what he deemed their favorable response to him. The next ship from London brought a letter telling of his visit to Foxley Manor. "Your father is quite feeble now. His eyes have grown so dim he must hire a clerk to read to him. Your mother, beyond a rheumatism that requires her to walk with a cane, is her old self, only grown more mellow toward me. By the by, your old love, Harbinson, remains unmarried. Still carrying the torch for you, I expect. There is talk of him for Parliament."

Each of the letters ended with love passages so intimate that Charlotte was embarrassed to show them to Higganbotham or the Lawntons. She kept the letters by her bedside and read them at night just before retiring, as fuel for her dreams.

But the most thrilling letter came just at Christmas time. It told of being taken by Lord Shaftesbury to meet the king at Whitehall.

After I had knelt he told me to arise and had me sit while we chatted away of several things. He recalled, or affected to, his knighting me. He asked many questions about Barbados and listened politely enough, and then he expressed his displeasure at the opposition of our Assembly to his 4½ percent tax. I had to sit quietly and listen to him complain of all the petitions and letters that come over to him about our need for naval protection and free trade and an end to the slave monopoly. "My dear Bolton," he said. "Wherever did you Barbadians gain the notion that you are a nation unto yourselves, independent of or at least only allied to England? I am weary of all this bickering over a tax that yields little enough to the royal coffers even when paid. I must tell you that I will brook no more opposition to it. You people out there have become too independent, I fear. You pass laws on your own. You appoint people to royal offices. I intend to tighten the leash, I must warn you. Now Shaftesbury tells me you want to become Governor."

I had practiced my speech well, taking care not to sound too cocky, just as you warned me, my love, and I flatter myself that the words came out smooth enough. He did me the honor of listening carefully. I expect to know before Christmas of his decision. I hope to return to you as Royal Governor, and my first act shall be to command you to go directly to bed without a stitch of clothing. Ah, my darling Charlotte, I yearn for you. You are in my every dream, and I can hardly bear our separation.

That letter was Charlotte's Christmas gift. By now he would know. If only thoughts could fly across the ocean. How could she wait until word came by ship?

Quaco received a Christmas present as well, even though he did not know what the season was all about. Harold Lawnton had a young female slave named Tippie just past puberty but already attracting the lustful attentions of other slaves and therefore becoming a problem. Tippie had been born in Barbados, and English was her only language. Hearing words of praise for "Sambo" from his overseer himself, Lawnton decreed that Tippie should be given to the African as his mate. Mandze explained it to Quaco.

"I have a wife."

"But she is in Africa. This girl will be your wife now."

"What shall I do with her?"

"Does a Fanti have to be told?"

He took the girl into the hut that had been assigned them. The other slaves laughed and called out rude remarks at the girl's squeals and cries. Quaco had kept his lust locked deep within his soul, but now it burst forth again and again savagely.

Tippie was a mixture of Whydah and Ga, so thoroughly Creolized that she hardly knew any African words. To Quaco, there was no comparison between her and his old wife, the mother of his children, a real woman. Although he was glad to have Tippie for sexual release, he took her without any feeling of love, treating her fearfulness with contempt, even laughing at her tears. Partly because she came from tribes his people despised and partly because he felt uneasy at being handed her by the white man rather than winning her for himself, he did not appreciate her as several other slaves would have. Indeed, that Christmas night, with his lust slaked and his loins wearied, a great sadness came over him. The other slaves were dancing about their cook fires, laughing and singing, and they did not miss him when he slipped away to go and sit by himself on a cart beside the cattle pen. Facing Africa, he was wondering what had become of his wife and children, when he heard the drum from the north. Holding his breath, he turned toward the sound.

There it was again, and this time there was no mistaking the rhythm that Cudjoe had learned in the foul hold of the *Mary Leigh*. Quaco ran to the other side of the cattle pen so that he could hear better. All doubt gone, he raced toward the sound.

Mirabel would not allow Cudjoe to beat on his drum when Charlotte or Richard were at home or when Clemmie was sleeping, and he was not permitted to wander away from the grounds. But this evening, while Charlotte was at the Lawntons, all the slaves were celebrating the white man's Christmas under the supervisions of Wilkens and Toby. They thought Cudjoe was already asleep, but there was too much noise coming from the Negro yard, and, feeling restive, he had stolen away with his drum to the great windmill. High up on the stone ledge just under the hub of the arms he seated himself and relearned the beats that had been taught him by the older Fantis. At first he tapped hesitantly, afraid that someone would come and chastise him, but when they did not he became bolder and bolder.

Running through his repertoire took him back to his mother and brothers, to those days of security and freedom. Louder and louder he tapped until a low voice spoke from the dark in Akan.

"Is that you, Cudjoe?"

Wilkens had got off on the wrong foot with Charlotte from the first, during the Dutch attack on Bridgetown, when he questioned her ability to ride a horse. She had formed a lasting dislike of him during their ride out to Bolton Hall on that momentous day. She had never forgotten his surly, offhand way of answering questions. And, perhaps unfairly, she associated him with her dismal introduction to her new home. It seemed to her that he had enjoyed her dismay at the conditions she found there.

The ensuing years had not made their relationship any warmer. She still disliked his drawling Suffolk accent and his slouching posture. Also, she sensed in him a streak of suppressed tyranny toward their slaves and a contempt for her because she was a woman. She sensed, also, his resentment of her cleverness at winning better rations and clothing for the slaves. Or was it jealousy that they respected her more than him?

Had Charlotte not been so prejudiced, she would have realized that Wilkens actually was an efficient overseer. And she would have recognized that he was devoted to her husband. But, no, in her view Wilkens was merely a little farmer's son who enjoyed far too much authority over the lives of a hundred other human beings.

Richard had been among the first planters to give their slaves Saturday afternoons off as well as Sundays. He had done so against the advice of Wilkens, who now brought up the question with Charlotte.

"I don't see how we can make this harvest with so few hands. I wish we had bought another parcel off that slave ship."

"Well, we did not, and the cutting will have to start next Monday morning."

"I had thought to begin Saturday."

"I see no point in spending but a half day in the fields."

"I did not mean to allow them Saturday afternoons off this season, seeing as we are so shorthanded. Nor Sundays either."

"That is a decision for me to make. We did buy six new slaves you know."

"So you did, but the two women are both with child now and unable to work very hard, and you took the boy as your yard servant. Without the master here, I will not be able to spend as much time in the field, and the work will not go as well."

"I can oversee the fieldwork myself."

"What? I mean, that would hardly do. It takes a strong hand to keep them at it."

"Nonetheless I intend to relieve you in the fields, so that you can spend more time at the sugar works. And I do not intend to deprive the slaves of their Sundays off in any circumstances and their Saturday afternoons only after we have demonstrated the harvest cannot be brought in any other way."

"Now see here, Lady Bolton. I am the overseer, and I have had considerable experience . . . "

"You see here, Wilkens. I am the mistress of this plantation. My husband and I are the owners of those slaves, and we will decide on their treatment. Further, I don't like the tone of your voice. You are forgetting your station."

Always before, Wilkens had knuckled under. Charlotte was unprepared for his "You can like the tone of my voice or not, Lady Bolton, but if you are going to pay no attention to my opinion, I am not sure I want to hang about taking orders from a woman."

Charlotte was enraged. "How dare you speak to me like that? You have no choice but to do as I tell you."

"I completed my indenture before you arrived here as a green girl from England, madam. I am not a slave. And there are other plantations that would welcome an overseer of my experience."

Richard would have known how to placate Wilkens with a joke or with a compromise that would have saved face for both, but Charlotte, besides being angry, lacked the skill to extricate herself, and so she pressed on.

"You must not threaten me."

"I am not threatening you. I am only telling you that I have had other offers for my services."

"And you wait until the eve of harvest, when my husband is across the ocean, to tell me this?"

"No, I waited until you ordered me to do something when you don't know what you are talking about. And I will leave unless you let me alone."

Charlotte felt ready to strike him with her riding crop. "Let you alone to do what?"

"Work the slaves straight through, yes, and flog them that don't keep up. They need some of that as an example."

"And if I relent my orders, would you remain?"

"I would," Wilkens said, but then he made the mistake of smiling and adding, "providing that you stay out of the fields as well."

Charlotte closed her eyes for a moment to shut out the sight of his smirk and to try to get control of herself. She remained so until Wilkens became impatient and demanded, "Well, what is your answer?"

She opened her eyes and smiled. "My answer very simply is that I want you off this land by sundown."

7

... There were many times during the next two months when I would have begged Wilkens's pardon and taken him back with an increase in pay if he had reappeared at Bolton Hall. But that first day was not one of them. I sat for a long while alone in the office wondering what to do. I was furious at the insolence of the little man and furious at myself for bungling things so. Then the thought occurred to me: "What would Richard do?"

Forthwith, I sent Toby to fetch Cromwell, our master boiler, and Caesar, the giant field hand. I invited them into the office one at a time, but said the same thing to each.

"You know Mister Ramsay who owns Gaelic Hall?"

Our Scottish neighbor was and still is notorious among both whites and blacks in the northern parishes for his cruel treatment of his slaves.

"I hear he wishes to purchase experienced slaves like you."

I hated myself for the look of fear that came over their faces, but I was desperate.

"I do not want to sell you to Mister Ramsay. I will not if you do as I tell you."

Now I had their attention, and I told them of Wilkens's dismissal. To Caesar I said, "The Master thinks you are a good worker. The other slaves respect you. I am putting you in charge of the cane cutting. You understand? You shall carry a stick but strike no one without my permission. Just make certain that the work is done properly. If it is, you shall receive a reward. You and your wife will get new clothing after the harvest, and I will ask the Master to build you a new hut with two rooms and give you a pig for your very own."

To Cromwell: "Everyone says you are the best boiler they have ever seen. You know how the grinding and curing is done, as well. I am putting you in charge of the sugar works."

"Everything, Mistress?"

"Everything. You will take your orders from me. If anyone lags, tell me, and I will have them whipped. You will direct the others. You understand?"

Cromwell had not smiled so since Wilkens awarded him the young Whydah wife.

In each case, I closed the interview with, "It will be necessary to work Saturday afternoons and Sunday mornings. The hands will have only Sunday afternoons free until we are sure the harvest is going well. Then, after the sugar is all in the curing shed and the molasses is barreled, everyone shall have three days free with rum and new clothing for all."

Thus did I step into the breach, which I had created. Many another woman had managed her plantation in the absence or at the death of her husband. There was no reason why I could not. People who thought me nothing more than a pampered wife and charming hostess would see what I was really made of.

There was no time for missing Richard after that. Dressed in a simple skirt and light cape and wearing a mannish hat, Charlotte became a dreaded presence, first in the fields talking to Caesar and then at the sugar works checking on Cromwell's progress. She stuck one of Richard's pistols, unloaded, in her belt and carried her riding crop like an officer's baton.

Higganbotham and John both stopped by to see her, but she made it plain she had no time to visit with them. While the field hands took their midday rest, she toured the sugar works. She napped briefly at dusk, then went back to make sure the furnaces were kept going into the night. Her only real sleep came after midnight. Every dawn the slaves awoke to see her sitting on her horse at the edge of the Negro yard, impatient to herd them out to the fields.

Caesar and Cromwell were awed by her. Until now she had showed a kindly interest in their health and housing, but now she was like a demon woman driving them on. They had passed word of her threat to sell laggards off to the dreaded Ramsay plantation, and after seeing her attention to every detail, they did not doubt her determination.

Charlotte no longer had time or energy to keep her diary. She was driven by a fierce will to prove that she could manage a plantation and by the belief that her putting Bolton Hall into good shape would leave Richard freer to concentrate on the governorship. Her other motive was to make the profits necessary to replace their old wooden house with a new one of solid stone, large and fine enough to serve as a governor's mansion.

She reflected often on what an excellent governor her Richard would make. He knew just how to handle people. And she would make an equally good governor's wife. Together they would transform Barbados into an outpost of English culture, complete with a theater and libraries. Who knew, in time she might win a dukedom for him. Wouldn't that be a title: Lady Charlotte, Duchess of Barbados?

These visions sustained Charlotte in the midst of a demanding reality and drove her to harder effort, until David protested. "I don't like those circles under your eyes. And you appear to be losing weight. Why not let me ask one of the larger plantations to lend you an overseer?"

"No, I brought on this situation, and I will see it through."

But, alone in her room, when she looked in the mirror and saw how haggard her face had become, Charlotte was tempted to relent. Even though exhausted, she often could not sleep for worrying about a broken cart axle or the scorching of a vat of syrup.

Clemmie got a tongue-lashing for remonstrating with her for not resting. Dispatched by Esther to offer advice and help, Harold Lawnton reported, "Except for looking so weary, the girl has things running as smoothly as if Wilkens were still there. I fear she is paying a high price personally . . . "

Esther laughed. "You said 'girl.' I think you mean 'woman.' "

At first a few slaves tested Caesar's authority, but a threat to report them to their mistress brought them in line. "The devil woman," some called her. If she would banish the powerful Wilkens, what might she do to them? And the female slaves noted with pleasure how the great oaf Caesar sweated with fear when she came about. Also, the women felt gratitude to her for winning them better clothing and more time to recover from childbirth. So Charlotte worked her will over Bolton Hall. She was glad no one could see the anxious wife hiding behind her stern facade.

By the end of March, with over half of the crop in, Charlotte allowed the slaves all of one Sunday free. Finding herself unable to relax in bed as planned, she rode over the fields to plan the next cutting. She had gained a fresh respect for Richard. Whereas she exhausted herself managing an already established plantation, he had cleared the land, built the mill, bought and trained the slaves, and scraped up the finances, all the while playing a large role in the political and military affairs of the island. He could not have achieved so much had he been overly solicitous for his slaves, nor could he have survived long in this politics-ridden land without being what some might call "an opportunist." He was right when he said this was no job for a fool or a weakling.

Near sundown she rode out again to the sugar mill. The great sails were disengaged and the furnace fires banked. To think that each vat, ladle, puncheon, and spider, every barrel stave, hoop, and piece of grinding equipment and pipe had to be brought by ship from England or North America. Even the oxen now lying about chewing their cuds were imported from New England. All this so that people in Europe could have sugar in their tea and on their strawberries.

She was surprised when she rode her horse around the corner of the curing shed and nearly ran over Cudjoe carrying his drum.

"What are you doing out here, Joe?"

"I play my drum, Missie."

"Well, don't play it too loudly."

When she looked over her shoulder a few minutes later, the boy was running toward the slave cemetery. In the growing darkness she could not discern a man in a loincloth leaning against a tree and watching her.

The day of rest restored the slaves' vigor, but Charlotte felt vaguely unwell all day. Her head ached, and her limbs were weak when she lay down at dusk to nap. Past midnight she awakened in a panic. She sat up and tried to swing her legs off the bed. She called in Clemmie and chastised her for letting her oversleep.

"Oh, Mistress, you looked so tired."

"Silence! Have Toby bring my mare to the door and help me dress."

Once clothed and on the veranda, Charlotte found her vision blurred. The brilliant tropical stars appeared like white splotches in the sky, and the glow of the furnaces at the mill formed indistinct streaks of red. She forced herself to breathe deeply of the cool night air, while Toby brought Nutmeg to the mounting block. She put one foot on the block but lacked the strength to step up. With Clemmie at her elbow and Toby looking on anxiously, she sat on the steps, frustrated and drained.

Clemmie touched her forehead. "Oh, Mistress, you are so hot. Come along, please."

Half carried to the bedroom and tenderly undressed by Clemmie, Charlotte drifted back into a sleep fraught with wild dreams. Wilkens smirked at her and mocked her weakness. Her mother refused to comfort her, saying, "I told you not to come crying on my shoulder." King Charles stood at the foot of her bed and declared, "Ah, well, if the fellow's wife can't manage his plantation for him, we can hardly make him governor." And in yet another dream, the field slaves gathered cane so rapidly that Cromwell could not keep pace and a mountain of stalks accumulated beside the mill.

With Esther looking on, John Martin checked Charlotte's pulse and listened to her breathing.

"She has been neglecting herself."

"I tried to warn her, but you know how obstinate she can be. I think she was trying to show that a woman can run a plantation as well as a man."

"She won't be able to do much of anything for a long while."

They left her sleeping. When she awoke, the Lawntons were arguing in the hallway outside her closed door.

"Damn it, Esther," Harold was saying, "I cannot afford to take the time to run Bolton Hall as well as Fulham. I know she can't find a good overseer in the midst of harvest, but it is not our responsibility."

"Would not Richard come to your rescue?"

"I think not. Not if you stupidly chased off our overseer and were too full of pride to ask for help earlier, when it might have been available. Not if you waited until he needed every hand for his own work. Not if you had always acted superior to other people, or if you spent your time pushing me in politics and then, without previous training, plunged yourself into supervision of a plantation. Do you really think Richard would drop everything and rush over to help you out of a situation you brought on yourself?"

"You are being too hard on Charlotte. She is a brave woman. We cannot let her down. Nor Richard."

Charlotte felt a surge of anger at Lawnton's words, but she kept quite while John mounted the stairs to shush them.

"I could hear you downstairs. You will disturb Charlotte."

"My wife thinks we must let our crop go to ruin to save Bolton Hall's."

"What is required?"

"Mainly a white man to serve as overseer. And I don't know where one can be found. Nor can I spare the time for searching."

"My duties are not overly heavy just now," John said. "I

could sleep in Wilkens's old cottage, keep an eye on Caesar and Cromwell, and look in on Charlotte from time to time."

"That may be the only answer," Lawnton said. "Charlotte should be thankful you are willing to bail her out of a difficulty she brought on herself."

Charlotte clenched her fists at Lawnton's words, but when Esther looked in on her, she pretended to be asleep.

Lawnton accompanied John to the Negro yard and addressed the assembled slaves. "Listen well. Your mistress has fallen ill. Doctor Martin will be in charge until your master returns. You will do as he says, or I will bring over a whipper."

The slaves looked sideways at each other.

"You shall have your Sundays off henceforth," John said.

"Mistress, she tell Caesar we get three days off and rum rations when crop over," a woman said.

"So you shall, Portia, if you work well."

"Enough!" Lawnton commanded. "To the fields."

Like other Barbadian slaves, those at Bolton Hall understood the white man better than he understood them. In the past thirty years, the blacks had developed great cunning in dealing with their masters. They had worked out a common language, a brand of English, spoken with the accent of the Irish servants from whom the early slaves had learned it. Most discerned that they got along better by pretending to agree with their masters and overseers and if they acted simpleminded. After all they were only one, albeit a major one, of the white man's concerns. They did not have to worry about borrowing money, buying equipment and animals, or finding sugar markets. They had far more time to observe and analyze the white man. At Bolton Hall, they knew just how hard to work so that Wilkens would not ask Richard to flog them. A few of the older ones remembered when Richard had become the owner, and, curiously, they felt a pride in him. Also he had sold off enough rebellious slaves in the early days so that he did not have to resort to threats. Justice, or rather discipline, had been evenhanded under Wilkens and Richard, and the slaves had accepted the status quo as the best they could expect.

They had regarded Charlotte's demanding regime as a temporary threat to their security. Everyone knew how erratic a woman could be. No one wanted to become the first to test her rule and find himself working under the lash of that devil, Ramsay.

But here was a new situation. They liked this young white doctor as well as they could any of his race, but they did not fear him. At the sugar mill, John had few problems. Cromwell worked to please himself, out of pride in his craft. He had a bad temper and now took to wielding a stick to enforce his rule. His temper grew worse very quickly, for he often ran out of cane to grind. The field hands, taking John's measure, worked at a leisurely rate, just fast enough to avoid a summons to Lawnton but slow enough to frustrate Caesar and infuriate Cromwell.

"Please, young master, take the whip to them," Cromwell said.

"I do not believe in whipping."

"Then let me go to the field. Caesar can hold them, and I will whip."

"You shall do no such thing. And you must not strike anyone here at the mill."

Thus Cromwell was forced to slow his production. The progress made under Charlotte's stern eye was lost.

John was so pleased to see Charlotte twice a day that he did not fret over the delays in the harvest. Always before, Charlotte had been in command of their relationship. First, when he was a green, frightened lad and she had seemed such a grand lady, then later, even when she affected to treat him as an equal, he had remained in awe of her wit and poise. He had never regretted his confession of love, but there, too, she had been in charge. Now he was controlling her. She ate what he told Clemmie to prepare, took the medicine he prescribed, followed his orders for rest, and, further, he was in command of her plantation. It pleased him mightily to see her lying listless and beautiful, still too weak to speak very long, seemingly content to hear him talk. And talk John did, more freely than he had to anyone since his father's death.

The work at Bolton Hall continued, slower than it should have, but the cane was not yet rotting in the field. The Negroes stepped up their pace when John watched, but slacked off when he left. The harvest fell even further behind during the second week of Charlotte's illness. John did not understand the danger of letting cane overripen. His mind was on Charlotte, not cane.

After two weeks, Charlotte was able to spend part of each day on the veranda. Her vision still blurred, she could not see well enough to discern the signs of slack work in the cane field. There was no reason for her to doubt John's naive reports that the cutting and curing were on schedule.

Then at midweek, John was summoned to a plantation near Speightstown to attend to an injured slave. This left Caesar entirely on his own to oversee the cutting crews.

On the veranda, Charlotte had fallen asleep over a book.

"Mistress."

Old Cromwell stood by the porch steps, leaning on his stick, a worried look on his face.

"What is it?"

"We got trouble in the yard."

"Trouble? What do you mean?"

"They no come out of huts."

Cromwell explained that the field crews had dragged their feet all morning. Then, when Caesar tried to end their midday break after one hour, the men pretended not to hear him. His threats of a whipping only made them laugh.

"I come. I beat them with stick. They run into huts. They still there."

Charlotte listened, shocked at his complaints of poor production for the past two weeks. She closed her eyes, wondering what Richard might do. A slave mutiny could not be ignored. She could summon the militia, but that would disturb the work at other plantations and advertise her own failure to manage Bolton Hall properly. Next she thought of sending Toby to ask Harold Lawnton's help. But she remembered the critical words she had overheard him say outside her bedroom when she had first fallen ill. No, she would not give him the satisfaction of witnessing her failure.

"What will we do?" Cromwell asked.

"Fetch an ox cart. Bring it to the steps here." She turned to Clemmie. "Bring down my robe and hat. The master's brace of pistols, too. Toby, I wish a large glass of wine laced with honey. And while you are inside, get me the old whip that hangs over the doorway."

Charlotte's head ached at every turn of the cart's wheels over the rutted lane to the line of huts that constituted the Negro yard. With her hat pulled low over her eyes to keep the brilliant early afternoon sun from her eyes, and Richard's pistols thrust in her belt, she braced herself with one hand on the cart rail while holding the whip in the other.

At the Negro yard, with Caesar standing on one side of the cart and Cromwell on the other, Charlotte took a deep breath. She prayed that the glass of sweetened wine would see her through.

Then, with a hand on a pistol butt, she spoke.

"Now listen carefully all of you," she said. "If you do not come out and return to work immediately, I will send for the militia. Come out of there."

Getting no response from the slaves, Charlotte handed Richard's old whip to Cromwell. "Take a brand from that cook fire. Now set fire to that hut on the end. You heard me correctly. Fire the roof."

The boiler waited with whip poised, until the flames caught the thatch. When a man and woman scurried out, he and Caesar lashed them until they shrieked for mercy.

"Now the next hut," Charlotte commanded.

"Wait, Mistress," the woman inside called. "We come out."

Within a few minutes, eighty-odd Negroes were standing sheepishly outside their huts. Charlotte pointed at the blazing roof with her pistol. "Put out that fire." There followed a scramble to beat out the flames.

"I shall return at sunset. Anyone who does not work this

afternoon will be whipped. You hear that, Caesar? Now back to the fields."

Exhausted, Charlotte returned to her bed. She slept straight through until dawn the next day. Although still feeling weak, she had Toby bring around the ox cart to transport her back to the Negro yard. She was addressing the slaves when John Martin hurried up from the overseer's cottage.

"We have fallen behind. You have been lazy. Today you will eat in the field and keep working. We must keep up. The master will return soon. He will sell you away from Bolton Hall, any of you who do not work hard."

Hearing of the trouble the day before, John apologized.

"I can't blame you, John. Running this plantation is too much for one person. If you would oversee the mill henceforth, I will manage the cutting through Caesar. I think I have their attention now."

John laughed. "From what I have seen, that is rather an understatement. Just don't tax your health."

"I am on the mend now, thanks to you, John."

There was no more trouble with the slaves, not that year. Reflecting on her behavior at the Negro yard, Charlotte again recalled Esther's words: "They are very different, and I fear their presence makes us different . . . "

Odd, how Charlotte had come to look forward to the sound of John's footsteps on the stairs. Just as he had begun to speak to her in a less hesitant way, so he walked with a surer stride. But, really, he was being presumptuous, clomping into her house as though he owned the place. He could at least send up Clemmie to announce him.

The door swung open, and there stood not John, but Richard, looking paler and grayer than Charlotte remembered, but Richard all the same, smiling rather sadly. Before she could say more than "Dear, Lord," he had seated himself on her bed and taken her in his arms.

All the anxiety of the past seven months came pouring out

in her tears, until he asked, in alarm, "Are you so grieved to see your poor old husband?"

"Not grieved, you lovable fool. Relieved."

She gained control of herself enough to blurt out the story of Wilkens's defection and her taking over the full management of Bolton Hall, but before she could finish he interrupted. "Don't fret yourself. I saw Harold on the road. He told me."

"Did I do wrong to dismiss Wilkens? I have dreaded your disappointment."

"And I yours."

His face sagged, and his eyes look pained. She held out her arms. "I cannot live without you. You don't know how I missed you."

"I am most sorry, Charlotte."

"For what? I brought this upon myself."

"No, the governorship. The king chose another of his courtiers. Jonathan Atkins. He will come over later this year." His voice broke, and for the first time she saw tears in his eyes, as he said, "Oh, Charlotte, I have been on a fool's errand."

She wondered at her own calmness. "It doesn't matter. It only matters that you are home again." She smoothed his hair and tried to put from her mind her dashed hopes for him and herself.

Later, at the sugar mill, Richard listened to Cromwell's complaints against Caesar and the field hands and against John Martin for his refusal to punish the laggards. He found John in the curing shed watching the slaves knock out cones of sugar from a row of pots. The youth glanced up, first with a look of recognition and then of disappointment.

"Sir Richard. You are back."

"So I am, *Doctor Martin*. I understand I am in your debt for overseeing Bolton Hall during my wife's illness."

"I was glad to do it."

"Yes, well, I need not detain you any longer. I will get things back in good running order again."

John flushed at Richard's cold tone.

"You must not be angry with Charlotte. She drove herself so hard I fear she harmed her health."

Richard frowned at this unaccustomed use of his wife's first name by one he considered his inferior. "Quite so. Well, Lady Bolton need worry no more. And we will not detain you any longer from your medical rounds. I should not like to cause you to neglect your other patients."

John waited for some further word of gratitude, but Richard had turned his attention to the sugar the slaves were spreading out to dry.

"If I may be of any further service . . . " John began.

Without looking up, Richard replied, "You have done too much already. Just add the charges for your time to your next bill."

John struggled for words to express his indignation at this offhand treatment, but he gave up the attempt and walked away. Anything he said would only make him sound foolish and guilty. How could his lovely Charlotte care for this selfish, arrogant man?

That night, feeling secure for the first time since Richard had left, Charlotte lay awake, treasuring his closeness. He had been too tired to talk for long but had told her enough to make her eager for him to awaken and answer more questions about her family, London, the king, and their new governor. She had that to look forward to and also the new books to be carted up from dockside in Barbados. They could not have come at a better time, during a convalescence. And she ached for him to know how efficiently she had managed Bolton Hall. At last she fell into a peaceful sleep with her arm across his chest.

She awakened when he started to rise. "Don't go. Not yet."

He turned on his side, facing her. "I have a thousand things to look after. You will have your books and other gifts to amuse you today."

"There is one gift I would like to have now, while the house is quiet."

"Surely, you are too weak for that."

"Let me be the judge." She kissed him, holding him close.

"Perhaps if I am very gentle."

"I cannot think of better medicine."

Later, in a pleasant stupor, she still would not let him go, and finally he relaxed and told her more about the way London was rebuilding from its great fire of 1666 and more of his meeting with King Charles and his visit to Foxley Manor.

"I had half a mind to remain in England and send for you after I learned of Atkins's appointment."

"That would have been stupid. We belong here, together."

During the rest of the cane harvest, Charlotte spent her days reading the books he had brought back from London. Lying on the veranda's bamboo couch, she found that she could savor life in Barbados in a new way. She took pleasure in little things such as a quickening of the breeze, smelling the fragrance of her long-neglected jasmine, and watching ships through the long glass Richard had brought her from England. And watching him, too, as he rode over the fields, directing the cutting crews. Sometimes he caught sight of her peering at him, and waved or made a face. She wondered if it were only her imagination that everyone from field hand to house servant felt more secure now that he was back. There were times when she ached with regret over his failure to become governor, but generally she was pleased simply to have him home again.

John was another matter. He came with Higganbotham to check on her progress. She did not know of Richard's rudeness to him, but did notice that John hung back and let David ask the questions. They agreed that she was mending nicely and would continue to do so, as long as she did not overtire herself again.

"John has been an angel to me," she said. Then, at the sight of his reddened face, added, "And we could not have got our crop made without his help."

"I am not sure your husband agrees with you on that point," John replied.

"Now, John, Richard is not given to effusive praise," David said. "Certainly he is grateful to you."

"Of course," Charlotte said. "We both are. Richard has had a rather severe disappointment, I fear. So have I."

"The governorship," David said.

"Yes, but he will be all right, so long as he stays busy. And so will I."

8

. . . It saddened me to discern in Richard a bitter streak after his return. The thing went beyond his natural disappointment at his ruined hopes for the governorship. He thought he had made a fool of himself for going to such lengths to seek the post. He imagined that folk mocked him behind his back for his ambition. And he was unforgiveably rude to poor Harold Lawnton when he tried to commiserate with him.

His drinking bothered me, too. It seemed to me that he consumed far more wine after he had been back to England, but I assumed that he would become more temperate as he settled back into his old way of life.

I would never admit it to him, but he hurt me with his lukewarm appreciation of the way I ran Bolton Hall in his absence. He remembered well enough my dismissal of Wilkens but made no reference to the fact that I got us through most of the harvest despite my breakdown, or that I put down a slave mutiny as adroitly as could have any man. Surely he recognized my ability to have completed a profitable crop, even if he had not returned in time to relieve me. Perhaps he simply did not like to admit a woman's competence. Anyway, I had proved to myself what I could do, and I was determined that henceforth he would treat me as a mature woman nearing thirty, and no longer as a girl bride.

It was curious how much more serene I had become. Women are, I think, more realistic minded than men. Although I had fairly lusted to be the wife of the governor of our land, once I saw it was not to be, I accepted the fact. But part of my acceptance grew out of a sense of having demonstrated my own abilities. In my youth I had been arrogant because of my supposed intellectual superiority. This feeling was different. I had been tempered by the fires of heartbreak and adversity.

Richard and I had our first quarrel after his return over my promise to give the slaves a three-day holiday at the end of the harvest. Because of their brief mutiny, he felt they should forfeit the reward. I pointed out what little pleasure they had in their lives and how it might feed their discontent to deprive them of something to which they had looked forward. He was quite adamant, but I got around him by enlisting Esther. She persuaded Harold to grant Fulham's slaves a similar respite on the assumption that Bolton Hall was doing so. She persuaded him further to combine the celebrations of the two planta-tions. I relayed this information to Richard with the comment that it would make him look exceeding mean in the eyes of the Lawntons should he refuse. And he then came around. Men do force women to be devious. And clever.

Quaco was pleased to learn that the slaves of Fulham Planta-tion would join those of Bolton Hall for a joint celebration. That would give him an opportunity to see his son in the open. Tippie was pleased, too. During the past few weeks her fear of the grim African had been replaced first by affection and now a sincere love. She liked seeing how other women admired him. It was an honor to be his wife.

*

In addition to the Lawntons, Richard invited a fellow militia colonel from near Speightstown, a bald, dropsical man named Bates, and his wife to join them for the "crop over" festivities at Bolton Hall.

Late in the afternoon Richard called the slaves together and thanked them for seeing the plantation through another harvest and then doled out a gourdful of rum to each adult who wished it.

Colonel Bates arrived in a coach driven by a paunchy, white-haired Negro with wise eyes.

"Hope you don't mind I brought Cuffee along. I have had to give up horseback. Piles, you know. Cuffee is too old to make trouble with your wenches, and he brought along his flute in case you want music."

Shortly before the sun went down, the Fulham Negroes marched over under the eyes of Harold and Witherspoon. The Boltons joined them and the Bates couple on a platform laid across two farm wagons in the Negro yard. At a signal from Richard, Witherspoon, the overseer of Fulham, set a torch to a huge pile of woodscraps and cane trash.

As the flames lit up the faces of the circle of black faces, Cuffee drew out his flute. Soon its discordant music was joined by that of a stringed calabash gourd. With the rum singing in their blood, the Negroes began to sway and chant. Then out came two bone rattles and, to everyone's surprise, the tattoo of a drum sounded.

Clemmie was watching with disdain what she considered to be an uncivilized spectacle. "Joe," she said. "Who said you could bring that thing down here?"

"Hand him up here," Richard said.

Embarrassed by the attention, Cudjoe sat at the feet of his master, dangling his legs over the edge of the wagon. Cuffee motioned for the other musicians to join him in front of the boy, and soon they were playing in unison. Faster and faster Cudjoe's hands struck the ends of the drum, and, at a command from Richard, all the slaves of the two plantations paraded past their owners, clapping their hands and dancing sedately. Afterward, they formed into circles and began in earnest. The slow-moving tempo quickened. Instead of merely clapping their hands and shuffling, first one and then another slave began jumping and twisting in the firelight. Soon the bodies of all except the oldest were going through what appeared to Charlotte to be primitive contortions. She was shocked at their violent to-and-fro pelvic motions, but the slaves were past minding what she thought. They were no longer chattel who could be bought and sold or worked to death like farm animals; their music briefly set them free, as free as they or their parents ever had been in Africa. The dipping and swirling bodies glistened with sweat, but Cuffee's face remained dry and his eye calculating as he shrilled his ancient melodies to the cadence of the boy's drum.

From the shadows on the other side of the bonfire, Quaco gazed upon his son and the whites on the platform and listened intently to Cuffee's flute. Near midnight, after the bonfire had died down and the dancers were exhausted, Witherspoon shouted for the Fulham Negroes to form up to march back to their plantation. Quaco edged close to the wagon, motioning Cudjoe to say nothing.

He spoke to Cuffee in a low voice. "You play like a Fanti."

"I am a Fanti, brother."

"Can we talk? In the dark."

"Yes, but we have little time."

In a few minutes Witherspoon bellowed, "Sambo. Where is he? Sambo?"

"Here, boss." Quaco grasped Cuffee's hand and stepped from the shadows to join his wife in the line.

The gift of a drum, the chance selection of one parcel of slaves over another, two women maneuvering their husbands into holding a joint crop-over festival, an offhand invitation for a third planter to join them—all these decisions, while inconsequential in isolation, began to form into a fateful chain. The vital link, it might be argued, really did not spring from anyone's conscious decision, however. Colonel Bates did not *decide* to develop hemorrhoids. And it was only because of them that Cuffee gained the opportunity to move about the lee coast of Barbados as a messenger for his master, with no white supervision.

As Bates liked to say, "Trust Cuffee to get a thing accomplished. If he was white, I'd make him my plantation manager and retire to London."

Yet another link was formed by Witherspoon's decision to put Quaco in charge of Fulham's cattle yard. After a generation of cane cultivation and erosion, the soil of Barbados was losing its fertility, and the only way to restore it was with manure. Some small landowners made a living by keeping livestock and selling off their droppings to large planters. Most plantations, however, kept oxen, sheep, pigs, and horses in pens that they shifted from field to field as a way of natural fertilization. The slaves who looked after animals got more freedom than the closely watched fieldhands. It was a mark of trust that Quaco was made a herdsman.

So, it was not thought amiss when Cuffee interrupted his ride to Bridgetown to pass a few words with his fellow Fanti at the cattle pen beside the road, or later, when his master and mistress again visited the Boltons, that he spent much time under the bearded fig tree talking earnestly with Cudjoe.

The first time Richard came home drunk from Bridgetown, Charlotte thought little of it; indeed, she enjoyed seeing him unwind. He rode into the rear yard, bellowing out a bawdy song, and after Toby helped him dismount she upbraided him in a mock Irish dialect.

"Sure, Richard Bolton, and it's a grand disgrace ye're making of yerself for all to see and hear. I'll not be able to hold up me head before others. Have ye no thought for the feelings of yer dear wife to bring upon her such shame?"

He fell into the charade with, "Aye, and it's lovely ye look when yer eyes flash so, me gorgeous colleen. Come, be not cold and uncharitable. Drink wi' me to show it's forgiven I am."

"Only a wee drop and no more. It's a good girl oi am. It's after debauching me that ye are."

She helped him undress and thought it amusing that he fell asleep in the midst of a fumbling attempt to make love. She was ready the next morning with a mug of strong coffee. Her only admonition was to warn him against riding abroad at night while drinking. "I'd hate to be a widow."

"Don't lecture me. This head is punishment enough."

Soon after her recovery and his return from England, Charlotte offered to take over the plantation books. Richard expressed surprise at her grasp of the affairs of Bolton Hall.

"Perhaps we should not be in a hurry to find a replacement for Wilkens," she said. "It would only be another expense, and I expect the cost of your trip must have run rather high."

"High enough."

Charlotte was hoping he would tell her the exact financial condition of Bolton Hall. The ledger and account books covered only the immediate expenses for supplies and the weight of the sugar sent off to warehouse. Records of bills of credit and merchants' loans were kept by a lawyer; Richard seemed reluctant to discuss these transactions.

But she pressed her point about doing without an overseer until he flared up with, "I'll be the judge of that. Surely I haven't come so low that I must drive Negroes into my old age."

"I only meant that I do not mind keeping the books if it would leave you free to oversee."

"I'm sorry. We could make do until the next harvest, but we should not wait until the last minute to start looking."

Although Charlotte cited the savings as an argument for postponing a new overseer, her deeper reason was to keep Richard busy. No longer did his old supporters come around to talk politics and, in his absence, command of his militia regiment had passed to a younger man. She wished that he shared her love of books but, no, it was all business and politics for him. She knew that he would mope with one of those avenues closed.

Meanwhile, it seemed that he welcomed excuses to be away. One night he came home late and drunk from Speightstown, and another time he remained away overnight, without advising her, at Oistin's Bay, talking to planter friends in taverns about prospects to take Wilkens's old job. So Charlotte was much relieved in July when he announced that he had found an overseer who would report to work immediately.

"Name's Croxton. About thirty. A Cockney who came out as a soldier with Brooks's regiment two years ago. Sent back for his wife. Worked last season as assistant overseer down in Christ Church Parish."

Richard did not tell Charlotte the circumstances of how he recruited Croxton, and it was fortunate for her peace of mind that he did not. It happened at the venerable Mermaid Tavern on Oistin's Bay, the site of peace negotiations twenty-three years before, between leaders of the Parliamentary expedition and Francis, Lord Willoughby, in which the Charter of Barbados had been forged. Croxton remembered Richard and his part in the invasion of Tobago but, mindful of their differences in station, did not presume to speak when he saw him sitting at a table with other planters. Another reason for Croxton's diffidence was the presence of his employer, whose father had been one of the most ardent Royalists in Barbados during the island's version of the English Civil War. This man and all his family hated Richard but, like many, feared him. What he did was explained in part by the rum he had drunk in Bridgetown before arriving at the Mermaid.

As he passed Richard's table, Croxton in tow, the man said in a loud voice, "Well, Bolton, we don't often see you down here in Christ Church Parish."

"No, Walrond, my place in Saint James keeps me well occupied."

"I thought you had been occupied at the Court of Saint James rather than the parish."

Encouraged by the laughter his jest drew, Walrond continued. "None of my business, of course, but what does bring you back to the scene of your old crimes?"

"Indeed, it is none of your business, but I am looking for a good overseer for Bolton Hall," and before the man could respond added, "Isn't this Sergeant Croxton? I remember you well from our little adventure in Tobago."

Enormously pleased by the recognition, Croxton said, "Sure, and every man as was there remembers you, Sir Richard. Saved us from a slaughter, you did."

Croxton's employer, stung at being thus ignored by Richard, groped for the last word.

"Croxton is a better overseer than he is a judge of character, I assure you," he said over his shoulder.

"Walrond!" Richard stood, no longer smiling. "What did you mean by that comment about the scene of crimes?"

"Why, just as Croxton cannot forget your opportune voyage to Tobago, so some of cannot forget that you joined Ayscue's expedition when he came to our shores in '51. It was at this very tavern, was it not?"

The talk in the crowded common room stopped. The men at Richard's table were embarrassed, but others within earshot nudged each other at this confrontation between two old adversaries.

"I am surprised that you would speak so glibly of crime. Some cannot forget how your father and his friends tried to purloin the estates of men who differed with them in politics. And none can forget the Spanish money he accepted from the sale of excess slaves in '62."

Walrond turned pale at this reference to a swindle his late father had attempted while president of the island's council. He had accepted a commission from Spanish traders for his aid in procuring four hundred Barbadian slaves from distressed planters. Upon his restoration as governor, Francis, Lord Willoughby, had forced him to return the fees. The elder Walrond had been disgraced.

"How dare you insult me so?"

"I did not mean to insult you so much as to warn a decent fellow like Sergeant Croxton of the danger to his reputation from public association with you." Richard said this with a smile calculated to infuriate Walrond.

"Look here, Bolton, are you seeking a quarrel?"

"Why, Walrond, I normally do not waste my time on poltroons. I would not be speaking to you at all if you had not first spoken to me."

"Damn you, sir! I will not suffer this outrage. To insult me so before my overseer is too much to bear."

"Surely you don't mean to challenge me?" Richard said in a level tone.

"I do, indeed. Name the time and the place."

"What weapons do you prefer?"

"Pistols, of course."

"Then it is up to me to specify time and place."

"Indeed, so."

Richard looked at the men with whom he had been drinking. "Please, gentlemen, stand aside."

After they had arisen, he took a handkerchief from his sleeve and spread it on the center of the table. Then he drew his pistol from his waistband, cocked it, and placed the butt against the edge of the cloth.

"If you will place your weapon on your side and take the chair opposite me, we can proceed."

"What are you about, Bolton?"

"You left the time and place for me to decide. I choose this table at this moment. I will give you time to check your weapon. We both know and respect Sergeant Croxton. Let him begin counting when you are ready. We will fire on the count of three. Unless you wish to withdraw your challenge."

Walrond pulled out his pistol, placed it opposite Richard's and sat down. He was sweating, and he gripped the edge of the table to steady his hands.

Except for Croxton, all the men had stepped back to the side walls to keep out of the line of fire.

"You think I am afraid of you, Bolton."

"I never think of you at all, if I can help it. Sergeant Croxton, tell us when you are ready to start the count."

All clinking of glasses and whispering had ceased. The little Cockney swallowed and wiped his palms on his trousers. Then suddenly he scooped up the two pistols and fired them into the floor.

Walrond leaped to his feet with a cry. Bolton simply looked at Croxton.

"I won't do it," Croxton said. "Sir Richard, he is not worth you risking your life. This is a foolish quarrel, and I will not be a party to it."

The proprietor of the Mermaid emerged from behind his counter. "He is right. You both have proved your courage. If you don't stop now, I will bring a charge of murder against the survivor. Please, gentlemen, shake hands and disturb my trade no more."

"I will not shake the hand of a turncoat," Walrond said. "Come along, Croxton."

The Cockney stood as though he had not heard, his eyes still on Richard.

"Damn it, man," Walrond said. "Let's get back to the plantation."

Croxton said to Richard, "You are looking for an overseer?"

"I am indeed."

"Do you think I would do?"

Richard told Charlotte only that he had observed Croxton in Tobago and felt particularly fortunate in persuading him to change jobs.

"I am glad you found the right man, Richard. I feared the search would turn you into a drunkard, you were spending so much time in taverns."

"That is not the first time you have made such a remark, Charlotte. I hope you will not go on repeating yourself."

"Or that I will have cause to."

Horace Croxton was a wiry little man who carried himself like the soldier he had been for ten years. He had a hawk's bill of a nose and dark eyes that dared the world to deceive him. His Cockney accent grated on Charlotte's nerves, but she saw instantly why Richard had hired him. He had been a sergeant in General Brooks's regiment, and it was obvious that anyone to whom he gave an order would obey it.

His wife was a plump little lass who lived to please her adored Horace. With the instincts of a nesting bird, she set about to make their cottage into a haven for the overseer, who accepted her coddling as no more than the due of a man of his station.

"At last I have someone on whom I can count," Richard said after the Croxtons had settled at Bolton Hall.

"How do the slaves take to him?" Charlotte asked.

"So far, so good. He has gone to the trouble to learn their names. And he has had Cromwell explain every step of our ways at the sugar mill. Fellow is something of a mechanic, as well."

"He understands we don't use the whip in the fields?"

"He accepts but does not understand. Points out our soldiers and sailors are flogged for even minor infractions, but he says, 'Hit's yer place, Sir, and hit's you as makes the rules and not hi.' The fellow may not be quite as intelligent as Wilkens, but he will follow orders better."

"So, no flogging."

"Not without my permission."

The summer rains began early that year, making Charlotte all the more glad that she had her trunkful of new books to keep her occupied. During a brief break in the weather, she returned to her garden with Cudjoe to weed and trim her long-neglected flowers and shrubs. The bearded fig tree had grown so that it cast a shadow over a corner of the garden much of the day. She wondered which would be the harder task, to trim back its huge branches or merely expand the garden to the east.

"Let's not hack away at it," Richard said. "I thought it stupid of old Simpson to want it set just there, so near the house, but I've grown fond of the ugly thing. After the final weeding in the fields, I'll lend you a crew to widen your garden."

John inexplicably turned the care of Bolton Hall's slaves back to David Higganbotham about that time. Charlotte missed seeing the handsome youth so often, but she treasured the few hours she spent each week with David. The sight of the stocky physician riding up the lane on his chestnut mare brought her a curious feeling of quiet happiness. He was a steadfast friend to both her and Richard. Although his manner was stolid and hers animated, they thought alike on many subjects. Their arguments were good-natured, never cutting too deep, and usually ending in a compromise of attitude.

Charlotte felt safe in having him about, even in Richard's absence, for while she felt that he was fond of her, he would never blurt out a declaration of love, as had John. She did not know that Higganbotham lived for the few hours he could spend in her company each week.

*Saccharum
officinarum*

(sugar cane)

Book Three

. . . Sir Jonathan Atkins arrived to assume the governorship of Barbados after the rainy season, in the midst of a new cane planting. Although we had little heart for it, Richard and I joined others in greeting him at dockside and escorting him to his temporary residence in Bridgetown.

Atkins was older than I had expected, well past sixty, gray haired, sharp featured like a fox, and possessed of a courtly manner that masked a quick and calculating mind. He dashed our hopes of an easier imperial yoke with the news that King Charles henceforth would choose the members of the Governor's Council and that all laws passed by the Assembly would have to be forwarded to London for his approval. There was much grumbling about tyranny, but as the new Governor said, "What country back home has its own Parliament as you do out here? Come, let us work together for the prosperity of all. I am here as your friend." Atkins made such a refreshing change from the high-handed Willoughby brothers that the Assembly voted him an appropriation of 200,000 pounds of sugar as a gift.

Although he had brought along the list of his court-approved Council members, Atkins was slow to reveal it. When I learned that Richard's name was on the list, my worries about his morale eased. Within a few weeks, however, I found myself wishing King Charles had chosen another in his place. Willoughby had used his Council members only as cat's-paws and errand boys, but Atkins kept his in constant session, and that meant much time away from home for Richard . . .

1

Although Croxton took quick control of the overseeing both of sugar works and fields, Charlotte, with Richard away so much, had to fill in at record-keeping. She did not mind either that or the loneliness at night, but it worried her for Richard to be so often in Bridgetown taverns, for she feared that he often went to bed drunk, and she had overheard references to his card playing with fellow politicians.

"I thought he would get over wanting the governorship, but I see now that it meant more to him than anything else in his life," she confided to the ever sympathetic Esther Lawnton.

"Oh, Charlotte, he once told me that you meant more than life itself to him."

"He doesn't act that way now. He comes home out of sorts, and when I try to discuss Bolton Hall affairs with him, he only half listens. If I did not know better, I would think he kept a mistress in Bridgetown."

"Don't be ridiculous, Charlotte."

"I certainly get little enough of his attention these days, or nights, I should say."

Esther looked at her with an expression that made her think of that awful morning when she had learned the truth about Richard and Mandze.

"Richard is how old?"

"He will be fifty in March."

"That is not an easy time for a man, Charlotte. He no

longer can pretend to be young, and when he looks at the future, he sees death waiting for him. It makes them desperate."

"I soon will be thirty myself, and I am none too happy about that. He might show some sympathy for me."

Esther laughed. "You poor, decrepit old lady. Stop feeling sorry for yourself. You make me look like a crone. You are luckier than you realize. Richard will come out of his slump, and all will be well again if you will be patient."

"I only wish to have my old Richard back in good spirits. I wish now I had not fueled the fires of his ambition."

Although she had said it in an offhand way, Charlotte really dreaded reaching thirty, just as Esther thought Richard dreaded his approaching fiftieth birthday. A thin streak of gray had appeared in her hair, and a decade of squinting in the bright Barbadian sunlight has produced crow's-feet around her eyes. In the mornings when Richard was not at home, she had taken to examining her image in the mirror, without clothes, looking for the first sign of sagging breasts or a double chin. But no, except for a trifle fuller waistline, her figure had not changed since the day Richard Bolton came charging into her life. At any rate there was some compensation in not having children. No babies meant no thickened abdomen or varicose veins. Damn Richard Bolton. A woman should not have to look in the mirror to reassure herself; that was a job for a loving husband. Could he be seeing another woman? If he were, she would kill him and the hussy.

Richard was not seeing another woman, but there were two hussies in his life and their names were loo and whist. He had got in the habit of gambling at these popular card games while cooling his heels in London, had continued it aboard ship back to Barbados, and now between the frequent sessions of the council in Bridgetown he found it stimulating to pass a few games with friends and sea captains at the Bow Bells. It took his mind off the nagging knowledge that he had gone as far in life as he was likely ever to go.

It never occurred to Charlotte to fear the Negroes at Bolton Hall; their one rebellion, against the authority of Caesar, had been easily put down. She regarded them as simple, timorous creatures who responded like children to firm but kind treatment. And so she was unprepared for what occurred one evening just before the start of the 1675 cane harvest.

She sat in the drawing room, reading by candlelight, waiting for Richard to return from a council session, when she got the feeling of being watched. She told herself it was only her imagination and resumed reading. But the feeling persisted, and then she heard a crunch outside that could only be made by a foot or hoof.

She blew out the candle and whirled to face the open window. "Who's there?" The silhouette of a man's head disappeared before she had said the second word, followed by the sound of running. Hearing her screams, Clemmie, who had been in the kitchen, was there within seconds. Charlotte quickly got control of herself, and when Richard arrived she was able to tell him about the incident calmly.

"If I knew which of our slaves it was, I'd make him rue the day he was born," he said.

"It may not be one of ours."

"True. Could be a runaway. Or even a white man."

"Well, whoever or whatever, it was very unsettling. If you are going to be away so often after dark, I need some protection. Perhaps a dog."

"I'll take steps tomorrow."

"A husband by my side would be the best protection of all."

"With a collar around his neck and the leash firmly in your hand, perhaps?"

"I only meant that you still have a wife and a plantation, and I question whether the affairs of your precious council should be placed so high on your list of duties that you neglect your basic responsibilities."

"Think how much more you would be neglected had I become governor."

"I like to think I might have been of some help to you. The role of governor's wife could be quite influential, I think."

"Whereas the wife of a mere council member is worth no sacrifice?"

"Please, Richard, let us not quarrel. What is troubling you? I have long wondered."

He sat down, slouched in the chair. "I despair of the Court ever understanding our situation out here. Now we must pay that damnable tax even on our exports to New England. And there is a big to-do between the council and the Assembly over which body may or may not introduce money bills. My friends in the Assembly refuse to consider appropriations that do not originate with themselves as has been our custom. I see their point, but here am I, trapped in the governor's council wherein I was appointed by the king himself."

"You are in a tight spot. But is not Governor Atkins in a worse one?"

"Perhaps. The poor man has no great personal wealth. He depends on his post for his living, unlike the Willoughbys, who had estates in Surinam and in England."

"Or yourself with a profitable plantation. You know something, Richard?"

"What?"

"I am glad you do not have the burden of Atkins's office. See the difficulties he has despite his years of experience in royal politics. It would be quite enough for me if you were content to be simply the master of Bolton Hall and my husband."

He looked at her for a long while, until tears came to his eyes. "I soon will enter my fifty-first year, and is that all I have to look forward to? Producing sugar until I am dead?"

"We spoke once of going back to England and agreed that was not a good idea. Why cannot you be happy with me here? Is there somewhere you would rather be? I know you are restless or you would not drink so much. Do you regret marrying me? Do you blame me for not bearing you children? Do you desire another woman?"

"Oh, Charlotte."

"Don't 'Oh, Charlotte' me. I have been living long enough on the fringes of your attention, and I demand to know what it is that you want, if you are so tired of Bolton Hall and weary of the politics of this island. Is there something else you want to do? Something attainable?"

"As a matter of fact, I have been thinking of something else, or someplace else."

"Dear God, please tell me, so that I can share it with you."

"Don't scoff until you have heard me out, but as you know Yeamans and others have borrowed capital or sold out here and taken up grants in the Carolinas. They have moved there with their families and their slaves, and they send back favorable reports. The weather is not so cold as in New England. The slaves thrive in the climate. And they can take up a thousand acres of virgin land there with less expense than a hundred acres here. Furthermore, they are secure from attacks by the Dutch. There are more trees than they ever could cut down. They can grow crops other than sugar. And they are not watched so closely and jealously by our greedy king."

"And you wish to sell Bolton Hall and move to the Carolinas?"

"I would like us to think seriously about it. We need another good crop here. I would like to have as much money as possible. I am too old to strive there as I did here to gain a foothold. I only wish I were a young man again."

"I would not love you so much if you were, Richard."

"You are not shocked by my talk of Carolina? You would be willing to pull up stakes and go with me?"

"I am not shocked, no. I must think about it. Let us not be hasty. You should be very sure before we take so drastic a step. Meanwhile, what are you going to do to ensure my safety while you are away?"

The next morning he brought up a gang of field hands and set them to planting night-blooming cacti outside each ground-floor window. "They will perfume the air and also discourage prowlers."

While the slaves were digging holes for the spiny plants, he pointedly called Charlotte into the garden, and there instructed her in loading and firing his pair of pistols. It turned out that she had a steady hand and a good eye for shooting, and she was pleased by his compliments.

"There you are, my dear," he said in a loud voice so the slaves could hear. "Next time anyone comes lurking about you can blow out his brains. And I will bury him face down in a cattle pen."

On his next trip to Bridgetown, Richard brought her a pair of finely crafted dueling pistols and a half-grown mastiff dog. "We'll call him Lucifer. With him about, you will have no more trouble with peeping Toms."

Charlotte felt better after that. She was grateful to the prowler, for he had provided her the opportunity to get into Richard's mind. While she thought the idea of their moving to the Carolinas was foolish, she regarded the possibility as remote. Anyway, she was glad that Richard had something to occupy his mind until he got over what Esther had called "a difficult time for men."

Charlotte had no intention of leaving Bolton Hall for the Carolinas or anywhere else. Where else would there be sunsets such as she enjoyed from her veranda? And she could not imagine another garden half so lush and colorful as the one she had patiently developed over the years. She would miss David Higganbotham, John Martin, the Lawntons, and their other neighbors. Back in England she had been only the daughter of a country gentleman, but here she was a person in her own right, respected and admired by others. From what she heard of the Carolinas, the land was flat, and, while Richard spoke of its freedom from foreign attacks, she heard stories of savage Indian tribes to the west who scalped their enemies and carried off white women and children. She could accept her childlessness here in a secure, orderly colony, but inevitably within the next two or three decades she would be left a widow, and that would be a lonely lot in a raw new land. She would humor Richard by listening to his dreams, but move to Carolina? No, thank you. All she desired was a contented husband and the grand new house he had promised her ten years ago.

2

... We had a good sugar harvest last spring, one of the best ever. Croxton paid closer attention to his duties than Wilkens, and while the slaves did not enjoy his sharp supervision, Richard was pleased by the results. The cane cutting went on schedule, field by field, and at the sugar works Cromwell kept his crews laboring day and night through March, April, and into May, until the last stalks had been fed into the creaking maw of the windmill and the final batch of juice had passed from vat to vat, through its various boilings and skimmings. The hands were exhausted by the time the last pot of sling had been poured into the pots to be drained of the molasses and converted into the brown crystals that represented such wealth to us.

Despite the exellent crop prospects, I heard much complaining about the shortage and consequent high price of imports from New England, particularly the scant supply of salt fish. There was some trouble there with an Indian uprising. Faint from lack of their chief staple foods, many of the slaves went about their chores like black zombies. I persuaded Richard to slaughter several sheep and an aged ox to feed our hands, but elsewhere on the island even normally benign planters relied upon the whip to keep the harvest going, and this caused David much distress, which he confided to Richard and me during an afternoon visit.

"It sickens me to see half-starved human beings beaten because they are too weak to do the work. I told a fellow down in Saint George

he was killing his slaves by driving them so hard, and he replied, 'I can always buy more. What's it to me if a few of the weaker ones die? The greater threat to me is losing part of this fine crop.' I tell you, Charlotte, I wonder sometimes at the patience of our Africans."

I agreed that starving slaves was both cruel and stupid.

Then David said something to which I now wish we had paid more heed. "It is a wonder to me they don't rise up and kill us all, the way they are treated."

Richard, who had been sipping his third glass of wine of the evening, laughed sarcastically. "What choice do they have but to be patient? David, you fret yourself too much worrying about what the slaves might think. Feed them adequately, give them their small pleasures, rule them with a firm hand, and there will be no trouble. But overfeed them and give them too much free time, and you invite difficulties."

"But surely you do not condone starving and indiscriminate beatings," David said.

Richard replied as I had often heard, with, "Indeed I do not. You must strike a happy medium. They are like children. They need evenhanded discipline. I have never had any serious trouble with my hands, and I don't expect any. As for those who starve theirs, I say simply that they practice bad economics."

I interrupted, "Yet, I wonder what may happen in later generations, as more of them learn English and as our population of Creole slaves and mulattoes increases. It seems to me inevitable that their resentments will increase. Consider Clemmie. She could easily be taught to read and write. She is always eager to hear the contents of my letters from my parents."

"I hope you have not taken it into your head to teach her," Richard said. "That is frowned upon here, you know."

"As you have told me, darling. And yet is it not pathetic to see her yearning to unlock the magic world my books contain?"

"Teach her to read, and you'd only spoil a good servant. What do you say, David?"

"I must admit that I am of two minds on the subject. Still, is it right to rip them from their natural ways of life and deny them access

to ours? We force them to live like brutes and then treat them with scorn for so living."

"You can't make bricks without straw, and you can't grow sugar cane without Negroes. If I thought teaching them to read and write would make them better hands, I'd be for it. But, alas, it would ruin them for our purposes. And it might truly make them dangerous—to themselves if not to us."

I chided Richard for his lack of sympathy, and he lashed out at me, saying, "Just look at the crazy old tailor who came out with us, your young chirurgeon's father. If he had not learned to read and write, he would be back in Bristol working happily at his trade and enjoying his grandchildren now."

"But Barbados would not have the benefits of his son's medical practice," David replied.

"Would that be so great a loss? From what I hear he has holed himself up in his hut on Apes Hill very like Old Tom Cochran himself. Shouldn't surprise me to hear one day that he has tacked up a prophecy on a church door as his father did."

I could not let him get away with talking such rot. "You are being ridiculous," I said hotly. "John is only moody. He is a good doctor."

He looked at me with an expression of contempt. "Well, you and David can sit about clucking like two old hens if you wish. I am going out to the curing shed." He walked a few steps and then turned and said something that shocked me with its cynicism. "The world belongs to the strong," he said. "Give up control over our Negroes and the lower order of whites, and our world will collapse. That is all I was trying to say."

"Oh, go look after your sugar works," I said.

"He seems embittered," David remarked after he was out of earshot.

I reminded David of Bacon's comment that ambitious men are busy rather than dangerous as long as they see hope for their ambitions, but that if they are checked in their desires they become secretly discontent "and look upon men and matters with an evil eye."

"Richard was far more ambitious than I realized when I mar-

ried him," I said. "Indeed it has occurred to me that he may have married me as much out of ambition as love."

"That is a hard thing to say, Charlotte."

"I would not say it to just anyone, David."

"Why did you marry him, then?"

"I would be embarrassed to tell you. And it is wrong of me to discuss my husband in a disparaging way. For all his faults, I love him beyond reason."

I did love Richard, I really did. Yet his behavior—his increased drinking and often bitter remarks, even rudeness toward me and our friends—weighed upon me heavily. It was as if he were becoming a different man. He grew more secretive, locking up certain records so that I could not see them and often going to Bridgetown on the pretense of business, when I knew there was none, then returning home late at night so drunk that Toby had to help him out of the saddle and into the house.

The best course, it seemed to me, was to remain patient, refraining from remonstrances, and give him time to recover from his political disappointment and adjust to the new circumstances of our lives, which, after all, were far better than most. So, despite his often boorish behavior, I held my tongue, for as long as I could.

"Mistress, I am concerned about Joe," Clemmie said to Charlotte.

"Whatever for?"

"He do go to the graveyard too much at night. He take his drum and stay a long time."

"I would rather he played it down there than in the yard."

"He act strange, too."

"You can't think he is meeting a girl. He is scarcely old enough for that."

"I wish you would take away the drum."

"That would be harsh when he loves it so. What is the harm?"

"I hear him down there at night, late."

"Bring him to me. And his drum."

Clemmie pushed him into the room, she holding his drum

and he looking down at the floor. Charlotte felt a stab of pity, rather as she had ten years before when John Martin had been led up to her cabin aboard the *Mary Leigh*.

The boy pretended not to understand Charlotte's questions.

"The graveyard. You do go there at night. I hear your drum sometimes."

"I don't know."

Clemmie cuffed him. "Don't lie to the mistress."

"No more of that," Charlotte said. "Give me the drum." She waited for Joe to raise his eyes.

"You want to keep your drum?"

"Yes, Mistress."

"If you do not answer my questions, I will take it from you."

"No, Mistress, please."

"Then tell me what you do at the graveyard."

"I like it there."

"Ask him who he meets there," Clemmie broke in.

A look of fear came over his face. "Nobody. Just me."

"Ask him if he got anything to do with Obeah magic."

"Oh, Clemmie, don't be ridiculous. He is only a scared little boy. Stop bullying him."

"Then take away his drum."

"No! Now, Joe, don't go to the graveyard so often, and don't stay long. The master would not like it if he knew."

She handed him his drum, and he left, followed by a disapproving Clemmie.

Charlotte considered telling Richard of the incident but decided that he might act on Clemmie's advice, and she saw no point in depriving the boy of his treasured drum.

Harold Lawnton was reluctant to allow his slaves a holiday to celebrate the end of the 1675 harvest, but at Charlotte's urging, Richard persuaded him to relent. "They have had a hard time of it this year. Short rations and all that. My hands are looking forward to another 'do,' and I expect yours are, too."

"They don't have to worry about the expense."

"You've surely enough rum. I can't find a market for mine with shipping from New England so sluggish. Come, Harold, don't be mean. Old Bates has promised to bring along Cuffee and his flute, all his slaves in fact."

"I would just as soon he left that old scoundrel at home. I don't like the way he is always lurking about. Bates allows him far too much freedom, if you ask me."

"Come, Harold, with the Bates's slaves present, it will be better sport even than last year."

"So many in one group? Ain't that asking for trouble?"

"We are having a militia company there to watch the fun, with arms. Don't tell me you are afraid of your slaves?"

"There is something stirring among them. Never had to whip so many in a season."

"You've overdone your economies. Here is an opportunity to let up on them. Surely you don't want me to tell Charlotte you are too stingy to take part in the celebration."

"I suppose not, but I'd feel better if we began in the afternoon and did not let it run on so late."

"Agreed. Frankly, I am looking forward to it, and it is a healthy exercise for them."

So it was that some three hundred blacks, with a hundred armed militia men looking on, gathered on a Saturday afternoon at Bolton Hall for their rations of rum and portions of roasted sheep, followed by several hours of violent dancing. There were so many slaves on hand this time that they broke into various tribal groups, and, although their white masters disapproved, it was too late to stop them without spoiling their fun.

Quaco, with a bit of mutton in hand, sidled close to Cuffee. Holding the meat in front of his mouth, he muttered, "When do we meet again?"

Cuffee did not look at Quaco as he muttered, "Tomorrow night at the graveyard. I will have others with me."

"And my son?"

"Tell him to come and bring his drum."

"Hey there, Cuffee, you black rascal," Bates yelled. "Start the music again."

Cuffee raised the flute to his lips and began a piercing melody he had learned from his grandfather in Africa. The Coromantees formed a circle, and this time they sang as well as danced. The whites did not understood the words, which mocked them. And at one point, the dancers, changing their rhythm to suit the words, walked in a circle, stiff-legged, with toes turned outward and mincing expressions on their faces. Then laughing derisively, they halted the charade and returned to their native steps.

Higganbotham, who had caught some of the words, winced, but Richard and Lawnton, half drunk, had not noticed, and Charlotte and Esther were pretending a polite interest in Mrs. Bates's account of her most recent bowel disorders. But Croxton, who had not approved of the celebration in the first place, sensed the mood of the dancers and stared at Cuffee until he, grinning at the overseer, launched into an English morris dance tune that delighted the other white guests.

"Clever blackamoor, that Cuffee," Richard said to Bates.

"I wouldn't take a hundred pounds for him."

After the dance had ended and the slaves were on their way back to their respective plantations, the Lawntons and Higganbotham remained at Bolton Hall and continued drinking until Richard and Harold both became drunk.

"Here, David, you seem down at the mouth. Have another glass. Toby, damn it, boy, don't let my guests sit about with naught to drink."

"Richard," Charlotte said. "David knows us well enough to ask for wine when he wants it. You don't have to shout so."

She was taken aback by the vehemence of his response.

"Who's shouting? And what if I do shout? This is my house."

Charlotte lowered her voice, saying quietly, "It is my house, too, Richard."

"Ah, listen to our well-bred lass. 'It's my house, too, Richard.' Hell, girl, it is your house because I married you and brought you out to be the wife of a real man. You should have seen the pipsqueak she was all set to marry. A mama's boy if ever I saw one. Shared books and secrets with him much as she does with you, David."

"Richard, don't be a boor."

He rose to his feet unsteadily. "Hear that? She calls me a boor. Maybe it takes a boor to turn a jungle into one of the best damned plantations on this accursed island. One thing is sure, your precious Marmaduke would not have survived a single season out here as I did. Mama's boy Marmaduke." He laughed at his crude pun, and when no one in the party joined him, he raised his glass defiantly and drained it off.

Charlotte frowned at him, shook her head, and tried to change the subject, but Richard would not be deterred.

"Now she thinks to silence me with her eyes. Oh, look there how she tries to shrivel me with her glance."

Even Lawnton was embarrassed now. "Come, Richard, don't you think that is enough?"

Richard turned his attention to his neighbor, saying balefully, "That is what you said to me in my last game in Bridgetown. 'Don't you think you have had enough?' You left too soon to see me take twenty pounds off that ship's captain."

Shocked by this revelation, Charlotte murmured, "That is the price of a prime slave."

"Ah, Mistress Bolton, you are learning. I bet Caesar against the fellow's twenty pounds, and you know what? I won. Richard Bolton always gets what he goes after. Toby, haul your black ass out here with more wine. The decanter is empty."

Their guests were glancing sideways at each other in embarrassment, and Charlotte blinked back tears. His outburst had taken her entirely off guard. She did not know how to handle this stranger who seemed to have replaced her husband.

"Here, Toby, damn it, over here with that wine." Richard stood up quickly and lurched toward the Negro, then stumbled and fell on his face.

Esther comforted the distraught Charlotte while Higganbotham and Lawnton, who was sobered by the scene, carried

Richard upstairs with Toby's help. There they removed his
boots and laid him across the bed.

"How long has he been doing this sort of thing?"

"He has never behaved this badly. He has been drinking
more than he should. And it seems to make him melancholy
rather than cheerful. Oh, Esther, what is happening to the man
I married?"

When the men returned, she apologized.

"No harm done, Charlotte," Lawnton said. "We all say
things we regret when we've drunk too much. Ought to watch
him about that gambling, though. Sooner or later one of that
Bridgetown gang will take advantage of him."

When they were gone, Charlotte went to the spare bedroom
and lay awake until near morning, too concerned for tears. She
had to do something to stop Richard from destroying himself.

The road that led from Bridgetown up across the upper
plateau of Saint Michael Parish and on past Fulham and
Bolton Hall had been stripped of earth down to the bedrock
recently, so that the hooves of the two horses rang as though
striking pavement. A full moon cast a silver glow over the cane
fields, outlining the windmills along the knolls and ridges like
giant ghosts against the sky.

Charlotte had warned Richard about riding at night,
whether drunk or sober, and here he was with a bottle of wine
in his stomach and a flask in his hand, astride his horse, and
singing an old Cavalier song with Harold Lawnton who rode
alongside him.

"Know something, Harold?" Richard said thickly when
the song ended. "I'd like to turn back the years. If I had known
in the fifties what I know now, I could own all of Saint James
Parish. Five hundred acres I could own and three hundred
slaves."

"You couldn't own Fulham. That is mine, bought and paid
for by me."

"Well, you know what I mean. I could have borrowed money
from the Dutch and built a fortune as large as Drax or

Modyford. Could have sold out at the Restoration and bought myself a peerage back in England. Gone into shipping and banking."

"You haven't done so badly, Richard. Neither of us has."

"Have another drink." Richard offered the flask.

"I've had more than my share."

"Then, Mr. Bolton—excuse me, Sir Richard—won't you have a drink? Why, I don't mind if I do." He turned his head back and drank deeply, ignoring the trickle of wine down his chin.

"What will you do this summer, now that the crop is in?" Lawnton asked.

"Do? See the new canes are weeded and manured. Repair the equipment. Buy fresh Africans maybe. Make peace with Charlotte."

"Still a strain between you?"

"She won't sleep with me. Hasn't since we celebrated the end of harvest." He took another swig from the flask. "Stubborn wench, always has to have her own way."

"Want my advice?"

"Not really, but go ahead if it will make you feel better."

"Go home and beg her forgiveness. Tell her you have considered what you did and have concluded that she is exactly right to be angry with you and ask for another chance. Be contrite."

"But I am not contrite."

"Doesn't matter. Act contrite. Tell her you have apologized to me for your behavior, and I forgave you and that you have asked me to relay your regrets to Esther."

"I won't. You can go to hell."

"Won't what, apologize to me or throw yourself on her mercy?"

"What are you talking about anyway?"

"Good Lord, Richard, you are acting the fool. Play on her sympathy. Nothing a woman likes more than to have the upper hand morally. You will melt her heart, I tell you. Never fails with Esther."

"Want to know something, Harold?"

"What?"

"You are an ass."

"At least when I get home I will not sleep alone."

"You really want me to apologize to you and Esther?"

"I don't care what you do."

"Tell you what. I'll just ride to your house and 'pologize right now to your good wife. That way she'll tell Charlotte about it. Now who is a fool?"

"I did not say you were a fool. I only said you were acting like one."

At the Fulham house, Esther came down dressed in a nightgown, wearing a sleeping cap, and carrying a candle with reflector to see what the ruckus in her yard was all about.

"It's Richard Bolton, dear," Harold said. "He has something to say to us both."

She held up her candle so the light fell on the still-mounted Richard.

"Mistress Lawnton, dear lady. It has been told me I did behave toward thee and thy good husband in a gross and boorish manner. The report is grievous unto me, and I do truly and sincerely repent of my transgression. If thou wouldst find it in thy heart to offer me forgiveness, I would be thy grateful servant forever. Amen."

"Richard, you are drunk again."

"But this time he is a happy drunk," Harold said. Then to Richard, "And me. Will you not beg my forgiveness as well?"

"Even you, yes." Richard raised his hat high above his head. "No matter what the truth of what I may have said to your husband, I regret saying that too. There now, how is that for contrition?"

"Saintly, positively saintly," Lawnton said, laughing.

"Richard Bolton," Esther said in a stern voice, "Go home to your wife and sober up."

"Not until you forgive me."

She chuckled. "All right. I forgive you. Now go and see if Charlotte will."

"I intend to do just that. The sinner is forgiven. Heaven doth rejoice. Good night."

The Lawntons laughed as he rode away.

"Do you think he will be all right, riding alone at night?" Esther asked.

"Certainly. There is no one abroad so late."

"I heard the sound of drums to the north. Two at least. First one and then another."

"Naught to worry about. Let's go to bed."

As he neared the junction of Fulham lane with the Bridgetown road, Richard began whistling a tune to the cadence of his horse's hooves.

"Master." It was a woman's voice, coming from a pile of cane trash beside the road.

Richard pulled his horse up short and by reflex drew his pistol from his belt. "Who's there? Come out, damn you."

"It is me, Master. Mandze."

She stepped onto the road so that he could look down at her.

"What do you want?"

"I want to warn you."

"Warn me? What is there to warn me about? Are you making threats? I told you if you tried to blackmail me, make any trouble at all, I'd have you sent to Jamaica."

"I am afraid for you."

Richard's brain was foggy from so much wine, and he felt an inexplicable anger at what he considered the woman's impudence, to accost him in this way, as if she had any claim on him, as if she had any right to speak to him.

"I told you ten years ago I was done with you. I treated you well enough. Warn me, indeed. Who are you to make threats against a white man?"

"Oh, Yellow Hair," she moaned. "You don't understand."

"How dare you call me that? Now stand aside, or I will report you to Major Lawnton. You aren't supposed to be out of the yard this late."

"Please, listen to me. Beware the dark of the moon. Let me tell you ... "

He lashed at her with his riding crop, missing and almost falling from the saddle. As she stepped back, shocked by his outburst, he recovered his balance and struck his horse's flank. "Goddamn black bitch, you could have ruined my life ... "

"Please listen," she called after the sound of the horse's hooves.

Sleepless from an aching head, Charlotte lay awake on the narrow bed in the spare bedroom. She longed to be at peace with her husband, but she was determined to show him no sympathy until he acknowledged his rudeness to her and their guests and foreswore his irresponsible drinking and gambling. For her to make the first overture would be to condone his general behavior. She was determined and miserable. She had regarded Richard as a mature man able to do anything, and it seemed to her he had reverted to a kind of juvenile folly, like a youth rebelling against his mother. Here he had a wife, a valuable plantation, and a hundred slaves depending on him, and he was neglecting them all and taking risks with both his health and his money. Yes, and with her happiness and his, as if he wanted to destroy their life together. No, she told herself over and over, she would give him the cold shoulder until he learned that he could not get away with such behavior. Let him be as miserable as she.

She stiffened at the sound of his horse clopping in the yard and lay quietly as he shouted for Toby to come and help him dismount. Now he was climbing the stairs and pausing at her door.

"Charlotte?"

She ignored first his call and then his light knock.

"Charlotte, are you asleep?"

She put her hand over her mouth and choked back a sob but did not answer, until she heard him pass down the hall to their room. No, it was *his* room and would remain so until he agreed to turn over a new leaf. But it took all her willpower not to rise and join him in the great bed. She put herself to sleep with prayers for his redemption.

She was awakened the next morning by a knock on her door.

"Who's there?"

"Me, Clemmie. I have brought your breakfast."

"I asked for no breakfast," Charlotte said, but she did open the door. There was Richard, already dressed, standing behind Clemmie.

"Put the tray over there, Clemmie," he said. "And leave us alone."

"What are you doing in my room?" Charlotte said.

"I have come to apologize."

Charlotte looked at him with suspicion. "It will take more than a glib apology."

"I mean it. I realize how badly I have behaved. Last night I apologized to the Lawntons, and they forgave me. Now I crave your forgiveness."

She listened and watched for a sign that he was mocking her, but no, he acted like an abashed schoolboy.

"It is more than what you said to me in the presence of our guests or to them. It is the way you have acted ever since you returned from England."

"I know. I have been a bastard, and I am sorry."

"And you offer no explanation, no excuse?"

"No defense of any kind. I desire nothing except to be back in your good graces."

She blinked against her tears, fighting to keep her apparent advantage over him.

"Why should I forgive you if you only take to drinking and gambling again?"

"I don't mean to. I shall give it up."

"Why this sudden repentance?"

"I have come to my senses. Last night I suddenly realized how wicked it has been of me to distress the dearest person in all the world."

"But you were drunk last night."

"True, I did drink a bit in Bridgetown after the council meeting, but my decision was a sober one, I assure you. Already I have apologized to the Lawntons, and now I beg your pardon."

She would not let him manipulate her again. Too often she had let him charm her into flying into his arms before an issue had been settled.

"There is more than just your drinking and gambling or your rude behavior."

"What may that be?"

"This talk of selling out and moving to Carolina. I want to hear no more of it. What about the house you promised me ten years ago? And I am tired of your concealing important matters."

She paused, conscious that she might never have another such opportunity to make him listen and heed. Then she continued.

"All of my life I have endured men who assume they are superior to women because they wear trousers. I put up with it from my brothers. I thought when I married you, 'Here is a man who wants a partner for his life.' Yet you have treated me like a girl. You have kept secrets from me. You toy with me in the matter of a new house. To this day, I don't know the true condition of our finances. Well, let me tell you this. I ran Bolton Hall while you were in England, and I ran it well. You may be better at some things than I, but do you think you would ever have been considered for the governorship without my help? I was as disappointed as you by the king's decision, but why cannot you be as philosophical as I? Let us accept our lot and get on with our lives. For God's sake, Richard, here is your chance to show the stuff you're really made of. Look, I sacrificed family and security in England to marry you and come to a strange land. I have swallowed some bitter disappointments. Oh, don't blanch. I shall not recount my old grievances. You once called me a spoiled little bitch. You are spoiled in many ways, yourself. You are handsomer and stronger and cleverer than most men. Yes, and until recently you have been more fortunate. Accept your lot, man. It remains a far better one than most humans enjoy..." She stopped, out of breath, amazed at her own loquacity.

"Dear Charlotte, please forgive me, and I swear I shall never again give you any cause to complain of me."

"You said you had apologized to the Lawntons?"

"Yes, and they both forgave me. What's more I shall beg Higganbotham's pardon as well, if you wish."

"And there will be no more talk of Carolina?"

"Not unless you bring up the subject."

"And my house?"

"We can dig the foundation after the rainy season."

"Richard, are you just mouthing these words, thinking to play on my sympathy?"

"Never have I been more sincere."

Then, shrewdly, he left her alone before she could obey her impulse to put her arms about his neck. He let her stew with satisfaction all day and that evening made restrained, polite conversation over the supper table. She was pleased that he sent Toby away with the wine. When night fell, she offered no protest when he took her hand and led her to their bedroom.

3

... *Neither that night nor afterwards was there any further talk of apologies or forgiveness between us. I drifted into a more serene happiness than I had experienced since coming out to Barbados. Finally, when Esther told me the true circumstances of Richard's apology, I merely laughed and said, "He is such an arrant scamp."*

"You won't tell him I told you?"

"Heavens no. I will let him go on thinking he pulled the wool over my eyes."

"My, you have suddenly become tolerant."

"'Assume a virtue, if you have it not . . . for use almost can change the stamp of nature.'"

"What does that mean?"

"Whether Richard really is contrite or not, it does not matter so long as he refrains from his folly and keeps his promises to me. If I had wanted a milksop for a husband, I would have married my original fiancé. 'Tis enough that Sir Richard now knows my feelings and will respect them."

After a decade of marriage, it seemed to me that Richard and I were finally coming to terms with each other. Neither his life nor mine had turned out as we dreamed, but we were well enough off, enjoyed the respect of our fellow Barbadians, and still had a comfortable future ahead of us, so it seemed. Alas, how was I to know the trouble that lay ahead?

There were seven of them in the graveyard, six men plus Cudjoe, and they sat in a circle, all hunched down so the light of the half-moon would not make them visible from the Bridgetown road. Cuffee spoke softly, in their own language, so softly they had to cup their ears to hear.

"They are cowards, I tell you. They are brave only when they have guns."

"But they do have guns," one African said.

"Just do as I have told you. Strike when the drums tell you. When there is no moon. They will be taken by surprise. Then their guns will become ours."

"But the militia . . . "

Cuffee snorted disdainfully. "We start in the north and march toward Bridgetown. Take every man of every tribe with their axes and billhooks, moving slow. Fanti and other Akans will run ahead and lie in wait beside the road for their militia to come along. Then we pounce. Once we have destroyed them, we go where we please and do as we like."

"There are so few of us here."

"You talk like a woman. Do you think me a fool? This is but one group. I have others, many others to the north. They are ready."

Another man spoke up. "We can overcome their militia, I know we can, but will they not send over ships with great cannon and real soldiers from England?"

"You have not been here as long as I," Cuffee said. "Soon after they brought me here, the whites quarreled among themselves. England sent ships and many soldiers to subdue the island. They had much difficulty doing so. They succeeded only because the white men were divided. Let me tell you this . . . " His voice became lower and more forceful. "We are far more numerous than they were then and are now. We cannot be divided. We will rule this island. The other tribes will do as we say. Let the English send their ships and their soldiers. We will have the forts and the cannon. They will never conquer us."

"You mean us to kill all whites?"

"All except for those women you want for yourselves. You may use them as they have long used our women."

Others raised different questions until Cuffee cut them off. "Do you want to go on toiling in the cane until you are old men, or until they starve you to death? If that is what you want, say so and I will find others, real men. I thought you were warriors."

"We only wish to understand clearly."

"Then understand this. Some who came here from our motherland with me thought if they killed themselves they would fly home. When they did, the white men chopped off their heads and stuck them on poles and buried the bodies. Then they said to the rest of us, 'See there. How can you return to Africa when your head is still in Barbados?' The white man was right. We cannot fly back to Africa. Here is where we must live and die."

The timid one interrupted again. "Could we not seize their ships and sail back to our homeland?"

"You are a fool. Which of us knows how to sail a ship? We

don't need to return to Africa. This has become our homeland. We shall make a nation of Africans on this island. Without the white man, it will be a better place than any in Africa. I offer to make you princes in a kingdom of black men, and you fret yourselves with foolish fears. Are you warriors or not?"

During these exchanges, Quaco had sat quietly with Cudjoe leaning against him, both thrilling to the words of old Cuffee. Now he spoke.

"I am ready to strike when you give the order."

"Good. And the rest of you?"

One by one, he called their names. Each said he was ready.

"I cannot linger here. I have others waiting. Remember, strike swiftly when the signal comes, and then wait beside the road to join the others in our march south. Spare no one."

"Except the women," Quaco said.

"Except the most beautiful of their women."

"And the young doctor," Quaco added.

"Why should we? One or two of you could sneak upon him with ease. He goes about unarmed."

"He would be useful to us. Some of us will be wounded. And later, when there is sickness, it would be well to have him."

"But he serves the white masters."

"He spared me once. I wish to spare him."

"Very well. Do not kill the doctor. But all of you remember: Say no word to anyone about this. Do not tell your women. Tell no other man of any tribe. Let the white fools spend their last few days untroubled. Now go quietly, brothers."

A few days later, Lucifer, the mastiff Richard had given Charlotte after the peeping Tom incident, fell violently ill. He went running about the back yard in agony, howling and snapping at the empty air. Charlotte had never cared for the ugly brute. She would not allow him in the house, and so he had been left in the care of Joe, but now she pitied the animal. She and the servants shut themselves in the house while Joe summoned Richard, who shot the dog between the eyes.

"Can't take a chance," he said. "May have had hydrophobia. I will have to get you another dog."

"Don't bother. With my pistols and the cactus hedges, I have no more fears."

Charlotte had spent most of the morning in the garden directing Cudjoe in trimming bushes and weeding flower beds. With a great straw hat shading her face and her arms covered with sleeves, she went about her work happily, humming to herself. She was about to go into the house when, to her amazement, John Martin came riding from the eastern fields and asked if he might speak to her in private.

"Of course, John. Tie your horse to the fig tree and come around to the veranda. I will join you there."

He was standing, staring out at the sea when she came out in a fresh dress with bare arms and her hair tied back.

"What a pleasant surprise. It has been too long since you have visited us. Do sit down. Clemmie will bring us mobby."

With sun-bronzed face averted, he tersely answered her polite questions about his life on Apes Hill and his medical practice, until she ran out of conversation.

"I suppose you are wondering why I have come."

"I should hope it is to chat with me. We have missed you."

"I am here to say good-bye."

"I don't understand."

"Good-bye to you and to Barbados."

"Oh, John. Whatever for?"

He stood up and walked about, slapping his riding crop against his boot top. "I have had a bellyful of this accursed island. I could labor here the rest of my life and still would be a nobody. Only the rich count here. I am weary of living in a land devoted solely to the getting and spending of money through producing sugar. All this sweating and suffering so a few rich people can live in ease and so folk in England can sweeten their tea and coffee."

"What a thing to say, John. I thought you were getting on so well. I hear good things about your work."

"What is the point of it? I go about trying to keep the slaves in fit condition so that they will produce a profit for their masters."

"Is that not a worthy occupation?"

"I might as well be a doctor of veterinary medicine, hired to look after a lot of farm animals. That is how I am regarded."

"You keep too much to yourself. It is not right for a young man to be such a recluse. You should get out more."

"I get out too much, and what I see sickens me. The owners cut expenses by starving their slaves, and they won't listen to me when I protest."

"But you know how short the supply of provisions has been this year. And how dearly they cost as a result. No one deliberately starves his slaves. It does not happen at Bolton Hall, certainly. I would not permit it."

"Oh, Charlotte, you should ride over to some of the plantations in the Scotland district or up in Saint Lucy. Many of the Negroes are walking skeletons."

"The planters are not so well off there."

"They are well enough off to furnish their houses grandly and to dress their wives in expensive silks and laces. Oh, I know all about the shortage of salt fish from New England. I have heard of their Indian war often enough. I hear it from men who, with small sacrifice, could band together and hire sloops to sail to North America for provisions. Or they could set aside more of their cane lands for growing food."

"But you are acting hastily. We have had a good crop, generally, and in time this situation will right itself."

"It goes deeper than that. I am sick of slavery. I thought my father was a fool to lose his life railing against what seemed to me only an efficient system of labor, but now I see how right he was. It is wicked. It is unnatural for a mass of human beings to be at the mercy of a handful of rich and powerful people. Who gives our planters the right to treat Negroes so? I do not wish to be a part of such a system any longer."

"Oh, John, you are serious then. Where do you mean to go?"

"Virginia. It is a well-established colony, even older than Barbados."

"But do not they have slaves there, too?"

"Only a few. And there is a great need for doctors."

"When do you mean to go, John?"

"Within the next few weeks. I have alerted the harbormaster, in confidence, to notify me when another vessel arrives from the James River."

"Does David know of your decision?"

"You are the only person to whom I have spoken of it."

"I am touched that you trust me so. But I am troubled for you, too. I wish you would stay here and be happy."

"I could never be happy here, even if I were not surrounded by so much misery."

"My, you are melancholy. What would it take to make you happy?"

He raised his eyes to look into her face. "I told you more than a year ago, when your husband was in England, and you forbade me ever to speak of it again."

"Oh." She paused to choose her words carefully. "I had hoped you had got over that."

"I have tried, but it is useless. I think only of you. You are in my thoughts when I go to bed. I dream of you at night, and I awake the next morning with you in my mind. Perhaps with an ocean between us, I can rid myself of this obsession."

"John, please. This is unhealthy. You will drive yourself mad. I would not listen to you if I were not concerned for your well-being."

"I would not have told you, but you asked what it would take to make me happy. And since I am leaving anyway ... "

"Oh, John, I am so sorry. This bitter talk about slavery is merely an excuse, then?"

"Barbados contains too many painful memories for me. If I stay on, I will become as mad as old Tom Cochran, or else will turn into a pottering old bachelor like Doctor Higganbotham. I must leave while I am young enough to make a fresh start."

"I had hoped you would marry and rear a family here."

"This is no place for a family. It is a place only to make money."

Loath to part with this handsome young man whom she had watched grow from a green West Country lad, she had to force herself to rise and extend her hand.

"Then I suppose there is nothing to do but say good-bye, with regret."

He made as if to take her hand and then, before she could react, he stepped close and put both arms around her and kissed her full on the lips, so hard that her head was bent back. She closed her eyes and did not resist for a moment, but then, when his grasp did not slacken, she turned her face and pushed herself free.

"John, really. I don't know what to say."

"There isn't anything to say, except good-bye."

"Not good-bye, John. Farewell, with affection. I shall never forget you."

Charlotte went into the house. She did not want to watch him ride away.

That evening at dinner Richard asked her why she was so pensive.

"Just one of my moods, darling. It will pass."

A rain had fallen in Bridgetown that morning, and now, with the sun out again, a moist, warm blanket of air lay over the town. In his sugar factor's reception room, Richard was nervously waiting to go over his accounts for the new crop when Harold Lawnton entered.

"Why so glum, Richard? Something the matter?"

"Just a bit anxious to see what the bloodsucker will pay. I need all the money I can lay hands on."

"Don't we all? I am glad it is only money that has you concerned. Feared it might be Charlotte again."

"No trouble there. Not anymore, except that she's hell-bent to build a new house."

"You took my advice, then?"

"Yes, I practically groveled, and it did the trick."

"Didn't overdo it, I hope."

"I don't think so. She extracted a promise or two before she accepted my surrender, but, truth to tell, I think she was looking for an excuse to make up, the wench."

"Esther says she seems aglow."

"I hope Esther did not tip my hand. What did she say?"

"Who knows what women talk about when we are out of hearing? What about yourself? Have you got over your low spirits?"

"I suppose."

"You don't sound too cheerful."

"She has taken to rationing my wine. And she pointedly asks what I mean to do when I go to Bridgetown and just when I expect to return."

"Got you on a short leash, has she?"

"For the time being I am playing along with her game. Lord, I am too old for domestic quarrels. Man must make some concessions for connubial bliss, I suppose."

"At any rate, you are not sleeping alone anymore."

"On the contrary. I may have to pick another quarrel to get some rest."

"A fellow of our age has to learn to pace himself, you know."

"Speak for yourself, Harold. But I do miss the wine and the cards."

"What's this about money? You've had two good crops in a row."

"Oh, my trip to England ran more than I meant it to. There were many hands out there, you know, to get to see this minister and that."

"Bribes?"

"Gifts to the right people, let's call them. And I had to do far more entertaining than I reckoned on. It all added up."

"Well, you always were the gambler."

Richard made a face. "Don't use that word. I have done too much of that, too."

"I did not mean it literally, of course."

Richard arose and stood in the doorway of the stifling office, turning his back on Lawnton and the subject of gambling. He noticed several red-uniformed militiamen running down Broad Street, peering into shops and taverns. And then one of them saw him.

"Colonel Bolton, sir," the fellow shouted. "I have a message for you."

The militiaman, out of breath, ran across the street to the factor's office. "And Major Lawnton. Both of you are wanted at Governor Atkins's office. Immediately."

"What's the matter, man?"

"I am not to divulge the reason. But the governor says it is urgent."

It was midafternoon, and Charlotte was reading on the veranda when she heard the sound of the horse's hooves pounding along the Bridgetown road. She arose and, with one hand shielding her eyes from the glare of the sun, watched Richard gallop up the lane and into the yard. He leapt from the saddle, shouting for Toby to come and take the sweating horse.

"Whatever is the matter?" she asked.

"No time to talk. I must have my uniform. Hold the horse. Have Toby water him. There is not a minute to spare."

In their bedroom, Charlotte watched Richard don his red coat and buckle the cross belts. "What is going on?"

"Load your pistols and keep the shutters closed."

"Richard, you must tell me what this is all about."

"Something is brewing among the slaves."

"Our slaves?"

"Maybe everyone's. We are mustering the militia in Speightstown. Keep your voice low. Don't alarm the servants. I will alert Croxton. Might be best for his wife to join you here."

He strapped on his sword and thrust two pistols in his waistband.

"What is brewing? For heaven's sake, tell me."

"There is a plot. We must move before it is too late."

She followed him down the stairs, pleading to know more.

"I'd tell you if I knew. Just keep your pistols at hand and stay indoors. I will send a squad out to guard the house tonight."

Before she could ask more questions, he was astride his horse again.

A little later, a bewildered Mistress Croxton came into the house. Charlotte seated her in the shuttered drawing room.

"I don't know what is going on, Lady Bolton. Horace says I am to stay here. Do you know what is the matter? Something to do with the slaves, Horace says." She broke into tears. "I don't feel safe here. I wish I had never left England."

"Whatever is the matter, Mistress Croxton, crying will not help. I would prefer that our servants see no evidence of alarm or fear."

"Do you think they mean to kill us?"

"I cannot believe that is the case. Now please compose yourself."

Near dusk a squad of militiamen riding dray horses and donkeys clattered up the lane and dismounted in the front yard. A sandy-haired sergeant with one crossed eye introduced himself in a strong Scots accent and announced that he and his men were there "to protect ye all."

"I am glad you are here," Charlotte said, "but am uncertain just what we are to be protected from."

"Why, the Naygroes, ma'am." He lowered his voice and looked about him. "They do say in Speightstown they mean to kill us all. Or make us their slaves."

In other circumstances, Charlotte might have been amused by the spectacle of ten unmilitary-looking militiamen in ill-fitting uniforms, but she had to admit that they made her feel safer this day. The sergeant, a Holestown carter, insisted on marching his red-faced, awkward fellows through the house and about the yard "to make a reconnaissance, ye know."

After agreeing that half of the squad should stand sentry duty outside while the others slept in the downstairs hall, they stacked their muskets against the bearded fig tree in the back yard and waited at the kitchen door to be fed.

These were part of the poor white population of whom Charlotte had heard so many complaints in her early days on the island and about whom she still knew very little. Several thousand had emigrated in the past decade, seeking a better life on other islands or North America and often fleeing debts. Those left behind operated small dung farms, raising cattle, sheep, or turkeys both for their manure and their flesh; or made a business of selling fresh water from their deep wells to ships; or hauled supplies from and sugar to Bridgetown; or grew tobacco or aloes; or worked as carpenters, boilers, mechanics, and overseers; or even lived by begging. Barbados had a far larger white population than any other British colony in the West Indies, and they made up the backbone of the militia.

Charlotte had brought from England her feeling of superiority toward the poor. There was a far higher proportion of wealthy persons in Barbados than back home, but a smaller one of energetic, prosperous folk of middle rank. In her aristocratic sight, most of the poor whites were a sorry lot indeed. And here she was, under the protection of just such a crew, all with rude manners and huge appetites.

After supper, they amused themselves by threatening Cudjoe with their guns, laughing to see him scurry behind the outraged Mirabel's skirts. Later, when Croxton asked the sergeant to post two of his men at the Negro yard, no one would accept the duty.

Croxton already had a low opinion of the militia, and he was incensed by what he regarded as a show of cowardice, but the sergeant refused to order anyone to do more than protect the house.

"Ye may have been in the English army, as ye say, but 'tis I who am in command here, and I'll nae force them."

"Then I will stand guard myself."

Charlotte showed the tearful Mistress Croxton to the spare bedroom. Even without the racket of half a dozen men snoring in the lower hall, her own mind was too unsettled for sleep. She had heard tales of two earlier rebellion plots, both among white servants, but each had been forestalled by the arrest and execution of the conspirators. None had yet involved African slaves. But, she thought as she lay awake, those slaves now outnumbered the island's whites more than two to one. And David had impressed on her their discontent over the recent shortage of provisions.

A shout from the yard drew her back from the edge of sleep.

"Halt! Stop where you are."

"What's up, Skinner?" the sergeant called out to a sentry.

"Someone in the bushes over there."

Charlotte arose and seized a pistol. She heard a scuffling of feet downstairs and then a hubbub in the yard. She opened her window to ask what was going on.

" 'Tis yer little yard Naygro, ma'am," the sergeant replied. "Caught him out here with a drum."

"He is my gardener. He belongs here."

"I know that. But what's he doing with a drum?"

"It is a toy. We allow him to keep it."

"Don't he know he ain't to go out tonight?"

"No one told him. He is just a little boy, as you can see."

"All the same, I'd like to keep his drum for the night."

"Very well, but please stop making so much noise. And I would think you and your men might be just as comfortable on the veranda."

The rest of the long night passed fitfully for Charlotte. She arose at dawn, feeling nervous and unrested. All during the forenoon, she saw troops of militiamen riding or marching along the Bridgetown road. Later, with her spyglass, she observed blacks in chains being driven north toward Speightstown.

Clemmie, Toby, and Mirabel spoke to her only when she asked them a question. Her lack of sleep, irritation at having Mistress Croxton underfoot, and the militiamen loitering about waiting to be fed all set Charlotte's nerves on edge. She was relieved during the afternoon by a brief visit from David.

"Just wanted to make sure you are all right, Charlotte," he said, still seated on his horse. "Richard has sent for me to come to Speightstown, as an interpreter."

"Whatever for?"

"He is sitting on a court-martial. They have rounded up scores of slaves, and they want me to help question them."

"Then there is substance to the rumors?"

"Apparently so. I for one am not surprised. I must be on my way. Just wanted to look in to see you are safe."

"You show more concern for me than Richard. He might as well have sent a swarm of locusts as these militiamen. We will have no food stores left if this emergency does not end soon and my protectors return to their accustomed pursuits."

Charlotte slept better that night. When she came downstairs the next morning, she was surprised to learn that the militiamen had departed, and to find Mirabel in tears.

"They take Joe," Mirabel said.

Clemmie confirmed it. "A man came on a horse and told the cross-eyed one to bring Joe and his drum to Speightstown."

"How dare they? Why did you not awaken me?"

"I am sorry, Mistress. The man said the master sent him."

"Gentlemen, we must apprehend and punish every slave who had the slightest part in this shocking conspiracy, even those who had guilty knowledge and did not speak. It were far better to execute a few innocent Africans than to allow a single conspirator to go undetected and unpunished."

The face of the provost marshal glistened with sweat as he addressed the militia officers facing him across a long table. The doors and windows of the warehouse were shut, despite the close, hot atmosphere, and the building was surrounded by armed militiamen.

"The governor's writ of oyer and terminer gives us a free hand. I remind you that the determination of the guilt or

innocence of individual Negroes is secondary. Our greater duty
is to root out the evil growth of rebellion and make certain that
the good folk of Barbados need never fear another such plot. Let
us proceed with our work."

Militiamen had whipped and tortured enough confessions
from the weaker-willed plotters so that the court had a general
idea of the aims and scope of the scheme. Sweltering in their
uniforms, Richard and his fellow officers listened with alarm
and indignation to the testimony. Some ground their teeth or
groaned at the revelations. One moved that the proceedings be
ended and all those arrested be summarily shot. Another questioned the wisdom of needlessly killing valuable field hands.
The interrogations continued into the night, until all slaves
who wished had either confessed or accused others.

Then the weary court turned its attention to those who
refused to testify. Quaco, his face swollen and his back a bloody
crisscross, now faced the court.

At his refusal to answer questions in English, the provost
asked David to translate.

"You belong to Major Lawnton, and your name is Sambo. Is
that correct?"

Quaco shook his head.

"What do you mean? I have treated you at Fulham Plantation. I know your name."

"I belong to no one."

"Your name is Sambo, however."

"They call me that. But I am Quaco."

The provost responded to David's translation with:
"Advise him not to jest with us. If he does not reveal all he
knows, he will be taken outside and roasted to death slowly."

Quaco smiled contemptuously. "If you roast me today, then
you cannot do it tomorrow. You can kill me only once."

The officers muttered in anger. The provost rapped his
pistol butt on the table. "Tell him he had best not try to bluff
this court."

"Why trifle with him further?" the man next to Richard

asked. "We know him to be one of Cuffee's lieutenants. Let's put a bullet in his brain and have done with it."

"Not so fast," Richard spoke up. "I remember this fellow. Harold Lawnton paid seventeen pounds for him. He will hardly thank us for depriving him of his investment without a confession. Besides, if he really was a ringleader, we must learn all he knows before he dies."

"I agree," the provost said. "Ask him if he knows Cuffee."

"Many know Cuffee," Quaco replied.

"Did Cuffee talk him into joining his plot?"

"No one talks Quaco into anything."

"Ask him if he is not a Coromantee slave."

"The white man calls us that, but I am a Fanti, and I am not a slave. I am only a prisoner."

The questions and the defiant or evasive answers continued for several minutes until the provost, in exasperation, said, "This is taking too long. Let the militia have another go at him. Bolton is correct. We must make that one talk."

From earlier testimony, the court learned that Cuffee had been at work for three years, patiently and craftily setting up cells of rebellion among his fellow tribesmen at plantations for several miles around Speightstown. He was to be crowned king of the island and his kinsmen were to control the other blacks after all the white males had been slain. He had meant to touch off the uprising the night of the end-of-harvest celebration, but the appearance of the militia company at Bolton Hall had caused a delay. All had been ready for the next moonless night when the house servant of a judge told her master of a conversation she had overheard between two male Fantis.

Between the appearances of witnesses or prisoners, the members of the court puzzled over gaps in their information. How had Cuffee kept in touch with his various groups of conspirators? How had he meant to signal them to start killing their masters? The provost despaired of making old Cuffee talk. Had they not been stopped, the militiamen would have killed him by now.

Outside the warehouse, they could hear the screams of slaves being beaten or tortured with hot pokers. The cries of a woman rose above the others, then died away to sobs as the doors opened, and two men led in Mandze.

Richard did not recognize her at first. Her hair was streaked with gray and her figure, once so supple and firm, had become gross. She had always had wide cheekbones, but now her face was grotesquely swollen. Suddenly he wished to be anywhere but sitting with his peers on this court facing his former concubine.

She needed no translator. In response to the provost's "Tell this court what you know," she replied, "I know very little. I knew that some of the men acted strangely. I heard talk they would take up arms but thought they were just bragging."

"Who was doing this talking?"

"I do not know. I heard their voices outside my hut one night saying something about killing our masters. It was like a dream."

"Did you warn your master?"

"Which master?"

"Major Lawnton, of course. Look here, woman, if you want to die, just keep up these evasions. Did you warn your owner or your overseer?"

"No."

"So you kept this guilty knowledge to yourself until now. Do you know Cuffee?"

"I saw him hanging about."

"Hanging about whom?"

"Quaco."

"Did you know Quaco was involved?"

"Not for certain, no."

One of the officers interrupted. "I don't understand. Is this woman here as a witness or as an accused?"

"What does it matter?"

"I just wondered why or how she was brought in. Well-spoken wench, I must say."

"I ordered all Coromantee women to be questioned. And, yes, she is well spoken."

Richard hated the officer beside him for leaning close and whispering, "Shouldn't wonder she speaks good English, considering who she learned it from, eh what, Bolton?"

"Well, is the woman on trial or not?" the first officer inquired.

"Hold, gentlemen," the provost said. "Mandze, we do not want to kill you. But we must if you know anything you are holding back. For instance, how did Cuffee and Quaco stay in touch?"

"You don't know?" she asked.

"If I knew, I would not ask. How did they communicate?"

"With the drum."

"Drum? What drum?"

"Ask Yellow Hair, there," she said bitterly. "He thinks he knows everything. Ask him."

Richard hesitated, pretending he did not know what or whom she meant, but with the eyes of his fellows on him, he shrugged and said, "She must mean the drum my wife's little garden pickaninny has. We thought it was a toy."

As they fumbled for questions, David intervened. "Excuse me, Richard, but you recall the day you bought your little Joe. He was clinging to this Quaco and his drum."

He turned to Mandze and spoke to her in her native tongue, but she replied in English, scornfully. "If you white men are so clever, why did it take you so long to learn the truth?"

He questioned her again, in her own language, and she nodded her head.

David faced the panel. "There it is. The Boltons have a nine- or ten-year-old yard boy who has a drum he brought over from Africa. He is the son of this Sambo or Quaco, and we never knew it. She says the boy can make the drum talk."

They were about to lead her away when Richard took a deep breath to steady himself and then called out, "Wait! There is something else she has not told you."

4

... That day, that dreadful, fateful, momentous, and monstrous day. Its dire consequences were to wrench my life apart.

I have written how my fate and that of others around me have turned on tiny, seemingly unimportant decisions such as mine to force my father to take me to Saint Paul's, or his to invite Richard Bolton to break bread with us back at the Rose and Crown, or Richard's to go out of his way to stop overnight at Foxley Manor, and now I was to see where other threads in the fabric of our life's tapestry began. And yet all those earlier coincidences and choices would have been rendered insignificant had I made a different decision late in that black day they hauled little Joe over to Speightstown.

I withstood my anxiety and uncertainty, yes, and anger, too, until near sunset, when I decided I could not bear another night alone at Bolton Hall. Ignoring the pleas of Clemmie, I did one of the most foolhardy things in my life, something for which I and others have paid a high price. I stuck my loaded dueling pistols in my belt and rode Nutmeg off to Speightstown. That is how desperately I wished to see Richard, wanted his reassurance that this ominous trouble would soon end. And I had to learn what had happened to little Joe.

At first I was comforted by the glow of bonfires burning in the town like beacons in the twilight. As I approached the Speightstown square and saw the shadowy shapes of hundreds of armed men milling about and smelled the odor of burning flesh, I thought the militia were holding another of their ox roasts ...

Halting her mare, Charlotte recognized the wife of a tavern owner on her second-floor balcony overlooking the square.

"Mistress Timmons. What is going on here?"

"Lord a'mercy, Lady Bolton, ye've no business to be here. Alvin, take her ladyship's horse and bring her up here with us where she'll have a better view."

Once on the narrow balcony, Charlotte had to fight to keep from fainting as the scene before her came into focus. The militia acted more like an armed mob than a disciplined military organization. Many of the men were drunk, laughing and shouting as though at a carnival. Charlotte tried to tell herself that the smoldering figures in the flames were not really human forms. But then the door of the warehouse across the square opened and a new victim, a muscular male wearing only a loincloth, was led out with hands bound behind him and was forced to his knees in the center of the square. Falling silent, the militiamen formed themselves into irregular ranks. A huge, bald corporal, wearing a butcher's apron, hefted a heavy broadsword for all to see. He held the blade directly in front, massive forearms perpendicular to his thick chest and gently, almost delicately, lowered the blade to touch the back of the Negro's bowed neck.

Charlotte put one hand over her mouth and with the other steadied herself against the balcony rail. The executioner held his pose until the militiamen had fallen silent. Then he raised the sword high above his head and rose on his tiptoes. Down came the blade with tremendous force, swishing clean through the victim's neck. The head spun across the cobblestones, and the body sagged to its side with blood geysering from the stump of the neck.

A hoarse, ugly cheer rose from the militia. Two men ran to pick up the head and mount it on a pole. While they raised the pole to give the crowd a better view, others carried the body to the bonfire and tossed it into the flames.

"One less Naygro to worry about," the tavern keeper's wife said as she turned to Charlotte. "Lord a'mercy, her ladyship has swooned. Here, Alvin, help me lift the poor dear onto the couch. There. Bring brandy. Quick now."

Charlotte came to with the woman bending over her. She gagged on the brandy, spilling it down her dress, but then, remembering what she had just seen, she asked for more and swallowed it with a grimace.

"Awful, simply dreadful."

"I am sorry, my dear. It is the best brandy we have. Should have cut it with a bit of water, I expect."

"No. What they are doing out there is monstrous. How long has it been going on?"

"Since midafternoon," the tavern keeper replied. "The court-martial is meeting in the warehouse. Questioned witnesses most of last night and throughout the day. Now they are carrying out the sentences one by one as they find them guilty."

"Feeling better now, my dear?" the woman asked.

"Somewhat, but oh, how brutal."

"Perhaps so, but you have to remember it is no worse than what they meant to do to us. You should not be riding out alone like this, you know."

"I must find my husband. Surely he will put a stop to this barbaric butchery."

"Why, Lady Bolton, begging your pardon, Sir Richard is on the court-martial."

"Where is he?"

"In the warehouse. What do you want with him?"

"They took away my little gardener. A boy of about nine. We call him Joe. I want my husband to give him back."

The man and his wife looked at each other in silence, and growing apprehensive, Charlotte demanded, "Have you seen the lad?"

"Did he have a drum?" the man asked.

"As a matter of fact, he did."

"Yes, well, you see, they learned he was sending messages for old Cuffee."

"Cuffee?"

"Yes, the old Coromantee as started this business. Belongs to Colonel Bates."

"That is ridiculous. Joe is a harmless child."

"They say he was under the influence of his father."

"Little Joe has no father."

"No one knowed it until too late, but his father belonged to Major Lawnton at Fulham Plantation. They brought the boy in, thinking that would make his father confess."

Fearing she was about to faint again, Charlotte sat down. "And did this supposed father confess?"

"I think not. That was him they just executed."

"Oh, my God. Please, Mister Timmons, I must see my husband. Would you take me to him?"

"They won't let a soul near the warehouse."

"Then take me to little Joe. The poor child must be frightened out of his wits."

Again the man and his wife looked at each other. Mistress Timmons poured another glass of brandy. "I think you may need a bit more, my lady."

"No, thank you. Well, Mister Timmons, I would be grateful if you would escort me to where they keep the prisoners."

The man cleared his throat. "My lady, I don't like to give you news that will distress you, but I do fear you will have to get yourself a new gardener."

Charlotte drank the brandy and then sat numbly while Mister and Mistress Timmons prattled on about the proceedings, assuring her that "we can all sleep sounder for this." They praised the dispatch with which Richard and his fellow officers had rounded up suspects, and they deplored the atrocities and indignities the Coromantees plotted to inflict on their masters.

"If your husband and others like him had not acted, right now my dear Alvin would be lying with his throat cut and some black monster would be having his pleasure of me." The woman sniffed and put her handkerchief to her eyes.

"There, my dear, it did not happen," her husband said. "But it makes my blood boil to think of it. I only hope they kill enough of the savages so the others will never dare try such a thing."

Charlotte closed her eyes, trying not to imagine little Joe's body lying on the bonfire.

"Your husband made a fine speech in the square this afternoon before the executions began," Mistress Timmons was saying. "He assured us that the ringleaders has been singled out. A grand man, is Sir Richard. I was that disappointed we did not get him as our governor, although I have no complaints of Sir Jonathan Atkins."

"Indeed we do not," her husband said. "After all, it was Sir Jonathan as nipped this thing in the bud."

Still in a trance, Charlotte only half heard the screams now rising from the square, followed by a woman's voice shrilling in English. "I have done nothing! I tried to give warning. He would not listen to me."

A fresh roar went up from the militiamen as the great sword fell across the back of Mandze's neck.

"That one was a woman as knew all about the plot and kept it to herself," Timmons said. "Should have followed the lead of Judge Hall's Fortuna and told what she knew from the first."

Unaware of the identity of the woman who had just died, Charlotte asked weakly, "Is this going on all night?"

"Only until midnight," the tavern keeper said. "They are saving old Cuffee and a few others until morning. They want to bring slaves in from the plantations to let them see that one meet his Maker."

"You'll not want to miss that, my lady," Mistress Timmons said. "Why don't you stay here the night? I'll just go and prepare a bed for you."

The couple went inside, leaving Charlotte alone on the balcony. When they returned to show her to her room, she was gone.

"I hope she don't do something foolish," Mistress Timmons said.

"Headstrong woman. Expect she has gone to give her

husband the message herself. Nothing we can do but wait. Silly woman, too, if you ask me. Took it hard about that little Naygro, and her husband rich enough to buy her a dozen more, I'm sure."

Although Charlotte had been upset by the reports of an uprising, she had regarded them as rumors. So, angered by the arrest of Joe, she had set out for Speightstown not unduly worried, still confident of the basic rightness of her world and sure of her place in it. There were inequities in English society in general, and special ones in Barbados, because of its growing population of primitive Africans, but just in her ten years on the island she had seen an amelioration of conditions. Barbados was becoming a more civilized island. Fewer owners now practiced needless cruelties on their slaves, it seemed to her. With kindly men in control of the government and enlightened people such as David Higganbotham coming over, there was a fair chance slavery could become a benign institution benefiting both slave and owner, rather like serfdom in Russia. It bothered her that custom forbade converting Africans to Christianity, or teaching them to read or write, but she thought that would change with time. Meanwhile, her conscience had been little more troubled than it had been by the treatment of her father's tenants in Bedfordshire or the sailors aboard the *Mary Leigh.* She and Richard treated their slaves well enough. And they scorned fellow planters who were cruel.

The Charlotte who rode away from Speightstown into the bleak night was a very different woman. What she had witnessed from the tavern balcony had shaken her very being. She had heard stories of the hangings of pickpockets and highwaymen at Tyburn outside London, but surely the crowds of the English curious did not act so bloodthirstily as had the militiamen. And they had done such a thing to her little Joe. No, not some faceless "they," her own husband had been a party to the atrocity. They were chopping off the heads of fellow human beings and tossing their bodies into bonfires when not one of the

Negroes, as she understood it, not one had lifted a hand against a single white person.

Richard often compared his slaves to children to be controlled with firmness but a measure of kindness. What hypocrisy! No, worse, what depravity, to slay even an innocent child. Moses Martin had been right after all. This island reeked of injustice and wickedness.

The darkness of the night was barely relieved by a fingernail of a waning moon. Charlotte rode with her head bowed, letting the reins hang slack, allowing Nutmeg to go at her own slow pace. She dreaded returning to Bolton Hall. She did not want to tell Mirabel about her beloved little Joe. And other thoughts troubled her. Clemmie had hauled the boy in to complain about his going off to play his drum in the graveyard. Why had she been so lax? Her kindness had cost the boy his life.

She made no effort to squelch the regrets and self-accusations with which her mind spun. They partially blocked the awful image of that huge man in the butcher's apron with sword raised above the kneeling African.

Another profound change had occurred in Charlotte's psyche. All day she had yearned to see Richard, who, for all his faults, had meant more to her than anyone, or anything. In the past, she had rarely hesitated to tell him straight out when he had offended her, but this thing went too deep for an easy confrontation. She did not want to hear his voice or have him touch her.

Charlotte's shock and disillusionment put her beyond tears. So Nutmeg plodded on, instinctively stepping around stones and potholes in the road until, near the lane into Bolton Hall, she broke into a trot. Charlotte took up the reins and halted the mare at the turnoff. She sat in the dark for a long time, debating what to do. She could not bear to return to that ugly house with all its wrenching memories. Esther would give her refuge at Fulham, but she dreaded the explanations that would be required, or the obligatory, platitudinous advice that she would receive. Where on this wretched, unhappy island could she find a refuge from her torment?

Her mind was so frozen that she was beyond either fears or tears. After long minutes of sitting on Nutmeg's back beside the slave cemetery there at the entrance to Bolton Hall, she struck the mare's flanks with her crop and continued along the main road.

The moon was higher now, and she could make out the way rising toward Mount Hillaby. More by intuition than sight, she found the point where the path to Tom Cochran's old hermitage began. She had enjoyed some almost mystically serene moments at this hideaway tucked into a patch of wilderness. John Martin would be on his way to Virginia now, she assumed. The old hut offered a place where she could hide and sort out her emotions.

Dismounting, she led Nutmeg gingerly into the bushes, straining to see, hand before her face to fend off branches. Twice her nerve nearly failed her and she started to turn back and ride down to Fulham and the comfortable sympathy that Esther would offer. But, not, it would be too easy for Richard to find her at Fulham.

She pressed on, groping for her way. She lost her hat, and her face smarted from scratches. Now she had gone too deep into the thicket to turn back. She flailed about, madly seeking the path, despairing of ever finding the old hut in this worst night of her life.

The choir of insects and tree frogs that had greeted her arrival and accompanied her penetration of the thicket suddenly ceased, and a voice called.

"Who's out there?"

Charlotte stiffened, and her hand went to the butt of one of her pistols.

They brought old Cuffee before the court-martial board early the next morning. His face expressionless, he stood in front of the officers, waiting with alert eyes to hear what they had to say. The provost had summoned Colonel Bates to hear the testimony. An injured look on his turkey-red face, Bates took his place at the table.

"Well, Cuffee," the provost said. "Your game is up. It won't do you any good not to talk, not anymore. We know all there is to know. Mandze told us all that she learned from Sambo, or Quaco, to call him by his African name. And the little boy with the drum talked."

"Did Quaco talk?"

"We will ask the questions here, but he did not need to talk. Others did. We know just what you meant to do and when."

"Then what do you want from me?"

"We want to know why you planned all this."

Bates had been listening with growing indignation. Now he interrupted the provost. "Yes, why? You black rascal. I took you out of the field and gave you a position of trust. Treated you almost like a son, I did. Let you go about freely, dressed you better than the others, never stinted on food. Trusted you, and this is how you repay my dear wife and me, by plotting to kill us."

The old man sputtered on about how shocked his wife was until the provost asked him to be quiet and nodded for Cuffee to continue.

Cuffee drew himself up straight and looked over the heads of the officers. He spoke slowly at first. "He says he treated me like a son. That makes me laugh. I would be ashamed to be the son of such a foolish father. Oh yes, he treated me better than many of my brothers. Gave me cast-off clothing and fed me on scraps from his table. But what he does not see, what none of you white men see is that when you mistreat one of us you make us all hate you. And there is not one of us who does not hate you."

"So, you feel no gratitude for what Colonel Bates did for you?" the provost said sarcastically. "We rather suspected that."

"Why should I be grateful? You white people brought me and my brothers to this place against our wills. You expect us to thank you for enslaving us?"

"You talk nonsense. Many of you were already slaves in Africa. Most of you are better off here."

"Slave or free, in Africa we were human beings. There, even a slave can marry his captors, and his children will be treated as real sons and daughters, not like possessions. Here you make us live like oxen or mules chained to the end of a millsweep, going round and round until we die, without hope. But we are men and women, not animals. This silly old man who calls himself my master says he treated me as a son. How many times has he insulted me by calling me a 'black rascal'? He used to make fun of me to his wife or other whites without even lowering his voice, as though I had no ears, no feelings. You are all guilty, you know it. You say we are like stupid little children, but let me tell you this: Not one of you could last for a month back in Africa where men are real men and women are real women. You could not last a month living as you force your so-called slaves to live here."

Richard smote the table with the palm of his hand. "Must we listen to this old scoundrel talk such rot? Look, you black ape, I came here as a prisoner myself. I would have sold my soul to have had a master as kind as Colonel Bates. I lasted far longer than a month, not only lasted but prevailed."

"Yes, and now that you hold the whip, you forget how it feels to be on the other end. Did you enjoy being a slave? Why are you surprised that we do not wish to be your human oxen?"

"Your race was intended for slavery," Richard replied. "You should accept your lot and make the best of it. We did not bring you to Barbados to be our brothers and sisters. We brought you here to work."

As Richard spoke, the corners of Cuffee's mouth drew down, and he looked into the faces of the officers. "You say Africans are meant by God to be slaves, and I suppose you think your colorless skins mean He intends you to be masters. I cannot think God would choose such a weak, sickly people as you. If you work in the sun without a shirt for even half a day, you turn as red as a lobster and break out in blisters. Your militia would not last half a day without their guns. My brothers would have torn them apart even with their guns. We would have scattered them like a flock of geese, had we not been betrayed."

The members of the court-martial were muttering angrily now. "Geese do not wield broadswords, as you soon will discover," one of them said.

"And not even geese are so silly as to expect someone you insult, mistreat, and force to live without hope of change still to love you. You despise us when we submit to you; you hate us when we resist. White men, you want to know what I think? I think beneath all your bluster you know how wrong you are, and you dread us because you know how much cause we have for revenge. You are afraid of us, and well you should be. Soon you will kill me, but do not think that will put an end to your fears. As long as you hold us in slavery, you cannot rest easy. You escaped our vengeance this time, but you cannot go on forever treating men and women like animals. You grow weak and foolish in this land. You drink too much, and you have few children. You think only of gaining wealth. But my people thrive here. We will endure, and sooner or later your power over us will end, and we will be the masters of this island. Lead me to your bonfire. I am not afraid."

The officers sat in silence for a moment. Then the provost called an aide over to inquire if the slaves had been brought in from nearby plantations as witnesses and whether new bonfires were ready.

There at Tom Cochran's old lair, each time Charlotte tried to tell John what she had seen and heard in Speightstown, she broke down, so that after an hour he still had only a sketchy idea of what had happened.

"Don't try to talk anymore. Just tell me what I can do to help."

"There is no one I can turn to. Richard ... oh, John, he sent little Cudjoe to his death and the others. They butchered them and the militiamen stood about laughing. My own husband ... "

She put her hands over her face. "Even David was involved. They called him there to question the slaves. You are the only person I know who is innocent in this awful business."

"None of us is innocent, Charlotte. The sin of slavery has infected us all. I, too, have profited from it."

"What is to become of us? I can't go back to Bolton Hall, not tonight, maybe never!"

"Stay with me for a while, then. Don't try to talk anymore. Have some hot tea."

The tea restored her enough so that she stopped trembling and became more coherent.

"You must think me a mad woman, but this place called to me. It is the one spot on Barbados that is free of slavery. I remember how peaceful it was when we came to visit your father and the old hermit when you were but a lad."

"I remember that day well. But do not apologize for coming. There is no one I would rather see."

"I must look like a wretch. See my scratched hands."

He came closer. "And your face, too. Let me attend to you."

She sat passively while he lightly applied an ointment to her welts. "May I have more tea?" she asked when he had finished.

He refilled her cup and then brought a blanket. "It gets cooler than you think up here."

"I didn't expect anyone to be here. I must have given you a start."

"I dreamed last night that you were in distress. I dreamed that you were crying out to me for help."

He drew his stool close to hers and looked at her until she grew embarrassed.

"But I did not dream you would come to me like this."

They looked at each other a long while. Later Charlotte could not have said for certain which of them first leaned forward. All she could remember was that his arms suddenly were around her, and she was sobbing against his shoulder without any pretense of control.

"My darling, darling, Charlotte, you have come to me at last. I have prayed for this."

She uttered no protest when he lifted her and carried her to his crude bed of rushes in a corner of the cabin, nor when he lay down beside her and drew the blanket over them. Ever since the day he had come to say good-bye to her and had taken her by surprise with his bold kiss, she had been repressing her desire for this very thing, and here it was. Yielding to him seemed a way to expiate the cruel wickedness of the Speightstown executions. At least it blotted the memory for the moment.

She awoke with the sun in her face and, raising herself on one elbow, examined his sensitive, yet strong young face. How guileless, untroubled, he appeared. He opened his eyes to see her staring down at him.

"Dear Charlotte. What have I done to you?"

She kissed him on the lips before replying, "You have restored my sanity, for one thing."

He sat up and put his arms around her. "What shall we do?"

"Just now I would like some breakfast."

They talked throughout the morning telling each other things they had never revealed to anyone. They laughed at their recollections of their first formal meeting aboard the *Mary Leigh*. "I thought you were some sort of goddess. I had never seen such a beautiful lady. And up in the crow's-nest I used to spend more time looking down at you than I did keeping the lookout."

"I thought you were a darling little boy. I knew you would grow into a handsome man, and you did not disappoint me."

"Last year, when you came up here with me, it was all I could do to keep from throwing myself upon you."

"You young fool. You could have any girl you want on Barbados. Why waste yourself on a middle-aged married woman?"

"I would spend the rest of my life with you."

"Don't let's think of the rest of our lives. There is only right now. I can't let myself think of anything but this."

"But you do love me?"

"At this moment I would not say no."

Later they sat by the same tree where they had picnicked once, now eating plantains and looking out toward the sea. He stretched out and put his head in her lap. "Could heaven be any more pleasant than this?"

She smoothed his hair. "Or hell any worse than what I witnessed last night?"

"Do you want to tell me about that now?"

She left out nothing in her account. When she had finished, he said, "You see now why I must leave this unnatural island?"

"Are you sure Virginia will be any better?"

"If you will come with me, Virginia will become my heaven."

"Oh, John, you can't want a woman so much older than yourself. And one already married at that."

"Who would know there? I can grow a beard and act very grave. And as a doctor I can provide for you. I am a good one, you know, and in Virginia no one need be told that I am only a tailor's son." He sat up. "Seriously, Charlotte, tonight we can make our way to Bridgetown and go aboard ship; any ship that will get us off this accursed island. Look, from what you say, things will be in a turmoil for a while. We'll never have a better chance to slip away. What do you say? I have enough money for our passage."

Charlotte kissed him lightly, then drew away to say, "Don't press me, John. I must think things through. Meanwhile let me savor this moment."

"If you won't come with me, then I will stay here and confront your husband. I will tell him you are mine now."

"Don't be a fool. He would kill us both. Here, take that look off your face and come into my arms again."

They were aroused by the sound of a horse's hooves on the

path and David Higganbotham's voice calling, "Halloo there, John, are you home?"

Charlotte barely had time to sit up and rearrange her clothing before the doctor led his horse into the clearing. John was standing with his back to her so that Higganbotham at first did not see her.

"There you are. Didn't you hear me calling? I am looking for Charlotte Bolton. She has been missing since yesterday."

"Here I am, David."

He dropped the reins of his horse and walked toward her, looking puzzled and worried. "My God, Charlotte, they are beside themselves at Bolton Hall. They thought you were in Speightstown."

"I was in Speightstown, David. I wish I had not been, but I was."

"During the executions?"

"During the murders."

"Then where did you spend the night?"

"I was in safe hands, David. It is touching of you to be so concerned. Did Richard send you for me, or is he too busy slaughtering defenseless slaves?"

He came closer, squinting into her face. He spoke slowly, choosing his words with care to give himself time to understand. "Richard is not aware that you are missing. He will not know until he returns to Bolton Hall this evening."

"Well, now that you know where I am you can resume your own role of Judas goat."

"What do you mean by that?"

"Were you not a part of the official proceedings? Were you not there to question them in their own languages? How many so-called confessions did you wring from them?"

Charlotte despised the man for his hurt look. His voice became soft, pleading. "Could we speak in private for a few minutes?"

"I have no secrets from John."

"Please, Charlotte. I must say something in private."

John started to protest but at Charlotte's nod he turned

without speaking and led Higganbotham's horse away to tether it beside Charlotte's.

"I am surprised at you, Charlotte," he whispered. "Surprised and disgusted. How long have you been up here? What would Richard think? What would he do?"

"I no longer care what Richard thinks or does."

"What has come over you, Charlotte? This is not like you at all. Don't you comprehend how wrong this is? And you a married woman."

"You speak of wrong? Was it not wrong when they butchered little Joe? And they say he had a father at Fulham all this time. I saw them chop off the man's head. And the militiamen cheered. How dare you speak to me of wrongdoing? You, and Richard and the others on that so-called court are guilty of the worst wickedness I can conceive of."

"What do you know of the conspiracy, Charlotte?"

"Only that some of the Coromantees talked of an uprising."

He repeated what the court learned, but he could see that she was not convinced when she interrupted with, "So it was necessary to slay even a child who happened to have a drum?"

"Perhaps not. The majority of the court-martial thought so. Do you remember earlier this year how you frightened away a peeping Tom?"

"Yes."

"That was Sambo, or Quaco, the Coromantee who was Joe's father."

"And for that they chopped off his head?"

"He had a reason for spying on you. He was one of Cuffee's chief lieutenants, and they were to have first choice of white women. You were his choice, Charlotte. And if the plot had not been uncovered . . . need I say more?"

Speechless, she looked at him incredulously as he continued.

"Joe was to open your house so that his father could slip in and slay Richard. He admitted it. He also admitted poisoning your dog."

Charlotte put her hands over her face. The man in the butcher's apron and the kneeling African, that image was too strongly imprinted on her mind for her to absorb these new revelations. Higganbotham squatted and drew her hands from her face. "Charlotte, they executed thirty-five slaves. Everyone who helped old Cuffee, or who knew and did not tell. They worked on this scheme for many months. Once set in motion, whether the uprising succeeded or not, there would have been a bloodbath. This island would be up to its knees in blood. The blood of white men and black."

"I cannot stop thinking of what I saw in the square," she murmured.

Charlotte had never seen Higganbotham angry. For a moment she thought he would strike her. "Damn what you saw in the square. Damn you for causing me so much anxiety. Have you any idea how I feel about you? I was sickened, too, by the way they whipped and branded to get confessions, but when I heard what that Sambo meant to do to you, I would gladly have taken over the job of executioner." He caught himself, and looked away with tears in his eyes. "I am most awfully sorry to have spoken to you like that. I am terribly fond of you. You must know that. And of Richard, too. Look, I know you and Richard have not been getting on too well since he returned from England, but confound it, Charlotte, he is still your husband and he loves you very deeply. The other members of the court had to restrain him when Joe confessed, or he would have slain Sambo on the spot."

"Did they have to kill the boy?"

"If it matters one way or the other, Richard voted to send him off the island, but the majority overruled him. He told them you would never forgive him if they executed the lad."

John came near. "You said you only wanted a word with her. What have you done to upset her so?"

"Stay out of this, my young fellow," Higganbotham replied.

"Don't call me young fellow. I am not your apprentice any longer. What do you think you are doing?"

"I am taking this woman back to her home. She is going to refresh herself there, and while she is doing so I am going to tell her servants what will happen if they ever speak of their mistress's absence to a soul. And when her husband returns tonight she will greet him as a man who performed a most unpleasant duty and who merits her love and respect. And her fidelity."

"You cannot take her from me. Nobody can ever take her from me again. I love her."

"So do I. And that is why I am returning her to her husband."

Higganbotham drew Charlotte to her feet.

His fists doubled, John moved between them and their horses.

"I will not let you take her away."

The physician half smiled. "John, I used to go about my rounds unarmed. But today, because of the uprising, I carry a pistol in my waistband." He drew back his coat so that the butt of the weapon showed. "If you do not stand aside, I will shoot you on this very spot."

"Charlotte," John implored. "You are not going with him, are you?"

"I am most dreadfully sorry, John."

Higganbotham lifted her to her saddle with a strength that surprised Charlotte. As David took his own horse's reins, John began shouting at them. "There it is. Just like Old Tom said. You use ordinary folk as servants and playthings for your own pleasure. Everything is bent to your desires. If you choose to amuse yourselves with us for a little while, that is all right. But then when the play becomes real you retreat to your wealth and station. Damn you, Charlotte. You have used me, and now you toss me aside."

"Get hold of yourself, John," Higganbotham said. "You are saying foolish things. You should thank me for intervening here. Richard Bolton would kill you without a second thought if he knew." He paused. "For that matter, I expect I shall be carrying this pistol for a long time. I once looked upon you almost as my son, but if you ever interfere with Charlotte again, much as it would grieve me, I will surely shoot you."

The young man ignored the threat. "Please, Charlotte, don't leave me. Come away with me."

Head still bowed, overwhelmed by her emotions, Charlotte allowed Higganbotham to lead her horse along the path. The last thing she heard when they reached the road was John's voice crying out, "Please, please, Charlotte, don't go."

Lying across her bed at Bolton Hall, a numb, confused Charlotte tried to convince herself that the events of the past twenty-four hours had not really happened, that she was just awakening from a nightmare. She felt confused and numb. Surely she had only imagined seeing the swordsman and the doomed slave. And the feel of the hard-muscled, smooth-faced youth's body pressed close against hers, thrusting wantonly, that had never really happened. If she went downstairs, she would find Joe waiting under the fig tree. Clemmie and Mirabel would be in the kitchen preparing dinner. Richard would return home with unbloodied hands, and she would say, "I fell asleep this afternoon and had the strangest dreams."

But the images would not go away. Not the sights and sounds of the Speightstown executions and not the memory of John's contorted face and his pleas for her to stay.

She had not spoken to Higganbotham on the ride back from John's hermitage and had let him go without saying good-bye. She could not put a name to her feeling for the earnest physician. Certainly it was not gratitude. He had made her feel like a little girl caught by an uncle playing dirty games with a neighbor lad. It had been none of his business to intervene, and yet there was a rational corner of her mind that told her the man had acted out of sincere love for her and concern for Richard. The firm way he had handled both her and John surprised her. She had regarded him as a stodgy bachelor without strong emotions. Yet she felt no shame, only relief that Richard did not know. Her conscience was in suspension. It would take her a long time to sort out her feelings about what both she and others had done.

Going down the stairs, she felt like an old, world-weary woman. She forced herself to speak to the servants in her usual way, calmly inquiring about the progress of the meal, looking at them so that they dared not ask her any questions. Then she went to the veranda and waited for Richard to return. But she could not control her thoughts. Here was where John had come to say good-bye, where he had kissed her with such passion. Here was where she had stood full of anger and regret watching the sails of Willoughby's Guadaloupe-bound fleet, thinking Richard was leaving her. And here was the spot where the cart had drawn up with him dead drunk. And now here he came riding up the lane in a wilted, wrinkled uniform. He stopped at the steps and shouted for Toby, then took off his hat.

"Home never looked so good to me," he said. "God, I am weary."

Charlotte remembered other times when he had sprung from the saddle and run up the steps to embrace her. Now it struck her how old he looked. His face was gray and lined, and he only took her hand briefly and kissed her on the cheek.

"It is all over now?" she inquired.

"All behind us. But do not ask me to talk about it. I never want to go through another such experience." He sighed, then looked more closely at her face. "You have some nasty scratches."

He accepted without question her excuse about having blundered into a thorn bush while gardening.

They ate in silence. Charlotte had rehearsed replies to his questions about what she had been doing, but he asked none until they had finished eating.

"Did David stop by?"

"Yes, he did."

"And he told you?"

"Yes."

"I am sorry about the boy."

"I am, too."

"Someday, perhaps I will tell you the entire story."

"No need tonight. I expect that you will want to sleep."

"To sleep and forget. That would be a blessing."

Several days later, after he had recovered his vigor, he said to her, "You have not seemed the same since I came back from the court-martial. Is something bothering you?"

"Well, the uprising was alarming."

"That is behind us now. Are you happy?"

"Relieved, certainly. Why do you ask?"

"You seem so distant. As if your mind is far away."

"The heat bothers me more than usual this summer. And I am sick of the rain."

That night in bed she forced herself not to refuse him. But she took no joy in the act. For the first time she was conscious of the slackness of his body. Her mind was back at the hut on Apes Hill and its bed of rushes. Could that ecstasy have lasted in Virginia?

"I never see David Higganbotham hanging about anymore," he said to her next day. "Croxton said he looked in on the slaves but left without coming to the house."

"I expect he is quite busy."

"Yes, and likely to be even busier. They say in Bridgetown that your young doctor friend has sold his place on Apes Hill and is packing himself off to North America somewhere. Strange fellow that one. Never fitted in quite. Remember how you wanted to buy his term and his old mad father's? I think he has a good bit of the old man's blood in him."

Charlotte did not reply, feigning an interest in her needlepoint.

"You heard what I said?"

"I am not deaf, Richard. And you are correct. He did not fit in. Let us hope that he will in Virginia."

"I didn't know that is where he is going. What makes you say Virginia?"

"David mentioned Virginia, I think."

"I'd sooner think it was New England. That place is full of

Puritans. He'd be right at home there. I wonder why David doesn't come about anymore."

"We agreed that David is very busy."

"Sorry. I didn't mean to repeat myself. Why are you so irritable?"

"It is just very hard to make these stitches and talk."

"Then you don't mind if I walk outside and smoke my pipe?"

"On the contrary."

At first Clemmie had acted normally. She apparently felt no sorrow at the loss of Cudjoe; she had regarded him as little more than a wild animal anyway. And she seemed to have taken to heart Higganbotham's warning not to mention Charlotte's mysterious absence. But then she began to avoid Charlotte's eyes, as though she herself had something to hide. Mirabel had gone off by herself and wept at the news of Cudjoe's death but had recovered and now went about her work with her usual stoicism. But Clemmie's behavior bothered Charlotte, and she did not know what to do about it.

Then one day, when Richard was away, Charlotte's afternoon nap was interrupted by a knock on her door.

"Mistress, I have something to tell you, and I am ashamed. I hope you will not beat me."

"Beat you? I have never laid a hand on you. What is it?"

"This." Clemmie held out an envelope. "He came several nights ago and gave me this. I thought about burning it, but I could not."

"A letter? From whom?"

"Master John. He told me to tell no one."

Charlotte snatched the letter from Clemmie's hand. "How dare you hold a letter so long?"

"You are angry?"

"It is all right, Clemmie. You will speak of this to no one."

"I am sorry. I could not help it. He is going away."

"Get hold of yourself, Clemmie. I am not angry. I will not punish you if you simply keep this between us."

Charlotte felt like pushing her from the room but did give her time to wipe away her tears and compose herself. Once Clemmie was gone, she bolted the door and sat beside the window to read the letter. She could hear his voice, still tinged with its West Country accent, saying,

My dearest Charlotte—

I regret the dreadful things I said to you when you left me. You are not heartless, I know that. I beg your forgiveness. Every night since you were here I have sat beside our tree in the dark, praying to hear the sound of your horse returning to me. A thousand times I have thought of sneaking across the fields to see if your husband is away so that I might speak to you. Yesterday I went down to Bridgetown and put this land up for sale. Coming out of the lawyer's office I saw a woman with long brown hair walking along Broad Street and I ran after her crying, 'Charlotte,' and when she turned around it was not you. I suppose that is how it will be for a very long time, perhaps forever. I went to see Doctor Higganbotham to apologize to him for my behavior, and he accepted my apologies graciously. He told me how you gave him the money to buy my indenture and wanted to do the same for my father. I loved you already, you know that. Now you are enshrined in my heart forever. What passed between us is something more precious than I can ever expect to occur again in my life. Perhaps it was too good to last. At least I carry from this island one memory that I shall cherish to the end of my days. I hope it shall be so for you, as well. I do not know what life will hold for me now. I only hope that I can keep myself from leaping overboard before my ship reaches Virginia. It sails the day after tomorrow. I will leave this letter with your yellow-skinned girl. You said she was trustworthy. Always, always, I shall love you. You did more for me than I knew. And you have given me a memory that will light up the rest of my life.

Charlotte read the letter three times and then hid it away at the bottom of a chest of her clothing.

After that, her garden became her refuge. She arose early and worked until it rained or the sun became unbearable. Richard offered to give her a new slave child to help, but she declined. Clemmie sometimes chided her for pushing herself so hard but, failing to persuade her to let up, finally began sending

Toby out to help. None of them understood how the garden comforted her that summer. Unlike reading, gardening left her mind free to wander and to wonder what John might be doing now, what David Higganbotham really thought of her actions, whether Richard felt any remorse for the wholesale slaughter of the slaves, and whether the passage of time would restore their happiness together.

She wondered, too, what went on in the minds of Clemmie and Toby. They had never mentioned her absence of that night. She marveled at their discretion. And she formed a new respect for Clemmie. The girl really had loved John Martin; if he had asked *her* to go to Virginia with him, there would have been no hesitation. Strange how John was an unspoken bond between them now. Toby did not know of what was in Clemmie's heart; and Richard did not know what was in Charlotte's.

She was mildly concerned about Richard. Several times he awakened her by muttering in his sleep. She listened carefully in the hope of discovering what troubled him. "I didn't know. I really did not," she caught one time, and another, "Go away. Stop deviling me."

Charlotte decided not to mention these incidents; she wanted to avoid personal revelations. She feared he might ask questions she would not want to answer.

It was Clemmie who first expressed concern for Charlotte's health. "You don't look right, Mistress. You driving yourself too hard. Your face is sunk in. I wish you would rest more."

Charlotte ignored her, but then Richard asked if she felt well.

"I am rather tired, I suppose. Does it show?"

"Your face is drawn, that is all. Hadn't I better bring up a buck to do the gardening?"

"With the rains coming on, I will get plenty of rest."

"Would you like me to ask David to look in on you?"

"No! If I need him, I'll say so."

A few mornings later, as they sat down to breakfast, she

became faint and nauseated and had to go back to bed. Again Richard offered to summon Higganbotham, and she forbade him to do so. Thereafter, she took to sleeping late, waiting until after Richard had eaten his breakfast to have hers. Later in the day she would become wolfishly hungry, eating great quantities of guava jelly and drinking lime juice. At the same time, a strange calm came over her. She still thought about the death of Cudjoe and the executions of the other slaves and the anguished departure of John, but was able to do so dispassionately. She wondered if she might be losing her mind, that she might be slipping into a kind of happy lunacy. Nothing irritated her anymore. And she found that she enjoyed sleeping with Richard again. Once, early in the morning, she took the initiative and they made love with the fervor of honeymooners.

"You are a minx," Richard said when they lay spent. "You make me feel like a boy again."

She sighed and put her face against his neck. "Don't talk, just hold me, Richard."

But the next time he approached her she refused him. The thought of sex was suddenly repulsive to her.

The rains fell almost every day during early and mid July, but toward the end of the month they ceased, and there was a period of fair weather, which Richard welcomed; Croxton could have the slaves make one last weeding of the canes planted the previous November.

Charlotte became content to work at her needlepoint and to read. She welcomed her afternoon naps, leaving the running of the household to Clemmie to a degree she never had before. She sometimes saw Higganbotham's horse tied up at the Negro yard and, in her new state of complacency, no longer cared that he did not come to the house. She was content to remain at home with her books and her thoughts, to wait out the long hot summer.

5

... It is embarrassing to admit how ignorant I was in some matters, and I can only lay my lack of knowledge at the door of my mother. She nagged me about the running of a large household and taught or tried to teach me more than I was desirous of learning about embroidery and so-called ladylike manners, but she neglected informing me about certain elemental facts that any farmer's daughter back home would have known, or, for that matter, any of our slaves at Bolton Hall. Even Clemmie, despite her relatively sheltered upbringing, knew more than I, as it turned out.

Richard, of course, was a man of the world. And so I learned what I learned from him, but he was a person more given to action than explanation. I thought it odd that he had never expressed a desire for children. Whenever I brought it up, he would change the subject, and I assumed this was to spare my feelings about my apparent barrenness.

My story nears its end. But there was one more day of rather confusing happiness left for me ...

"Mistress."

"Yes, Clemmie. What is it?"

"The doctor be here to see you."

It was midmorning, and Charlotte was reading in the drawing room. She started, thinking for a moment that the girl meant John Martin had returned. But then she saw David in the doorway.

"David. It has been a while."

"Yes. I was at your Negro yard, and Clemmie came down to say I should call on you."

"Really? Well, of course I am glad to see you."

"I don't mean socially. She says you have not been yourself of late."

"It is nothing that requires a doctor."

"They say you seem tired."

"Oh, David. There is nothing wrong with me. But, now that you are here, do sit down. I have missed you."

He put down his bag and sat, still holding his hat. "I have missed you, too, Charlotte, but I thought you might prefer that I stay away."

"What is past is past. Have you been well and happy?"

"Anyway, well. And too busy to think of whether I am happy."

There was a long silence, which she broke by saying, "Come, David, you must not act ill at ease. Why the troubled look?"

"I don't mean to pry, but Clemmie said you had been ill in the mornings. And that you have been rather listless."

"David, I really do not want to discuss my health with you. Have you kept up with your reading?"

"No, but Clemmie says you spend half your days reading and the rest napping."

"It is not for Clemmie to discuss me outside the house."

"Oh, confound it, Charlotte, don't play games with me. She thinks you are with child."

It took a moment for his remark to sink in.

"How preposterous. And embarrassing."

"I am embarrassed myself, but now that the subject is broached, are you?"

"How would I know? I have never experienced pregnancy."

"The first sign is, I don't know how to put this, Charlotte, but one begins to suspect if the woman misses her menses."

"Menses?"

"Yes. Her time of month. If it passes with no effusion, that usually is regarded as an indication." He paused, his face beet red.

"Oh. As a matter of fact, it has been quite some weeks."

"You are a married woman, past thirty, and you did not know?"

"My mother never discussed such things with me."

"Oh, dear God. Let me ask you a bit more."

She told him more about the morning sickness and the cravings for certain foods and the strange sense of peace that had come over her. When she had finished, he said, "Charlotte, if you are not with child, then I am no doctor."

Then Charlotte began laughing hysterically until he grew alarmed and went to her.

"Don't mind me," she said. "This summer has brought me more than I can bear."

"It could be a false pregnancy. They happen sometimes."

"I am not unhappy about it. At least I don't think I shall be when this sinks in. A baby may be just what we need at Bolton Hall."

"You mean to tell Richard?"

"Of course. Why not?"

Higganbotham looked at the floor for a moment before replying. "Tell him I reckon that you are but a few weeks gone at the most and that I would not expect the child before the end of March. Now that you know, do get lots of rest and eat enough without overeating. All's well between you and Richard, I trust."

"Quite well, David. And now that the ice is broken don't act like a stranger again. You are always welcome here."

After he had left, Charlotte sat quietly, absorbing the news. A child *would* make a difference for her and Richard. Surely it would draw them close again, give them something to live for. She and Richard had existed too long for themselves only. They needed a family. Clemmie found her looking out the window, smiling.

"What did the doctor say?"

"He said that you talk too much for your own good, and I agree."

At first Charlotte felt foolish, not to have suspected the cause of her early morning sickness and her increasingly placid mood of late. Only a few weeks earlier, she had been caught in a maelstrom of conflicting emotions and had feared she was going mad, and now the longer she thought about it the happier she became. Well, how was she to know the signs of pregnancy? The youngest child of older parents; the daughter of a woman who gave her only the most perfunctory explanation of how to deal with her monthly periods when they first appeared. She had stood by while slave women had babies, but she had not learned from them the symptoms of morning sickness. It seemed to her that they simply started swelling a few months before labor began.

When they went to bed that night, Richard asked why she acted so happy, and she nearly told him. But no, she would like time to enjoy her secret alone. After all, David had said it might be a false pregnancy. When she was sure and when the time was right, she would tell Richard. Meanwhile, let him sleep on in his ignorance.

She lay beside him in a state of euphoria. Now she did not fear Richard's growing old. A child might even keep him young. And when, inevitably, he did leave her a widow, she would have a child for her own old age. Charlotte thought, too, how it was better to bear the baby now than it would have been, say, during her first two or three years on Barbados. Then she might have resented the interference with her life, while now it would enrich her existence.

The more she thought about it, the more Charlotte wanted to tell someone. She considered for a moment awakening Richard. No, but she might invite Esther over next day and share the secret with her. Sleep would not come, and at last she slipped out of bed, lit a candle, and opened her writing desk.

She had not written to her parents since the discovery of the slave conspiracy. Her description was matter-of-fact and rather offhand, barely mentioning that their gardener lad had been executed. She told about the weather, the state of the cane crop, gossip of the island, saving her news to the end.

> *... you are to become grandparents. I expect to deliver my baby between Christmas and the beginning of next year. I feel like such a ninny, Mother; you never instructed me in these matters, so I did not recognize the meaning of my early morning sickness and cravings for unaccustomed foods. So far only Clemmie and our physician-friend, David Higganbotham, know. I am saving the news as a surprise for Richard. A child will make such a difference in our lives. I do not know whether to pray for a boy or a girl. I suspect that Richard will want a son to carry on here at Bolton Hall ...*

Suddenly it struck Charlotte how oppressive the night air had become. She set the letter aside and opened the shutters. No wind was stirring, yet she could hear the sound of the surf pounding a mile away. After staring out the window into the blackness of the night for a long while, she returned to bed and snuggled contentedly against Richard's back. He shifted and moaned. "No. She didn't really tell me. How was I to know?" Charlotte started to awaken him but thought better of it and soon drifted off.

Charlotte awakened at first light to the sound of the shutters slamming against the house and a limb of the bearded fig tree lashing the kitchen roof. She lay awake for a few minutes, puzzling over the way the fitful wind seemed to be coming from first one direction and then another, and then arose to close the shutters. The dawning sun cast an eerie, reddish light over the landscape. The sky was dappled with a pattern of high "mare's tail" clouds crowding in from the west.

With Richard still sleeping, she dressed quickly and stole downstairs to find a worried Clemmie preparing breakfast.

"I don't like the sound of that wind, Mistress. Birds aren't even singing this morning."

"Clemmie, you sound like an old Obeah woman."

"I just don't like the feel of this weather."

"Don't let your concern delay breakfast. I'll be on the

veranda. When the master comes down, ask him if he would like to eat there."

Charlotte could not fix her attention on any one thing very long. Although the sea did not look particularly rough, powerful swells were crashing against the beaches so loudly that it made her think of the sound of the cannon when the Dutch attacked Bridgetown on her first day on Barbados. Just above the western horizon, she could see the edge of a high cloud curtain obscuring the more distant mare's tails. Ten years she had lived on this island, and she never tired of its changing beauty. There had been turmoil and disappointments, but now that she had come to terms with her life here, now that she was carrying a child, she did not see how she could live any other place.

Clemmie interrupted her with coffee.

"Has the master come down yet?"

"No, Mistress, but I did hear him stirring. I believe he is getting dressed."

Clemmie paused to listen to the pounding of the surf. "They getting a heavy sea down there."

"We have had heavy seas before. Nothing to worry about."

"We ought to do something about that big tree at the back. Cut off some branches or take down the whole thing. That limb over the kitchen has knocked loose some shingles."

"I will mention it to the master."

The two women did not hear Richard come down the stairs. They were watching the slaves being herded by Croxton from the Negro yard toward the lower cane fields when Richard came riding around the house on his horse. Without glancing back at them, he lashed the animal into a gallop down the lane away from the house.

"That is strange," Charlotte said. "Where is he off to in such a hurry without his breakfast?"

"And he is wearing his sword."

Croxton threw up his hand as the horse drew near, but Richard rode right past him to the end of the lane and turned south toward Bridgetown.

"What about breakfast?" Clemmie asked.

"You might as well bring mine out here. That is very naughty of the master to ride off without a word to anyone."

By noon, the wind settled down to a steady gale from the north. The sheet of high clouds had spread across the sky, and rain splattered down occasionally. The pounding of the surf had grown heavier, and along the horizon there now appeared a fringe of angry-looking clouds. Charlotte began to share Clemmie's concern about the weather. She wished desperately for Richard to return from his mysterious, apparently urgent, errand. She was baffled by his abrupt departure.

Charlotte went to her bedroom, but the howling of the wind would not let her rest. As a rain squall swept across Bolton Hall, Charlotte lay on her great bed and wondered if Richard might be caught in the downpour. When the rain stopped briefly, she arose with the notion of completing the letter she had begun to her mother the night before, but now it had grown so dark she could not find the paper. Downstairs Clemmie, Toby, and Mirabel were huddled in the kitchen, their faces reflecting their concern.

Charlotte scoffed at their fears.

"You go and look out front and see for yourself, Mistress," Clemmie said.

All along the western horizon there advanced a bank of dark clouds touched here and there by orange and green highlights. Deep within the ominous mass, as though emanating from some colossal furnace, lightning pulsed. A steady growl of thunder rolled across the ocean.

The clouds directly overhead had grown thicker. A lower scattering of dark puffs raced along like pickets fleeing before an awesome army advancing from the west.

Still coming from the north, the wind was bending the palms along the lane and stripping leaves and small limbs from other trees. Croxton had given up the day's work and sent the slaves to their huts. Now he approached the house, leaning against the steady pressure of the wind, one hand holding his hat in place.

"I wish Sir Richard would come back, Lady Bolton."

"So do I. He must have been detained in Bridgetown."

"I am wondering what to do with the Negroes if this thing gets worse. I have seen storms in my time but nothing like that building up out there. We are in for a rough night, in my opinion."

"Let us not go borrowing trouble, Mister Croxton. I am sure Sir Richard will return soon. If your fears are realized, I suppose you could evacuate the slaves to the boiling room. They should be secure within its stone walls."

"How about yourself, ma'am? Are you not worried? Is there aught you wish me to do?"

"There is nothing I wish you to do except see to the safety of the slaves if the storm does indeed grow worse. I only hope Sir Richard does not get caught in this."

6

... *Despite my brave words to Croxton and the servants, by midafternoon, I realized that a hurricane was aimed directly for us, and with the wind growing in force and heavier clouds now obscuring the afternoon sun, Richard himself might be in danger if he did not soon return.*

Hiding my fears as best I could, I directed Toby and Clemmie in battening down our house. Even though we securely closed the shutters, that did not keep out the swirling wind or even the rain which now gushed down. We lit candles against the growing darkness but had to shield the flickering flames against the aggressive wind.

Throughout the afternoon, as the hurricane rushed upon us with ever increasing violence, the lightning flashed faster and more brilliantly, and the thunder grew into a nearly constant rumble.

Alone in the drawing room. with debris rattling against the house at an alarming rate, I prayed for Richard to return and save us from this malevolent, raging force. I was afraid for myself, the child within my womb, and for him. Where could he have gone for so long and in such weather?

David Higganbotham had spent a miserable night in his lonely bedroom, his thoughts as restless and shifting as the wind that rattled his shutters. He had known few happy moments since he had discovered Charlotte at John's hut and returned her to Bolton Hall. Almost from the moment he had met Charlotte Bolton aboard the *Mary Leigh,* he had looked upon her as the model of what a woman should be: intelligent, poised but high-spirited, independent of mind but considerate of manner, witty in a ladylike way, and while she was not a conventionally pretty woman, in his eyes she was beautiful of face and form. He had reveled in their innocent little confidences, taken pride in the sure way she had established herself in the social hierarchy of Barbados, and treasured their conversations about literature and drama. He had been impressed, too, by the way she had matured through the years. To him she was a flawless Guinevere, and Richard, despite his faults, was a gallant Arthur. Serving as a platonic Lancelot to this favored couple had made the physician's lonely life bearable. Now he felt empty, disillusioned, not only with the Boltons but also with the Galahad of his life, that wretched little ingrate, John Martin. Higganbotham could forgive John for having outgrown and left him, but several times during his sleepless night he wished he had shot the youth that day after the Speightstown executions.

With dawn breaking and all hope of rest departed, he dressed and went to the one-room office at the rear of his house.

He had meant to make his medical rounds in Christ Church Parish, but with this rising wind he feared he would be caught away from home in heavy rain. Instead he would work on his book on tropical diseases. Perhaps if he concentrated hard enough, it would take his mind off Charlotte.

He refused the cook's offer of breakfast and was sitting at his desk when he heard a horse's hooves on his lane. As he stood in his office doorway, Richard Bolton rode into the yard.

"Why, Richard, what brings you here?"

Richard did not reply. His horse, sweating and laboring for breath, dropped his head in relief as Richard dismounted, still without speaking. Then, with his sword in his right hand, Richard approached the office door and, putting his left hand against Higganbotham's chest, shoved the amazed physician into his chair.

"You two-faced quack! I smoothed the way for you on this island. I extended the hospitality of my house to you."

"What is the matter with you?"

"Don't play innocent with me. It is here in this letter I found on her desk this morning. 'So far only Clemmie and our physician-friend, David Higganbotham, know.' You might as well confess. I know the truth."

"Oh, she has not yet told you? Well, it does appear that she is pregnant, but that hardly gives you the right to manhandle me."

Richard shifted his sword to his left hand and drew his pistol from his belt. "It gives me the right to kill you for deceiving me. I should have known better than to encourage all the sharing of secrets between you. Always running back and forth with your precious books."

"Richard, you are not yourself. You are being absurd."

Higganbotham started to rise, but Bolton shoved him back into his chair and put the pistol to the doctor's forehead.

"You shall die no matter what. First you and then her. You might as well tell me the truth. When did you and she first betray me? Was it when I was in England?"

"Oh dear God, no."

"You want to die with a lie on your lips? You think me a fool? Why then, after always being underfoot, have you been avoiding our house of late if it were not from a guilty conscience?"

"Richard, I never ... Why would you suspect such a thing?"

"It had to be you. You are the only man who had access to her in recent months. It will do you no good to deny it."

Higganbotham's mind raced, thinking of some way to make Bolton put away his pistol long enough to listen.

"Why would you think such a thing of Charlotte or me?"

Bolton, with his pistol muzzle now pressing into Higganbotham's forehead, bent low so that their eyes were only a few inches apart, and said through clenched teeth, "You are a doctor. You know what the clap is. I caught a raging case years ago from an Irish servant girl in Bridgetown. I can father no children. So if you have anything to say before you die, speak now. I can see it in your eyes that you are not telling me the truth."

Thinking that any second would bring the fatal bullet into his brain, Higganbotham closed his eyes and said quietly, "I will tell you more if you will put away your pistol and listen. Just for a few minutes. Then if you want to kill me, it doesn't matter. I have nothing to live for anyway."

Richard backed away and sat on a stool but kept his pistol across his lap. "All right. I know it was not me. If it was not you, then who? The second I think you are lying, I will shoot you."

The sweat streamed down Higganbotham's face and neck, soaking his shirt. His hands trembled, and his voice shook, but he took a deep breath and fumbled for a way to tell Richard the truth without throwing him into a fresh rage.

"Gonorrhea does not always render a man sterile, you know, Richard."

"Don't play games with me. I have had enough women to have got one or the other with child long before my marriage."

He raised his pistol again, and Higganbotham held up his hand.

He began again. "Charlotte did not send for me yesterday. Clemmie did. Charlotte, for all her erudition, is a naive and innocent woman, Richard. She had no idea that she was with child."

Richard laughed sarcastically. "Naive, perhaps. Innocent, hardly. You are running out of time, *Doctor.* You promised to tell me the truth. Shall I begin counting?"

Again the pistol came up cocked and Higganbotham looked into its muzzle. "One, two, three . . . " Richard began.

"All right. If I tell you the truth will you promise not to harm Charlotte?"

"No."

"Then go ahead and shoot me. I don't care that much about living."

Richard's finger tightened on the trigger, and then he hesitated. "All right, I will not kill her. It *was* you then?"

Higganbotham closed his eyes again, wondering what might happen if he made a false confession. Would Richard slay him and spare Charlotte? Could he trust this madman to keep his promise not to harm her?

"Richard," he said at last. "Listen to me carefully. You have threatened my life, but you have made me a promise not to harm your wife. I am going to tell you what happened, but first I take a solemn oath. If you do touch a hair of Charlotte's head for what I am about to tell you, I swear to Almighty God that I will kill *you.* You understand me?"

"I hear you."

"And do you promise?"

"I promise. Now out with it."

Bolton's face sagged as Higganbotham, choosing his words carefully and making sure that he explained the horror Charlotte had experienced in Speightstown, told of her brief affair with John Martin. "She was not herself, Richard. You did not tell her what you knew about that Quaco and his son. I talked to the people who were with her when she saw some of the executions. They said she fainted briefly, came to, and rode off like a crazy woman."

At the story's end, Richard sat dazed, then muttered, "That little pipsqueak. She gave herself to the son of a pricklouse . . . " Then, growing agitated again, "If she was gone all that night, why did no one tell me? You protest that you are my friend, and you kept me in ignorance? You are lying. Wait, is that why he left Barbados so abruptly?"

"He wanted Charlotte to go with him, but she would not desert you."

Richard stared at Higganbotham until he began sweating again. "You are a clever man, friend David. First you wring from me a promise to let her go unpunished and then tell me that her loverboy is safely out of my reach in Virginia. Do you really think that Richard Bolton will suffer himself to be cuckolded by a tailor's son, or gulled by a quacksalver, and take no action?"

"No one will ever know. Listen, Richard, think how you deceived Charlotte in marrying her when you knew you were sterile. I know too, about Mandze. You did not tell her about that. You have hurt Charlotte deeply on many occasions. She has forgiven you and gone on loving you. Your best years are ahead, if you can but see it. I implore you to act as though none of this ever happened. She has no reason to think you could not be the father, don't you see?"

"You are a simpering fool." Richard started for the door. "Do you really think I will let her get away with this?"

Higganbotham waited until Richard had put his sword back in its scabbard and was in the act of returning his pistol to his belt as he stepped through the doorway. Then he hurtled himself out of his chair and on Richard's back. The two men went sprawling out into the yard. Crying, "Damn you, you promised . . . " Higganbotham grappled for his throat, but Richard twisted away and got to his feet. He had one foot in the stirrup and was about to mount his weary horse when the doctor flung himself on him again.

Richard thrust him back with his left hand and, with his

right, drew out his pistol. As Higganbotham pressed forward again, hands groping wildly, the pistol barrel smashed against the side of his head and he went down into a whirlpool of crimson and black.

No matter how hard Richard lashed his poor horse, the exhausted beast could manage no more than a trot. At last he gave up the effort and let the animal proceed toward Bridgetown at his own pace. Richard had been a tormented man ever since the court-martial of the slaves three months earlier. If he had it to do over, he would have kept quiet about Mandze. It had done neither him nor her any good, his telling his fellow officers that, yes, the woman had made some remarks to him about danger, which evidently he had misunderstood. They felt that since she did not carry her report directly to her master, Harold Lawnton, she had kept guilty knowledge to herself and therefore deserved to die with the others. But, night after night, her face had appeared in his dreams, sometimes swollen and aged but often as smooth and young as when she first attracted his attention aboard that slave ship. Always, her words were the same, upbraiding him for casting her out of his house and permitting her to be killed. That alone was enough to drive a man mad. Now he had this new knowledge, that the wife in whom he had taken such pride, his lovely if at times exasperating Charlotte, had played him false, and with a youth for whom he felt contempt. And that fool Higganbotham expected him to keep silent, to go on living with her as if nothing had happened. Even if it were true, that she really did think he were the father, the knowledge of her carrying another's child was more than he could bear. Damn her. He would strangle her.

Throughout Bridgetown, people were securing their windows and looking anxiously out to sea. In Carlisle Bay, ships were rocking in the great swells as their crews reset their anchors and tied down all loose gear. At the Bow Bells, the proprietor, wondering at Richard's wild look, brought him the bottle of rum he demanded.

He still sat at a corner table drinking while the winds

settled down to one direction and mounted in intensity, while the lightning began to play on the western horizon, and the first squall splattered down upon the town.

The proprietor shook his shoulder. "Sir Richard, they do say we are in for a real hurricane. Two ships already driven ashore in the bay. If you mean to return to your plantation before it strikes you'd better get started."

Richard brushed away the man's hand and rose to his feet unsteadily. "Hurricane?"

"That is what it has become. You've been here quite a while. Shall I prepare you a room?"

"No. There is something I must do. Don't you see, I must. There is no other course for me."

"Really, sir, I don't think you are in a condition to venture forth. You don't know how bad it is out there."

But Richard staggered out the back of the tavern, bawling for his horse. With the force of the hurricane behind him, he rode up the slope from the town like a ship with a strong following wind. Shingles from the roofs of Bridgetown and palm fronds went hurtling past him. Trees writhed and danced like the slaves at their last end-of-harvest celebration. After he had gained the road that led toward Bolton Hall, his body caught the wind from the side and it took all his strength to hold on to the saddle. The rain that followed soaked him within seconds, but it also sobered him so that he could think more clearly. Now the horse had to fight to keep his footing. Time and again, Richard had to turn the animal's head into the wind and lash him toward the left side of the road, only to find himself soon shoved back to the right side. And thus by this slow zigzag course they fought their painful way north.

By the time he reached Saint Thomas Church, Richard was leaning forward with his face against the horse's neck. He had long since lost his hat, and it seemed to him that his coat and shirt soon would be torn from his body. Twice the horse had been driven to his knees, and upon his third collapse, Richard realized that the animal was only an impediment to him. Not bothering to remove the saddle, he freed the horse and, his head now clear, continued toward Bolton Hall in a crouch, using his sword as a walking cane, while the rain fell in wind-lashed torrents and lightning played around him in blinding, explosive sheets.

By nightfall, gigantic bolts of lightning crisscrossed the sky, filling the interior of Bolton Hall with a light so bright Charlotte could have read a book by it. The thunder crashed nearer and nearer. The wind shrieked about the house, like a blind madman groping for a throathold.

Taking pity on them, Charlotte allowed the fearful servants to come and huddle with her in the drawing room, but soon regretted doing so, for Mirabel's wails increased with the velocity of the wind.

"If you don't stop that howling, I shall send you back to the kitchen," Charlotte threatened her.

Soon it did not matter, for no one in the room could hear anyway. The rain gushed upon the roof like a waterfall. The wind became a palpable thing, like a great hand pressing upon the groaning house. The thunder crashed around them like a ceaseless barrage of artillery, and the lightning sent wave upon wave of white and blue light dancing through the room.

As a child in Bedford, Charlotte had enjoyed summer storms, had liked to climb to a top floor dormer room and watch the play of the lightning and thrill to the thunder. Now she closed her eyes and put her hands over her ears. All nature had gone wild, it seemed to her; it had turned into a maniac seeking to destroy her personally. Numbness replaced terror. But raw terror returned near midnight when the veranda gave way. The raging wind ripped it off and flung it into the night and then drove sheets of water against the great exposed front door like a liquid battering ram.

The house shook more violently than ever, as if all that mighty force were directing its fearful energies against this one spot. And then the front door burst off its hinges and the hurricane rushed into the room like a herd of wild beasts. Chairs and tables crashed against the walls. Clemmie screamed.

In another minute the roof cried out as if in pain, and in another the wind had pried it off, and the rain was cascading from the ceiling of the drawing room, drenching the three women and snuffing out their candles.

"The kitchen, the kitchen," Charlotte cried and, taking Clemmie's hand, felt her way through the hall toward the rear of the ravaged house, their way lit by the constant flashes of lightning, their bodies thrust along by the force of the wind rushing in the front door.

They huddled in the kitchen, while the storm, having breached the house's defenses, went about the business of stripping away the rest of the front roof. Charlotte closed her eyes and tried not to think of the ruin of her precious books or the destruction of the furniture they had brought from England. The storm was only momentarily diverted by the sack of the house. Like an army of vandals, soon it was probing their bastion in the kitchen. The wind screamed with renewed force, rattling Mirabel's pots and pans in a maddening cacophony.

"I'm not ready to die," Charlotte thought. "Dear God, spare us." The storm paused for a second, as though catching its breath, just long enough for Charlotte to think the worst might have passed, and then it slammed into the rear remnant of the house. The kitchen roof sailed up and away, and the rain came pouring in upon them so heavily they could hardly breathe.

Her clothing plastered against her, her hair hanging in sodden ropes, Charlotte felt paralyzed, without hope, not knowing what to do, not even caring anymore, oblivious to the screams of the two Negro women.

Toby had remained quiet throughout the storm, simply following Charlotte's orders. Suddenly he was speaking, or rather shouting.

"Stop that. Be quiet." He slapped Clemmie across the face, hard.

"Here, Mistress." He held out one hand to Charlotte and with the other gripped Clemmie's arm. Thus he led the three women out into the fury of the storm. They were instantly driven to their knees by the wind. In the midst of a gigantic flare of lightning, Charlotte raised her head and, with a hand keeping the rain out of her eyes, looked up at a mass of ugly clouds boiling so low overhead it seemed she could touch them.

The cabin of Toby and Clemmie was gone, but next to it there still stood a little building made of solid coral stone and roofed with tile. The structure measured only about four feet square and it housed Bolton Hall's water filter or "drip." This consisted of two large porous stone receptacles set one over the other. Water passed from the upper receptacle to the lower by the process of condensation, and in that way was considerably cooled and purified when it dripped into the receiving basin.

On hands and knees, Toby led them to the little house and, using every scrap of his strength, forced the tiny door open against the pressure of the wind.

"Inside."

He thrust Charlotte in the doorway. "Hunch in the corner, Mistress. Now you, Clemmie."

Charlotte squeezed herself against the vats. There was scarcely room for Clemmie, but she finally wedged herself on the other side.

"Now you, Mirabel," Toby shouted.

"I can't get in there," the woman wailed.

He struck her across the face. "Shut up and get in before the wind takes the door off."

It was a miracle that Mirabel did fit in. She had to lie on her side with her head on Charlotte's hip and her knees bent against Clemmie's. Both Negro women were crying, and Charlotte barely could keep from doing so herself. She wondered how Toby could possibly wedge himself in, but, before she could ask, the wind slammed the little door shut, and he lowered the heavy bar, locking them inside.

Charlotte was barely able to breathe. The odor of fear, from herself as well as the two Negro women, sickened her. There was no way to shift positions and soon the pain made her want to cry out. Meanwhile the storm howled and raged around them without pause, until in spite of her discomfort, exhausted by the long hours of fear, Charlotte fell asleep.

She awoke to dead silence from the outside and inside only the heavy breathing of the other two women. The wind had died away, and the rain had stopped.

"Clemmie."

"Yes, Mistress."

"What is happening?"

"The storm let up a little while ago."

"Then why didn't you awaken me?"

"We can't get the door open, Mistress. So we let you sleep."

"Did you call?"

"Yes, ma'am. But there ain't nobody out there. Toby must have locked us in. Maybe everybody is dead."

Charlotte ached in every joint. Her neck was turned at an unnatural angle and the weight of Mirabel's head tortured her hip. She called out. "Toby. Help! Someone help us!"

"It's no use, mistress. We just going to have to wait until daylight.

"I'm thirsty," Mirabel said.

"So am I," Clemmie said. "But there's nothing to do but wait."

Charlotte gritted her teeth. She thought: I must not scream. I must be an example. If I begin to scream, I will not be able to stop until I have gone completely mad. Dear God, please help me to keep my sanity . . . That was when she felt the stirring in her abdomen for the first time.

"Mirabel, have you ever had a baby?"

"Yes, Mistress, when I was young. The baby died before it was weaned."

"Did it move inside you?"

"Oh yes, it did."

Clemmie spoke up. "Oh, Mistress, that's a good sign. We will be all right now."

Charlotte relaxed a bit. She prayed again, this time for the safety of Richard and the resumption of their life together. She lay in the cramped, stinking darkness and thought about her life in England, of her old love for London, the honeymoon voyage to Barbados, and her growing affection for Bolton Hall, until the eye of the hurricane passed and the winds arose again, from the south this time, and quickly mounted to their former intensity. Debris peppered the stone hut. The thunder crashed about them. The rain gushed down as heavily as before, but now Charlotte felt almost calm. Bolton Hall could not suffer any more damage. Whatever harm might have befallen Richard was done; possibly he was safely holed away in Bridgetown. At any rate her worrying would make no difference. The essential thing was that she and the new life she had felt stirring within her were secure here in this little womblike structure. The hurricane could rage until its maniacal powers were spent; she and her baby would be safe. Surely someone would come to let them out once the storm ended.

"Mistress," Clemmie said, "where do you think Toby ran off to? He should not have shut us away like this."

"You hush about Toby," Mirabel said. "He saved us."

"You are right, Mirabel," Charlotte said. "Toby did a brave thing. You should be proud of him, Clemmie."

The worse part of the ordeal came after the storm had died away and daylight shone around the door of the water filter, when no one came to release them, and they began to fear they would die jammed like this in the tiny chamber. Charlotte ordered the two Negro women not to talk about this possibility, but Clemmie got around her by saying, "Well, Mistress, if we were going to die what would you be sorry about?"

Charlotte thought the question entirely too personal, but she was tired of playing the stern mistress. "I would have to give that much thought."

"I wish I had been born white, like you."

"One cannot change the circumstances of one's birth, Clemmie."

"I ain't had any power over my life, but if I had I would like to be able to read and write. I see you with a book, and I can tell that it takes you off to another world. And I know I could learn."

Charlotte, thinking the conversation had gone too far, did not reply. And if her nerves had not been near to breaking and her back and neck not been aching from their cramped position, she might have noticed that Mirabel had not spoken for an unnaturally long while. So, when the African woman began screaming and shouting in her native Pawpaw, Charlotte was shaken. The cries rose and fell in waves of hysteria. She banged her head against Charlotte's already bruised hip. Nothing either Charlotte or Clemmie said stopped her banshee shrieks.

All her life Charlotte had been taught not to show extremes of emotion, to remain in control of herself and those for whom she was responsible. But the persons who had instructed her had never been through the horrors of seeing mass executions and suffering through a hurricane of a force beyond imagination, nor had they ever been jammed for hours, nearly smothering, in a dark hole. All this her nerves had withstood. The shrieks of Mirabel brought a new test.

I will go mad if she doesn't stop, she thought.

Deliberately filling her lungs with the stale air of the enclosure, she screamed even louder than Mirabel.

"Stop it. Stop it," she shouted, and then screamed again.

When she stopped to catch her breath, to her amazement, not only had Mirabel fallen silent, she felt better herself.

After a few minutes Clemmie asked hesitantly, "You all right, Mistress Charlotte?"

"No," Charlotte replied. "I am not all right. I am sick of this black hole."

"I never heard you yell like that," Clemmie said.

"No, but if you or Mirabel don't keep quiet, you will hear even worse."

"I am sorry. You know what a fool Mirabel is."

"Don't you call me a fool."

"Both of you hush, or I will scream again."

"Wait, mistress, you hear that?"

"What?"

It was a man's voice, calling, "Charlotte. Charlotte. Is that you?"

Now it was Clemmie's turn to shriek. "In here," she shouted. "Here in the water filter."

They could hear someone fumbling with the bar. Suddenly the door burst open from the weight of Mirabel's ample rump and light flooded in around the great stone urns.

Clemmie wriggled out after Mirabel and, unable to stand, lay on the sodden earth while Charlotte was tenderly lifted from her tortuous position and placed on a cape spread beside the little house.

... They say that no such storm has ever struck Barbados, and I can well believe it. From one end of the land to the other, almost every church, dwelling, warehouse, office, shop, windmill, or sugar works either has been destroyed or severely damaged. Along the lee coast the normally placid Caribbean surged deep inland, damaging low-lying areas worse than the wind, rain, or lightning. There were twelve ships anchored in Carlisle Bay, and every one of them was driven ashore and wrecked. Among them, alas, were seven laden with much of our annual sugar crop. The surging sea ruined the houses and other buildings near Bridgetown's waterfront. Those farther from the bay got off lighter.

They tell me that Speightstown suffered even more damage proportionately. The warehouse in which the court-martial was held was swept off its foundation and reduced to a rubble. In all of Speightstown not one roof remains in place, and many of the buildings themselves are smashed flat. I wonder if traces remain of the blood spilled on the cobbled surface of the square.

The land looks as though a malicious Almighty has placed His heel upon the island and ground down buildings, crops, trees, and the people themselves. The cane stalks are either uprooted or flattened beyond recovery. Great gullies have been gashed across our laboriously tended fields. In some places the roads are washed out and in others filled in with topsoil and debris. Stripped of their leaves and branches, the few remaining trees look like skeletons.

The hurricane respected neither class nor color. In Speightstown a man and his bride were plucked from their nuptial bed by the wind and dumped many yards away in a pimploe hedge, where they huddled in terror throughout the violent night. We have heard that, over in the Scotland district, seventeen members of a single family died in the collapse of their house.

The generally flimsy slave huts were the first dwellings to be swept away. Our Negroes here at Bolton Hall were fortunate to have an overseer with the foresight to evacuate them early to a more secure building. Elsewhere, most spent the awful night in the open. The next morning found them cowering like dazed cattle, unable to follow orders.

And many of their masters and mistresses, like me, were too befuddled to give intelligent directions anyway. We white Barbadians resembled corpses, with our complexions bluish and wrinkled from the long exposure to the drenching rains. The hair of some actually turned gray overnight, and I am among them.

No one can say for certain just how many died in this worst calamity in our history. So far, according to David, more than two hundred bodies have been found. Many more are missing.

David found Richard lying under a fallen branch of our fig tree beside the collapsed wall of our kitchen. He would not let me see him, but I overheard Clemmie telling Esther that Richard had been stripped of clothes, and that he still clutched his sword in his hand. "Trying to rescue us, he was," Clemmie said.

The body of poor, brave Toby was found face down in a ditch near the ruins of the windmill. I can write no more at present. I cannot bear to think of my dear Richard ...

More than a month passed before her grief let up enough for Charlotte to think clearly again. By that time, Croxton and the slaves had built a two-room hut from the debris of Bolton Hall and furnished it with a few salvaged chairs and tables. During the first few days, Charlotte had sat about numbly, but gradually, under the solicitous attentions of Clemmie and Mirabel, she began to recover.

Having provided shelter for Charlotte, Croxton replaced the roof on the boiling house and converted it into a kind of slave dormitory. Food presented a worse problem. The hurricane had destroyed their stores of provisions, and they were forced to slaughter two prime oxen. But the same providence that had sent the destruction now dealt more kindly with Barbados. Each year about this time, flocks of wild pigeons visited the island, but more of these birds than usual came that September. Unable to find their normal supply of berries, they huddled dispiritedly in the fields and fell easy prey to nets and stones.

At Fulham, all that remained of the great house was the kitchen. The Lawntons offered to share it with Charlotte, but she refused.

"What will you do?" Esther asked. "With a baby on its way, you can't go on like this, Charlotte."

"Don't fret yourself about me. You have troubles enough of your own."

Higganbotham shuttled back and forth over the ruined landscape between Bolton Hall and his own house, which had escaped with the loss of its front roof. He was careful not to press Charlotte to make decisions until he saw clear signs that she was coming out of the fog of her grief.

"Dear David," she said. "You have been so kind. I fear that I am being a burden to you."

"You are not, and even if you were, I would not mind. I only wish I could do more."

"Is everyone in our condition?"

"Some are in worse. I could name you a dozen plantations that lost their masters, and there is no one to provide for the slaves, nor to control them. Governor Atkins has called out the

militia to patrol the roads and to guard the remaining food
supplies. You are fortunate to have Croxton. I have formed a
great admiration for that brave little man."

"He has been most kind. And so has his wife. I am sorry
that I am so broken down."

"Let us not speak of it, Charlotte. We should be looking to
the future."

"I have thought about that. I would be most grateful if you
would see Richard's lawyer in Bridgetown. I want to know the
exact state of our accounts. Richard was never very precise."

The worst time for Charlotte came at night when she lay
on the rude, narrow bed the plantation carpenter had fashioned
for her. That was when she missed Richard the most. She
yearned, not just for their old life together, but for his presence
in these circumstances. Croxton kept Bolton Hall from disinte-
grating, but Richard would have been magnificent in such a
crisis. And, curiously, she felt that he would have been happy
facing up to the challenge. She hated herself for having
thought he had deserted her. He had died trying to reach her
side again in the midst of the hurricane, had died without
knowing about the baby. How cruel fate was to strike him down
just when she needed him most. Except for a falling tree limb,
he would be here with her. Would there ever be another such
man?

Higganbotham returned two days later with his saddlebags filled with coffee, bread, and other foods. They set chairs
under the fragment of the fig tree and drank their coffee.

"You saw the lawyer?"

"And the factor."

"How much is there?"

"Oh, Charlotte, I do not like to bring you bad tidings. You
really thought Richard left you in good condition?"

"Of course. We have had many good crops. This has been a
very profitable plantation. I would be much surprised if there
were not several thousand pounds in credits."

"Alas, there are several thousand in debts, I fear."

"You cannot be serious."

"I am. I cannot give you a precise reckoning, but were you not aware that Richard borrowed a thousand pounds before he sailed for England to conduct his campaign for governor?"

"I thought he had repaid whatever it was he borrowed."

"And he lost more than you might have thought in the convoy the Dutch intercepted in '72. And did you not know he had advanced money to Yeamans for land in the Carolinas?"

Charlotte began to feel faint. "Go on, tell me everything."

"The worst are the gambling debts. He lost heavily when he was going through that bad period after he returned from England. I can't tell you exactly how much, but I know of at least two thousand pounds."

Charlotte closed her eyes and put her hand over her face. "Then all I have is this land."

"And the slaves, but all are mortgaged."

Charlotte raised her head and looked across the ruined fields that led up toward Mount Hillaby. "I have been thinking how cruel it was of God to take Richard from me. Now I think He was cruel to have spared my life. I wish I had died with Richard."

"Please, please, do not say that."

"I have nothing to live for. Nothing to live with. There is no hope for me. I should return to England."

"No, Charlotte. Don't say that."

Higganbotham arose and strode about agitatedly. He stopped as if to speak and then walked around the fig tree again.

"The news is not all bad. Governor Atkins means to ask the Assembly to pass an act suspending creditors' rights to foreclose on widows such as you until you have time to rebuild. That would give you a breathing space."

"But without money, I cannot buy provisions for the slaves."

"Charlotte, please do not take this amiss, but my plantation is debt-free. My medical practice has been rewarding. There are some advantages to being single, you know."

"What are you implying?"

"My providing you with a thousand pounds."

"Oh, David, I could not accept charity from you."

"Call it a loan then. Call it whatever you like, but stop this talk of wishing to be dead or of leaving Barbados."

"You dear man. I am touched. But I am not certain I have the energy to rebuild. Croxton thinks we cannot have another full crop here for three years."

The physician looked down at his boots, started to speak, but halted at her further words: "I will consider what you say, David. No matter how I may decide, thank you for your generous offer and for your friendship."

Charlotte, who had never experienced the loss of anyone she loved deeply, could not understand the emotions that buffeted her from first one direction and then another. She felt a wrenching sorrow at the loss of Richard, and, although she fought against it, she was often overcome with a deep bitterness toward him, a kind of anger for leaving her in these circumstances. Her feelings ran beyond her natural disillusionment in learning of his deception about his debts. She yearned for his presence, rich or poor. She felt abandoned by Richard and misunderstood by those who survived. How could anyone expect her to remain on Barbados with all its memories of him?

She did not like this swinging of her moods like a pendulum between self-pity and anger. Yet she lacked the energy to take charge of her affairs, and she resented the interference of others. She was embarrassed, afterward, by her irascible flare-ups toward Clemmie, Croxton, and even Higganbotham, but she really could not help herself. She needed time to come to terms with her bereavement. And being pregnant in the midst of a ruined land with the responsibility of scores of slaves upon her shoulders added burdens that would have challenged the strongest of women.

"Mistress?"

"What do you want, Clemmie? You can see that I am trying to rest."

"I want to talk to you."

"It can wait."

"No, it can't. I got something to say, and you can have me whipped, but I am going to say it. I have been loyal to you for ten years. I married Toby even though I didn't love him just because that was what you wanted. And now you speak of going back to England and leaving us here."

"You have been eavesdropping."

"Call it what you want, but I am going to have my say. We are not sheep and oxen, you know. Maybe your laws will allow you to sell us all to somebody else, but what about your duty to us? I always thought you was a brave woman, braver even than the master, but now, when you don't have your soft bed and all your comforts, you are talking about giving up and going back to England. Don't you owe us some loyalty too?"

"If you are so wise as to criticize me, what do you think I should do?"

"You would have me whipped if I told you."

"In that case, hold your tongue."

Clemmie withdrew, but Charlotte could catch wisps of an animated conversation going on in the other room of the hut between her and Mirabel. She slept poorly that night, and each time she awakened there was that nagging question waiting to be answered. Did she really want to rear her child on the charity of her father? To return to Foxley Manor as a penniless widow, again under the thumb of her mother? Remarriage after a decent period of mourning? Who would want a woman past thirty and looking even older with this gray hair? Yet she would be trapped if she delayed her return, would be condemned to an endless struggle to operate a sugar plantation profitably enough to pay off Richard's debts.

Only near dawn, as Clemmie and Mirabel arose to boil corn meal for her breakfast, did a solution occur to her.

Nutmeg had survived the hurricane, although Charlotte's

sidesaddle had not. Clemmie was horrified when her mistress placed a bridle on the aged mare with her own hands and then, with the help of a mounting block, straddled the animal's bare back. Ignoring her protests, Charlotte rode with her skirt up about her thighs, across the gullied fields toward Fulham.

Esther Lawnton was aghast at her appearing so, but Charlotte ignored her remonstrances.

"I am well enough to ride. Where is Harold?"

Lawnton listened as she recited the bad news she had received from Higganbotham. She did not tell him of the physician's offer, but made one of her own.

"If you will promise to look after the Negroes, you may have them. And the land, if you are willing to stand for the debts with which it is encumbered."

"I'd have to put on my considering cap about that. Do you really mean just to give me Bolton Hall?"

"And its slaves and its debts."

Before Lawnton could respond, Esther spoke up. "Harold, before any more is said on this subject by either of you, I want a word in private with Charlotte."

When her husband was out of hearing, Esther began calmly. "I remember nine years ago, when you did not get your way, you were ready to pack up and return to your parents."

"You mean when Richard meant to go on that foolish expedition? What has that to do with my offer?"

"You thought Richard was shirking his duty to leave Barbados. I think you are being foolish, yes, and cowardly, too, to desert the island now."

Tears came into Charlotte's eyes. "It is impossible for me to live here without Richard. I have no money. The debts are enormous. I am with child. What choice do I have?"

"You are not alone in your predicament. At our ages, it will not be easy for Harold and me to rebuild, but we will. Barbados is our home. I could name you many widows who remained here after the death of their husbands. Most succeeded. Not a few did better than their husbands, for they were more temperate in their habits and were better managers. I recall that you did well enough when Richard was in England."

"These are quite different circumstances. I have no money."

"Yet, David Higganbotham is willing to provide you with a thousand pounds of capital."

"How do you know that?"

"He has told me so. He would give you much more if you would accept the gift."

"I wish charity from no one."

Before Esther could reply, Charlotte untied Nutmeg's reins, and Harold came running to lift her onto the mare's back.

"My offer is very simple," Charlotte pointedly said to him rather than Esther. "Bolton Hall and its slaves are yours, if you will promise to provide for them and to pay off the debts."

Lawnton was about to ask how much the debts totaled when Esther intervened.

"No, Harold. Charlotte has something else to think about before she takes such a step. She must decide whether she wishes to complete her growing up."

"Esther Lawnton, you are a bitch."

"It remains to be seen what you are, Charlotte."

Too angry to reply, Charlotte kicked Nutmeg in the ribs and set off at a canter for Bolton Hall.

Croxton was waiting for her under the fig tree.

"I thought we ought to talk about new quarters for the Negroes. They are getting restless, shut up in the boiling room at night."

"Then you ought to start building new huts."

"What with? We need to buy lumber and supplies."

"I have no money, and, even if I did, until shipments arrive from New England, there is no building material available. You'll have to use tree limbs, or debris from the stables. I don't care what you do. Just do it."

Croxton looked hurt. "It would go faster with proper lumber. And what about food? The slaves are so hungry they can't work."

"I told you to let them put in their gardens first, then repair the erosion in our fields."

"Their spirits are low. It's not just the lack of food, you see. Forgive me for saying so, but word has spread that you mean to sell out and go back to England. They are worried."

"Indeed?"

"Yes, ma'am. And they have asked me to beg you not to go."

Charlotte left Croxton standing with his hat in his hand while she went into the hut to compose herself. He was still there when she returned.

"Tell the slaves I am touched. Tell them that I will not leave them in the hands of a cruel master, however I decide. Now do get on with building their huts."

Whatever the validity of the advice Esther had given, it was good for Charlotte in one way. It made her furious. She lay awake most of the night thinking of responses to her neighbor's cruel frankness. Yes, Esther owed her an apology. How disrespectful both to her and the memory of Richard to drag up unpleasant reminders and to pass judgment so harshly.

Charlotte reserved part of her anger for David Higganbotham, too. What business did he have, telling the Lawntons of his offer? He had made it impossible for her to accept his money, even as a loan. Damn all meddlesome people.

The next morning, Clemmie and Mirabel would have welcomed a return of Charlotte's former sorrowful mood. She lashed out at them repeatedly. She charged Clemmie with disclosing her thoughts of returning to England. "You have never learned to keep your mouth shut. I ought to sell you to one of those establishments in Bridgetown where they rent women to sailors. You could talk as much as you like to them."

When Croxton came to consult with her she ordered him to "Get on with your work. You know well enough what wants doing."

At noon she brought tears to Mirabel's eyes by criticizing the pudding she had taken great pains to make from a carefully guarded cache of fruit and cassava roots. And she was still in this savage mood when David Higganbotham came riding up.

Charlotte barely looked at him. Without bidding him to dismount, she said, "You offered to make me a loan."

"Not a loan, exactly ... "

"Don't interrupt me, sir. I cannot accept money from you, even as a loan. Ten years ago I gave you a purse with which to buy the indenture of two bond servants. You enjoyed the services of one of them for five years. If you wish to calculate the value of that purse, with accumulated interest, I will accept it and no more. It will pay my passage to England."

"Charlotte, what is the matter?"

"The matter is that I am tired of people interfering in my affairs. I am tired of free advice. And I am fed up with so-called friends who cannot keep a confidence."

She would not look at him. She did not want to see his earnest face, did not want to have this welcome mood of anger melt into pity.

"Back to England? That's what you mean to do?"

Charlotte was too absorbed in her own feelings to notice his slurred speech.

"It is is none of your business, but, yes."

"Then I will come with you."

"What?" She shaded her eyes from the sun and then saw how flushed his face appeared.

"You heard me. If you go back to England, I will book passage on the same ship. If you stay here, I will remain to help you."

"Are you mad?" And then with narrowed eyes, "Or are you drunk?"

"I did enjoy a few drinks with Harold Lawnton and Esther. What is wrong with that?"

"So they put you up to this?"

"Nobody has to put me up to anything."

"Well, the last thing I need is a drunken quacksalver

hanging about. Go back and tell Esther Lawnton to mind her own business hereafter."

He released the reins and crossed his arms. "I am not budging until I have your answer."

"I have told you I will not accept money from you."

"Not about that, you idiot girl. Your answer to my proposal of marriage."

"Marriage?"

Hearing giggles from the servants' end of the hut, Charlotte whirled around and yelled, "Clemmie, Mirabel, I will have Mister Croxton whip both of you. I swear I will."

"I'm sorry. I didn't mean it that way. I meant, when should we get married and where?"

"You have lost your mind, David Higganbotham. The sun has got to your brain. If Richard were here, he would kill you."

"If Richard were here, I wouldn't ask you, would I? So what is your answer?"

He still sat with that fatuous look on his face, arms folded across his chest and the reins hanging about his horse's neck, when Charlotte, infuriated by his effrontery and what she imagined to be Esther's part in it, shouted, "Get out of here. You are trying to take advantage of my predicament."

With that, she struck the horse on its rump, causing the animal to shy and throw the unsteady Higganbotham out of the saddle.

He landed on his back, and it took so long for him to recover his breath that Charlotte, fearing he was dead, asked his forgiveness. She held his head in her lap while Clemmie fanned him and Mirabel ran for a basin from the water filter.

"Dear David, I have killed you. I did not mean to," Charlotte moaned.

Drunk as he was, Higganbotham kept his wits enough not to speak when his breath returned. He lay with his head in her lap, until he made the mistake of opening one eye slightly to peer into her face. Charlotte stood up abruptly and took the basin.

Higganbotham arose, sputtering. "You could drown an unconscious person doing that."

"Or one only pretending," she said.

They looked at each other, and both burst out laughing.

Strong coffee and a brief rest cleared Higganbotham's brain. Charlotte forbade further mention of marriage, but throughout the afternoon, they spoke with increasing ease and frankness of other things.

Richard had never had the patience or the interest to ask about her childhood, but David seemed fascinated by her account of growing up in Bedford. She, in turn, enjoyed hearing his stories of studying medicine in Edinburgh and an early trip to Italy.

For the first time, he told her of his forlorn love for the sister of one of his fellow medical students.

It struck Charlotte what a sad life he had led, devoting himself to other people, never claiming anything for himself, always living up to his responsibilities. She marveled, too, at the quiet, unselfish strength of the man.

They fell into a long silence. And then Charlotte brought up a subject they had always before avoided.

"It has all come to pass, hasn't it?"

"What, Charlotte?"

"The things of which Moses Martin prophesied, first in his broadside tacked up on the cathedral door in Bristol and then on that dreadful day at Saint Michael. The plague in England. The great fire of London. The loss of the expedition to Saint Christopher. Bridgetown nearly wiped out by the magazine explosion. One loses track of the lesser calamities. And now this awful, awful hurricane. Tell me, David, do you think Barbados is under some sort of curse, as he said? If so, I would be foolish indeed to remain here."

"It would hardly cure the wrongs and ills of this place for us to abandon it. One cannot undo the past. Our slaves are here to stay. They may not always remain in servitude, but they are, or will be, Barbadians just as we are. They have no choice. Your

Negroes and mine would be better served by our remaining than our leaving. We owe it to them."

Frowning at his use of "we" and "our," Charlotte changed the subject.

"Have you never regretted coming here?"

"Now and then. I have known some lonely times. Duty aside, however, I would miss the warmth and beauty of Barbados."

"You surprise me saying you have been lonely. I know of no one who is more often invited to dinners. Everyone likes you, David."

"I have been lonely for you, Charlotte."

"David, you promised you would say no more in that vein."

"I cannot help myself. And you do need someone to look after you."

"You are exceedingly kind. I can't think why anyone would want a used piece of goods in my condition, gone gray and . . . "

"Stop it, Charlotte!"

She was taken aback by his tone.

"Don't say such things. You don't realize how I feel about you, how I have felt since we met aboard the *Mary Leigh*. I don't care about your condition or who is the father of your child. If that is the price of having you at my side, I would pay it gladly."

He walked away and stood beside the fig tree, with his back turned. She moved close and lowered her voice, so they could not be overheard.

"What did you mean by that remark, about not caring who is the father of my child?"

His face scarlet, he turned. "I should not have said that. I cannot say what I meant."

"But you have said it. I notice you change the subject whenever Richard's name comes up. Now you must tell me why."

"I cannot. I will not."

"Then, that settles it. Tomorrow I depart for Bridgetown to book my passage back to England."

"No, Charlotte!"

"Then tell me what you meant. Surely you are not jealous of Richard."

"I am afraid to tell you. I fear it would turn you against me."

"It will turn me against you irrevocably if you do not speak the truth."

With contorted face, not daring to look into her eyes, the physician blurted out the story of the day before the hurricane, of Richard's visit to his house, and part, but only part, of their confrontation, and nothing of their altercation.

Charlotte, humiliated and shocked, listened with her hands first over her mouth, and then her face. At last she looked up.

"Did you know about Mandze?"

"It was common knowledge."

"I swore never to mention her to Richard, and I kept my pledge, but I did wonder why they did not produce a child. Oh, I wish he had not died with that knowledge ... "

Higganbotham made no reply.

She blew her nose and straightened her shoulders. "What did Richard say or do after you told him all that?"

With great effort, Higganbotham kept his face straight and his voice even.

"He simply uncocked his pistol, put it in his belt and left without another word."

"Poor, poor Richard. He never quite found what he was looking for in life. I wish I had been a better wife to him. I wish he had not died knowing such a thing about me. He deserved a happier ending to his life. There will never be another like him. Faults and all, I wish ... "

She caught herself and said, "You know about John and me and still you wish to marry me. I cannot believe you."

"Believe it or not, it is a fact. It doesn't matter whether you love me or not. I would devote the rest of my life to your happiness."

"Richard said something very like that in the presence of my father when he asked for my hand."

"Did you know Richard very well?"

"Not then. Indeed, it seems that after living with him for ten years, I did not know him as well as I thought."

"Did he know you well, then?"

"Frankly, he never took the trouble."

"There is my advantage. I have studied you like a book for ten years, Charlotte. I appreciate your mind, yes, and your good judgment. I do not look upon you as an adornment for my arm, for a possession to declare to all the world what a powerful and rich man I am to have such a wife. No, I value you for yourself. Nothing pleases me more than to be in your company, to discuss our mutual interests as equals, not man and maid, not master and servant. I love you, Charlotte, no denying that, but I also like you as a person."

Charlotte could not bring herself to reply.

"I don't expect you to love me so soon after Richard's death. If you never love me, that will be all right. Just let me love you, let me look after you and your baby. No, let us call it our baby."

Higganbotham took her hand and put his face closer to hers.

"If talk of love pains you, let us speak of practical matters. I have replaced the roof on my house. We can live there with Mirabel and Clemmie until the baby is born. The Croxtons can move into this hut. Later, I can sell my plantation and conduct my medical practice here. Are you listening, Charlotte? You would be in charge of Bolton Hall. With Croxton as your overseer, you could have this plantation restored soon enough."

"Restore this plantation?" Charlotte said with a bitter laugh. "Suppose that I and our fellow planters all rebuild, what then? You know, David, the morning you paid me that visit I was reading from Thomas Hobbe's *Leviathan*. He wrote something about the state to which mankind reverts when it has no

moral restraints. He said there would be no commodious buildings, no arts, letters, society, and that all folk would live in
constant fear and danger of violent death. As he put it, the lives
of people would be 'solitary, poor, nasty, brutish and short.'
There, does not that apply to Barbados? Does it not sound very
like what poor old Moses Martin said on the eve of the expedition to Saint Christopher, before he fell to his death? How can
there be any stable, civilized way of life when everything
revolves around greed for profits and material things?

"I know you see good in everything and everybody, but
you know the history of this place as well as I. It could have
been a garden of Eden, a place where families cultivated their
little farms, followed their religious bents without persecution.
Truly we could have been a little England of the tropics. A few
of our cleverer poor whites have risen to wealth, but most have
died early or moved away in despair. Those who remain are a
sorry lot. And the poor, poor Africans we have brought to take
their places. I still have nightmares about those executions in
Speightstown. How can we have peace when so many human
beings harbor resentments, justifiable resentments against us?

"We have stripped away the trees and established one huge
sugar plantation. Think of it, David, here we are half-starved in
a land that could feed us a dozen times over if we were not all so
intent on the production of sugar, sugar, and more sugar. How
laboriously we have wrung profits from our slaves and soil, how
foolishly we have wasted it just to sweeten England's tea."

"I repeat, Charlotte, with Croxton's help and mine where
needed, you could make this one of the finest plantations on
Barbados. And who knows, perhaps the happiest. Someone will
operate Bolton Hall. Your conscience bothers you about the
inequities of this place. Will it bother you any less living back
in Bedfordshire, when you think of some hardhanded, greedy
planter wielding the whip with a vengeance to pay off Bolton
Hall's debts and realize the profits to join you in England? Face
the fact of Barbados's existence as a sugar colony. Like it or not,
Charlotte, you have become a part of this land. You would miss
it. You would long for the soft yellow sunrises, the brilliant

sunshine of midday, even the rains and the heat. Some other woman would cultivate your garden; some other woman would live here in a new house, Charlotte, while you exist on the charity of aged parents in dull, cold, gray England."

Her smile gave him pause. He wondered if she were mocking him.

"Go on, David. Finish your piece."

"Forgive me for saying this, but you have your child to think of, too. Whether you consider yourself Barbadian or not, it will be so. Do not forget that you carry within your body a true Barbadian. The child belongs here."

"I take your meaning. Is that all?"

"I have said enough. But you mentioned something about no commodious buildings. You long have dreamed of a grand new house, Charlotte. See what I have here?"

He drew out a large folded sheet of paper. "Come, let us sit together."

Genuinely amused at first by his ardent speech and now this sudden tack, Charlotte asked, "Whatever is it?"

"Plans for a new Bolton Hall. It must be built strong enough to withstand another such hurricane. Walls of good coral stone, two feet thick and set on bedrock. See the floor plan here. I propose a porch across this end, opening into a twenty-by-twenty-five-foot hall, large enough for dancing. Here is a parlor, not quite so large. Kitchen attached to the rear. Above on the first floor we will have a hall and four large chambers. Finally a top garret floor. The roof will be of tile, pinned and laid in mortar. We will use the best seasoned timber for the beams and joists ... "

"What is this room projecting to the rear?"

"Your library. We will have to order more books, of course, but I want you to have a proper place of study."

"It is shown here as occupying the spot where the bearded fig tree stands."

"What is left of it. I thought we would remove it."

Charlotte studied the drawing.

"When first I came here, I used to hate that tree. It seemed a grotesque, unnatural thing with its ugly, gnarled trunk and those hideous tendrils hanging down like bearded serpents. Richard planted the tree with his own hands, for his then master."

"Really?"

"Yes. He was a white slave on this plantation, you know. He tried to warn the Roundhead who owned it how quickly the tree would grow and the problems it might cause, but, no, the planter's wife had her heart set on a fig tree for her backyard. She pictured herself gathering the kind of sweet, chewy Spanish figs they sell in London. Poor, simple woman. She did not remain on Barbados long enough to learn that the fruit of the bearded fig tree is small and unpalatable. I have often thought the tree to be like the slave system that has grown up here in the same period. Each puts out tendrils. Each is too firmly rooted now to be easily got rid of. Each produces a bitter fruit." She sighed. "Ah, well, at least it has provided a comfortable shade for those of us with the leisure to sit out here. No, the tree should remain. It belongs there."

"What about the library, then?"

"There is room a'plenty on the upper floor. With only three of us, we would not need so many bed chambers."

"I was looking forward to the future. But we will do as you wish."

"No, as *we* wish. And we don't have to decide right away. I am impressed by your plans. You are a man of many parts, David."

"For a drunken quacksalver, I suppose I am."

Mirabel and Clemmie came out of the kitchen end of the hut to see what all the laughter was about.

Further Reading

These are the basic older books on Barbadian history:

A True and Exact History of the Island of Barbados, by Richard Ligon (1657, 1673, reprinted by Frank Cass, 1970); *The Natural History of Barbados*, by the Reverend Griffith Hughes (1750, reprinted by Arno Press, 1972); *The History of Barbados*, by John Poyer (1808, reprinted by Frank Cass, 1971); *The History of Barbados*, by Sir Robert H. Schomburgk (1848, reprinted by Frank Cass, 1971).

More recent books include *A History of Barbados, 1625-1685*, by Vincent T. Harlow (Clarendon Press, 1926) and *The Economic Geography of Barbados*, by Otis P. Starkey (Columbia University Press, 1939).

Several even more recent works by American authors deserve special mention: *Vexed and Troubled Englishmen, 1590-1642*, by Carl Bridenbaugh (Clarendon Press, 1968); *No Peace Beyond the Line: The English in the Caribbean, 1624-1690*, by Carl and Roberta Bridenbaugh (Oxford University Press, 1972); *Sugar and Slaves: The Rise of the Planter Class in the English West Indies, 1624-1713*, by Richard S. Dunn (University of North Carolina Press, 1972); *Plantation Slavery in Barbados: An Archeological and Historical Investigation*, by Jerome S. Handler and Frederick W. Lange (Harvard University Press, 1978).

Finally, these books by Barbadian authors should be noted: *Barbados, A History from the Amerindians to Independence*, by F. A. Hoyos (Macmillan Caribbean, 1978); and *The Barbados Book*, by Louis Lynch (Andre Deutsch, 1964, 1972).

Anyone wishing to delve even more deeply into Barbadian history should consult Jerome S. Handler's *A Guide to Source Materials for the Study of Barbados History 1627-1834* (Southern Illinois University Press, 1971).